The Perils of
Peppermints

ALADDIN PAPERBACKS BY BARBARA BROOKS WALLACE

The Barrel in the Basement

Ghosts in the Gallery

Miss Switch Online

Miss Switch to the Rescue

Peppermints in the Parlor

Secret in St. Something

Sparrows in the Scullery

The Trouble with Miss Switch

The Twin in the Tavern

The Perils of
Peppermints

BARBARA BROOKS WALLACE

ALADDIN PAPERBACKS
New York   London   Toronto   Sydney

ALADDIN PAPERBACKS
An imprint of Simon & Schuster Children's Publishing Division
1230 Avenue of the Americas, New York, NY 10020
Text copyright © 2003 by Barbara Brooks Wallace
All rights reserved, including the right of reproduction in whole or in part in any form.
ALADDIN PAPERBACKS and colophon are registered trademarks of Simon & Schuster, Inc.
Also available in an Atheneum Books for Young Readers hardcover edition.
Designed by O'Lanso Gabbidon
The text of this book was set in Bembo.
Manufactured in the United States of America
First Aladdin Paperbacks edition May 2005
10 9 8 7 6 5 4 3 2 1
The Library of Congress has cataloged the hardcover edition as follows:
Wallace, Barbara Brooks.
The perils of peppermints / by Barbara Brooks Wallace.
p. cm.
Sequel to: Peppermints in the parlor.
Summary: Left at a New York boarding school by Aunt and Uncle Twice, eleven-year-old Emily finds horrors even greater than those she faced at Sugar Hill Hall, especially after she gets word that her inheritance is lost.
ISBN 0-689-85043-3 (hc.)
[1. Boarding schools—Fiction. 2. Schools—Fiction. 3. Swindlers and swindling—Fiction. 4. Inheritance and succession—Fiction. 5. Orphans—Fiction.] I. Title.
PZ7.W1547 Pd 2002
[Fic]—dc21 2001046361
ISBN 0-689-85045-X (pbk.)

For the two royals of Clan Wallace,
Victoria and Elizabeth,
with love

Contents

1

Terrifying Arrangements

The black cab rumbling through the city at nightfall swayed and shook with every gust of icy wind that blasted down the streets. Its roof was piled so dangerously high with bundles, boxes, and baggage that the cab further distressed its three occupants by very nearly tipping over each time it rounded a corner.

Inside the cab, no one spoke, each one being deep in thought. The only sounds heard were the drumming of the horses' hooves, the *chink-chinking* of their harnesses, and the clicking of sleet hurling itself against the windows.

Emily Luccock, one of the three inside the cab, sat rigidly by one window, clutching the seat in fright with each lurch and shudder of the cab. Why was she not the one seated in the middle between her Aunt and Uncle Twice, their arms around *her* comforting *her*? Did she not deserve that now when within the hour she was to be abandoned to who knew what fate? Had they chosen to dismiss from their minds all recollection that she was a young girl of still but eleven years, and that they were all the family she had left in the world? It seemed so to Emily, because it was Aunt Twice who sat in the middle of the seat, with Uncle Twice's arm about *her* shoulders, his arm tightening protectively each time the cab seemed in danger of turning over.

It tightened again when suddenly Aunt Twice began to tremble. "Oh, William," she moaned, "if it is this bad here, how will it be on the high seas? How will we be able to abide it?"

"My sweet girl," replied Uncle Twice, "I've been assured that we are sailing on the most modern of ships. Our cabin will offer every comfort. As for this weather, why, when we reach India it will be so warm you'll soon be longing to see a snowflake!"

Uncle Twice's attempt at humor to cheer his "sweet girl" was clearly not very successful. She only sighed deeply and shook her head. Emily, for her part, could only think, *India . . . with the warm sun, the elephants, the tigers, and the temple bells. India, where they are going without me!*

Was it possible that at the very last moment, when the time for parting actually arrived, Aunt and Uncle Twice would have a change of heart, would relent and tell Emily she could go with them? She would cling to that hope until they reached the very docks, though it was a fast-fading hope. After all, had she not pleaded with them endlessly all the way on the train trip to New York? And what had that availed her? Nothing!

Why was all that Emily had already suffered not enough to persuade them that she should accompany them? Was it not enough that her mama and papa were no more, lost in a terrible boating accident? Orphaned once, was she to be made to feel orphaned again? And what of all the horror that had happened afterward? Was that not misery enough? Perhaps they did not see it all as clearly as she still did, each scene in her mind so terrible and real.

She saw herself, an orphan arriving at Sugar Hill Hall, the grand mansion in San Francisco that was home to Aunt and Uncle Twice, so named because Aunt Twice was sister to Emily's own mama, and Uncle Twice brother to her papa. With the loss of Mama and Papa, Emily was to live with them.

Then there she was in that terrifying moment, stepping through the doors of Sugar Hill Hall. In the parlor were standing those who turned out to be two of the most wicked, cruel, evil ladies ever to be met in this world, Mrs. Meeching and Mrs. Plumly.

The parlor itself had become shabby and desolate, for Sugar Hill Hall had been turned into a home for sad old people abandoned by their families, with Meeching and Plumly, Inc., the proprietors. Aunt Twice herself had become shabby and downtrodden as well. No longer the golden-haired, sparkle-eyed beauty she once was, she was now their servant. And there was no sign, not then, not at any time, of handsome, dashing Uncle Twice!

The scenes marched grimly on. There was Emily in her tiny, dank cellar room where she was to live, having now herself become a servant in Sugar Hill Hall. There was the dismal dining room, where the old people feasted on moldy bread and fish-head stew and tea made from a single tea bag passed around the table. There was the scene of Emily being tormented by Tilly, the other servant girl. And then came the chilling vision of herself imprisoned in the dreaded Remembrance Room in the cellar, the place where the old people were locked up for stealing a peppermint.

Oh, those murderous peppermints! Emily would never, never forget, no never, that table in the parlor with the red velvet cover decorated with gold tassels, on which rested that bowl of puffy, tempting, tantalizing, delicious pink-and-white-striped peppermint drops, placed there deliberately to entice some poor old person into reaching out a hand and taking one. More than anything else, Emily would never forget *that!*

But then, at long last, everything had miraculously come to rights. The confession of a dying sea captain had revealed that Uncle Twice, who through gambling and a wild life (later sorely regretted) had lost all his fortune save Sugar Hill Hall itself, was not guilty of the murder of which he was accused by Meeching and Plumly, Inc. It was they themselves who were guilty of the murder of a seaman, along with the captain himself. So Uncle Twice could return safely from exile working as a seaman aboard the ship *Silver Sea* and take his place as the rightful owner of Sugar Hill Hall. Meeching and Plumly, who proved to be smugglers as well as murderers, not to mention their making plans to do away with Emily and Aunt Twice, were taken off to jail in chains.

Oh, what joy and happiness then reigned in Sugar Hill Hall for Emily; Aunt Twice; the old people; Kipper, the fishmonger's son, who was Emily's true friend throughout; and even Tilly, who proved to be not nearly so wicked as Emily had supposed.

But, alas, the happiness lasted for only a few paltry weeks. Uncle Twice was soon to be seen wandering the grand rooms of Sugar Hill Hall, silent, sunk in somber thought, his brows often drawn together in a deep frown. Aunt Twice's face began once more to look pale and drawn. But nobody explained why, until one sad afternoon, when Emily was finally invited to sit down before both of them.

"Do you remember, Emily, when you first came to Sugar Hill Hall, and I said you must try to be a brave little girl?" Aunt Twice asked.

Emily nodded solemnly. How well she remembered those very words!

"Well," Aunt Twice continued, "once again, I must ask you the same thing."

"But—but why?" stammered Emily. "All is happiness now, isn't it?"

Uncle Twice shook his head sadly. "The happiness is that I have been able to return to my family a man no longer accused of any crime," he said. "But as for the rest, I'm afraid I must now pay for all those early years when I carelessly squandered my fortune until there was nothing left."

"Not nothing, Uncle Twice," said Emily. "You still have Sugar Hill Hall."

"No longer, Emily," said Aunt Twice with a sob. "Oh, tell her, William!"

"Sugar Hill Hall has been sold," said Uncle Twice, his face twisted with grief.

"S-S-Sold?" Emily felt as if her heart would stop. "Why?"

"To pay all my terrible debts, Emily," replied Uncle Twice, "waiting for me when I returned. With no money left to pay them, and none with which to run this mansion, I had no choice but to sell it."

"But what about the money left to me by Mama and Papa?" cried Emily. "Kipper once said

I was a 'hairess.' Doesn't that mean I have lots and lots of money? Can't you take that, Uncle Twice?"

Uncle Twice shook his head firmly. "Never, never would Aunt Twice and I touch that, dear Emily. *Never!* That money is a sacred trust to be used for your future needs. Nothing more is to be said about it. No, I have made my bed, and I must lie in it!"

"But where will we live?" Emily moaned. "What of the old people who were to stay here? What of Tilly?"

"Welcoming homes have been found for them all, as we shall now tell them," replied Uncle Twice. "There are no worries on that score."

"Well," said Emily with a firm bob of her head, trying to be a "brave little girl" as Aunt Twice had requested, "at least *we* shall all be together!"

But at this, Aunt and Uncle exchanged telling glances. Each seemed waiting for the other to speak. At last it was Aunt Twice who said hesitantly, "Not—not *all* of us, Emily darling, at least not for now."

Not *all* of them? Could it be that Uncle Twice must leave Aunt Twice and Emily again? No, not even just Emily, for the happy announcement had been made that there was to be a Baby Cousin Twice!

"Oh, Uncle Twice!" cried Emily. "Must you go away once more? How can you leave Aunt Twice *now*?"

Once again, Aunt and Uncle Twice exchanged glances. Aunt Twice's hands were clasped so tightly together, her knuckles had grown white. "Uncle Twice will not be leaving *me*, dear child," she said. "I will be going with him."

Emily's breath caught in her throat. "But—but what about *me*?" she gasped.

"William," said Aunt Twice, tears in her eyes, "you must explain what has happened to Emily so she will understand everything."

Explain what has happened? Understand everything? Understand *what*? It sounded frightening. And by the time Uncle Twice had made his explanations, Emily did indeed understand all . . . and it was more frightening than ever!

It appeared, said Uncle Twice, that though they were to receive a handsome sum from the sale of Sugar Hill Hall, there would not be enough left to pay all his debts and still provide a means for their livelihood, especially now with the forthcoming arrival of Emily's Baby Cousin Twice. But then a remarkable solution to their dilemma had come about through the lawyer who represented the purchaser of Sugar Hill Hall. Although the purchaser was from another city and was someone neither Aunt nor Uncle Twice had known or ever met, Uncle Twice had been taken with Mr. Slyde, the lawyer, and had struck up a friendship with him.

Learning of Uncle Twice's predicament, Mr. Slyde told him of a small British company the elderly owner of which had died, leaving heirs who had no interest in the business. Uncle Twice could buy it for the money provided by Sugar Hill Hall, and would thus own a business and have income as well to support his growing family. It meant Uncle Twice must go to India for an extended period of time, but it was too splendid an opportunity to be dismissed.

India! India, where it appeared that Aunt Twice could accompany Uncle Twice, but not Emily. British families in India sent every school-age child back to England, and Emily would have to be sent away as well. Oh, not to England, but to New York, where one day Aunt and Uncle Twice would return. So it was best for her to remain behind and be placed in a boarding school. And it turned out Mr. Slyde could be of help there as well, for he was acquainted with a very exclusive, elegant establishment, so exclusive and elegant, in truth, that one young girl who attended it was a member of a royal family! Emily had already been registered there, and so it was all settled that she was to be a student and boarder at the exclusive, elegant Mrs. Spilking's Select Academy for Young Ladies.

Emily cared not a whit how exclusive and elegant it was. She did not wish to be separated from Aunt and Uncle Twice. She did not wish to go there. But her arguments against it could not change anyone's mind. Even the one about money! For where, pray tell, would that come from to pay for this exclusive, elegant establishment? Well, in this worthy case, Uncle Twice would allow for her own fortune to be used, it seemed. He had seen to it that it was all safely invested, and Mr. Slyde entrusted with full authority to administer it while Uncle Twice was away in India.

When Emily argued that, after all, she had not been attending school when she was living in the cellar as a servant girl, she was only met with the reply that it was all the more reason she should miss no more. Her insistence that she could read lots of books in India and be as educated as she needed to be fell on deaf ears. In the end, these and every other argument she could think of were rejected. And Emily began to suspect why.

All concentration was to be on Baby Twice, and there would be no time left over to worry about Emily. This was only Emily's suspicion, of course, but more and more she was hearing "Emily darling" being replaced with "Baby darling" in Aunt and Uncle's conversations! Emily, once the only child in their lives, was to be the only child no more.

And even in the rattling black cab taking them to the docks, it was Aunt Twice who was of greatest concern to Uncle Twice. Further, though Emily knew the train, arriving when it did, made them believe they must go directly to the docks rather than first take Emily to her school, could they not have tried a little harder to arrange for that? Why must she now have to be met and transported to the school like a piece of baggage by a strange man, also arranged by the accommodating Mr. Slyde?

But it was clear that Aunt and Uncle Twice's thoughts were entirely on what lay ahead of them, and Emily, whose future they considered settled, was already as far from their minds as if they had already arrived in India.

The horses' hooves drummed on. Through the windows of the cab, Emily could see men with their collars turned up against the sleet and icy wind, and women clutching their coats around themselves, all fighting to get to their warm homes as quickly as possible. The rattling cab piled high with boxes and baggage meant nothing to any of them. And it certainly meant nothing to them that one of the three passengers within that cab was a young girl who sat there in silence, her heart breaking.

2

Ichabod Crawstone

They reached the docks at last. The cab, swaying precariously, came to a groaning stop before a bleak gray building strung across with windows so encrusted with grime that they served no purpose at all. Herded by Uncle Twice, along with Aunt Twice, Emily entered a dank, cavernous room of the building. Ugly gas lamps overhead glared down upon swarms of dockworkers wheeling carts loaded with crates, ships crewmen shouting orders, and prospective passengers, all looking frozen and miserable as they huddled around their portmanteaus and carpetbags, looking vainly for help in boarding the waiting ship. The ship could be seen through wide openings that fronted the dock. It appeared a dark, mysterious hulk that even rows of lighted portholes could not make inviting in the icy wind and sleet howling past it.

But as they cautiously made their way across the room toward a glass enclosure bearing a sign that read INFORMATION AND ASSISTANCE, Emily's attention was suddenly caught and held by one thing, the man standing in front of the enclosure. He was dressed entirely in black, a color that extended even to a heavy, clipped beard. Unlike others around him, he appeared indifferent to the cold. He was not hunched down into his coat, nor did he even have his rich fur collar pulled up about his neck. Tall and narrow, black leather-gloved hands motionless at his sides, he may well have been a steel post as he stared at the three of them threading their way across the room.

For no reason that she could explain, the sight of this man frightened Emily. Was he a ghastly portent of dreaded things to come? No! No! He was only a stranger who happened to be standing there. He had nothing to do with her, and she was letting her fears get the better of her. Yet before they had even quite reached the glass enclosure, to Emily's horror, the man stepped forward.

"Would you be Mr. and Mrs. Luccock?" he asked.

"Why, yes, indeed!" Uncle Twice replied quickly. "And you must then be—"

"Ichabod Crawstone, at your service," the man interrupted, bowing slightly.

"Mr. Crawstone, we do apologize for keeping you waiting even a moment. We were slightly held up in tending to our baggage, which had to be unloaded from our cab and dealt with by a porter. We wouldn't want to inconvenience you for the world. Mrs. Luccock and I are so grateful to you for taking care of our niece for us. We don't know what we would have done if . . ." Uncle Twice shook his head, his voice trailing off.

"Think nothing of it," said Mr. Crawstone. "And you must know there is little I would not do for Josiah Slyde. I am deeply indebted to him for past kindnesses, and when he asked of me this small favor for a friend, I was only too happy to oblige. This, I presume, is the young person to be put in my charge?"

"It is, indeed!" said Uncle Twice, putting his arm about Emily and propelling her toward Mr. Crawstone.

"How do you do, Emily," said Mr. Crawstone, smiling at her.

But it was a smile that made Emily feel an icy chill creep over her skin. It was a smile formed by the thinnest of lips drawn back over unnaturally tiny yellow teeth. It was a smile that traveled no further than the mouth, for the eyes behind narrowed lids were dark and hard, with no trace of any smile ever having been in them.

"H-H-How do you do," Emily barely whispered, and quickly dropped her own eyes.

Aunt Twice, who as they crossed the room had done little but cast fearful glances at the foreboding hulk that was to carry them across the storm-tossed ocean, now at last turned her full attention to Emily.

"Oh, Mr. Crawstone!" she cried. "This is not what we would have wished, to send our beloved niece to a school without even being able to see it ourselves."

"Madam, you need have no fear," replied Mr. Crawstone. "For although I have never visited the school myself, it comes with the highest of recommendations. And so I was pleased to be able to tell Josiah when he made inquiries on your behalf. You have my assurance, madam, that your niece will be provided with the best education in the most pleasant surroundings. And I also assure you she will be in a school with other young ladies whose families demand the absolute finest."

"I do hope all you say is true! Oh, I do hope so! If for a moment we were to think that . . ." Unable to go on, Aunt Twice wrung her hands, a sob caught in her throat.

But if she *had* gone on, what could she have said, anyway? That if things were not as Mr. Crawstone had described them, she and Uncle Twice would return to fetch Emily and whisk her off to India? Why not just take her now and be done with it?

Emily wanted to throw her arms around Aunt and Uncle Twice, begging them one last time to take her with them. Yet how *could* she under the cold, unsympathetic eyes of Mr. Crawstone? All she could do was stand and listen to Uncle Twice explaining to him that her trunk had been sent on to the school, and that the little portmanteau at her feet was all that needed to be of any concern. And then the terrible moment came when it was clear that time had run out, and all hope with it. With promises from Aunt and Uncle Twice of long and frequent letters, Emily's replies to which they would eagerly await, Aunt Twice tearfully hugged her. After one last hug from Uncle Twice, they were gone. Looking back once as she left the building with Mr. Crawstone, Emily could no longer see any sign of Uncle Twice's fair head or Aunt Twice's ruffled blue velvet bonnet bobbing along beside him. They had vanished entirely.

Whatever charm Mr. Crawstone had seen fit to draw from his small supply of that commodity in her aunt and uncle's presence, he clearly saw no reason to waste any more on Emily. He did not even offer to carry her portmanteau, as Uncle Twice had done. And he appeared entirely indifferent to the bumping and thumping of the portmanteau against her knees as she struggled to keep up with his long strides.

And while Emily might never have imagined a more miserable ride than the one she took to the docks with Aunt and Uncle Twice, the one to Mrs. Spilking's Select Academy for Young Ladies surely surpassed it. Mr. Crawstone seemed totally committed to sitting in stony silence, staring out the window. This left Emily no choice but to do the same.

How, she asked herself over and over again,

could Aunt and Uncle Twice have left her in the charge of such a person? Were they so blinded by their own affairs that they had failed to note Mr. Crawstone's thin-lipped smile that was not a smile and his cold eyes? Worse yet, had they indeed noticed, but were so afraid something might go amiss in disposing of Emily that they were willing to overlook the qualities of anyone who had come to fetch her, no matter how dreadful they were?

But who was there in that cab to answer these questions? As Emily sat with white, high-button shoes crossed and hands folded politely in her lap, the answers came only in the *clop-clopping* of the horses' hooves, the *click-clicking* of the never-ending sleet against the windows, and the lonely gaslights winking palely at her as the cab rolled by them.

On and on the cab rolled, with Emily losing all sense of how far they had gone, how many streets crossed, how many corners turned. All this without a word spoken. Some of the streets were crowded with cabs, wagons, and throngs of people, despite the lateness of the hour. But when the cab finally drew to a stop, it was on a street that was deserted.

Feeble gaslights barely lit up lonely skeletal trees, their ghostly reflections dancing eerily on darkened windows that gave no evidence of life behind them.

They had stopped before the most ordinary of narrow brick houses, with no distinguishing features whatsoever. Further, it was attached to a row of other ordinary narrow brick houses that stretched from one end of the block to the other. In truth, the whole street as far as the eye could see was made up of very nearly identical houses.

Emily's heart fell like a stone. Although she had not formed any firm opinion of what the school she would attend should look like, somehow she did have the idea that any school attended by a member of a royal family ought to be at least partly as grand as Sugar Hill Hall. That was the only thought that from time to time had helped lift her sagging spirits. So how could this plain narrow building on this dreary street be the right place? Could the cabdriver have misunderstood the directions? Surely Mr. Crawstone, to whom the school had been so highly recommended, would be as puzzled as Emily by this and would question the driver. But instead, he simply threw open the door and climbed down from the cab.

"This is it. Come along!" he said tersely. "You will wait here for me, please," he ordered the cab-driver. Then he swiftly climbed the brick steps to the plain painted brown door and raised the knocker.

If there was any remaining question in Emily's mind as to possibly being in the wrong place, it was instantly dispelled by the brass plaque hanging beside the door. Therefore, she knew when she stepped through the doorway that she had indeed for the first time stepped into Mrs. Spilking's Select Academy for Young Ladies.

But as for the owner of the academy, Emily never noticed that the woman who answered the door was not in a costume befitting the caretaker of a member of a royal family. Never noticed that she was in only a dull gray dress, with a narrow white band at the collar the only form of adornment—unless one was to consider the narrow belt from which dangled a large assortment of ominous keys on a dull brass ring. And never noticed that dark hair twisted into a stern bun pierced with a plain black comb atop her head did nothing to improve upon the pinched, sharp, bloodless face beneath it.

No, what Emily *did* notice was that the woman instantly lowered her face, pursing her lips in a way that suggested she had caught Emily in some wicked misdeed. With ice-green eyes flaring, she fixed Emily with an unblinking stare, seeming to be completely indifferent to the presence of Mr. Crawstone. In confusion, Emily quickly lowered her eyes. That was when she first saw the large black dog by the woman's side. Emily barely heard the door click shut behind her, because at the same moment, the dog growled, a deep, throaty, frightening growl.

Its collar was attached to a heavy iron chain, held with such white-knuckled intensity by the woman that it was evident if the dog were released, anyone in its way would be in grave peril. All of this—the pursed mouth, the flaring eyes, the tightly restrained dog—was certainly for Emily's benefit and clearly to serve as a warning. Oh, yes, a very clear warning, indeed!

But of what? And, oh, most particularly, why?

3

Mrs. Spilking's Select Academy

Any fleeting thought Emily had that this might be only a housekeeper and not Mrs. Spilking herself who had come to answer the door was quickly put to rest.

"I am Mrs. Spilking," she said. "And this is Emily Luccock, whom I have been told to expect, is it not?" She looked questioningly at Mr. Crawstone.

"It is, indeed," he replied with a small, stiff bow. "Allow me to present myself. I'm Ichabod Crawstone, commissioned by a friend of Miss Luccock's aunt and uncle to escort her here. And now that I've fulfilled my duty . . ." Mr. Crawstone put his hand on the door as if to leave.

"Oh, Mr. Crawstone," said Mrs. Spilking quickly. "You must permit me to invite you into my humble parlor to warm yourself by a small fire before going back out into this icy storm. Please do consider it."

Mr. Crawstone hesitated, then withdrew his hand from the door. "That's very kind, Mrs. Spilking. Why, yes, I do accept your kind offer."

"Splendid!" Mrs. Spilking pursed her lips again, but it was a purse that contained something far more inviting than was offered to Emily. "Come along, Emily. We will go into my parlor, where I will ring for the housemaid to escort you to your room. You may bring your portmanteau with you."

Keeping the dog tightly at her side with the chain, Mrs. Spilking proceeded down the narrow hallway, followed by Mr. Crawstone and Emily, *thump-thump-thumping* along with her portmanteau. The hall was only dimly lit by two fluttering gaslights set high in the wall, and furnished with but one stiff-backed wooden bench and a strip of carpet underfoot, Oriental to be sure, but thin, worn, and frayed at the edges.

But at the end of the hall, not too many feet from where stairs rose up to a dark landing, Mrs. Spilking led them into a room warmed by a fire crackling invitingly in the fireplace. On a hob in the fireplace, a teakettle hummed merrily. This room, her own private parlor it seemed, was cozy with plump, flowered chintz armchairs, lace doilies decorating tiny walnut tables, and at least a dozen bright, cheerful pictures of country scenes. On one of the tables reposed a fluted pink dish holding an array of miniature frosted cakes.

As soon as they entered the room, Mrs. Spilking quickly pressed a button, which produced the sound of a jangling bell somewhere in the far reaches of the building.

"Allow me to take your coat and hat, Mr. Crawstone," she said, as she carefully attached the dog's chain to a ring in the wall. "And won't you be seated? I hope you won't refuse a nice cup of hot tea?"

"I would be delighted, Mrs. Spilking," replied Mr. Crawstone, removing and handing her the garments requested.

"It's much too late to show Emily the school," said Mrs. Spilking. "That can all be taken care of tomorrow. You might be interested to know, Mr. Crawstone, that while the buildings appear narrow, we do have two of them."

"You have nothing to be ashamed of here, Mrs. Spilking," said Mr. Crawstone. "Your school came very highly recommended, as I was pleased to tell my friend, who sought my aid in behalf of Miss Luccock's aunt and uncle."

"Highly recommended!" exclaimed Mrs. Spilking. "That is flattering, indeed!"

Now, throughout all this exchange of pleasantries, Emily was left standing in her coat and bonnet, her portmanteau at her feet. She might well have been a girl standing in the middle of one of the paintings hanging on the wall for all the notice she was being given. And it was certain she was never to be invited to remove her coat and bonnet, to avail herself of a cozy chair, or to be offered a "nice cup of hot tea," much less one of the little frosted cakes.

But it was also certain that Mrs. Spilking was well aware of her presence, because at last she rose impatiently and rang the bell once more. "Now, where *is* that girl!"

The bell had no sooner finished jangling than "that girl" appeared, a lanky fifteen-or-so-year-old in a faded gray dress with part of the hem dragging and a disreputable white apron streaked with soot. Wisps of hair stuck out untidily from under a wrinkled mobcap that sagged around her sallow, thin face.

"Bella, this is Emily, a new student," said Mrs. Spilking. "I wish you to take her up to the room she is to occupy with Sarah and Lucy, as I am entertaining a guest at the moment. Where is your lantern? You know you must always be prepared with your lantern."

"I was, mum," said Bella without a flicker of an eyelash. "Saw lamps on in the hall, so left it in the dining room."

"Well, you may go then," snapped Mrs. Spilking. "Good night, Emily."

Emily was so startled at having her presence finally noted, she could barely mumble, "G-G-Good night, Mrs. Spilking. And—and thank you, Mr. Crawstone, for bringing me here."

Mr. Crawstone nodded his acknowledgment.

"And, Bella," said Mrs. Spilking as the two girls started from the room, "please do not appear in that condition again when you answer my bell."

"Yes, mum," replied Bella, rolling her eyes upward. She was careful, of course, to do this with only the back of her head visible to Mrs. Spilking.

Leaving Mrs. Spilking's room, Bella led Emily through a door across the hall where a plain long table with several straight-backed chairs around it were evidence that this was the dining room.

"Fancy a bisk?" Bella asked as she picked up a small lantern, already lit, sitting on a table against the wall.

"Bisk?" asked Emily, having never heard the word before.

Bella snickered. "Bisk-it, o' course. I figger you ain't had anything to eat. No chance in this world Mrs. Spilking would o' offered one o' them fancy little treasures she buys for herself and her royal majestry." Bella produced another telling roll of her eyes upward. "Anyways, offer still stands. You want a bisk?"

Emily had actually had nothing to eat since the noon meal aboard the train, and then only a hard roll and bit of cheese. Even a dried "bisk" sounded good at this point. She quickly nodded.

"Well, then," said Bella, "you wait whilst I go fetch it. I'll just snitch a couple o' bisks from the bisk basket and hope Madam S. don't go counting. Everything 'round here got a flippin' number on it."

Emily's breath caught in her throat. "Everything 'round here got a number on it." Wasn't that what Tilly had said on that first terrible night when Emily had arrived at Sugar Hill Hall?

"What—what would happen if you got caught?" she asked, trying to keep her voice from shaking.

Bella shrugged. "Oh, I might get sent back to Pa for a day. He'd wallop me 'round for a bit, then shoot me back here. He ain't having me home no more than Mrs. Spilking has intentions o' losing cheap help like me. But don't you worry. I'm good at not getting caught. Had lots of experience at it. You go park yourself on that bench out there. I'll be right back."

The bench was the one in the hallway. It was set against the wall between the door to Mrs. Spilking's parlor and the staircase. As soon as Bella had disappeared, Emily wished that she had asked to wait in the dark dining room instead of where she was. The door to Mrs. Spilking's room was not tightly closed, and a sliver of light streamed into the hallway. Further, Emily could hear the voices of Mrs. Spilking and Mr. Crawstone quite clearly. What if Mrs. Spilking were to come from her room and find Emily sitting there, for all intents and purposes eavesdropping? But Bella had told her to "park herself," and so, not certain if she should move, Emily remained "parked" on the bench. And though trying not to listen to the conversation coming from Mrs. Spilking's room, she was, despite herself, listening.

"Splendid cup of tea, Sophronia," said Mr. Crawstone.

"Thank you, Ichabod," replied Mrs. Spilking. Then she added coyly, "You may have noted a little drop of something added to keep you warm on your journey home."

"I have indeed noted it, Sophronia," said Mr. Crawstone, stealing a little more from his well-guarded supply of charm.

Sophronia? Ichabod? What was this all about, Emily wondered, rigid on her hard bench in the hall. How could Mrs. Spilking and Mr. Crawstone arrive in such a short time at the point where they were addressing each other familiarly by their first names? Even cold and unfeeling as he appeared to be, had Mr. Crawstone not questioned how a school so "highly recommended" could be so shabby and run by such a person as Mrs. Spilking? How could he now be sitting with her enjoying a cup of tea with "a little something in it"?

"I must say, Ichabod, it's a relief not to have had to put on the usual charade of showing the . . . um . . . *room* and all the rest," said Mrs. Spilking. "This is a great deal more pleasant."

"It is, Sophronia!" replied Mr. Crawstone. "It is!"

"Well, you certainly put on a convincing act in front of our little friend," said Mrs. Spilking. "You should go on the stage, Ichabod."

"I *thought* I did rather well," he replied. "Still, in the end, I suppose it doesn't matter much since, as you say, she'll never have the chance to tell all, even assuming she comes to know all."

"I'll take care of *that*, you may be sure," said Mrs. Spilking. "You *are* quite certain they are safely aboard the ship?"

"I saw them on their way with my own eyes," replied Mr. Crawstone. "I don't doubt at all that they are minutes away from being on the high seas."

"Splendid! Splendid!" said Mrs. Spilking.

What more they had to say Emily was not to know, because at that moment Bella tiptoed up and beckoned her toward the stairs. But as she followed Bella up, Emily's feelings were a mixture of rage and horror and pure terror. Had not Mr. Crawstone told Aunt and Uncle Twice that he had never visited this school? A lie! And everything that happened thereafter apparently a lie. Sophronia and Ichabod, indeed! They had known each other all along!

Yet what was the point of the lies? What difference could it make whether or not it was known that Mr. Crawstone was already acquainted with Mrs. Spilking? But most ominously, why would Emily never have the chance "to tell all," presumably to Aunt and Uncle Twice, who were now "safely aboard the ship"? And more ominously still, what was the "all" that Emily was not to tell?

Oh, why had Aunt and Uncle Twice so trusted Mr. Slyde that they had also put their trust in Mr. Slyde's friend Mr. Crawstone? Should they not have investigated the school more closely? Something sinister and terrible was happening to Emily, and she was powerless to stop it. Or was she?

Was not Mr. Crawstone's cab waiting for him in front of the school? Why not jump in and order the cabman to take her back to the docks? Yes, and then find the ship steaming away? Also, pay the cab with what? Aunt Twice had sewn into her trunk lining the two gold coins Uncle Twice had given her, and her portmanteau held nothing but a few of her necessary garments.

As soon as she could, she would write Aunt and Uncle Twice and tell them of the terrible mistake they had made. What they could then do about it she had no idea, but surely they would think of something. They would not possibly wish her to remain in such a place as this.

In the meantime, however, she was a prisoner of Mrs. Spilking's Select Academy for Young Ladies. There was no other way to put it. But the question was again . . . the question was *still* . . . why?

4

Sad Revelations

"Her flippin' majestry's room's that one," announced Bella when they reached the top of the stairs. She jerked a thumb over her shoulder toward a closed door at the front of the building. "Next door's the washroom, which she gets first go at when she wants it. No standing in line for *her*. If the other washroom's in use, everyone else just got to hold their breaths till she's through here. Hmmmph!" she snorted. "Only one gets to keep her door shut, too."

Bella now jerked the same thumb at the next door, which was, in truth, several inches ajar. Room sleeps two," she said. "Them are older girls been here longer than they ought, if anyone cares to know my opinion."

Emily actually cared very much to know Bella's

opinion about a great many things, but this was hardly the time to be asking—or even to be sharing confidences with someone she knew so little. At any rate, after struggling up the stairs with her portmanteau, she now had to give all her attention to simply keeping up with Bella.

Bella's thumb went back to work again as they turned at the head of the stairs and went through a doorway that must have been cut to join the two narrow buildings that made up the school. A second set of stairs just beyond the wall confirmed that. "Not for use excepting for me doing donkey work carrying laundry and the like," said Bella. "Madam S. wishes to know every girl what has to use stairs, so no sneaking up and down here. Now," again Bella's thumb was impressed into service, "there's the same room up front what's like her majestry's, only sleeps five. And here's the washroom for the rest. You take the lantern and go have a wash. I'll wait."

Grateful for the opportunity, Emily quickly availed herself of a room that did not invite anyone to remain there any longer than was absolutely necessary, with its bleak gray walls, cold linoleum, and worn granite basin with no mirror over it.

This without doubt insured the minimum of overflow into the room particularly reserved for royalty. Needless to say, Emily's washroom visit was speedily accomplished.

"This here's yours," said Bella, leading Emily through the door next to the washroom.

She found herself in a small room barely large enough to hold its one small pine chest of drawers and three brown-painted iron cots with a spindly pine chair next to each. Over the chest of drawers hung a little oval mirror so age spotted and clouded, the lantern flame hardly reflected in it at all. On the wall across from each cot was a coat hook, on two of which hung identical gray dresses. These clearly belonged to the occupants of the cots, two young girls at present fast asleep. The third cot, one under the window on the back wall, was empty.

Finger to her lips, Bella led Emily to the empty cot. "This is as far as you go. You got night stuff in that satchel?"

Emily nodded, setting her portmanteau on the piece of rag rug by the cot.

"Hey, what's this?" Bella lifted something from the foot of the cot. "Hmmmph! Looks like

Madam S. ain't wasting any time. It's your hew-nee-form waiting right here for you. Just hope it fits! I'll hang it up for you, then I'm out o' here. Don't want to be here when Madam makes her flippin' doggy run. Think you can finish up without the lantern?"

"Yes, I think so. B-B-But what's a doggy run?" Emily's voice quavered.

"Oh, it's just her cute little trick o' coming 'round with that dog o' hers, checking up on everyone." Bella shook her head with disgust. "Oops, almost forgot your bisks!" She dipped into her pocket and then thrust three hard little biscuits into Emily's hand. "Here you go. Just be careful 'bout crumbs. Eating in your room ain't 'lowed. You might o' guessed."

"Th-Th-Thank you, Bella. It's . . . it's—" Emily faltered, overcome by this small act of kindness.

"Aw, it ain't anything," Bella interrupted. "No need to go on about it. You take care o' yourself. Ain't anyone else going to!" And with that warning, Bella was gone.

Gone with her, of course, was the friendly lantern light. Darkness closed in around Emily. Nightdress on, clothes piled on the chair beside her, she climbed cautiously into her cot. The hair mattress was so thin she could feel the sharp springs under it, and her pillow was a hard lump under her head as she lay on her back staring up at the ceiling. Waiting!

Sure enough, it was not too long before she heard footsteps treading softly up the hall, with the occasional *click* of a dog's nails on the floor. As the footsteps came closer, Emily rolled on her side and snapped her eyes shut. In moments, she felt the heat of a lantern being held over her face and the sound of a dog panting beside her. One. Two. Three. Four. The seconds ticked by. It was unbearable. Finally, she felt the lantern heat leave her face, and then heard footsteps, accompanied by clicking nails, stealthily leave the room.

But even with this terror safely out of the way, Emily could not drop off to sleep. She felt as much alone as she had been when she had first arrived at Sugar Hill Hall and had been consigned to that grim little room in the cellar inhabited by only herself and rats. But at least there she always had Aunt Twice, as much a prisoner as Emily was, to be sure, but at least she was there. Now her aunt was on a ship already bound for far-off India, so that

Emily could not possibly "tell all," that mysterious, ominous "all"! Oh, why had Aunt and Uncle Twice abandoned her? Why had they left her here with no one to turn to?

Emily could hold back the tears no longer. But she did not want to waken the two strange girls in her room or let them know of her misery, so she turned over and buried her face in her hard little pillow to stifle her sobs. As a result, she never heard the squeak of bedsprings, the sound of a match being struck, or the bare feet padding softly across the floor.

It was not until she felt a hand on her shoulder and turned to see the tiny flutter of lantern flame turned low that she knew anyone was standing by her bed. Mrs. Spilking! It must be Mrs. Spilking returned to her room! With a start, Emily turned over, her heart in her throat. But she found herself looking not into the deadly face of Mrs. Spilking, but into the frightened faces of two young girls. The one holding the lantern glanced nervously over her shoulder at the doorway.

"We're not supposed to be up," she whispered. "I mean, unless we have to use the washroom. Mrs. Spilking says Wolf—that's her dog—will rip us to shreds if we're caught. Anyway, my name is Sarah." The weak flame in the lantern lit up a pair of remarkably clear blue eyes, but they were set in a pasty, narrow face with a pinched nose so red rimmed it must have been subject to frequent applications of a wiping rag. Her hair, a nondescript brown, dangled thinly around her shoulders.

"I'm Lucy," said the second girl, whose face, while equally pasty, featured a pug nose peppered with freckles and cheeks puffed out like pale apples. This was all topped with an untidy mop of red ringlets.

"We decided we were going to let the new girl, which is you, know in case she cried that it was all right," said Sarah.

"*We* cried when we came," said Lucy. "You're Emily, aren't you, the new girl?"

Emily nodded, quickly sitting up in her cot.

"Who—who is it who didn't want *you*?" Lucy asked timidly.

"I—I don't understand," stammered Emily.

"Well," said Sarah, pausing to wipe her nose on the sleeve of her nightdress, "we're both here because of stepmamas who don't want us around. Mine is really pretty, and she doesn't want anyone thinking someone as plain as me belongs to her. That's not what she says, though. She just made Papa believe I ought to be in boarding school. It was easy. She's so pretty, and now with the baby coming, she has Papa twisted 'round her little finger. I guess it's the way papas are. So here I am!"

"*I'm* here because my stepmama is not just pretty, but is lots, lots younger than my real mama was," Lucy said. "She doesn't like having anyone thinking she's the mama of someone who's as old as eleven. She thinks it makes *her* seem old. I'm not even certain she wants the baby that's coming in case it makes her look old as well, though she can't very well send the baby to boarding school. But Sarah's right. The real reason is never what they say. *Everyone* is here because someone doesn't want them, we think."

"Even—even the person of—of royal blood?" asked Emily.

"That's Princess Delilla," replied Lucy. "At least that's what we're expected to call her. But we don't know why *she's* here. We don't know anybody who does. It's a big mystery."

"But lucky for Mrs. Spilking she *is* here," said Sarah. "It makes the school sound grand to tell people someone royal is here. I expect your family was told that, weren't they?"

Emily nodded. That's exactly what they were told!

"Yes," Lucy chimed in, "and Mrs. Spilking gets to show off the princess's big pretty room to the families. But the other girls actually get put in rooms like this one. Mrs. Spilking is so afraid someone in Princess Delilla's country will take her back, we expect, she gets all the special treats. Sarah and I think she's spoiled as she can be, don't we, Sarah?"

Sarah nodded, scowling. "Yes, we do." Then she added wistfully, "We sometimes wish *we* were the princesses here. Then it might not be so bad."

"The way it is . . . ," Lucy began, first looking at Sarah, then fearfully back again at the doorway, "we—we *hate* it here!"

"Your families might take you back. Can't you write a letter to them about it?" asked Emily. After all, that was what *she* intended to do.

Lucy shook her head. "Mrs. Spilking reads all our letters, even those of the older girls, and mails them herself. Every morning we have penmanship, and that's when once a week we write letters.

She checks every one before it gets sent. It's for spelling and grammar, she *says,* even though we write the same things every time."

"We ask how everyone is at home," Sarah broke in. "Then we tell them how happy we are and how much we're learning. Well, it's what they want to hear, anyway, and it's what Mrs. Spilking expects."

"And if anyone comes to call on us, we have to sit in Mrs. Spilking's parlor with Mrs. Spilking right there," said Lucy. "So how would we dare complain about anything?"

"Papa came to visit me at the beginning . . . once," Sarah said. "I had to tell him how glad I was to be here. I write that as well, and Papa always writes back how happy he is to hear it. I mean, when he remembers to write."

"It's exactly the same with me," Lucy said, and then hesitated. "But you never have said who it is who doesn't want *you.*"

"It—it isn't anyone," said Emily. "At least, I don't have a stepmama. My mama and papa are both no more, but my aunt and uncle who look after me had to go to India. All English children in India my age get sent back to England to go to school."

"Do American children get sent back to America as well?" asked Lucy.

"I—I guess so," replied Emily. "It's what they said, anyway. So they just left me here."

Sarah considered this a moment. "Well," she said, "it does seem as if you didn't get put here because you weren't wanted. I mean, unless your aunt's to have a baby and you'd be too much trouble to take along. She's not, is she?"

Slowly, Emily nodded.

"Oh!" said Lucy and Sarah, looking at her with sympathetic, pitying eyes.

Well, was that not what deep, deep down Emily had been thinking all along? No wonder the great Mr. Slyde had recommended Mrs. Spilking's Select Academy for Young Ladies. Everyone there was not wanted . . . a perfect choice for Emily!

"How—how long does everyone have to stay here?" Emily asked, remembering what Bella had said about the older girls.

Sarah shrugged. "We don't know, but we guess it's until our families marry us off to some old man wanting a young wife. Or perhaps we'll have to go off to be a governess or something like that."

"Well, that's never going to happen to me!"

cried Lucy, a sob in her throat. "I'll run away first. I haven't seen my grandpapa since my mama died. He's been at sea all this time. But perhaps if I can find him, he'd think of something."

"Lucy, you mustn't talk about running away," breathed Sarah, shuddering. "You know what Mrs. Spilking says. If we ever so much as set foot outside the school without her, she'll set Wolf on us. He can find us wherever we are, she says, and will tear us to shreds. But now we'd better get back to bed. What if they were to come again?"

Lucy's eyes flew open with fright at the thought of this possibility. "We'll see you in the morning, Emily," she whispered. And with one last trembling smile, the two girls ran swiftly back to their cots.

Once again in the darkness, foreboding thoughts began again to crowd into Emily's head. There was little question now as to why she was in Mrs. Spilking's Select Academy for Young Ladies. Not wanted! Every girl in that school was not wanted! Still, Aunt and Uncle Twice would surely write to her from India, and she would write back. Remembering Aunt Twice's tearful eyes at the boat dock, and Uncle Twice's warm hug, she could hardly believe they no longer cared for her, even if at the moment she was not wanted in their lives. Still, what exactly could she tell them?

All letters read by Mrs. Spilking! Is that not what Sarah and Lucy had said? Now Emily knew the meaning of Mr. Crawstone and Mrs. Spilking's assurances to each other that she would never be able to "tell all." Oh, how that ominous "all" kept returning to her thoughts! And though she could not explain why, except perhaps for "Sophronia" and "Ichabod" lying about knowing each other, she had the terrible feeling that the "all" applied only to her, and not to Sarah or Lucy or any other girl at the school.

Yet was there not something else that applied to her as well? The sudden thought made her heart beat faster. Was she still not an heiress? For the time being, Mr. Slyde was to manage her fortune, but she would come into it at seventeen. Marry an old man or become a governess, indeed! No, all she had to do was stick it out. Five years plus some months seemed an impossibly long time, but other girls had made it here that long, and she would do it. Yes, she would do it!

Her spirits considerably repaired, Emily now remembered all at once the "bisks" so kindly provided her by Bella. She wished now she had offered to share them with Sarah and Lucy, although they might well have been too frightened to accept them. So Emily pulled them out from the pocket of her coat lying on her chair, where she had hidden them, and lay nibbling on them in the dark. And thinking.

And when her eyes finally closed for sleep, her cheeks were dry. She had cried her first night at Sugar Hill Hall, and not again. Now she had finished with crying here. For she was remembering how she had survived the early horrors of Sugar Hill Hall: a wicked servant girl who only later proved to have a heart of gold as Bella did, a dank little cellar room, peopled only by rats, down the hall from the grim Remembrance Room, as opposed now to being in an upstairs room with two friendly young girls, and nothing more threatening down the hall than a spoiled princess. So if she could survive her introduction to Sugar Hill Hall, she could certainly survive all the charms provided by Mrs. Spilking's Select Academy for Young Ladies, including a vicious dog who might "tear her to shreds"! Yes, she could do it. She *would* do it! But, oh, if only there were not that short, terrible word hanging over her head.

"All"!

5

Oh No!

The loud, piercing sound of a jangling bell woke Emily rudely in the morning. Her mind still clouded from sleep that had been so long and late in coming the night before, she raised herself up to see that it was barely light outside her window. The window framed a frozen picture of ice-clad rooftops, a tiny, barren backyard, and beyond that an unkempt, empty lot. Emily shuddered at the sight of this cheerless landscape. She quickly turned from it to see that Sarah and Lucy had already made up their cots and were scrambling into their gray dresses.

"Hurry, Emily, hurry! We mustn't be late!" Even the dress being pulled over Sarah's head could not disguise the fear in her voice.

"It's three demerits if you're late to breakfast!"

Lucy breathlessly added her own dire warning. "It's on Mrs. Spilking's rule list right here on the door. You'll have to study it later. She expects us to know the rules by heart, every last one!"

Emily lost no time in dropping her feet to the floor and throwing her coverlet up over her cot. Climbing out of her nightdress and into her petticoat, she scurried to retrieve her own gray dress hung up by Bella. Bella's hopes that it would fit were in vain. The dress was way too large, and it was only by lifting the skirt and knotting the belt tightly around her waist that Emily was able to keep it from dragging on the floor. Then after pulling on her stockings and fastening her high-button shoes with trembling fingers, she hurried from the room with Sarah and Lucy.

But it was only to have to stand at the end of a line, breathless, waiting to enter the washroom. The closed door signaled that the room was already in use, with four other girls queued up behind it. Through the doorway to the adjoining building, Emily could see two girls, older ones, who undoubtedly were the two referred to by Bella as having been there "longer than they ought." It seemed they were taking their chances on "her majestry" finishing before the other wash-room became available.

Each girl, when she emerged from the wash-room, went flying down the stairs. But when Emily had finished with her "turn," she was happy to see that Sarah and Lucy were waiting for her, though clearly frightened at doing so. Others were now standing there as well, the two older girls who had given up waiting for Princess Delilla to emerge from her washroom. That door was still tightly shut.

Her heart thumping, Emily followed Sarah and Lucy back to the hall she had entered the night before, and was led through the door behind the stairs into the dining room. The five other girls were already seated in straight-backed chairs at the one long table in the room. They sat in absolute silence, their hands folded on the table before them. At the head of the table sat Mrs. Spilking. From the time Sarah, Lucy, and Emily entered the room and took chairs across from the five girls, she stared at them with her eyes flaring and lips com-pressed. It was as if they were all being accused of something. Of what? Being late? How could they possibly have been down any sooner? The two oldest girls arrived moments later, one to take the chair next to Mrs. Spilking, the other the one next to the empty chair at the other end of the table.

The only other person in the room was Bella. She stood leaning on the wall beside the kitchen door, indifferently puffing on her fingernails and polishing them on her apron. Beside her was a serving cart, on which now lay only a large tin ladle.

As Emily could see, however, there was to be something more arriving, because in front of each girl was an empty china bowl, five matching and the rest plainly unmatched replacements. Beside each bowl was a spoon, and *none* of these matched. A white enamel pitcher was set in front of Mrs. Spilking, as well as a small, worn china bowl with only the memory of any painted design still remaining. This bowl contained . . . was it actually sugar? Emily was astonished. She had no idea what was finally to go into the bowls, but so far this was more promising than the fish-head stew and moldy bread lumps served the old people at Sugar Hill Hall. Yes, perhaps she really could stick it out at Mrs. Spilking's Select Academy for Young Ladies!

But so far, nothing was being served for them to eat. The girls continued to sit in silence, hands folded on the table before them, hands now including Emily's. The silence continued, until at last footsteps were heard on the stairs.

"Bella, you may now serve!" ordered Mrs. Spilking.

Bella immediately came to life and grabbed the handle of the serving cart as she prepared to race back with it to the kitchen. But before she could even get started, the kitchen door flew open. Out stumped an enormous woman in a faded pink dress, split at almost every visible seam. A mobcap drooping way to one side of her head and a sagging apron both made no pretense of ever having been anything but filthy and grease stained. Her face, round as a pot lid, and at the moment an angry red, was the setting for a pair of squinted eyes and several quivering chins. She was carrying a great, black iron pot, which she proceeded to slam down on the serving cart.

"I ain't got all day to stand la-da-da-ing in the kitchen stirring a blinkin' pot, waiting for her majesty to show up in the dining room!" she announced furiously. "I got a other job to go to and better things to do there. I should go and let this stuff burn on the stove. One day I will. Mark my words!"

"I am sorry for the inconvenience, Mrs. Slump," said Mrs. Spilking coldly. "But that will be quite enough."

"Not *nearly* enough!" growled Mrs. Slump, as she went thumping back through the door, giving it an extra shove to leave it swinging savagely behind her.

Mrs. Slump had no sooner disappeared, although the door was still trembling on its hinges, than "her majestry" the Princess Delilla came strolling in as if she had nothing whatsoever to do with the cause of the eruption.

If Emily had ever given any thought to what a princess should look like, she might very well have pictured her as this girl, except, of course, for her gray dress matching those of the others. Probably no more than fifteen years of age, she was tall and slender. Overshadowing an imperial nose and a perfectly formed mouth and chin were startlingly brilliant eyes, so green and slanted as to be almost catlike. A black ribbon tied back her glossy dark hair to reveal shapely ears wearing something probably not allowed any other girl there, earrings! They were only tiny gold balls, but earrings nonetheless. And finally, her cheeks could only be described as interestingly pale, not pasty as in the case of the other girls. All in all, it could not be denied that this princess was most decidedly . . . pretty!

But she was also decidedly pampered and, just as Lucy and Sarah had said, spoiled. Well, here she was never even opening her mouth to say she was sorry for being late. And Mrs. Spilking said not a word to her about it as she sauntered over and dropped into the chair at the head of the table. This was despite the fact that she had kept ten girls waiting for their meal, not to mention Mrs. Spilking herself, and created a major uproar on the part of Mrs. Slump.

As she was settling herself at the table and adjusting her skirt, however, Bella was already wheeling her cart to the head of the table, and had begun ladling gray, gluey lumps of porridge from the iron pot into the bowls, starting with Mrs. Spilking's. Emily was further astonished that Mrs. Spilking was to share the same unappetizing fare as that given the girls. This was a far cry from Sugar

Hill Hall, where Madams Meeching and Plumly ate nothing at all with the old people and then dined in high style in a private dining room later. But Emily finally decided that Mrs. Spilking eating with the girls was nothing but a sham, for Bella put such a small portion of the porridge in her bowl it was all but invisible.

Nonetheless, she continued the pretense by pouring milk from the enamel pitcher into her bowl. Or at least Emily supposed the substance pouring from the pitcher to be milk, though it was so thin and watered down as to be almost blue. Then, as this traveled down the table, Mrs. Spilking lifted the sugar bowl, and with a spoon no larger than a salt spoon, carefully sprinkled one spoonful into her bowl. Under her watchful, piercing glare, each of the five girls opposite Emily did the same.

But when the bowl reached the princess, she simply dumped a heaping spoonful into her bowl. Then a second. Then a third. She had helped herself to at least seven spoonfuls before passing on the bowl. But if Emily had any ideas of imitating this act, they soon evaporated when the older girl next to the princess, like all the other girls, carefully sprinkled one tiny spoon of sugar into her bowl.

Sadly, the few grains of sugar in connection with a thin, nearly blue liquid not much improved over plain water, did little to enhance a large, steaming lump of gluey, tasteless, gray porridge. Probably because they had finally become used to it, or simply because they were hungry and knew they could expect nothing better, the older girls seemed able to get most of it down. But Emily could choke down only a few bites, and she could see that Sarah and Lucy did not do much better. If only she had some of Kipper's pa's fish syrup that had done so much to increase the appetites of the old people of Sugar Hill Hall! But at last all spoons were laid down, and the dismal meal was ended.

"Bella, you may now clear," said Mrs. Spilking. "Adelaide, you will please fetch the stationery and pens for letter writing. Eudora, you will fetch the pots of ink."

So as Bella rushed the cart around the table collecting the bowls, spoons, milk pitcher, and sugar pot, two of the girls hurried to the sideboard. They returned to the table with the articles ordered by Mrs. Spilking, and passed them out to the girls still seated.

"Now," said Mrs. Spilking, "you will note that

our new girl, Emily Luccock, is with us, so I must explain what we are about to do, which is write letters. Time is allowed for this every week because I know all the girls' families long to hear from them, as I'm sure Emily's own family does." Mrs. Spilking paused to flare her eyes in Emily's direction. "You may begin now, girls."

Mrs. Spilking had, of course, said not a word about the fact that she would be reviewing the letters for spelling, grammar, or anything else. Nor had she even mentioned that the letters would pass through her hands for mailing. The other girls must know this, as did Sarah and Lucy. So the omission could only have been to let Emily hang herself from the very outset by writing her exact opinions of the school thus far. But thanks to Sarah and Lucy, Emily was quite prepared for it. So this is the letter she finally wrote:

> *Dear Aunt and Uncle Twice,*
>
> *How was your exciting voyage to India? I hope it was fun and that you are both well.*
>
> *I am so glad you learned about Mrs. Spilking's Academy from Mr. Slyde. I have only just come, but I believe I am going to like it a great deal.*

I have a nice room that I share with two other girls, and we all wear neat gray uniforms.

My first breakfast has been a delicious porridge with milk and sugar, but I could not even finish mine, because we were all given such grand portions.

I expect to enjoy my lessons very much.

Hoping to hear from you soon, I remain your loving niece,

Emily

While Emily was writing, she once looked up to see Mrs. Spilking watching her with an eager gleam in her eyes and a half smile on her face. *Oh, yes,* said the look, *she is pouring her heart out to her aunt and uncle with every complaint she can think of. Well, we shall see about that, Miss Emily Luccock!*

When Emily had drawn her letter to an end and laid down her pen, she dropped her eyes guiltily, as if she had actually written the dreadful report expected by Mrs. Spilking.

"Well, I see we are all now finished, so just as we always do, we will now pass our letters in to me for spelling and grammar approval," said Mrs. Spilking, all the while never for a moment taking her eyes off Emily. "Now," she said as soon as all letters had been passed to her, "I shall first look at our new student's letter to see if she measures up to our academy standards."

From the way Mrs. Spilking's mouth twitched as she read Emily's letter, it would be safe to say that she was receiving a shock of a very unexpected and unpleasant nature. In the place of the frown and stinging rebuke she was prepared to deliver, she had instead to apply a forced smile to her face and tell Emily that she had, indeed, written a very nice letter. Further, as the spelling and grammar were flawless, she did not even have the pleasure of remarking on that. All that remained to be said was that she would see the letter was mailed at once to Emily's aunt and uncle in India.

Her plans in total disarray, Mrs. Spilking rushed through the other letters and then announced they would adjourn to the next room for their other studies and activities. Emily had begun to think the dining room was to be their sole classroom, but as the girls now rose from the table, Mrs. Spilking opened the wide pocket doors that led to a larger room at the front of the house.

Straight-backed chairs, each with a thin pillow on the seat, circled the room. In front of the chairs were long, low tables. On the table, before each chair, was a large cardboard box. At the head of the room, facing all the other chairs, was a faded purple, worn velveteen, high-backed wing chair. In front of the chair was also a table holding a large box. And to the side of that chair and table was . . . was . . .

Oh no! No! No! No!

Emily felt as if something had struck her hard in the chest. She struggled to take a breath as her legs began to buckle and finally give way entirely. Then blackness rolled over her, and she fell to the floor, senseless.

6

No Explanation

Emily had only the vaguest recollection of being helped up the stairs by two of the older girls. She could not remember being helped into her cot, however, or having someone undo and pull off her high-button shoes. But those things must have happened, because when she finally returned to her senses, she was indeed lying in her cot with her shoes off. But before then, she had been drifting in and out of a dark fog, not aware of anything. Later, she thought she remembered opening her eyes for a moment and seeing Mrs. Spilking peering down at her with narrowed, calculating eyes. Then the dark fog had rolled over her again.

When at last the fog lifted and did not return, Emily finally opened her eyes to see two scared faces looking at her, the faces of Sarah and Lucy.

"Oh!" cried Sarah, "you are all right, Emily. You had us so frightened."

"What happened to you?" asked Lucy. "Was it the dreadful porridge? Did it make you ill?"

"You—you'll get used to it," said Sarah uncertainly. "You just have to, Emily."

"I'll try. I really will," said Emily. "But—but it wasn't the porridge."

"What, then?" asked Lucy. "It could not have been because you were afraid of what you wrote in your letter. Mrs. Spilking said it was a nice letter. You were clever to write one like that, Emily."

"I remembered what you told me," said Emily. "But it wasn't that, either. It was—it was . . . the peppermints!"

The peppermints! Yes, *peppermints*! Peppermints in that very building! Peppermints in the room under the very floor where Emily lay in her cot! *They* were what had robbed Emily of all her breath, what had turned her legs to rubber, and finally sent the dark cloud rolling over her when she had walked into the room.

In that room, next to the wing chair, sat a round table hidden under a rich, full-skirted, red velvet cloth. Trimmed in an elegant gold fringe, it reached all the way to the floor, contrasting curiously with the worn carpet beneath it. And on this grand setting reposed a sparkling, crystal bowl holding the peppermints . . . tantalizing, tempting, pink-and-white-striped peppermint drops. The whole was a close cousin, if not an exact twin, to the one that had once sat in the parlor of Sugar Hill Hall! Had they been put there just for Emily's benefit? By whom? Certainly not by Mrs. Meeching or Mrs. Plumly, both now safely locked up in prison. By whom, then? Had those two . . . had they anything to do with "all"?

Sarah and Lucy's eyes flew wide open. "Peppermints?" they gasped together.

"Why?" asked Sarah.

"It—it has something to do with what happened to me before I came here," Emily replied, sitting up in her cot. "It's a long story, and later I'll tell it to you. But—but were they only just put there before I came?"

"Oh, no!" said Lucy. "They were there when we came months ago."

Months ago? Well, then, perhaps they had nothing to do with Emily alone, nothing to do with "all." But there still seemed something mysterious about it, something ominous. What?

Emily faltered. "Wh-Wh-Why are they there?" she asked.

"Mrs. Spilking tells you," said Sarah, and then paused to reconsider. "Well, she doesn't *exactly* tell you. It's like our stepmamas never *exactly* telling us why they don't want us. What her rule *says* is that the peppermints are there for guests only, and we're never to take one."

"Sarah and I have never seen a guest in the Front Room . . . not ever," Lucy said. "What we believe is that the peppermints are there for a temptation."

"It's no wonder," Sarah said, drawing her shoulders up and shuddering. "I wouldn't take one for my life! It's not like demerits, where what you get for punishment is mostly staying outside all alone when everyone else has come in, or extra lines in penmanship. And you have to have at least fifty demerits before you face dire consequences, the rules say. It only takes *one* peppermint to face them!"

"And we all know what dire consequences are," Lucy broke in, "because Mrs. Spilking always announces it when someone has to face them. It means the Cupboard!"

"Th-Th-The Cupboard?" stammered Emily. "Whatever is that?"

"It's a very tiny room in the cellar with a cot in it," replied Sarah. "When you get the Cupboard, it means spending the night there, with Wolf outside guarding the door just waiting to rip you to shreds!"

A very tiny room in the cellar with a cot in it! Was that not the very description of the grim Remembrance Room in Sugar Hill Hall? But terrible as that one was, it did not have a vicious dog posted outside that was panting to rip a person to shreds. Mrs. Spilking's Select Academy provided some very select horrors, indeed. And Emily had the prospect of facing them for more than five long years that seemed to be growing longer by the minute!

But now Sarah tugged anxiously at Lucy's arm. "We must go back down, Lucy. Mrs. Crumble will be here by now. We were only sent to look in on Emily, not to stay all day."

"Are you well enough to come with us?" Lucy asked Emily.

"I—I think so," replied Emily, climbing from her cot and managing to remain standing. "But who is Mrs. Crumble?"

"Mrs. Crumble comes in to watch over us while we do our embroidery and knitting and drawing, which we do mostly all day. She lives in a house nearby, she says. We expect she doesn't get paid much because she's Mrs. Spilking's sister. But she's nice, and we think she only pretends to be strict because she's as afraid of Mrs. Spilking as we are."

Well, it was certain that Mrs. Crumble did look very nice, indeed, sitting in the wing chair in the Front Room below. Her head was bent over an embroidery hoop, as were those of all the girls. Atop her head was a dainty lace doily, and perched on her nose was a pair of tiny spectacles. When Emily entered the room with Sarah and Lucy, she looked up to reveal blossom-pink cheeks and a tremulous smile. Sister to Mrs. Spilking she might be, but she appeared a far cry from Mrs. Spilking.

But did she not also present a picture as cozy as that presented by Mrs. Plumly when Emily first came through the doors of Sugar Hill Hall? And did Mrs. Plumly not turn out to be more evil, more treacherous, more wicked even than Mrs. Meeching, named "the snake lady" by Emily's friend Kipper, the fishmonger's boy? And, oh yes, had Mrs. Plumly, a splendid actress, not won Emily over by what turned out to be a totally false appearance of being terrified of Mrs. Meeching?

And there was Mrs. Crumble, sitting and smiling so sweetly, as if she were quite unaware of the table with the red velvet cloth and the sparkling bowl full of those deadly, seductive peppermints right beside her—quite unaware that anyone taking one would be led to a room in the cellar guarded by a dog that was fully prepared to tear a person to shreds.

So how was Emily to sit there calmly doing embroidery with fingers that had suddenly turned to lumps of ice? Well, she would do it, for she could pretend as well as anyone could. And while Sarah and Lucy and all the girls might think Mrs. Crumble was just as "nice" as she could be, Emily intended to be on her guard. For everything at Mrs. Spilking's Select Academy, including Mrs. Crumble, was whispering, *Beware, Emily Luccock. Beware!* And never for a moment forget . . .

"All"!

7

A Trip to the Cellar

"Watch your step. Ain't the best light down here," Bella warned as she led Emily by lantern light down the steep, narrow steps to the cellar. "And I been informed you're only to collect a clean nightdress and what goes on under the flippin' hew-nee-form. Anything else what might pass for pretty stays in the trunk. Hmmmph!" she snorted, passing judgment on this order.

Emily hesitated. "Is—is this where you have to live, Bella?"

"Where else?" said Bella with a shrug. "Servants' quarters is servants' quarters, and far as I know, the cellar is where they're mostly at."

Upon hearing this, Emily felt a sudden chill. When, after the evening meal, she had been attempting to learn to knit in the Front Room, with four lamps on the wall barely providing enough light to cast a shadow, she had been happy to be rescued by Bella, come on Mrs. Spilking's orders to fetch her to pay a visit to her trunk in the cellar. Now Emily wondered how she could have been so eager to come. Better to have remained in the Front Room learning to knit under the watchful eyes of Mrs. Crumble, struggling with impossibly long knitting needles, than to be where she was now.

Another cellar, oh so familiar, dank and dark, and heavy with the odors of mold and mildew! Servants' quarters! All reminders of her frightening introduction to Sugar Hill Hall! So what she must keep reminding herself now was that she was not a servant, that she did not have to live in a cellar, and most important of all, that she did not even have to stay at Mrs. Spilking's Select Academy forever, for she was still an heiress. Yes, an heiress possessed of an immense fortune!

"My room's that one," said Bella, once again putting her valuable thumb to use. "Over there's the laundry. Up front's the steps to the street what's used by me and Mrs. Slump. Trunk room's next building . . . this way."

Brushing aside dusty cobwebs, Bella now led Emily through a door into a small corridor matching the first. There was a door, as well, to steps leading out the front of the building.

"Where is the—the Cupboard?" Emily asked faintly, not entirely certain she really wanted to know.

"You heard about that already?" Bella asked. "Well, small wonder. Stuff like that gets 'round early on. Anyways, that's it." She jerked her head toward a closed door. "Always gives me the creeps just thinking 'bout it. Well, this here's the trunk room, and this trunk's the one got your name on it."

Bella leaned down and lifted up the lock of the trunk. "Hmmmph! Already been pried open, by Madam S., I presumes. No surprise why she never said you was to bring a key. Hope you ain't got anything in here you don't want her nose into."

Emily was all too familiar now with her trunks being broken into or even stolen in their entirety. She was actually happy to have her trunk even make an appearance. Quickly, she knelt down to unlatch and throw open the lid, with Bella holding the lantern over her head. It was clear that somebody had rifled through her belongings, but done so very carefully.

There was surely one thing Mrs. Spilking would have a great interest in finding. But when Emily looked at the place where Aunt Twice had carefully stitched in the two gold coins given her by Uncle Twice, she could see at once that the stitching had not been touched. Aunt Twice had done her work well!

And there was Abigail, the beautiful doll given her by Aunt and Uncle Twice! Emily picked her up and hugged her, but when she looked at Bella, Bella only shook her head and sighed. No, Abigail had to remain in the trunk. All Emily was to take from it, as Bella had said, was a nightdress and what she would wear under her gray uniform. Her red velveteen party dress, her navy blue sailor dress, and her green plaid skirt and yellow silk blouse must all remain behind. Without even pulling them out, Emily slipped her hands under each one, comforted in knowing they were there.

But what was that curious bundle she felt? It was hard, shaped like a flattened bottle, and in a thick wrapping of cotton cloth. If someone had not put their hand in just that exact spot, they might have missed it entirely. Emily pulled it out, carefully unwrapped the cloth, and then gasped. For what she found was, in truth, a bottle, flattened on opposite sides. On one side was pasted a label with somewhat rough, untidy printing: PA'S FISH SYRUP—TAKE IN CASE OF NEED. ALSO, TELL PIPER HELLO IF YOU EVER SEE HIM. KIPPER.

For a moment, Emily was too startled even to speak. How had Kipper managed to get this in her trunk? And then all at once, she remembered, and could hardly keep tears from springing into her eyes. Kipper had promised to send something along for her to remember him by when she left Sugar Hill Hall. Emily thought he had forgotten the promise, and with all that was happening to her, she had forgotten it herself . . . until now. Kipper must have secretly given it to Aunt Twice to slip into Emily's trunk, which, along with the gold coins, Aunt Twice had done most successfully.

"What in tarnation's that?" asked Bella, reading the label over Emily's shoulder. "Fish syrup! Ugh!"

"It isn't bad at all, really, Bella," Emily hurried to say. "It's something my friend Kipper's pa makes, to improve the appetite. And it works, too. I expect Mrs. Spilking didn't look carefully enough or she would have found it and then thrown it out. But, oh," Emily said wistfully, sighing. "I suppose I can't take it with me anyway."

"My eyesight ain't too good, and I ain't seen a thing," said Bella, pretending to gaze at the ceiling. "Wrap it up in your nightdress and bring it along. Just hide it good and proper in your room. Your appetite needs all the help it can get till you get used to Mrs. Slump's kwee-zeenee."

But it wasn't until Emily was back in her room and looking at the bottle once more that she puzzled over Kipper's message: "Tell Piper hello." Piper? Who was Piper? And then she remembered!

When Kipper's pa had left New York for San Francisco, his brother had stayed in New York. Piper was his brother's son, and therefore Kipper's cousin, although the boys had known each other only as babies. But Emily knew she had as much chance of meeting Piper to deliver the message as she had of making a trip to India . . . or the moon. She was a prisoner of Mrs. Spilking's Select Academy for Young Ladies, and that was that. Further, she could not even write Kipper to tell him she had the fish syrup, or write him anything at all. Just how would such a letter get past Mrs. Spilking? But at least Emily had the fish syrup. She would even share it with Sarah and Lucy, for Emily could see that their appetites needed improving as well, despite what they said.

So in the end, the trip to the cellar had proved worthwhile after all. Fish syrup! Seeing Abigail! Emily could hardly wait for Sarah and Lucy to leave the Front Room and come up to bed so she could make her report!

Emily's trip to the cellar turned out to be one of the happiest events of her long, dreary days at Mrs. Spilking's Select Academy. Even the friendship of Lucy and Sarah provided few happy moments, for they were both frightened of everything. Emily could not even persuade them to take more than a taste of the fish syrup. Oh, it was not that they thought it was unpleasant. It was because they actually were afraid Mrs. Spilking might catch a whiff of fish in case they should have to pass by her!

And how could Emily blame them? Mrs. Spilking's presence, whether or not seen, was felt everywhere, even when they lined up in the morning, shivering outside the bleak, icy washroom. For was she not waiting right below them in person to make certain no one was one moment late in arriving at the table? And was she not there to preside over the gray, tasteless, gluey lumps called "porridge" and to clear her throat threateningly if one extra grain of sugar found its way into a bowl?

It was also Mrs. Spilking who graced the noon table, where the girls were treated to slices of bread that had clearly departed a bakery days earlier, and that was hardly improved when spread with "butter" that was more likely pure lard, if color and flavor were any signs. Accompanying this tasty fare were cups of tea so weak they rivaled the milk that had come from the same pitcher that morning.

Needless to say, Mrs. Spilking also presided over the dinner table, where the same menu was provided day in and day out, potato and turnip stew, a dish as tasteless and unappetizing as the morning porridge. However, whereas the girls had to knit in the Front Room every night until bedtime in near darkness, Mrs. Spilking clearly believing money should not be wasted on anything so frivolous as eyesight, the food, such as it was, was always plentiful. It could only be concluded from this that girls were of no value to Mrs. Spilking if they perished from hunger, as then all payments from their families would perish with them.

In addition to the meals, Mrs. Spilking was also present to conduct the "class" in penmanship. She sat at the table with her eyes calculating not only what was being written, but also the amount of ink used to write it. One morning, one of the girls spilled two drops of ink as her pen traveled from the ink pot to her paper. Mrs. Spilking's eyes flared as she watched the poor offender try to mop up the spill with shaking hands, using a small rag of a handkerchief from her pocket.

"So," said Mrs. Spilking when this sad performance had ended, "it appears that Alicia has never learned the motto 'Waste not, want not' and has carelessly spilled valuable ink on the table. Alicia, would you like to repeat for the benefit of all rule number fifteen?"

"I-I-Ink spilled during penmanship, four demerits," recited Alicia, her pitifully thin, bent shoulders trembling.

"Very well," said Mrs. Spilking, instantly opening the black notebook on the table before her. With lips compressed into a tight, disapproving line, she found the right page in the book, and *tick-tick-tick-ticked* on it with her pen. "Hmm, that makes twelve demerits, all for the same misdemeanor! Tomorrow morning, Alicia, you will stay behind to provide me with thirty copies of that rule in perfect penmanship, with *no* drops of spilled ink!"

After this pronouncement, Mrs. Spilking treated everyone at the table to a flare of her eyes, and then proceeded to narrow them. "Perhaps it is now time for another rule review. It has been several days since the last one, and we don't want to forget them, do we?"

Each girl at the table dutifully shook her head, as who there would have dared to do otherwise?

"All right, then," said Mrs. Spilking. "Adelaide, rule number nine, if you will?"

"Being late for breakfast, three demerits," replied Adelaide in a nervous rush of words.

Mrs. Spilking then waited a few moments, allowing her gaze to move around the table, resting briefly on each girl as if she were to be the next victim. "Rule number three . . ." Her eyes snapped back to a girl she had just passed. "Imogene?"

"T–T–Taking too long in the washroom, four demerits," quavered Imogene.

"Rule number nineteen, Eudora," said Mrs. Spilking so quickly that it caught the next victim off guard.

"I—I—I—," stammered Eudora, swallowing and swallowing, unable to go on.

"Perhaps, Emily, you would like to help Eudora?" said Mrs. Spilking. "She seems to have lost her voice. I hope you have yours."

Emily hesitated. Oh, it was not because she did not know the rule. With the help of Sarah and Lucy, she knew them all by now, backward and forward. So, undoubtedly, did Eudora, had she not been taken so by surprise. Now the look of fear and desperation on her face almost made Emily want to "forget" the rule as well, out of sympathy for a fellow student in such misery.

"Well?" Mrs. Spilking's sharp finger tapped on the table. Her eyes glistened as she anticipated the collapse of another victim.

"Wasting thread in embroidery, three demerits," Emily rattled off, for any thoughts of "forgetting" the rule in support of Eudora's feelings would have been quite mad, and accomplished nothing.

But with this moment of triumph denied to her, Mrs. Spilking lost no time in returning to pounce on her earlier prey.

"Now, Eudora, having failed with rule number nineteen, perhaps you would care to enlighten us with your knowledge of rule number one?"

"F–F–Failure to know the rules by heart, ten demerits," replied Eudora in a fading voice.

"Quite right! And don't you think you then deserve what I am about to enter in my demerit book?" inquired Mrs. Spilking with all the sincerity of a fox asking the opinion of the hen he is about to make his next meal.

Eudora's head now hung so low, she was barely able to nod.

With a great flourish of her pen, Mrs. Spilking *tick-ticked* Eudora's demerits into her black book, and the inquisition continued. When at last it had ended, Mrs. Spilking reminded them it was letter-writing day. So Emily, after all the misery of what had just transpired, had to write Aunt and Uncle Twice her usual letter telling them how much she continued to love being at Mrs. Spilking's Select Academy. She still, of course, had not received any letter at all from them.

But, oh, how she would like to have been able to tell them of the dismal, dreary days marching by, one exactly like the other. Mornings spent with embroidery and mending; afternoons spent with more embroidery; drawing, in which they took pencils and tablets from their boxes and drew with no instruction whatsoever; grammar, in which they simply studied ancient grammar books entirely on their own; and reading from deadly dull books so dilapidated their covers were all but falling off.

These "lessons" were interrupted only by the horrible meals, by a one-hour nap in bed in the afternoon with all conversation forbidden, and by two grim "exercise" periods, where they were required to march around and around a small, barren patch of ground called a "garden," but where surely no daffodil, daisy, or rose had ever bloomed. There they were not allowed even to whisper to one another but had to march in silence to the accompaniment of a barking dog. For in the very same amount of small space allotted the girls, separated from them by a brick wall, was the space allotted to Mrs. Spilking's vicious dog, Wolf!

And though, excepting meals, penmanship, and

letter writing, not to mention the rule inquisitions, it was Mrs. Crumble who watched over the girls, still, who was to know when Mrs. Spilking might suddenly appear in person?

One morning, having spied from a rear window, she arrived in the "garden" to accuse two girls of whispering. Four demerits each! And on another never-to-be-forgotten afternoon, she rushed out to ask a girl to place in her handkerchief something she had been seen putting in her mouth. Mrs. Spilking passed the offending object under her pinched nose, sniffing suspiciously.

"What is this?" she inquired. "Do I detect the odor of peppermint?"

"A—A—A cough drop I've been saving since I came here," replied the girl, looking as if she might faint. "I—I—I have a sore throat."

"Well, take it, then!" said Mrs. Spilking coldly, in no way able to equate the dark little lump in the handkerchief with a forbidden pink-and-white-striped peppermint. "See that it does you some good!"

Oh, yes, Mrs. Spilking's presence was everywhere! It was no wonder the girls were all so quiet, and wore such sad faces most of the time.

For what did any of them have to look forward to but more of the same dreary days, all with the frightening specter of Mrs. Spilking hovering over them? For Emily, it would come to an end when she came into her fortune, but the five and more years continued to look longer and longer to her.

The only girl there who did not appear sad and forlorn was Princess Delilla. And why should she? She clearly had nothing to fear from Mrs. Spilking, and did not even have to learn the rules, much less mind them. She could get up and walk out during embroidery or grammar or penmanship, with neither Mrs. Spilking nor Mrs. Crumble saying a word to her about it. She never even bothered to take part in the "exercise" periods. Let other girls parade around the barren yard with the icy wind freezing their noses. She simply took her aristocratic one up the stairs and disappeared into her room.

Well, as the girls all sat in the Front Room working, had not Emily often looked through the open door into the hallway and seen Mrs. Spilking accompanied by the princess parade down the hall and out the front door? Then had they not returned carrying boxes and full shopping bags?

Exercise in the backyard, indeed! Why should the princess bother with that when she could have her exercise in such other pleasant ways?

As for food, "her royal majestry" simply picked at that, and yet she managed to look perfectly healthy and well fed. Emily, it must be said, was not terribly surprised. She remembered how Bella had remarked on Mrs. Spilking sharing the precious little frosted cakes with "her royal majestry." And no doubt other delicious food was shared with her, as well: fresh fruit, cheese, and butter from the grocer's, freshly baked bread and cakes from the baker's. It was certain Princess Delilla did not have to rely on Mrs. Slump's kitchen for her nourishment any more than Mrs. Spilking did.

The princess could not have had more attention paid to her in her royal palace in her own country, wherever that was. Sarah and Lucy often said that Mrs. Spilking's academy was as much a palace for her as her own in that mysterious country. And Emily would have been hard put to disagree with that!

In the meanwhile, the dreary days went on. And on. And on. Would there be no end to them?

8

A Royal Favor

They had just come in from morning exercise when Emily decided she needed a visit to the washroom. She raised her hand, made her request, and was given permission by Mrs. Crumble to leave. Laying down her embroidery hoop, Emily hurried to the door, only to realize that Princess Delilla had stood up and was following right behind her. The princess, of course, never had to receive permission for much of anything. She just came and went as she chose. Emily thought nothing of it.

When they reached the top of the stairs, she turned to go to her washroom, and the princess turned in the opposite direction. Whether she went to her room or not, Emily did not know, nor for that matter much cared. But what she did know was that when she left the washroom, Princess Delilla was standing at the head of the stairs, waiting. As soon as she caught sight of Emily, she beckoned to her. At the same time she put a finger to her lips, a sign for Emily to keep quiet. Tiptoeing to her room, she signaled Emily to follow her.

Now, although Emily had once or twice caught Princess Delilla staring at her in a calculating manner, she had believed that the princess probably stared at the other girls in the same way. Now she was not so certain. Princess Delilla clearly had something in mind for her all along. The question was . . . what?

The princess closed the door very carefully and softly behind them as soon as they entered the room. And what a room it was! Why, it was impossible to believe that there even *was* such a room at Mrs. Spilking's Select Academy, especially considering the rooms in which all the other girls lived.

"Nice, isn't it?" said Princess Delilla with an indifferent shrug.

Nice? Why, it was so startlingly nice that Emily could do no more than nod as she looked around the room with wide eyes. In it was a proper bed complete with carved walnut posters, not the iron cots enjoyed by everyone else. On the bed were piles of pillows and a puffy down comforter with a cover of pale pink rosebuds. Rosebuds twined in profusion in a painted frieze that reached all around the walls. And there was more.

Against one wall, in addition to a handsome, gleaming chest of drawers, was a dainty, mirrored dressing table. And as if a round, pink wool rug were not enough to warm the floor, beside the bed where the princess would first put her royal toes in the morning lay a white bearskin rug. On the tops of the chest and dressing table sat pretty little china dishes and figurines beside displays of photographs in silver frames—without doubt, photographs of the princess's royal family.

But the centerpiece of the room was a delightful slipper chair in pink velveteen. Beside it was set a small, round walnut table holding a flowered glass oil lamp and a pink china bowl.

"Would you like one?" Princess Delilla asked.

Emily felt her face grow hot, for she realized she had been staring at the china bowl. It was heaped with an assortment of delectable fancy biscuits. For a moment, she was in such a state of confusion, she could not reply.

"Go ahead, take one!" said the princess. "Lots more where that came from. Go on! I won't tell."

"Th-th-thank you, but I'd better not, Your—Your Royal Highness," stammered Emily.

"Whyever not?" asked Princess Delilla. "And you may call me 'Princess.' That's good enough."

"Thank you, P-P-Princess, but I . . . I *must* get back downstairs," said Emily.

"Oh, no. What you *must* do is stay here for a few more minutes," said Princess Delilla airily. "I didn't invite you in just to visit my room, you know."

Well, of course she had not! Did the princess really believe Emily was so stupid as to think that? Not knowing what she was expected to say to that, however, Emily remained silent as the princess made a big pretense of choosing a biscuit, while stealing a glance sideways with her cat-green eyes to see what Emily had made of her revelation.

"I have something I want you to do for me," she said, taking a nibble from her biscuit. "I expect you could call it a favor. It isn't much, really. I could ask one of the other girls, but I don't fancy asking the older ones, and the younger ones like you always look so frightened. I've been watching you, and I've decided you're much smarter and braver than they are. So now, would you like to know what the favor is?"

Though she could not help but be curious, Emily was not at all certain she *did* want to know. Somehow, she did not like the sound of any of this. The princess had indeed been studying her all along, just as she suspected. But what had she done to make the princess think she was brave and smart? Nothing, that was what! Was it not more likely that she had been selected because she was new in the school, and also a younger girl who could be easily twisted around a wily older girl's finger? Was not being told she was smart and brave only an attempt to butter her up?

What she should do, then, was simply call the princess's bluff by thanking her for the great honor bestowed upon her, but then politely state that she was not as smart and brave as the princess supposed, and prove it by saying how frightened she was to stay any longer. Then she would quickly escape the room.

But it was easier to think all this than come out and say it when the cat eyes of a member of royalty were staring right through her. Emily's thoughts, all neatly strung out in her head, instantly fell into disarray. And almost before she was quite aware of what she was doing, she found herself nodding her head.

"Good!" Princess Delilla pounced with lightning speed. "I knew you would! But first, I must tell you it has to do with chocolate. Now, that's not so bad, is it . . . chocolate?"

"Ch-Ch-Chocolate?" stammered Emily. The princess was right. What could be bad about chocolate? Oh, but there must be more than that. The princess had dropped the first shoe. There *must* be a second yet to be dropped, but what could it possibly be?

"Yes, chocolate!" repeated Princess Delilla. "You see, I *love* chocolate. I truly *long* for chocolate. Only Mrs. Spilking won't let me have any."

"But Mrs. Spilking lets you have anything you want, doesn't she?" asked Emily, and then threw a hand to her mouth in horror at her boldness in having said this. What would a princess have to say to such rudeness from a mere commoner?

Not much, it appeared, for she had more important things on her mind. "Not chocolate," she said. "Mrs. Spilking won't let me have that. She says it would spoil my complexion. She believes she has a sacred trust placed upon her by my family not to let that or other disagreeable things happen to me. So, that's what my favor is . . . to get me some chocolate!"

Well, the second shoe had now been dropped. Emily was to get the chocolate!

"How—how am I to do that?" she asked.

"Weeell," drawled the princess with a sly look at Emily, "when you leave the school and go left for two blocks, there's Binkwig's Grocers. That's where the chocolate—I mean, *chocolates*—are."

"But—but I'm not allowed to leave the school," said Emily faintly.

"Oh, I *know*," said Princess Delilla, looking at her with the greatest sympathy. "But I have it all worked out. It will be easy. I heard Mrs. Spilking telling Bella she would be away until late this afternoon. All you have to do is slip out the front door at nap time, leave the door unlocked while you run and fetch my chocolates, and then slip right back in again."

All Emily had to do! It would be easy! Was the princess mad? Why, there were all sorts of things that would not make it easy at all.

"What about Sarah and Lucy, my roommates?"

asked Emily. "What shall I say to them if they ask where I'm going?"

"Just say you're going to the washroom," replied the princess airily. "They're supposed to be sleeping anyway, and not asking questions, aren't they?"

"Oh, Princess!" cried Emily. "Why is it *you* can't go?"

"Because," said Princess Delilla, "despite what you think about me being allowed everything, I'm not allowed out either, unless I'm with Mrs. Spilking. Besides, Mr. Binkwig knows me, as I've been there often with Mrs. Spilking. He'd report to her in a minute."

"But he'd know I was a Spilking Academy girl from my uniform, and report that as well!" said Emily, desperately grasping at reasons why she should not go on this errand.

"Not if you're wearing your coat and bonnet," said the princess coolly.

Now Emily could think of but one more reason. Fortunately, it was the best yet and should surely end the matter: "How can I buy chocolates?" she said. "I have no money. We're not allowed to have any."

"Oh, I've thought of that. Here!" replied

Princess Delilla, and whipped an envelope out of her pocket. "Take this with you. It's a note requesting a sack of chocolates, the ones Mr. Binkwig keeps in a glass case. But whatever you do"—the princess paused to look hard at Emily—"*whatever you do*, do *not* give this note to Mr. Binkwig. He'll report both of us to Mrs. Spilking if you do. Mr. Binkwig is short and fat and bald and wears an apron, so you'll know who he is. What you're to do is give it to the grocer's boy. The grocer's boy will wear an apron as well, but he's tall and thin and has dark hair and is much, much younger. He knows me well, too, but he won't say a word to anyone. He'll sneak the chocolates, and nobody will know. Now, is that all clear?"

Oh, very clear, indeed, and very clearly something Emily most certainly did not wish to do. But she had been artfully led into agreeing to it by a very cunning, crafty girl who happened to be a member of royalty held in the highest esteem by Mrs. Spilking. If Emily were to back out now, who could know what misery the princess might arrange for her later? Better to do what she had agreed to and be done with it.

If only Mrs. Crumble had sent someone to look

for her. After all, Emily had been missing for more time than it took to visit the washroom. But Mrs. Crumble must have been dozing, as she often did. So Emily had not been sent for, and now there was no escape. She must do the "favor" for the princess.

Princess Delilla—"her royal majestry"—so spoiled, so bent on having her own way, and so very, very clever in arranging it! Princess Delilla, who was perfectly willing to put a young girl at risk all because she had to have chocolates! And it was "smart" and "brave" Emily who was the lucky one chosen to get them for her!

9

A Deadly Surprise

Emily continued to hope that some miracle would happen to keep her from the frightening trip to Binkwig's Grocers for Princess Delilla's chocolates. But no miracle *did* happen. She had even thought it might be possible to stumble during exercise period and injure an ankle, but she had been unable to manage that. No, the minutes simply marched safely by. Even Sarah and Lucy, always dutifully obeying every rule to the letter, had their eyes snapped so tightly shut Emily easily tiptoed from the room without a murmur from either of them.

Then there she was, her heart thumping, creeping down the stairs, fetching her coat and bonnet from the dining room, and then quietly letting herself out the front door. It was possible Bella might have made an entry into the hall as Emily slipped from the building, and successfully put a stop to the whole venture. But even that did not happen. She was on the street with nothing at all that could then come between herself and Binkwig's Grocers. Drawing in a deep breath, she began her journey.

Fear made her want to run, but she knew running might attract attention, so she simply walked as fast as she could down the street. The store, just as the princess had said, was only two blocks away, and so it was but minutes before Emily was cautiously opening the glass door with BINKWIG'S printed on it in bold black letters.

What if Mr. Binkwig presented himself to wait on her? What was she to do? But to her intense relief, the short, fat, bald man in the apron was already busy waiting on another customer, and someone else was in line to be waited on by him. The tall, thin young man was at work on a ladder, rearranging tin cans on a shelf in the back of the store. Pretending to examine the other shelves, Emily sidled up to the ladder. When the young man caught sight of her staring up at him, he quickly climbed down. Before he even had a chance to speak, Emily silently handed him the envelope. He opened it and read the note at once.

"Right this way, miss," he said when he had finished it. Princess Delilla was entirely right. There was going to be no problem with this young man, that was now certain.

Well, it was hardly surprising. The princess was very pretty and was royalty as well. This was an enticing combination, and the young man had no doubt been smitten with her when she had accompanied Mrs. Spilking to the store. The princess, likewise no doubt, was quite aware of this and knew she could count on him to keep a secret.

Mr. Binkwig was so busy with his customers, and yet a third coming into the store, that he paid no attention to what was going on at the glass case that held the chocolates. There the young man carefully lifted some out with a tin scoop and poured them into a small, brown paper sack. Then he handed the sack to Emily.

"Tell her I hope she enjoys them," he said with a broad smile.

So nervous she could barely smile back, Emily hurried from the store, clutching the bag tightly against herself. Then she hurried back to the school, flew up the front steps, and with shaking fingers, twisted the door handle. It would not turn, which could only mean . . . No, oh no, the front door was locked! She rattled the handle. How was she ever to get in the building? Must she remain on the steps waiting for Mrs. Spilking to return and let her in? Terrified, she rattled the handle again. The door remained tightly shut. Well, she could ring the bell, and Bella would answer it and very likely ask no questions. There would be the end of it.

But before Emily could even raise her hand to ring the bell, she heard a key being turned in the lock inside. The door slowly opened to reveal someone standing behind it, someone in a gray dress who was wearing keys on a dull brass ring dangling from a narrow black belt. And Emily found herself staring, like a rabbit caught in the glaring light of a carriage lamp, directly into the flaring eyes of Mrs. Spilking!

"So now I know why it was that I returned to find the front door unlocked!" she said, coldly furious. "I looked out my office window, and what did I see flying down the street but one of my

Select Academy girls, and the newest one at that. And what have we here?"

Mrs. Spilking snatched the paper sack from Emily and peered into it. "Chocolates! I see. The food here is not good enough for you or plentiful enough for you, so you must sneak out when I am away to purchase chocolates at the grocer's. And may I ask, Miss Luccock, how you were able to purchase these when it is clearly stated in the rules that girls are not allowed to have money?"

"Oh, but I *didn't* buy them!" cried Emily.

Mrs. Spilking threw a hand to her throat as if gasping for air. "That can only mean, then, that you *stole* them! Worse and worse!"

"But I didn't steal them!" Emily was now almost hysterical. "I *didn't*!"

"So then," said Mrs. Spilking, "you didn't buy them, nor did you steal them. I suppose someone in the store simply *gave* them to you? Is that what you're expecting me to believe?"

"But—but someone *did*!" Emily replied with a sob. "I had a note from the princess to the young man. *She* wanted the chocolates and—"

"*What?*" Mrs. Spilking's eyes flared again with burning rage as she drew her face close to Emily's.

"Are you now trying to tell me that the princess had something to do with this? Well, we shall see about it. You will please follow me!" she snapped. Then, turning, she marched angrily up the stairs.

Emily trailed after her in total misery and horror. For in very truth, she would never have intentionally revealed to anyone what the princess had asked of her, and certainly not to Mrs. Spilking. Emily had decided she did not care much for Princess Delilla, and she knew the princess had taken unfair advantage of her. Still, she also knew this was a secret, and as she had agreed to do the favor, it followed that she must keep the secret . . . she must keep the pledge.

Could she ever make the princess understand how Mrs. Spilking had led her right into breaking it? Could the princess realize how terrified she had been when Mrs. Spilking had met her at the door when she returned with the chocolates? Not keeping a secret, breaking a pledge made to royalty was unthinkable. Emily had done this, but she would try in every way to make it up to the princess. In every *possible* way!

Emily had once heard Uncle Twice use the expression "noblesse oblige." When she had asked about it, he had explained that it meant the honorable, generous, responsible behavior associated with high rank or birth. So there was no question about Princess Delilla admitting to her part in this wrongdoing. There was, of course, no way that she could keep Emily from most surely receiving some kind of punishment, although it might be nothing worse than a few extra demerits if the princess pleaded her case. The princess would, happily, receive only a slight scolding from Mrs. Spilking, and be warned again about the evils of chocolate in regard to her complexion. And there it would all end. Still, Emily was trembling when they were admitted to the princess's room.

"I am sorry that we must disturb your nap time, Princess," Mrs. Spilking began at once. "I have been told a story by Emily Luccock, standing here before you, which I do not believe for one moment. She claims to have had a note from you to a young man at a store requesting that he give you chocolates. That would be Binkwig's Grocers, I presume."

"I have no idea what you're talking about, Mrs. Spilking," said Princess Delilla, looking Emily dead in the eye without so much as blinking.

"Then you never did write such a note?" inquired Mrs. Spilking.

"Absolutely not!" replied the princess coldly. "I would never do that, or go hunting for chocolates when you have forbidden me to have any. How would anyone dare to say such a thing?"

"Well, *somebody* did!" said Mrs. Spilking, turning to Emily with a look of triumph. "And this behavior certainly deserves an appropriate reward, which I intend to announce when we return downstairs. Would you care to be present, Princess?"

"I don't believe so," the princess replied with a shrug. "I'm sure you will deal with this in any way you think best." Her cat eyes had no expression in them whatsoever as she watched Emily leave the room with Mrs. Spilking.

Nap time had ended, and the girls were all back in their places in the Front Room. Emily was still in her coat and bonnet, with a sharp finger in her back propelling her forward to notify her that she was to continue with Mrs. Spilking to the head of the room, where Mrs. Crumble now sat.

"You are to remain standing and facing the girls, Emily," ordered Mrs. Spilking. "Girls, please put down your work. I have something of extreme importance to announce, and it requires your full attention."

In a moment, the slight rustling that attended the laying down of embroidery hoops ended. The room now fell so silent it almost seemed as if no one was even breathing.

"Girls," began Mrs. Spilking, her eyes traveling around the room, fixing on each, one by one. "You see here before you someone in a coat and bonnet, the coat and bonnet she was wearing when she left the school with *no permission from anyone!*"

Her eyes flaring, Mrs. Spilking waited a suitable length of time for this shocking news to settle before continuing. "But this is not her only crime, for there are worse to come. Do you see this?" She raised her arm, dangling in front of her the brown paper sack she had continued holding. "Chocolates! It contains *chocolates!* Not content with the food so generously provided by our Select Academy, Miss Luccock has seen fit to avail herself of chocolates from the grocer's. And not even purchased with forbidden money, which is bad enough, but stolen, girls, *stolen!*"

Mrs. Spilking snapped the sack down by her

side as her lips tightened to an angry, pencil-thin line. "Compounding this crime," she continued in a deadly, low voice, as if the next was too terrible to be uttered aloud, "she has lied . . . *lied* about it. And, worse yet, she has attempted to place the blame on someone else. Yes, on someone else . . . our very own princess, the Princess Delilla, who honors us by gracing our Select Academy with her presence!"

If the looks on the girls' faces had gone from dread at the words "someone else" to relief at hearing that the blame had been placed on the princess, lest someone in that room be called upon to defend herself, Mrs. Spilking was happily too intent on describing Emily's wickedness to notice. She relentlessly drove on.

"So it appears that we have here someone who has broken one of our most sacred rules, has stolen, lied, and ended by accusing an innocent person of her crimes." Mrs. Spilking drew herself up, pursed her lips, and flared her eyes, waiting for this list of horrors to be registered and permanently recorded by all present. It was clear that she was now approaching the high point of this trial.

"And now I ask you . . . I ask *each* of you what

you think might be a suitable punishment for all this, bearing in mind that not one but four . . . *four* crimes have been committed, some of which are of such magnitude they are not even on our rule list!"

If anyone in the room had any ideas along these lines, it was certain she would not have suggested them for her life. So, needless to say, nobody raised a hand, nor, also needless to say, had Mrs. Spilking expected anyone to do so. The very room itself seemed to stop breathing when she turned to the bowl of peppermints, delicately picked one up with long, white, bony fingers, toyed with it a moment, and then let it slide back through her fingers into the bowl.

"Well, then, I *do* have an idea," she said silkily. "It seems to me that a basket of four such crimes is worth at least as much as one peppermint. And so, I must sentence her to our beloved Select Academy's most extreme punishment. One guilty of such wickedness should pay the price as others have done for far lesser crimes.

"Therefore, you, Emily Luccock, will remain here until the evening meal, of which, out of the kindness of my heart, you will be allowed to partake. You will then return here for the remainder of the evening. When, however, the other girls prepare to retire to their rooms, you will be led by me from this room to the cellar stairs. You will descend those stairs as other culprits have done, be led through the door and down the corridor to ... the Cupboard. There you will remain under the guard of my dog, Wolf, until I come for you in the morning."

The Cupboard! Emily had thought she was being so clever with her glowing letters to India, making a big show under Mrs. Spilking's watchful eye of never taking a grain more than the allotted amount of sugar on her porridge, and not only minding every rule, but knowing them so well that she could have recited them in her sleep. Yet "smart" Emily Luccock had somehow managed to get herself sentenced to the "beloved" Select Academy's most extreme punishment.

She had clearly failed in "smartness." Would she fail in "bravery" as well? She had survived the horrors of the Remembrance Room, but how much bravery was required to sleep near a dog that was prepared to rip you to shreds? How was she ever to survive *that*?

10

The Cupboard

There was *something* there. In the suffocating darkness and deep silence, unbroken by even a whisper of air, Emily knew there was *something*. And it was right outside her door! There was no other sound but that, for the creaking of footsteps overhead had long since stopped. Now there was no sound but that one, the one outside the door.

She knew something was there because Mrs. Spilking said there would be. And if Emily had had any doubts about it, they came to a sudden end when earlier she had heard the door to the corridor open and then close. This was followed by whining and scratching on that door. When this proved fruitless, there came the sounds of metal chinking up and down the corridor, and then that, too, ended. For a while there was silence, and then

Emily began to hear the sounds outside the door.

She lay in the small room, rigid as the cot under her, staring at the ceiling. Sleep was impossible. Every time she closed her eyes, ghostly shadows flitted across her eyelids. And it seemed that the thoughts she could not keep away only became worse when her eyes were shut.

She had determined that she *would* be brave. And so she had managed to be when Mrs. Spilking had marched her down to the Cupboard. After all, she had been marched to the Remembrance Room by Mrs. Meeching, and so was experienced in such marches. Lucy and Sarah would have been in tears. Emily had marched out dry eyed and with her jaw set. Brave Emily! Well, her bravery had all melted away in the dark cellar room! Even the Remembrance Room, after all, did not have something outside the door waiting, perhaps even hoping, to rip her to shreds. Emily was not simply frightened now. She was terrified!

What would Aunt and Uncle Twice think if they knew of this? Would they not be angry, and repent at having so carelessly left her in such a horror of a place? But they never would know— not while they were in India, at any rate. For

Emily must go right on writing them the same cheerful letters reporting how much she loved being at Mrs. Spilking's Select Academy for Young Ladies, just as she had been doing every week. And yet so far, she had still not heard from them. Not one single word!

And what of the girls who had listened to Mrs. Spilking's accusations? Four terrible crimes! Did they really believe she had committed them? And, oh, most particularly, did Sarah and Lucy believe it? She had not had a moment to talk with them before her sentence was carried out, as the only time they ever had for conversations, albeit the very shortest imaginable, was just before they went to bed at night. Further, everyone had kept their eyes cast down in front of her, as if frightened to be seen looking at her. Emily Luccock, arch criminal! And defiant, as well. Perhaps she *should* have shed tears . . . tears of repentance. But, no, she had had to be Emily the brave. If they could but see her now!

As for the princess, Emily traveled back and forth between a state of terror and a state of rage. That Princess Delilla! Noblesse oblige, indeed! What country did she come from that she had never been taught the meaning of those words? Well, Emily must remember never, never to visit it. And if she did, she would certainly visit the palace and express her opinion about it. Her opinion about it . . . her opinion about it . . . the palace . . . the palace . . . girls think of her . . . think of her . . . Lucy and Sarah . . . Lucy and Sarah . . . Emily's thoughts were getting more and more muddled, as at long last, she drifted into a troubled sleep. And sometime during the night, she had a dream.

It was a terrible dream. She was in a tiny boat, all alone, rowing and rowing, but all the while staying in one place. Somewhere way ahead of her, masked by a thick fog, were two people. She could not tell who they were, but she knew she must reach them. Keep rowing, keep rowing, harder and harder. And then, the waves began to swell in front of her, and heavy spray washed over her face. It washed and it washed and would not stop. Suddenly, she woke with a start. But the washing went on. *Slosh! Slosh! Slosh!* Right over her chin and the tip of her nose.

The washing had not stopped with her dream, but what did almost stop, in truth, was Emily's heart. For the washing came from a very large, very wet tongue! Emily lay absolutely motionless, stiff with fear, and hardly breathing. The licking continued, and then something came over the side of her cot and began determinedly pawing at her shoulder. It took very little thinking on Emily's part to realize that this was the dog. This was Wolf! The door to the Cupboard must not have been tightly closed, and he had succeeded in pushing his way in.

But his actions were hardly those of a dog who had entered with the idea of ripping her to shreds. No, he gave every sign of wishing to be friends— and to get petted in the bargain! Emily drew in a deep breath and held it as she shakily reached out a hand and began to scratch behind a big, floppy, velvet-smooth ear.

"G-G-Good boy!" she whispered.

The "good boy" whined his approval and flopped his large head down beside her on the hard mattress with a sigh of contentment.

So this was Wolf, who, thanks to Mrs. Spilking, was held in such dread by all the girls. Suddenly, Emily now realized that although she had heard him barking behind the fence and accompanying Mrs. Spilking on her nightly bed checks, she had never actually seen him again after she had arrived at the academy that first night. At that time, of course, he had only been exhibited to her attached to a heavy black chain held tightly by Mrs. Spilking in a most ominous way. Could the way she was holding him be the reason he had growled? At any rate, it was more than likely the other girls had not had personal encounters with Wolf, either, so knew as little about him as Emily did.

It appeared that Wolf's interest in ripping anyone to shreds was simply a clever invention of Mrs. Spilking's cruel mind, which rippled through the school, spreading terror as it went. Why, Wolf was no more threatening than Clarabelle, the kitten that Kipper had brought to Emily, and that had ended up brightening the lives of the old people at Sugar Hill Hall.

Only now Emily was presented with a dilemma. If Wolf remained by her cot, and Mrs. Spilking were to find him there in the morning, she would know that her deception had been discovered. What terrible things might she invent to take its place? Emily must do something about this.

"Good boy!" she whispered again, and while continuing to rub Wolf's ear, cautiously put one foot on the floor, and then the other.

"Come along, boy! Come along, Wolf!" Emily said, taking the dog by his collar and gently tugging on it.

He padded right along with her as she felt for the door in the dark. It was open, just as she had suspected, and she led the dog through it.

"Good boy! Down!" Emily said. Although they were in total darkness, she could sense that he had dropped to the floor. "Good boy! Now stay!" she said, and with one last rub behind his ear, she stepped back into the Cupboard, closed the door, and climbed back onto the hard cot.

Emily was thoroughly pleased with herself for remembering how her papa had trained the dog they once had, for repeating the words he had used. But more than that, think of it, Wolf such a gentle dog and now lying quietly outside the door! She could only hope that if she ever did encounter him with Mrs. Spilking, he would not wag his tail and reveal their secret. It was a good thing she made her bed checks in the near dark and was less able to see a tail wagging! That was the last thing Emily remembered thinking before she fell into a deep and dreamless sleep.

• • •

"Sarah and I never did believe you'd done all those things!" declared Lucy.

It was the next night, and they were in their room before bedtime. Now Emily could finally have the conversation that would explain all that had happened to her.

"That princess! How could she tell such a lie!" Sarah was furious. "How *could* she, an actual member of a royal family!"

"Well, we all know she doesn't care about anyone but herself," said Lucy, scowling. "You can tell. Sending you into such danger just because she fancies chocolates. I wish you'd got them for her, Emily, and she'd broken out all over in spots. I do, indeed. Serve her right!"

"But, oh, Lucy and Sarah," cried Emily, "what of the other girls? Do you think they believe everything Mrs. Spilking said about me?"

Sarah and Lucy exchanged glances. "We don't know," replied Sarah. "But what we believe they think is that if you really did what she said, you're about the bravest girl they know, and they wish they'd had the courage."

"It's what Sarah and I thought, anyway," said Lucy, with an eager bob of her head. Then she added quickly in great confusion, "I mean, it's what we *would* have thought if we didn't really believe you hadn't done those things."

"And we do think you were so brave being led to the Cupboard without even crying," said Sarah. "I expect you'll be the school heroine, though no one would ever dare say so."

"But, oh, that Cupboard!" Lucy clasped her hands together in anguish. "How did you bear it? Sarah and I would have perished."

"Oh, yes!" agreed Sarah, moaning. "We would indeed have with that—that horrible dog just aching to rip us to shreds. How were you able to sleep listening to him panting his hot breath outside your door? Didn't you just faint dead away?" Both girls threw their arms around themselves and shuddered.

Now, Emily had not been at all certain that she should tell them about Wolf. She desperately wanted to, but she knew that the more people who knew a secret, the less likely it was to remain a secret. But it was rapidly becoming unbearable, not telling what she knew about Wolf when she saw the looks on Sarah's and Lucy's faces.

"He wasn't outside my door," Emily blurted. "He was right inside the room!"

Lucy and Sarah both gasped, looking as if *they* were the ones who were going to faint dead away. Emily, who had no intention of frightening them so, rushed on breathlessly.

"Oh, it was all right, really it was! He managed to push open the door, which turned out not to be closed tightly. But all he wanted was to be petted! He came over to my cot and put his head down beside me. So I scratched his ear, and he was as content as could be. I don't believe he has ever wanted to rip anyone to shreds in his life. Mrs. Spilking has been lying about him to frighten us to death!"

"Well, she has!" declared Lucy. Then she hesitated. "Did—did he stay with you all night?"

"No, I couldn't let him do that," explained Emily. "I knew he shouldn't be there when Mrs. Spilking came to fetch him in the morning. So I just led him out, and he lay down like a lamb. Then I closed the door and went back to my cot and went to sleep."

"Oh, Emily, I wish all the girls could know," said Sarah wistfully. "I wish we could find a way to tell them."

"Oh, no! No! No! You mustn't even think about it!" cried Emily. "Mrs. Spilking must never know what I found out. It's too dangerous, and the more people who know about it, the more likely it is she'll find out. I was even afraid to tell *you* about it!"

"But we're so glad you did!" exclaimed Lucy. "And I don't care what you say, you must have been scared out of your wits when Wolf came in. I still think you're the bravest girl ever!"

"I do too!" echoed Sarah. "And even if we can't say anything about Wolf, I do know what I *am* going to say. I intend to whisper to someone during exercise about how you did *not* do all those terrible things that Mrs. Spilking said you did. So . . . so there!"

"You'll do no such thing, Sarah!" ordered Emily, hearing the quaver in Sarah's voice. "Some day they're sure to find out one way or another, and all you'll do is get demerits for whispering. Say you won't do it?"

"Well, all right," agreed a clearly relieved Sarah. "I promise I won't."

"But if we don't get into bed right away," said Emily, "we'll be caught when Mrs. Spilking comes around on her bed check."

"But just think," said Lucy. "For the first time since I've been here, I won't be trembling, wondering if I might be the one ripped to shreds!"

"Oh, Emily," Sarah said breathlessly, "nor will I!"

The looks they gave Emily came very close to making up for all of it. Nobody in that room would have anything to fear from Wolf ever again. Wolf, who would no more rip anyone to shreds than . . . than Clarabelle. Yes, it did indeed come very, very close to making up for all of it!

11

A Startling Midnight Conversation

Mrs. Spilking had come around with Wolf for the bed check, and it was all Emily could do not to roll over, reach out a hand, and rub Wolf's ear when he came sniffing up to her cot. But she remained motionless on her side with her back to the door, her eyes tightly shut, and her hands safely under her coverlet. If Wolf's tail was wagging at an unusual rate, it was not noticed, just as Emily had hoped.

But after Mrs. Spilking left, she kept reviewing her conversation with Lucy and Sarah, and no matter how hard she tried, she could not drop off to sleep. The ponderous tolling of the hideous old clock in the Front Room, which could be heard in the rooms above it, first announced the hour of half past ten. Then eleven. Then half past eleven. And then, at last, twelve.

Emily now had to use the washroom. This was always an unpleasant thing to contemplate in a cold, dark room, but in the end, she reluctantly folded back her coverlet and dropped her feet onto the icy floor. Determining that she could make her way without a lantern, she tiptoed from the room in her bare feet so as not to waken Sarah and Lucy.

To her dismay, she found the washroom in use, for the door was tightly closed. And from behind the door came the sound of a girl sobbing bitterly! Emily's breath caught in her throat. The older girls had always appeared so composed, even though they were almost never seen to smile. She had thought they must be adjusted to the deadliness of Mrs. Spilking's Select Academy, but now she knew that they had simply taught their faces not to register their true feelings. Still, she could do nothing about it, and surely the girl would not wish to come out and find that someone had been standing outside the door listening.

Emily's first thought was that she should return to bed, forget her need for the washroom, and try to go to sleep. But then she looked through the door to that other washroom and had a bold thought. Why not use the princess's washroom?

There were no rules about it not being allowed when she was not using it, were there? Brave Emily ought not to be afraid to do something that did not require all that much bravery. But, in truth, brave Emily's heart was in her throat as she tiptoed toward the princess's royal washroom.

In the washroom, she was so intent on accomplishing her mission in the shortest possible time, she did not notice at first that she could hear voices coming from somewhere. As she listened, the voices grew louder. They were angry voices, and they were not just coming from "somewhere"; Emily now knew *exactly* where they were coming from . . . the room of Princess Delilla! She could even tell who owned the voices. One was that of the princess herself, and the other was that of . . . Mrs. Spilking!

And what Emily was hearing was most certainly an argument. Further, because no one was bothering to lower her voice, she could hear every word of it.

Eavesdropping, Emily believed, was no more acceptable now than it had been when she had overheard, through no fault of her own, the conversation between Mr. Crawstone and Mrs. Spilking weeks ago. Further, she was in even more danger now if she were discovered than she had been then. Quickly she started to leave the washroom. But with a hand already on the door handle, she suddenly dropped it. For she had heard something that made her determined to listen to more of the conversation. Oh, yes, very determined, indeed!

And so she remained in the washroom, still as a stone statue, listening. And it was not until the voices had lowered enough so that she believed the argument had abated, and Mrs. Spilking might soon be leaving the princess's room, that Emily scurried back to her own room. But by then she had heard everything she needed to know. Everything . . . and a great deal more!

The days had always passed slowly, but the day following Emily's bold excursion to "her royal majestry's" washroom seemed to drag by more slowly than ever. She was exploding with excitement and impatience to report what she had learned to Sarah and Lucy. She could hardly wait to see their faces when she told them.

The day finally came to an end. There was far too much to tell, however, in just the few minutes they had before they must climb into their beds. Therefore, Emily informed them they must positively try to stay awake and only feign sleep when Mrs. Spilking came around. Sarah and Lucy, of course, were so excited themselves, they could not have fallen asleep if their lives had depended on it. So at last they were all three seated cross-legged on a coverlet spread between Emily's and Sarah's cots. Emily had placed the oil lantern in the middle, and now its small flame fluttered on Sarah's and Lucy's eager faces.

"Well," began Emily, pausing to make the most of this thrilling moment, "it all began last night after you both were asleep, and I needed to use the washroom. When I arrived there, I found the washroom was already in use. The door was closed just as tight as it could be. But, oh, Lucy and Sarah, whoever was in there had not gone for the same reason I had. She was in there to cry! She was crying so hard, it quite broke my heart to hear her."

Emily's listeners, hanging on her every word, shook their heads in sympathy. "Did you find out who it was when she came out?" asked Sarah.

"Oh, I didn't wait until then," said Emily. "I didn't think whoever it was would like to know someone had been standing outside the door listening. So I didn't stay."

"Is—is that all that you wanted to tell us, Emily?" asked Lucy.

"Oh, no!" exclaimed Emily. She was hardly able to keep a cat-who-swallowed-a-mouse smile from her face. "That's only the beginning. There's lots, lots more. You see, I decided to use the princess's washroom!"

Sarah and Lucy gasped in delicious horror. "You *didn't*!" Sarah cried out.

"Yes, I did!" declared Emily. "And it was when I was in there that I heard voices. They came from Princess Delilla's room. One voice was hers, and the other belonged to Mrs. Spilking!"

Emily was again rewarded by horrified gasps. "Weren't you just terrified?" asked Lucy hopefully. "Did you fly back to your room then?"

"Oh, I would have," replied Emily. "And I was going to. But their voices were very loud, because they were having an argument. And I could hear every word they were saying."

"Do you mean Mrs. Spilking was actually having an argument with her pet?" asked Lucy, wide eyed with disbelief. "What was the argument about?"

"It . . . was . . . ," said Emily, drawing out the words as slowly as she could, "about . . . the . . . note!"

"The note?" Sarah repeated, gasping.

"Oh, yes, the note!" said Emily with a firm nod of her head. "And I shall tell you exactly what I heard Mrs. Spilking say. Well, not exactly, but as close as I can remember.

" 'You little fool!' is what she said. 'You stupid little fool!' "

Lucy's jaw fell. "Are you certain she was calling the princess *that*?"

"It's the person she was talking to," said Emily. "So of course it was the princess. But you mustn't interrupt, Lucy. Now I shall have to start from the beginning," she added pleasurably.

" 'You little fool! You stupid little fool! Did you think Mr. Binkwig was so blind he would not be paying attention to what was going on in the store even if he was waiting on another customer? Do you think he would not notice a young girl hand a note to the grocer's boy, who then gave her a sack of chocolates from the precious glass case without taking any money from her to bring to the counter?'

"Then the princess said, 'Well, he shouldn't have asked to see the note. It's unfair, and it's prying.'

"And Mrs. Spilking said, 'Unfair and prying, is it? If you are going to come up with excuses and reasons, you had better do better than that. It's his business, and he has every right to see such a note. And he was quite right to show it to me.'

"Then the princess said, 'I don't see how he even knew I wrote it. I was very careful not to sign my name.'

"This made Mrs. Spilking even more angry. 'You silly idiot! Mr. Binkwig was not born yesterday, my good girl. He has seen you and that grocer's boy of his making calf eyes at each other. He would have had no trouble figuring out who signed the letter "D," even if he had not been able to pry it out of the boy. Love notes to a grocer's boy! Oh, what folly! Stupid! Stupid! What could you have been thinking?' "

Emily paused to take a breath. "Well, as I said, that's not *exactly* what I heard them say. But it's close."

"A love note?" Lucy asked breathlessly.

Emily nodded. "Oh, yes! That's exactly what she had me carry in my pocket . . . a love note!"

"So the note never said anything about chocolates at all?" asked Sarah.

"Well, it *had* to," replied Emily. "But it must have said other things as well."

"A love note!" Lucy repeated. "Oh!"

And then she and Sarah giggled nervously, for it was hard to know whether one should find this funny or shocking.

"Is—is the grocer's boy really handsome?" Sarah asked hesitantly. "He would have to be handsome, wouldn't he? I mean, think of all the handsome princes Princess Delilla has met."

Emily tilted her head, considering. "Yes, I believe he is. He is very handsome."

"What does he look like?" Lucy asked eagerly.

"Oh, he has very blue eyes and very dark wavy hair," replied Emily. "I should think he might pass for a prince."

"Well, I don't care how handsome he is," declared Lucy. "The princess shouldn't have let you be put in danger. I don't suppose *she'll* get put in the Cupboard for writing the note and then lying about it."

"Of course not!" replied Emily.

"But didn't Mrs. Spilking even say she might

tell you she's sorry she put you in the Cupboard by mistake?" asked Sarah.

"Not likely!" replied Emily with a toss of her head. "What she said was that a night in the Cupboard was a good lesson for a mealymouthed young girl, and all the other girls would profit from it, as well. So there you are!"

"Is that *everything* you heard?" Sarah asked, clearly hoping Emily's exciting report had not ended.

"Oh, no!" said Emily. "The very best part is still to come. Because guess what?"

"What?" asked both Sarah and Lucy breathlessly.

"Well," said Emily, "I now know who Princess Delilla is. And I know where she comes from. And I even know why she's here!"

12

A Very Suspicious Offer

The best part yet to come, Emily had announced. Elbows on their knees, Lucy and Sarah leaned forward, their glowing eyes riveted on Emily. Her midnight adventure had already provided enough thrills to make up for many dismal days past and many more to come. Now, unbelievably, there was yet another discovery to be reported, most amazingly the result of a simple trip to the washroom. It was almost too exciting to bear.

"Well," said Emily, "after Mrs. Spilking had finished with calling the princess stupid, she went on to say, 'To think of all the effort I have made to see that you might grow up a lady, and see how you repay me. A grocer's boy, Dolly! A grocer's boy!'"

"Dolly?" Sarah broke in. "Why was she calling the princess 'Dolly'?"

"Do you suppose it might be a short name for Delilla?" Lucy asked.

Emily smiled mysteriously. "Wait and see! I'm coming to that. Anyway, Mrs. Spilking went on, 'Look at all the things you're given here, everything you could possibly want. If you mind me, you might marry a rich man who can give you the same. Just what do you think a grocer's boy could provide for you, I ask you?'

"Then the princess said, 'Well, I love him. I do!'

"And Mrs. Spilking said, 'Pshaw! What do you know about love? You have a very good life here, with prospects. Yes, prospects, Dolly, my girl, and you had better be careful what you do.'

"And then the princess said, 'But it's so dull. Sometimes I think I will quite die from dullness, Ma.'"

With this, Emily stopped, waiting expectantly. She did not have to wait long.

"D-D-Did you say 'Ma'?" asked Lucy.

"That's exactly what I said!" replied Emily.

At this, both Sarah and Lucy threw their hands to their mouths, trying, albeit unsuccessfully, to repress squeals.

"Ma!" They both gasped.

"Yes!" Emily affirmed. "And she said it several

times, so I know I didn't make a mistake hearing it. Princess Delilla is no other than plain Dolly Spilking, and no more a princess than any of us. What do you think of that?"

The girls hardly needed to tell Emily what they thought of it, for the looks on their faces all but said it for them—looks of shock, surprise, disbelief, and total delight. Princess Delilla no more than plain Dolly Spilking! Who could ever have believed such a thing?

"Did they say more?" asked Lucy hopefully.

"Yes," replied Emily, "but I couldn't hear them very well after that, for they dropped their voices. I believed they had stopped arguing, and I was afraid Mrs. Spilking would come out at any moment, so I hurried back to our room."

"I don't suppose we can breathe a word to anyone about this either if we ever have the chance, can we?" asked Sarah.

"Oh, no!" cried Emily. "Not *anyone*! And we must never call her Dolly either, not even when we're alone. We might get into the habit of it and say it when we're in the washroom line or some place like that. We must go right on calling her Princess Delilla."

"Hmmmph!" Lucy said, sniffing. "It doesn't seem we have to worry about what to call her to her face. She never even *looks* at us. The stuck-up thing. She must really think she *is* a princess, but being called one doesn't make you one."

"Why, we could just call ourselves princesses, too, if we liked," said Sarah.

Emily thought a moment. "Yes, we could," she agreed. "When we're by ourselves, that's just what we could do. This can be *our* palace as much as hers and . . ." Emily began to get excited. "And we could have special names and—"

"And we could have royal meetings like this one," Sarah broke in.

"And think up adventures," added Lucy excitedly. "Mrs. Spilking could be the wicked stepmother queen and—and . . ." Lucy was too overcome to go on.

"But whatever we do, we have to be very, very careful that no one finds out. We can't be princesses anyplace but right here at night," Emily warned. And then, hearing the clock tolling the hour of twelve, she said, "But now we ought to get back to bed, or we'll fall face first into our porridge in the morning."

"Gruel provided by the wicked stepmother queen," Lucy corrected her.

"Yes, gruel," said Emily. "But does anyone have any ideas what they'd like to be called?"

It was remarkable how quickly the ideas arose. Instead of Emily Luccock, Sarah Tibbits, and Lucy Goodbody, who had climbed into bed the first time that night as three unhappy students of Mrs. Spilking's Select Academy for Young Ladies, it was now Princess Everbold, Princess Strongspirit, and Princess Lionheart, who climbed into bed for the second time as three happy princesses of their own private palace!

"The third meeting of the Palace Princesses will now come to order!" announced Princess Everbold, otherwise Emily Luccock.

It was after Mrs. Spilking and Wolf had made their nightly visit, and the three princesses were seated on the floor between Emily's and Sarah's cots again, the light from the flame of a fluttering lantern dancing in their eyes.

"Good thing Mrs. Crumble was dozing away again today," continued Princess Everbold. "I managed to hide the three strands of embroidery thread we each need. Did anyone else get any?"

The hands of the two other princesses instantly flew up.

"I got three pink ones," Princess Strongspirit, otherwise Sarah Tibbits, said eagerly.

"I got three yellow ones," said Princess Lionheart, otherwise Lucy Goodbody. "But you never did tell us what they're for. Do we get to know now?"

Princess Everbold grinned. "Well," she said, "they're for this!" She pulled from her pocket her three strands of embroidery thread, braided and knotted together to form a circle, which she set on her head. "There, you see, a crown! It was easy to make. I even made mine in the dark before Mrs. Spilking arrived."

"You *didn't!*" Princess Lionheart and Princess Strongspirit cried out, gasping.

"I did," said Princess Everbold. "But you can make yours now, and then we'll wear them at every meeting."

"Oh, Princess Everbold." Princess Lionheart sighed after she and Princess Strongspirit were wearing their crowns as well. "You *do* think of everything. You're the cleverest princess of us all!"

"No, I'm most surely *not!*" declared Princess Everbold. "Think of our last meeting, when we'd managed to get pencil stubs and folded pieces of drawing paper. The portraits Princess Strongspirit did of the wicked stepmother queen and her wicked stepdaughter looked exactly like Mrs. Spilking and Princess Delilla. You really are the best artist of all, Princess Strongspirit. And, Princess Lionheart, you're by far the best story-teller. I think we ought to go on right now with the story where the wicked stepmother queen and her wicked stepdaughter kidnap Princess Strongspirit."

"And then Princess Everbold and Princess Lionheart have to find a way to rescue her," said Princess Strongspirit. "I suppose they'll have to have the aid of a handsome prince, won't they?"

"A blindingly handsome prince," Princess Lionheart corrected her, "disguised as a grocer's boy with deep blue eyes and dark wavy hair."

"But *he's* the one yearned after by the wicked stepdaughter, isn't he?" asked Princess Strongspirit.

"Of course he is, silly," said Princess Lionheart. "But he's in love with only Princess Everbold, Princess Lionheart, and Princess Strongspirit."

Princess Strongspirit's eyes widened. "All *three* of them?"

"Well, maybe just one of them," replied Princess Lionheart after some consideration. "But don't forget, he probably has two blindingly handsome royal friends. I'm certain we can work something out, can't we, Princess Everbold? Is that too many complications?"

"Oh, no!" exclaimed Princess Everbold. "We need lots of complications!"

And they did. The more the better, for that was just something to look forward to at their meetings. And how much more wonderful all this was than looking forward to nothing but gray porridge, endless hoops of embroidery, dull books, and walks that passed for exercise, all repeated over and over again.

But Princess Everbold, as Emily, warned them over and over how the old people at Sugar Hill Hall had aroused suspicion when they began to look too cheerful and happy. So Emily, Sarah, and Lucy were very, very careful to go about during the day looking as downcast and dispirited as ever. They never exchanged telling glances over porridge or embroidery or during exercise or when they heard "terrifying" Wolf barking on the other side of the fence, and not even when they noted the looks of unbridled hatred Princess Delilla cast at Emily.

All the while, Emily had to fight to keep from her mind the fearful thought that she had yet to hear from Aunt and Uncle Twice. She kept telling herself that it must have taken a long time for them to reach India, and so it must take an equally long time for a letter to come in the opposite direction. But had not that long time come and gone? Was this not sure proof that she was indeed "not wanted"? How was she expected to forget about *that*?

She had by now, however, almost managed to forget about the ominous "all" until one afternoon, when she was coming into the dining room with the other girls after exercise in the yard, and Mrs. Crumble came up to her. After looking nervously over her shoulder toward the hall and Front Room doors, she put a hand on Emily's arm, stopping her before she could even hang up her coat on her wall peg.

"Please wait a moment, Emily," Mrs. Crumble said in a low, urgent voice. Then she added in a louder voice, "Girls, please return to your seats and begin your work. I shall be there in a moment."

Mrs. Crumble waited until every last girl had left the room before beginning to speak. What was it to be about? Emily's embroidery or knitting? She had never thought that Mrs. Crumble, so often dozing in her wing chair, ever paid a great deal of attention to the girls' work. Was Emily's so bad that she needed to be spoken to about it privately?

Mrs. Crumble dropped her voice again. "Emily, dear child, your aunt and uncle are in India, are they not?"

Totally unprepared for any question that was not to do with her embroidery or knitting, it took Emily a moment before she cautiously nodded. Cautiously, because, in truth, Mrs. Crumble continued to remind her so much of Mrs. Plumly . . . Mrs. Plumly, who had so deceived her at Sugar Hill Hall, feeding her little cakes and, in the end, tea that had something in it that caused Emily to reveal dangerous secrets. Embroidery and knitting? Oh, no. Mrs. Crumble must be leading up to something, and Emily intended to be very, very careful about what she said.

"Have you no relatives in New York, no friends you could go to if the need should ever arise?" asked Mrs. Crumble, an anxious frown creasing her pink cheeks.

Oh, if there were ever a trick question, this one was surely it! If Emily said "yes," then she might be asked to name them. And whom could she name? Mr. Crawstone, the only person she knew? Better to name a crocodile! So, no, she could not name a friend or relative, because she had none to name. There was nothing she could do but tell the truth. Even more cautiously now, she shook her head.

"Oh, my dear child, I was afraid of that!" said Mrs. Crumble, wringing her hands in anguish.

Actually wringing her hands . . . as good an actress as Mrs. Plumly! *Say nothing! Reveal nothing!* Emily warned herself.

"I had so hoped you would have a place to go if you should flee this place," Mrs. Crumble said sadly.

"Oh, but I don't wish to flee," promptly returned Emily, becoming as good an actress as Mrs. Crumble and Mrs. Plumly ever were. "I do love it so here!"

To that grand lie, Mrs. Crumble only shook her

head and sighed. "So frightened! Oh, so frightened!" she said under her breath. "Well, if anything should ever happen that you need a place to
go, I want you to have this, child." With another
quick, cautious look at both open doorways, she
removed a bit of paper from her own pocket and
slipped it into Emily's.

"Oh, I don't believe I shall ever need it," said
Emily earnestly. "But I do thank you so much. I
do, indeed."

Emily did not need to look at the bit of paper
to know that it contained the address of Mrs.
Crumble's home. What she had told Mrs. Crumble
was the absolute truth, that she would never need
it. For even if she ever had to do such a dangerous
thing as fleeing the school, she would as soon have
run to Mrs. Crumble's home as named Mr. Crawstone as a friend! But what was behind all this in
the first place? Finally, Emily came up with the
answer.

Mrs. Spilking wished to know if Emily could be
as easily persuaded by Mrs. Crumble to do something as she had been by Princess Delilla! Would
not that be another fine excuse to send Emily back
to the Cupboard as a further example to the other

girls? Well, Mrs. Spilking had better try something else. Emily had been hoodwinked by Princess Delilla. She would not be hoodwinked by Mrs. Crumble!

Satisfied that that was the answer to Mrs. Crumble's mysterious behavior, Emily was able finally to put it from her mind. All she knew was that she must be very careful about such tricks being played on her. Further, Mrs. Crumble was to be trusted as little as Mrs. Spilking.

That night, Lucy and Sarah were greatly inclined to agree with Emily's appraisal of the situation. They were, of course, dreadfully disappointed that Mrs. Crumble, fearful though she was of Mrs. Spilking, could be persuaded by her to do something so wicked. And while they had always doubted Emily's comparison of her to the hideously evil Mrs. Plumly of Sugar Hill Hall, they were beginning to believe that Emily might just be right.

It was not until much later that night, however, as Emily lay staring into the dark, once again unable to drop off to sleep, that she began thinking. And thinking. And wondering. And then suddenly, she shivered. It was not from the cold, but from suddenly beginning to consider that she might have been entirely wrong about the reasons for Mrs. Crumble's offer of her home in case Emily should ever need it. Oh, not that Emily trusted Mrs. Crumble. Not one bit. But what if . . . what if, in some frightening way, this actually had something to with "all"!

13

Doomed!

A week passed by, and nothing further happened to make Emily believe one thing or another about Mrs. Crumble's "kind offer" of her home should Emily need it. Then one morning, when letters had been written and passed to Mrs. Spilking for inspection, she flared her eyes in Emily's direction. "Before going to the Front Room, Emily, you will please meet with me in my office. That will be all, the rest of you."

A private conversation with Mrs. Crumble now being followed by a private conversation with Mrs. Spilking! Lucy and Sarah cast anxious glances at Emily as she followed Mrs. Spilking from the dining room.

In her office, Mrs. Spilking pointed a sharp finger at one of the two stiff, unwelcoming wooden chairs that stood at attention before her desk. "You may sit, if you wish," she said. And while Emily perched timidly on the edge of one of the chairs, hands folded, Mrs. Spilking pulled open a drawer and lifted out two envelopes.

"I have two letters here," she said, her long, bony fingers toying with them. "One is actually addressed to me, but I wish you to read it. The second, which you may read first, I believe is from your aunt and uncle in India."

A letter from Aunt and Uncle Twice at long last! Emily eagerly reached for it, barely noticing the calculating look given her by Mrs. Spilking when she handed it over. Nor did Emily care that the envelope opened so easily there was not much doubt it had been opened earlier. Never mind, it was a letter, the longed-for letter! But Emily's heart was not nearly so light when she finished reading it as when she had begun. For this is what she read in the letter written by Aunt Twice:

Dear, darling Emily,
    What was our delight in finding a letter from you waiting for us when we arrived in India, along with a letter of welcome from Mr. Slyde! Our ship had experienced serious difficulties and delayed us

to such a degree that the ship bearing your letter actually arrived before we did. And now a second letter from you has also arrived. But the best part is that you love your school so much. Uncle Twice and I cannot tell you how happy that makes us!

There are unfortunately many things that have to be seen to, so many arrangements made, which is why this letter is so short. And, sadly, it may be a very long time before you hear from us again.

Now I must go. I pray that, for your sake and ours, you will continue happily in your school. And try always to be a brave girl, no matter what!

Your loving Aunt Twice and Uncle Twice

Here was the letter Emily had awaited for such a very long time, a letter that should have set her heart dancing. Why was it that it filled her with such foreboding? "Be a brave girl, no matter what!" Why those ominous words once more? And why must it be such a long time before Emily would hear from Aunt and Uncle Twice again? All Emily could think was that Baby Cousin Twice was to take up so much of their time, there would be none left for writing to *her*. And they did not have to suffer a shred of guilt because, after all, was not Emily reporting in her letters that she was as happy as she could be in school?

Well, Aunt Twice was certainly true to her word. For the date on the letter revealed it *had* been a long time since it was written. If Aunt or Uncle Twice had written every week, as Emily did, several letters should have arrived by now, not just one. Emily had to fight to hold back tears, for to weep in front of Mrs. Spilking was unthinkable.

"I trust your aunt and uncle are well?" she asked.

Emily dutifully nodded, knowing full well that Mrs. Spilking had already read the letter.

"You may, of course, keep that letter," she said. "But now I wish you to read this one, the one written to me." She handed the letter to Emily, pretending to be busy with papers on the desk, but looking at her the whole time from under lowered eyelids. The letterhead announced that it was from "SCREWITCH, CHIZZLE & SLYDE—Attorneys at Law," addressed to Mrs. Felonius Spilking of Mrs. Spilking's Select Academy for Young Ladies. And this is the letter Emily read:

> *My very dear Madam:*
> *It is with the deepest regret that I must write this letter to you regarding one of the young girls who is a present student and boarder at your most*

highly regarded academy. That girl is Miss Emily Luccock. I must tell you that a most excellent friend of mine, Mr. Ichabod Crawstone, to whom your fine academy was unreservedly recommended, in turn recommended it to Miss Luccock's aunt and uncle, Mr. and Mrs. William Luccock, via myself.

You, of course, were apprised from the outset that all money due you on Miss Luccock's behalf would come from me. I believe I have to this date been faithful in fulfilling that obligation.

Perhaps you should know that it was only the most unfortunate of circumstances that led to Mr. Luccock's decision to remove to India with Mrs. Luccock, a decision that entailed the sad necessity of leaving their niece behind in this country.

Unable, however, to provide the means to place his niece in your highly esteemed academy, he regretfully agreed to allow her fortune to be used for this purpose. After making certain investments on her behalf, he honored me by placing that fortune, in its entirety, in my trust.

Now a calamitous event has occurred, the catastrophic sudden failure of all the investments Mr. Luccock made on behalf of his niece. It is with the deepest regret, my very good madam, that I must tell you Miss Emily Luccock is now penniless. She is no longer an heiress. Her entire fortune is, alas, lost.

As Mr. Luccock is totally unable to support her at your most valued academy, I must ask that you temper with mercy any action you may deem necessary to take in regard to this young girl, and ask that she not be simply put out, for she has no place to go. Recognizing that you do not operate a charitable institution, and need income for your most superior academy to remain in business, might I ask that you perhaps find something for Miss Luccock to do there to assist you in some way?

I have already written a letter to Mr. and Mrs. Luccock, a letter that went out in the very same mail as this one. Unfortunately, as you know, a reply as to their intentions will take some time in reaching me. I must beg your indulgence in this. If you have further questions about this most unfortunate situation, please do not hesitate to write me.

In the meantime, my very, very dear madam, we must throw ourselves on your mercy.

> *With the utmost regard, I remain*
> *Your respectful servant,*
> *Josiah Slyde*

Emily, a pauper! Thrown on the mercy of Mrs. Spilking! And for how long was that to be? The two months or so it might take to hear from Uncle Twice? And hear what? That Emily was to be immediately placed on a ship and sent to India? To an aunt and uncle who were too occupied with their present affairs even to write her more than one, pitifully short note? That is to say, provided they even had the money to pay her passage, which it appeared they did not.

Emily had made up her mind that she might be at Mrs. Spilking's Select Academy for a very long time. But the "very long time" had had a number attached to it, five and one half years, at which time she would come into her fortune. Now, suddenly, she was no longer an heiress. There was no fortune. She was penniless! The question was what was to become of her now, being thrown upon the mercy of Mrs. Spilking?

Mrs. Spilking was in no hurry to make her pronouncement. Keeping Emily in agonizing suspense, she retrieved the letter, very, very carefully folded it up, slid it back into the envelope, and laid it on the desk before her in Emily's full view. Then she placed her elbows on her desk, rested her sharp chin on her knuckles, and flared her eyes at Emily.

"Well, and what *are* we to do with you?" she asked with a coy little smile, as if what Emily thought made the slightest bit of difference.

Emily could only shrug. What else was there to do?

"Now, as you read in Mr. Slyde's letter, Emily, this is not a charitable institution," said Mrs. Spilking. "While the families of each girl do pay us, each girl also costs us a great deal of money."

As Mrs. Spilking paused for Emily to digest this financial revelation, Emily thought of the gray porridge, stale bread, and potato and turnip stew, the dog-eared books, and the pencil stubs that cost Mrs. Spilking such "a great deal of money" and could not help but suspect that a much *greater* deal of money from the girls' tuitions was reserved for Mrs. Spilking herself, and particularly for the luxuries enjoyed by her daughter, Dolly.

"So," continued Mrs. Spilking, satisfied that enough of what she had said had sunk into Emily, "you can understand why I cannot keep a girl here for charitable reasons. However, as Mr. Slyde has written such an eloquent appeal on your behalf, I shall give no thought to sending you to some institution where girls with no visible means of support are placed. No, I shall allow you to remain here, certainly until Mr. Slyde has received some word from your uncle in India." Mrs. Spilking paused to flare her eyes again at Emily.

"Th-Th-Thank you, Mrs. Spilking," mumbled Emily, recognizing that an expression of gratitude was expected of her.

"But . . . ," said Mrs. Spilking with another warning flare, "as Mr. Slyde suggested that I might find something for you to do here, to earn your keep, as it were, I shall do just that. Since I have no need for an assistant, as Mr. Slyde has mentioned, you will be allowed to remain here as a servant, Emily, but no longer as a student. You will, therefore, no longer be permitted to attend classes. You will, however, remain in your room upstairs until I can make arrangements for a cellar room, all of which are in use at the moment. In fact, you may remain upstairs until a new student comes to take your place or until something is heard from your uncle, whichever comes first. But never forget, not for one moment, that you are now a servant. Is that understood?"

How could it not be understood? Nothing could have been clearer. And while Emily was to be allowed the privilege of remaining in the room with Lucy and Sarah, she was always to have the fear of being removed. Oh, yes, it was understood! Emily Luccock was once again to be a servant with a future that included living in a cellar. It was as if nothing had changed. Nothing!

Understood? Yes, indeed, it was understood! Slowly, Emily nodded.

14

Bella Speaks Out

Lucy and Sarah, as was to be expected, were shocked and horrified by the new development.

"Oh, Emily!" cried Sarah. "A servant at Mrs. Spilking's dreadful Select Academy!"

"It's bad enough to be a student here!" exclaimed Lucy.

"And—and we won't be able to be princesses anymore," said Sarah, tears in her eyes.

"Whyever not?" asked Emily, who, as it turned out, found herself having to cheer up a totally downcast Lucy and Sarah, instead of the other way around.

"How can we be?" asked Lucy. "You'll be in the cellar, where Bella lives, and we'll be up here. How will we be able to have our royal meetings?"

"Well, we *will* be able to," declared Emily,

attempting a smile, "because I haven't told you the good part."

"You mean there's actually a good part?" asked Sarah.

"There actually is," replied Emily. "Mrs. Spilking says there's no room to put me in the cellar, so I'll get to stay right here!"

"Oh, Emily!" exclaimed Lucy and Sarah, breaking into smiles.

"Of course," Emily hurried to say, "it might not be forever. It depends on what Uncle Twice writes back after he has heard from Mr. Slyde. And if Mrs. Spilking gets a new student for this room, I'll have to move out. Then, I suppose, she'll have to find a place for me in the cellar. But for now, we can go on having our royal meetings right here!"

"Then let's hope the old stepmother witch never gets another student!" said Sarah.

"We'll hang a sign in front telling everyone who comes that this is a horrid place and that they shouldn't apply!" added Lucy.

"Do you suppose what Mrs. Crumble said to you had anything to do with this?" Sarah asked.

"Sarah, it couldn't have," Lucy said. "That happened days ago, and the letter just came. Perhaps

Mrs. Crumble was really trying to be helpful."

But to this, Emily could only shake her head. "I saw the date on the letter. It must have come days before Mrs. Crumble talked to me about fleeing. I think it was Mrs. Spilking's idea, hoping I might try to run away. If she caught me and then told me about being a pauper, she would have a good excuse to put me in a . . . in a home for wayward girls—or even a workhouse."

"A home for wayward girls or a workhouse!" Lucy repeated, gasping.

"You're probably right, Emily," said Sarah indignantly. "But now look, she's got herself a nice free servant!"

"Well, she *does* have to pay for my food," said Emily.

Upon hearing this, Lucy and Sarah looked at her with disbelief. "Then don't eat too much porridge," said Lucy. "You really are quite amazing, Emily. You're so . . . brave."

"I've been a servant before, and I lived to tell about it," said Emily. "Remember?"

"I don't care, Emily. You *are* brave," said Lucy. "I'd be in a puddle if it happened to me!"

But the truth was that Emily *was* in a puddle.

She had to fight back tears that night, the last night before she began her role as a servant girl. She had been a servant when she first came to Sugar Hill Hall, with very little hope that she would ever be anything else. But somehow, this was different. She had endured so much before, but she had finally begun a wonderful new life with Aunt and Uncle Twice. She was even returned to being an heiress again, one day to be possessed of an enormous fortune.

Now all that had been snatched away with the arrival of two letters. She had been lightly dismissed by Aunt and Uncle Twice by the "many things that have to be seen to," and the little over five years until she would come into her fortune had been turned into never!

If only she could stop thinking of both these things, especially when she lay in bed each night, she might not have minded quite so much her new life at Mrs. Spilking's Select Academy. At least she no longer had to develop a stiff neck from bending over embroidery hoops, poke her eyes out knitting in the near darkness, read unbelievably dull books, or march 'round and 'round the dismal yard. But when she tried to persuade Sarah and Lucy of the one or two benefits provided by her new role as servant, purely in order to raise their spirits, she had very little success. They simply could not see anything beneficial about it.

Then one night, as they sat on the floor holding their meeting of the Palace Princesses by the light of the lantern, Emily suddenly had an idea. Scrambling to her feet, she went to her dress hanging on its wall peg and drew a key from the pocket. Then, asking a puzzled Lucy and Sarah if she could borrow the lantern for a few minutes, promising to return with a surprise, she left them in darkness as she tiptoed from the room and down the stairs. No, not the front stairs, which as a student she was required to use, but the stairs Bella used, which did not pass right by Mrs. Spilking's parlor. Well, as a servant like Bella, was it not perfectly proper that Emily should use those stairs as well?

The only light in the hall at the foot of the stairs came from the lantern Emily held, for not a single lamp fluttered on the wall. Mrs. Spilking had turned them all off for the night. And as Emily crept through the dining room and looked through the hall doorway, she could see that there was not even a sliver of light coming from Mrs. Spilking's parlor. Once in the kitchen, key in hand, she made for a cupboard on the back wall. But then she came to a sudden stop, her heart pounding. Through the deep silence, she had heard the sound of footsteps!

Swiftly, Emily dove under the kitchen table against the wall, turned off her lantern, and pushed herself back as far as she could, drawing her knees up under her chin. Afraid even to breathe, she waited, as the footsteps drew nearer and nearer. Then they came right through the kitchen door, accompanied by the dim flicker of lantern light. Holding the lantern and wearing a gray flannel robe and outrageously bright pink beaded slippers was Mrs. Spilking!

Yawning hugely, she headed straight for the very same cupboard that had been Emily's destination. With a key drawn from her robe pocket, she unlocked the cupboard and took from it a round tin box with a small china plate sitting on top. Then she carried the box and plate, along with the lantern, and set them right down on the table under which Emily was cowering. *Plunk! Plunk!* She could hear them come down right over her head. Then there was the *plunk* of the plate coming down from the tin. This was followed by the sound of metal scraping against metal, accompanied by a grunt from Mrs. Spilking as she labored to pry the lid off the tin. Then she began to mutter to herself, clearly counting something.

"One, two, three, um, um, um. Well, they're all still here. Bella hasn't been helping herself. Now, let's see, which ones to choose, um, um, um. I believe I'll have two."

This conversation with herself successfully completed, Mrs. Spilking replaced the lid on the tin and returned it to the cupboard, which she carefully locked. Then she retrieved the plate left sitting on the table and, finally, with another shuddering yawn, left the kitchen.

Even after the *flap-flapping* of Mrs. Spilking's pink beaded slippers had faded, Emily remained under the table, too frozen to move. What if Mrs. Spilking had brought Wolf along, wagging his tail and sniffing under the table, as he would most assuredly have done? That would have been the instant end of Emily. Off to the school for wayward girls for *her*! And would Mrs. Spilking not have had an excellent excuse now to send her there? Skulking around the kitchen late at night, prepared to steal. Yes, to *steal*! For was not the key in her nightdress pocket intended for the very cupboard where Mrs. Spilking kept locked the treats reserved for herself and her precious Princess Delilla?

And where, pray tell, had that key come from? In truth, it was from Bella, who had found an extra key and given it to Emily. But Emily would have allowed herself to be sent off to join the wayward girls rather than disclose this to Mrs. Spilking. For when Bella had given Emily the key, she had said it was for no particular reason, "just be certain that whatever disappears from the cupboard"—wink, wink—"is not something Mrs. Spilking can easily count."

Well, this was not something Emily needed to think about now, because neither she nor the key in her pocket had been discovered under the kitchen table. But after she had taken a few minutes to begin breathing properly again, her first thought was that she had better forget her grand plans and fly back to her room. Her second thought was the same. But by the time she had arrived at her third thought, she had entirely changed her mind. Mrs. Spilking would surely not return that night, and Lucy and Sarah were upstairs waiting patiently in the dark for a big surprise. And had Emily's whole plan not been to impress on them that being a servant had its benefits? What kind of benefit was it that she had had a terrifying near encounter with Mrs. Spilking, and risked a possible one-way trip to the home for wayward girls? No, Emily decided at last, she must complete the mission.

Of course, having had to turn off her lantern, she was now in total darkness. But she did know the shelf on which Mrs. Slump kept the matches for lighting the stove. Cautiously feeling her way over to it, she soon had the lantern lit again and once more approached the locked cupboard. Her hand was shaking as she fitted the key into the lock. This, after all, was where Mrs. Spilking had been, doing the very same thing only minutes before.

The cupboard door open, she found herself looking at the very same tin that Mrs. Spilking had just held in her hands. That one Emily would not touch for her life, for she was certain it contained the little frosted cakes, counted "one, two, three, um, um, um" by Mrs. Spilking. There were other tins and boxes as well, but in the end, Emily took only some dry "bisks" from the basket heaped with them. Just as Bella had said that first night when she had brought some to Emily, no one would miss them. Still, Emily was careful to take only three to put in her nightdress pocket, one for Lucy, one for Sarah, and one for herself.

Smart, brave Emily! On her way back to their room, fearing every second that Mrs. Spilking might just put in another appearance, Emily considered having "smart" win out over "brave" and never trying this again. But she knew that when she saw how excited Lucy and Sarah would be over this late-night royal feast, she might very well decide to reverse the "smart" "brave" order, and perhaps "brave" would win out!

Lucy and Sarah, as it turned out, were not nearly so thrilled with Emily's "royal feast" as she had thought they would be. After all, it *was* only plain, very dry biscuits, one each. They were both terribly polite, of course, and did say "thank you" over and over. But when Emily told them about the encounter with Mrs. Spilking, Lucy actually used the word "stupid" when referring to the risk taken by Emily.

As for ownership of the key changing anyone's opinion of her becoming a servant at Mrs.

Spilking's Select Academy, Sarah only allowed weakly that it *might* improve upon it a bit. Lucy said flatly it did no such thing, and the sooner someone discovered a terrible mistake had been made, and returned Emily to her proper place in the school, the better. So "smart" finally won out over "brave" after all!

Bella, on the other hand, although just as certain that Emily was "done wrong" by someone, was far more interested in the fact that Emily had so readily taken to her servant's role. Bella, in truth, never ceased to be astonished by it, and she told Emily so on every possible occasion.

"I ain't ever!" she declared once more as she and Emily stood at the sink one evening "doing up" the end results of Mrs. Slump's dinner preparations after she had gone. "Washing, ironing, dusting, scraping pots and pans. You're a wonder is all I can say." Bella paused to shake her head. "Ain't ever seen the like! Now, tell me more 'bout Tilly what you said taught you all you know. Was she really as mean as all that?"

Emily, of course, had by now had plenty of time to tell Bella about the early horrors of Sugar Hill

Hall, and Bella never tired of asking more questions about it, Tilly being of special interest because she was a servant just as Bella was.

"Oh, she was dreadfully mean, Bella," replied Emily, busy polishing a dish. "But, as I said, she turned out to be kindhearted as she could be, and we ended up the best of friends."

"Was that Mrs. Meeching 'bout the same as Madam?" asked Bella.

"Probably close to the same," said Emily.

"I ain't surprised," said Bella grimly. "But hard for me believing anyone's so wicked as Madam here is. Keeping that dog just to scare the wits out o' the girls. That dog scare you, Emily?" While seemingly giving all her attention to scraping something off the sink, Bella gave Emily a sideways look.

Emily, herself suddenly intent on polishing another dish, mumbled something and then quickly darted a sideways look at Bella as well.

Back and forth went the sideways looks, until at last Bella could contain herself no longer. "You know, don't you?"

Emily bit her lip and nodded.

"How'd you find out?" asked Bella. "You ain't

ever been 'round that dog excepting maybe once when you first come here."

"He pushed the Cupboard door open when I was in there being punished," said Emily. "I just knew he was going to rip me to shreds, but instead he came up and licked my chin. He's gentle as a kitten, Bella! I—I just don't understand why he growled at me when I first arrived here."

"Hmmmph!" Bella snorted. "'Twasn't you, Emily. 'Twas that flippin' Mr. Crawstone. Dog growls its head off every time that man gets too close when he comes visiting Madam S. *He's* the one most likely to get ripped to shreds one day, if you wish my opinion. Anyways, you know the secret 'bout Wolf, and now you got your answer 'bout the growling."

Bella hesitated, then looked sideways at Emily again. "Would you like to know another secret?"

Emily quickly nodded.

"All right, then," said Bella. "The secret is that Wolf ain't a he at all. Wolf's a she, and Wolf ain't even her name. It's Willa!"

"Willa!" Emily exclaimed.

"That's right!" said Bella. "A real jewel she is, and belonging to someone who don't even like dogs. Just kept for the purpose o' scaring everyone. She's left outside in that flippin' yard with that old dog-house o' hers most o' the time or else tied up in the cellar. But I see she gets her walk most nights, poor thing. Mrs. Spilking lets me take her out after you're all gone to bed. I feel real scared going 'bout nights most times, but never when I'm with Willa."

"Does Mrs. Spilking know that you know?" asked Emily.

Bella shrugged. "It ain't anything we have discussions 'bout. She slipped once and said Willa 'stead o' Wolf, which is why I know her name. But 'round Madam, I just keep pretending I don't know a boy dog from a girl dog, and go on calling her Wolf."

Bella now paused to deliver yet another sideways glance in Emily's direction. "You in on any other house secrets?"

Emily started, very nearly dropping the cup she was polishing. Then she again mumbled something that could have passed for "yes" or "no," and did not look Bella in the eye. But Bella had no intention of letting this pass.

"Well, which is it?" she demanded to know.

"I . . . I guess it's 'yes,'" replied Emily faintly.

"All right," said Bella. "This place got two secrets. You already found out 'bout one. How'd you find out 'bout the other? I mean, it's her majestry we're talking 'bout, ain't it?"

Emily nodded. "I—I heard an argument she had with Mrs. Spilking when I went to use her bathroom late one night. She—she called Mrs. Spilking 'Ma.'"

To this, Bella shook her head and sighed. "Took me three years 'fore I found out. You ain't been here but a few months and already know it all. And good at keeping secrets, too. Too bad you ain't going to be in service permanent. But you ain't, Emily. I got a serious feeling in my bones that you ain't!"

15

An Unexpected Visitor

Well, Bella's bones might be telling her that Emily's days as a servant were numbered, but as more days went by with nothing changing, Emily concluded that she must make up her mind this was to be her life forever.

It had been a shock at first, especially waiting on the girls at mealtimes instead of sitting down with them. And she had to endure the looks of triumph Princess Delilla gave her at every opportunity. Once she even nudged Emily's arm deliberately when she was trying to pour some watered-down tea into a cup on the table. The tea naturally sloshed all over the girl sitting next to Princess Delilla, and Emily had to endure a grand lecture on clumsiness from Mrs. Spilking. But now she was getting used to waiting on table and had learned how to avoid Princess Delilla's elbow when passing near her.

Emily knew, however, she would rather return to being a student in a minute, even if it meant suffering through endless hoops of embroidery, dull, ragged books, and deadly "exercise" periods. Perhaps it was only because she once had hope for her future as a student, whereas now there was none. All she had left to count on was the feeling in Bella's bones. In the meantime, she must try to keep up her spirits, reminding herself how fortunate she was to have such staunch supporters and friends as Bella, Lucy, and Sarah.

But Emily did not feel quite so fortunate about her now-closer acquaintance with Mrs. Slump. She was so very large and violent, and the kitchen so very small, that when she began banging pots and pans around, as was her usual manner of preparing food, Emily often feared serious injury if she were in the kitchen at the same time. Still, her job included helping Mrs. Slump, so help her she must.

Mrs. Slump being as large as she was, and the cellar stairs being as narrow as they were, one of Emily's chores was to go down to the cellar and fetch the potatoes, the turnips, the lard, and the dry cereal. The latter, of course, then required that Emily pick out the weevils. This job was once done by Mrs. Slump herself, if she even thought about it before preparing the porridge. Otherwise, she would boil the porridge, weevils and all. But Emily never minded the trips to the cellar to fetch supplies for Mrs. Slump or, for that matter, to help Bella with the washing and ironing, which took place down there. At least she did not mind them as much as she thought she would. But she would not want to *live* in the cellar. Never again! Not then . . . not *ever*!

Another task Emily performed for Mrs. Slump was peeling. Mrs. Slump hated peeling. If it were up to her, the potatoes and turnips would undoubtedly be hurled into the stew in their original state.

"Peeling comes close to goormette cooking. If Madam wishes my goormette cooking, she pays for goormette cooking," Mrs. Slump announced to Emily, slamming a pot on the stove. So while Emily peeled or picked weevils from the cereal, Mrs. Slump lowered herself into a chair at the kitchen table and sipped tea from her favorite cracked green china cup while regaling Emily with stories of her life. In truth, Emily came to enjoy these more peaceful moments with Mrs. Slump, who could be jolly and entertaining when she was not rampaging around the kitchen.

But when Mrs. Slump was at the height of her cooking fervor, Emily stayed out of her way and came into the kitchen only when all was quiet. Which is what she did one day to fetch a cup of water before Mrs. Slump was due to arrive to pre-pare the stew for dinner. When Emily entered the kitchen, however, she found somebody already there.

It was a boy about her age, standing at the sink, intent on the job of cleaning a large fish. He was attacking the task with such energy that fish scales were flying all over the counter. Some even seemed to be flying into his red curls and the green scarf he had wound around his neck.

Bright red curls, brighter even than Lucy's, and a familiar green scarf! Emily threw a hand to her mouth to repress a shriek. "Kipper!"

The boy turned around, saw Emily, and produced a wide grin. But while he most definitely did have red curls, blue eyes brighter than the sea, and ruddy cheeks, he just as definitely was *not* Kipper.

"Wrong boy," he said cheerfully. "But close 'nough. Kipper's my cuz."

"P–P–Piper?" stammered Emily.

"The very one!" replied the boy, wiping his nose with the back of his hand, paying no attention to the fish scales decorating it. "You must be Miss Emily."

Emily could do no more than nod, for her brain was still spinning. Piper, her friend Kipper's cousin, actually standing right before her!

"I never thought as how I'd find you here so easy," said Piper. "I decided if I arrived at the front door o' this place asking for you, they'd just slam it in my face. So I figgered I'd come to the servants' entry, *not* asking for you, but selling fish from my pa's shop. There's more than one way to trap a tuna, as Pa always says.

"But wasn't so easy getting in that way, neither. Appears like the owner ain't willing to spend two cents more'n she has to feeding the inmates, and the cook ain't willing to clean a fish. Too much like peeling, and smelly besides. Leastways that's what someone named Bella, who answered the bell when I rung it, said."

"So how *did* you ever manage to get in here?" asked Emily.

"Well, this Bella told me that I had to practically offer the owner, name of Mrs. Spilking, a fish for just 'bout nothing and then offer myself to clean it. So I offered one, and then I offered th' other, and here I am. Didn't have a idea how I was to see you, howsumever, you being a student, like Kipper's pa wrote. Then here you go and show up slick as a sardine what found its way through a hole in the net, as Pa always says. But why are you out here in a apron what looks like you been housecleaning? Ain't you supposed to be studying your lessons?"

Emily bit her lip, hesitating. "I—I'm not a student anymore. I've become a servant again, the way I was when I first met Kipper."

"Wheeoo!" Piper whistled. "How come, Miss Emily? What happened?"

"Oh, you mustn't call me Miss Emily," she said quickly. "Kipper never did, and you mustn't, either. But what happened is that my Aunt and Uncle Twice went to India, and—and didn't take me with them because I don't believe they wish me to live with them anymore. Then the fortune I had, which was to pay for my school was all lost. Someone has written to my uncle about it, but I don't believe that will change anything. So there you are. It—it's really very simple."

"Don't sound simple to me," said Piper. "And I know Kipper won't like it when he hears. He ain't much o' a hand at writing, but his pa, who's my Uncle Ab, wrote my pa, so I know Kipper was pleased as the mackerel who swallowed the minnow, as my pa always says, when your uncle got found, and you got to be a hairess. Now, quicker 'n any wink, your uncle's gone again, taking your aunt with him, and you ain't got a penny left. You know, something don't sound right to me 'bout it. Can't help thinking what I come to tell you 'bout's got something to do with it."

"I was wondering why you had come looking for me," Emily said. "Kipper gave me a note telling me about you, but I never thought I'd ever see you, even when I was still a student here. Mrs. Spilking keeps all the girls practically prisoners. This isn't a very nice place, Piper. But what is it you came to tell me?"

"Might be something, and might be nothing," said Piper, thoughtfully pulling on an ear, his fingers leaving a few fish scales in their wake. "But seems as how Kipper went back to that big old mansion he says got the name o' Sugar Hill Hall.

He wanted to see if whoever bought it from your uncle might want to be reg'lar customers buying his pa's fish. But when he got there, he rung the bell at the back, and then he banged on the door. But nobody came to answer. Then he got brave and went out front and did the same. Still nobody came. He figgered as how everybody was out, but seemed pecoolyar—a big place like that ain't got a servant to come to the door. Anyway, back home Kipper went."

"Perhaps if the owners were away," said Emily, "the servants were just taking naps or something."

"You mean taking a few winks on the sly?" said Piper. "Might o' crossed Kipper's mind, 'cause he decided as how he'd give it 'nother try. So back he went, ringing and banging, banging and ringing. Then, getting to wondering, he went and hoisted himself up to look in a window. Then he looked in more windows. And guess what, Emily?"

"I couldn't," replied Emily.

"Nothing in the house!" said Piper. "No people, no furnishings . . . not a blamed thing but dust lying all over. Ain't anybody living there, Emily, and that's the truth! Thinking something ain't right, and wondering if it got anything to do with you, Kipper had Uncle Ab write my pa and asked him to try to find you to tell you 'bout it. Lucky you told Kipper the name o' this school. Pa dug 'round and 'round, and somehow or other found out where it was. But you got to wonder as how Kipper, who ain't got any notion o' your present situation, got it in his head 'bout something not being right with that old house sitting there all dark and dusty and empty as a shell with the crab missing, as Pa always says, and thinking as how it got a connection to you. Now, that's mighty pecoolyar, ain't it?"

"It really is, Piper," said Emily. "But I don't know what connection there could be. My Uncle Twice sold Sugar Hill Hall, and he and Aunt Twice are already in India. Mrs. Meeching and Mrs. Plumly, who used to be there, are now in jail for all their wrongdoings. My fortune got lost because . . . because Uncle Twice didn't manage it very well. So now I've become a servant. I can't see how nobody living in Sugar Hill Hall could have much to do with all that."

"Maybe not," said Piper uncertainly. "But now that I know how to find you, I'll let you know if we hear more 'bout it from Uncle Ab. And if you ever need anything, here on this bit o' paper is where Pa's fish shop is. Pa and me live over it. It's a pretty long ways away. Had to take a bunch o' trolleys to get here. But good for you to know 'bout it anyways. Sorry 'bout the paper being all crumpled and smelling so powerful of fish. Oops! Sounds like someone's coming. Never mind, I'm 'bout done, anyways."

Someone was indeed coming, and moments later Mrs. Slump thumped into the kitchen. She eyed Piper suspiciously as she hung up her coat and removed a great, squashed red hat from her head.

"I'm Mrs. Slump, the cook," she said sourly. "And who might you be?"

"I'm Piper," he said. "You got bought some nice mackerel, fresh as you please. And I'm cleaning it for you. Comes with the price, you might say."

"Now, ain't that nice!" said Mrs. Slump, rewarding Piper with an expansive beam. "Cleaning it and all. Good thing, or it might o' gone into the dump. Don't like cleaning. Don't like peeling. Might just cook up a goormette dinner tonight. You can run along now, fish boy. Emily will let you out. Emily, you hurry back. We got work to do!"

Mrs. Slump was already slamming a pot on the stove as Emily led Piper out of the kitchen, down the cellar steps, and on to the stairwell leading to the street. She hated to see him leave, for who knew how long it would be before she would see him again. But Piper promised he would be back even if there was no further news from Kipper. Then with a smile and a wave, he was gone, and Emily had to fly back to the kitchen to help Mrs. Slump with her "goormette" meal.

And, oh, what a grand introduction Mrs. Spilking gave the dinner that evening. A very, very special treat, she informed the girls, and she but hoped they would appreciate what it had cost her to provide this outstandingly fresh fish from the sea. One might have thought Mrs. Spilking had rowed into the ocean herself to catch the fish—a fish that might well have been a charitable donation from Piper's pa's fish shop for all it cost her, a fish cleaned by Piper so Mrs. Slump would then deign to cut it up for the potato-turnip stew, and finally, a fish that would not have been there at all but for Emily, who had the great pleasure of serving it to Mrs. Spilking and Princess Delilla before she could even taste it later in the kitchen with Bella.

But Emily hardly minded, for she had now actually met Kipper's cousin! And while he did not have *exactly* the same bright red curls or blue eyes or ruddy cheeks, Kipper and Piper came as close to being two peas in a pod as they could be without being twins. Besides, in Emily's dress pocket, at that very moment, was a crumpled bit of paper that smelled beautifully of fish! If Piper had but known it, there was hardly a need for him to apologize for the condition of that bit of paper. For to Emily, it was the most wonderful reminder of the fishy smell that accompanied Kipper whenever he arrived from his pa's shop. And at that moment, it was worth more to her than any crown jewel from anywhere in the whole world!

16

The Final Proof

It was several days before Piper returned with a fish. "Even fresher'n the last!" he informed Mrs. Slump.

Of course, this second time around, Piper needed no "credentuals," as he put it, because Mrs. Slump welcomed him with open arms. For, in truth, she not only enjoyed "goormette" cooking, but also enjoyed "goormette" eating. And considering the prodigious amount of taste testing that went on, it could be said that she particularly enjoyed her new specialty of the house, potato, turnip, and fresh fish stew. She even went so far as to give it a name, Slump's Supreme Surprise!

Mrs. Spilking, for her part, as was later reported to Emily by Bella, appeared ready to call out "a flippin' brass band" when informed that Piper had returned with yet another fish. It was "a crying shame," said Bella, that "that penny-pinching old witch" was getting an all-but-free fish because of Piper needing to "bribe" his way in to see Emily.

Bella, needless to say, as well as Lucy and Sarah, had all been joyfully apprised by Emily of Piper's connection to her old friend Kipper. But all three agreed with her that his report from Kipper regarding Sugar Hill Hall probably had nothing whatsoever to do with the fate that had befallen her. Perhaps another letter from the same source would simply announce that furnishings, lights, and people had returned to Sugar Hill Hall, so there would be no mystery left to connect to Emily.

In any event, when Piper returned, he had no report to bring of another letter from his uncle Ab. When Emily hurried into the kitchen, however, having been advised of his presence by a nudge and a wink from Bella, he was thoughtful and far less bright and cheery than he had been on his first visit. It was as if he *did* have something important to relate, and was just trying to make conversation until he got around to it.

At last, looking up from a not-too-successful

attempt at cleaning fish scales from the sink, he hesitated and then blurted out, "Emily, don't know as how I should be saying anything 'bout this, but Pa was telling me 'bout a man what come into his shop th'other day. Pa figgered he was a dockworker from the way he was dressed. Pa ought to know. His shop being down by the wharves, dockworkers come in all the time. This one had his wife with him, and begging your pardon, Emily, Pa said as how she looked like she was just 'bout getting ready to increase their family."

Piper's already-ruddy cheeks turned even ruddier at this. He shifted in embarrassment from one foot to the other. "Anyways," he finally continued, "this man and Pa got to talking a bit, and he tells Pa as how he's a dockworker all right, as Pa guessed, but he's been working 'board ships and just come all the way from India. He said he ain't been back long. Told Pa how glad he was to find Pa's shop, on 'count o' they live nearby."

Piper stopped to take a breath, and suddenly started staring at the toes of his shoes as if finding it difficult to look into Emily's eyes. Then at last he looked up. "Emily, . . . you don't got any reason to suppose this is your aunt and uncle, do you?"

"No, no!" exclaimed Emily. "Uncle Twice has a business in India. He's not a dockworker or even a ship's sailor. Just because the man your pa talked to has come from India doesn't mean anything. I expect there are lots of sailors on the wharves who've come from there."

Piper then turned his attention to flicking a fish scale from the sink with his fingernail. "Lots of dockworkers who are tall and handsome and got hair the color o' corn silk, like yours, Emily? And maybe a pretty little wife with dark curls as well?"

"Maybe not lots, Piper," replied Emily, finding herself becoming a trifle upset with Piper for going on with this discomforting subject. "But I'm sure there are enough."

Piper then raised his eyes, looking directly at Emily again. It appeared that he had no intention of giving up. "Dockworkers and their pretty wives who—who call each other 'William' and 'Fanny'? Ain't those names got any meaning for you, Emily?"

Emily's heart jumped to her throat. William and Fanny! Aunt and Uncle Twice! But it could not be. How could it *possibly* be? Uncle Twice was a businessman in India, not a dockworker on the wharves of New York, just as she had told Piper.

This had to be a very strange quirk of fate. It could not possibly be anything else.

"Emily," said Piper, "Pa, taking note of the condition of this man's wife, asked them if they might like me to bring a fish or two 'round to where they live, it being close by and all. Then she could choose what she likes, and ain't got to walk to Pa's shop to do it. Pa said you couldn't believe as how they thanked him for his kindness. Then he whipped out a piece o' paper so the man could write down his name and where they lived. Pa put it in a drawer and never looked at it till this morning. Then he showed it to me. We talked 'bout it, and Pa and me both decided we shouldn't do anything 'bout it till it got showed to you. So, Emily, here 'tis!"

Emily looked down at the scrap of paper handed her by Kipper and saw there, besides the address, a name in oh-so-familiar handwriting:

William Luccock

"You ain't going to faint nor anything, are you?" Piper asked anxiously. "Blood's all gone from your face, Emily."

Emily shook her head, although, in truth, she

felt almost as stunned as she had when she first saw
the peppermints in the Front Room. Aunt and
Uncle Twice back in New York! And while they
may not have been there very long, surely it was
long enough to come see *her*.

"Pa knows your story from Uncle Ab's letters,
Emily," said Piper. "And I told him what you said
'bout your aunt and uncle not wishing you to live
with them anymore. Pa says he don't understand
it, that nice couple being so mean. But he says we
ain't going to say anything to them 'bout seeing
you 'less it's what you want. Pa thinks, though, it's
what ought to be done."

"Oh, no! No! No!" cried Emily. "You and your
pa mustn't tell them anything! They may not wish
to see me. But—but perhaps they intend to come
and just have not had the time."

Just have not had the time! Oh, what a very
sorry excuse that would be! For if Aunt and Uncle
Twice still cared deeply for Emily, would they not
have rushed to see her the very moment they
returned? But just to have not had the time! The
words lay like stones in the room, and for several
moments silenced them both.

"Please don't tell them what's happened to me

if you see them," Emily pleaded. "I—I want to wait a while longer for them to come. I'm certain they will! Promise me you won't tell them, Piper. Please promise me!"

"All right, I promise. And I'll tell Pa to promise, as well. But he ain't going to like it, Emily. I'll tell you that right now!" said Piper.

Piper left with yet a second promise that he would be back soon, no matter what. No matter what! Ominous words again. For to Emily, "no matter what" meant that Aunt and Uncle Twice might never come to see her. And if they did not come to see her, it could hardly be because they did not have the time but more likely because they did not wish to see her and then have to decide what was to be done with her. In a word, they did not wish to be bothered!

Mingled with all these thoughts that kept tumbling through Emily's head was the question, why had Uncle Twice returned with Aunt Twice from India? And why not as the businessman he had gone to India to be, but as a dockworker living near the wharves? The question kept coming back and coming back, until at last Emily came up with the answer. Uncle Twice had lost her fortune by not managing it properly. Did it not stand to reason that he might have lost his business for the very same reason? Still, whatever that reason was, and whatever the sad results, should not Uncle Twice at least have come to tell Emily how sorry he was for what had happened to her fortune? And know about it he must, for had not his friend Mr. Slyde sent him a letter asking him what was now to become of Emily?

These questions ended up in such a muddle in Emily's head that finally she could not bear to think of them anymore. At any rate, what difference did the answers make? What did she care that she was no longer an heiress or that Uncle Twice had become a dockworker? All she wanted was to be back with him and Aunt Twice and, yes, Baby Twice as well, and she might never be. Not ever again! And so for the first time since she had been sent to Mrs. Spilking's Select Academy for Young Ladies, the night following Piper's return visit, Emily cried herself to sleep.

Emily found it impossible to keep her mind on her work the following two days. Perhaps this was because she had kept her thoughts and her questions all to herself, somehow unable to reveal to Bella, Sarah, and Lucy what Piper had told her. But that night, she intended to tell Sarah and Lucy, and the following morning to tell Bella when they were doing the laundry together.

That afternoon, when the girls had left for their "exercise" period, Emily was deep in thought as she dusted the Front Room. Not paying enough attention to what she was doing, she rose too quickly from cleaning the legs of Mrs. Crumble's wing chair. Her shoulder struck the red-velvet-covered table, and at least seven peppermints parted company from the rest and plummeted to the floor. Horrified, Emily snatched them up and quickly began to set them back in the bowl, trying to remember exactly how they were placed. But she was not quick enough!

"So!" said a chilling voice from the doorway.

Emily whirled around to see Mrs. Spilking standing there with her arms folded and her eyes flaring.

"Some people never learn lessons!" she snapped. "And what do you have to say for yourself, Emily Luccock, for this act of disobedience? You know the peppermints rule, I believe? Will you please explain yourself?"

Explain the peppermints, when she stood there holding the evidence in her hand? Why, there was no excuse or explanation in the world that would do the slightest good, unless it was perhaps accompanied by dropping dead at Mrs. Spilking's feet, and there were even grave doubts about that.

Emily simply stood there barely able to breathe, much less provide an explanation.

"I thought you could not possibly have anything to say for yourself," said Mrs. Spilking with relish. Then she offered up a sigh no doubt manufactured for the occasion. "Well, you already know the punishment for this particular crime, so at least I need waste no time in describing it to you. However, in this instance, you will not only be spending one night in the Cupboard, but perhaps several nights while I make arrangements for you to occupy another of the cellar rooms. For as it appears that the kindness and warmth of my heart have not influenced you in the least, we shall no longer be awaiting word from your uncle, nor the arrival of a new student to take your place in your present room.

"You, Emily Luccock, will now be assigned to the servants' quarters in the cellar, where you should have been put in the first place. I shall personally see that your clothing is removed to the cellar before escorting you to the Cupboard tonight. And, as you are not to be trusted, you will now in my presence please replace the peppermints stolen from the bowl!"

Silently, Emily did.

Spending the night in the cellar, needless to say, no longer frightened Emily at all. She was in the cellar so much now, fetching and carrying, she was quite used to it. Then, too, she would be seeing Wolf—no, Willa—again. What if Mrs. Spilking knew about *that*! But Emily desperately did not want to spend the rest of her life in a cellar. And now that Aunt and Uncle Twice had not even come to inquire about her welfare, was that not final proof of their intentions? More and more, it looked as if life in a cellar was what was in store for her.

That night, this one grim thought chained itself inside her head and would not let go. The rest of her life to be spent living in a cellar! The rest of her life! But all the while, as she lay awake on the hard cot, unable to go to sleep, she was rubbing Willa's soft ear. For, of course, as soon as Mrs. Spilking had left, Emily had crept to the door of the Cupboard and let Willa in. Then all at once, Emily remembered something Bella had said. "I feel real scared going 'bout nights most times, but never when I'm with Willa."

Then Emily began thinking of the outlandish idea Mrs. Crumble had once tried to put in her head, the idea of fleeing. Well, suppose she were to flee now? She need no longer be afraid of Wolf... no, Willa again... tracking her down and ripping her to shreds. No, for she would actually take Willa with her, to protect her! But if that were to be the case, it meant she would have to leave that very night. For even if she were to remain in the Cupboard for several additional nights, it would not be as a "punishment," so "Wolf" would not be posted outside to guard the room.

Fleeing! Emily's heart began to race. Fleeing! But to where? She had but one place, Coddy's Fish Shop that belonged to Piper's pa. She had the address right on that fishy bit of paper she had kept in her dress pocket. But what after that? She could hardly just appear on their doorstep and expect to live there indefinitely. No, but Uncle Twice had given Piper's pa his and Aunt Twice's address. She could appear on *their* doorstep and plead with them not to send her back to Mrs. Spilking's Select Academy. Surely they would not send her back to be a servant there and live once more in the cellar, as she had in Sugar Hill Hall. They *could* not! They would have to think of something else to do with her.

Was the thought of fleeing rash, reckless, and stupid? Lucy and Sarah would think so, and they would be right. Yet even as Emily was thinking that "smart" should win out over "brave" and that she should remain right where she was, she knew "brave" was nudging "smart" right out of the way.

"And you'll come with me, Willa," she whispered in the dog's ear as she climbed from the cot. "Yes, you will!"

The part of the cellar that held the Cupboard was in total darkness, but Emily had been down there enough now to know how to make it to the door leading to the street, exactly where the trunk room was, and where in that room she had seen a rope that would serve as a leash for Willa. As for the coat and bonnet Emily would need, they were in the heap outside the Cupboard with her other clothes, spitefully thrown there by Mrs. Spilking.

The first thing Emily did was put on her coat and bonnet. Then she felt her way to the trunk room, with Willa docilely following right beside her. She found the rope easily and tied it to Willa's collar. The big dog's tail started wagging furiously, for she recognized what this meant.

The last thing Emily did was look for her trunk. This proved more difficult than she had thought, but when she finally found the trunk she believed to be hers, she opened the lid and felt the lining. And they were still there, the two gold coins! Quickly she tore open the stitching and pulled out the coins, dropping them into her coat pocket. Now she was ready!

By the time she and Willa reached the door to the street, her heart was pounding so hard she was finding it difficult to breathe. It would have been much easier to simply turn around and head back to the Cupboard. But she unlocked the door and opened it without even hesitating, for she knew if she hesitated for even a moment, she and Willa would indeed be heading back.

With the door closed behind them, she leaned down and whispered into the dog's ear, "Come along, Willa. We're going for a nice long walk!"

17

Something Fishy

Emily had been out late at night but once in her life. That had been when she was escaping from the Remembrance Room in Sugar Hill Hall to Kipper's pa's fish shop. Now she was escaping from the Cupboard in Mrs. Spilking's Select Academy to Piper's pa's fish shop. But whereas she had Kipper by her side on that earlier occasion, she did not have Piper by her side now as she hurried up one street and down another, most deadly dark but for the occasional tiny pool of light fluttering timidly around each post holding a gas lamp. Now all Emily had with her was Willa. So when a hulking shadow emerged from a black stairwell, she was nearly paralyzed with fright as the shadow drew closer and became a man. But met by a deep, throaty growl, he all but ran past them. Oh, yes,

Bella was indeed right about having Willa by one's side at night!

Emily was worried, though, that Willa might present a problem. Remembering how very long the ride was when Mr. Crawstone brought her to Mrs. Spilking's Select Academy from the wharves, not to mention Piper saying he had had to take a "bunch o' trolleys" to get there, Emily knew she could not walk to Coddy's Fish Shop or find her way there by trolley, assuming she would be allowed on one with a large dog in tow. So she must take a cab to her destination, but what cab-driver would accept a large dog as a passenger any more than a trolley? Well, she must find any cab at all, and that meant seeking a busy street.

As very large cities have countless streets that remain awake all night, Emily soon found one, but it proved to be more frightening than streets that were dark and deserted. Cruel faces with shifty eyes, painted faces with glittering eyes, and flat faces with no expression at all in their eyes all swirled around her. There was not much doubt that the gold coins in a young girl's pocket, at least one of which must be used to pay her cab fare, would not have remained in her pocket long but for the large black dog attached to a rope wrapped firmly around her hand. As it was, everyone coming in her direction carefully described a wide circle around her on the sidewalk, especially when Willa delivered her deep, warning growl.

Emily was quite right, however, in thinking no cab would take her and a big dog. They all turned her down. But in the end, she came upon one cab-driver who was actually nodding in his seat for lack of business. Emily reached up and tapped his shoe. She had to tap again before he came to with a start.

"I—I'd like to hire your cab?" she said, her voice quavering.

"You and your pet both, I presumes?" said the cabdriver. "Does he bite?"

"He's never bitten *me*," Emily replied firmly, though her knees were shaking.

"You got the money to pay?" the cabdriver asked suspiciously.

"I—I have a—a gold coin," said Emily, reaching in her pocket to draw it out and show it to him.

"Never mind," the cabdriver said quickly. "You don't better go pulling anything like that out for this lot 'round here to see, dog or no dog."

"I need to go to the wharves," said Emily. "Do you know where they are?"

"Do I know where the wharves is?" The cabdriver looked at her in disbelief. "This is New York, young lady. Just tell me where on the wharves."

"It's Coddy's Fish Shop," Emily said, and gave him the address.

"All right, you and your pet hop on in, and be quick about it," said the cabdriver. "I ain't got all night!"

The ride to the wharves was as long as Emily remembered it. In truth, even longer—or at least it seemed so, because it was getting later and later, and Piper and his pa would most certainly have long since closed up the shop and gone to bed. But at last the cab pulled to a stop, and Emily climbed out with Willa.

When she handed the cabdriver a gold coin, however, his eyebrows raised almost to his hairline, and he whistled. "Wheeoo! So you really do got a gold coin. But I got to tell you, I don't got change for a king's ransom. Maybe somebody here can help out, but looks like the place is closed down for the night."

Coddy's Fish Shop was indeed closed, and it was

dark upstairs as well as down. And if there was any doubt about the matter, a streetlight lit up a sign on the door that unmistakably read CLOSED!

The cabdriver frowned. "Young girl like you oughtn't to be traveling 'round this hour. You certain somebody's expecting you here?"

"In—in a way," replied Emily, which was a half-truth after all. For had Piper not given her this address with the idea that some day she might need it? And was this not that some day?

"You best make certain, miss," replied the cabdriver, leaping down beside Emily. "I'll come with you while you go knock."

So it was the cabdriver and Willa who accompanied Emily to the door of Coddy's Fish Shop, where she timidly knocked. Then, noting a small brass button beside the door, she hesitated but then pushed it.

Somewhere in the shop a bell rang. Several anxious minutes passed before Emily saw through the glass in the door a light descending a stairwell at the back of the store. It was followed by a man and a boy, both in their nightclothes. Yawning, they came to the door, and the man unlocked and cautiously opened it. If the man was not Piper's pa, it must be said that considering his red hair, blue eyes, and ruddy cheeks, he was certainly a fine imitation of that person.

"Shop's closed," he said, scowling. "Can't you see the sign?"

At this point, Piper, for it was indeed he, gave his pa a sharp dig in the ribs. "This here's Emily, Pa," he said, and then produced a sunny grin bright as the middle of day. "Evening, Emily!"

"Emily? Well, I never!" exclaimed Mr. Coddy, his expression changing from the very cold north one hundred eighty degrees to the warmest south imaginable. "But, child, what are you doing out at this time of night?"

"Same as I was wondering, sir," said the cab-driver. "I being the one what brung her and her dog here. But if it ain't too much trouble, she give me a gold coin I ain't got any way in this world o' changing. Might I be asking if you got any way o' changing it for her, and helping me out? Much obliged if you could."

"I could, indeed!" said Mr. Coddy. "You are an honest man not to be taking a child's gold coin and driving off with it. Now, if you can just tell me the fare for her ride here?"

In no time at all, Mr. Coddy had turned over to the cabdriver not only the fare and a generous number of extra coins, but a large fresh mackerel as well! Then, with a promise to return to Coddy's Fish Shop at the earliest possible moment as a customer, the cabdriver climbed back onto his cab and, with a smile and a tip of his cap, drove off whistling.

"I—I'm very sorry to have put you to so much trouble, Mr. Coddy," said Emily. "And it's—it's so very late at night."

"No trouble at all, child," said Mr. Coddy. "And it ain't all that late. Piper and I only just climbed into bed, being late cleaning up and closing the shop. On top o' that, you got a invitation to come here with no date nor time on it, far as I can recollect. So now's as good a time as any. Ain't that right, Piper?"

"Right, Pa!" agreed Piper, nodding his head so hard his red curls bobbed on his forehead.

"But I must pay you for my cab ride," said Emily.

"Oh, we'll have to see 'bout that!" said Mr. Coddy, with a broad wink at Piper saying clear as any words that the subject was not to be mentioned again.

"But what you need to tell us is who your friend is," Mr. Coddy then said, leaning over to rub Willa's ear. That ear and the other, of course, had already been getting a good deal of attention from Piper, and Willa's tail was flagging the air at a great rate.

"Piper never did get 'round to making mention o' any dog," said Mr. Coddy.

"That's because I never got around to telling him about her," said Emily. "Her name's Willa, but I only learned that a while ago. Mrs. Spilking, who owns the school, always tells everyone she's a boy dog named Wolf, who will rip us to shreds any chance he gets. She posts Wolf—only it's really Willa—outside the Cupboard, which is where you get put to be punished. It's where I was when I ran away here tonight, and . . . oh, it's so complicated, and it's such a long story!"

"Which you shall tell us now!" declared Mr. Coddy.

"To-Tonight?" stammered Emily.

"Why not?" said Mr. Coddy cheerfully. "We're all properly awake now. But I think it best be told up in our quarters over the shop, if it pleases you."

"Should I bring Willa?" asked Emily.

"Piper wouldn't like it if you didn't!" replied Mr. Coddy, his eyes twinkling, as he started for the stairs.

So Piper, Emily, and Willa followed Mr. Coddy up the narrow stairs, leaving behind the neat and tidy little shop that smelled of fish, and arriving at the neat and tidy little apartment above it, where the smell of fish was almost equal to that of the shop below. Emily was enchanted, for it was just as if she had been transported right to Kipper's pa's place!

They had no sooner arrived upstairs than Mr. Coddy turned to Emily and asked, "What is it you call Kipper's pa, who is also my brother Abner and Piper's uncle? You call him 'Mr. Coddy,' as well?"

"Oh, no!" said Emily. "He said he'd be pleased if I was to call him 'Pa,' which I always did."

"Well, then," said Mr. Coddy, "I'd be pleased as the crab what crawled out o' the crab pot if you called *me* 'Pa,' same as my brother Ab. Ain't any reason as I can see why you can't have two pa's. Any reason as you can see, child?"

"Oh, none at all!" replied the delighted Emily.

"Then that's settled," said Mr. Coddy, now to be known as Pa. "Piper, I'd take it kindly if you'd heat up some o' that milk we just got in fresh this morning. Then pour Emily here a cup. One o' our old saucepots will do fine for holding some water for Willa."

Those things speedily accomplished, Pa, Piper, and Emily sat down around the small table with the blue checkered cloth over it that served as Piper and Pa's dining table.

"Now," said Pa, "you're to tell us everything, starting way back with that place you call Sugar Hill Hall. Piper's told you we already been told a lot by his Uncle Ab, writing for Kipper, so it ain't all new to us."

So Emily began her story, going back to the very beginning, from when she first arrived at Sugar Hill Hall after her mama and papa had been lost in the boating accident, and she was an orphan come to live with her Aunt and Uncle Twice. She was only interrupted a very few times when Pa mentioned that, well, he already recollected being told that by his brother Ab or when he had a question about something. But there were no interruptions when she came to the part in her story where Uncle Twice had sold Sugar Hill Hall, and she had been left at the terrible Mrs. Spilking's

Select Academy for Young Ladies as Aunt and Uncle Twice departed for India. Again and again, as the sad story unfolded, Pa would shake his head, especially at the end of her tale, when Emily related how she had been condemned to the Cupboard for having stolen peppermints that, in reality, she was trying to put back in the bowl.

Pa exploded at that. "Blamed peppermints! We heard o' them wicked Sugar Hill Hall things from Kipper, writing through Abner. But where I got to come in here is to say what I told Piper, that something ain't right 'bout you thinking the nice couple I met, what turns out to be your Aunt and Uncle Twice, not wanting you 'round anymore. Can't help it, but I smell something fishy going on what ain't what's coming from down below. Just can't put a finger on it."

"But I still think I should have waited to see if they'd come to see me," declared Emily.

"I don't b'lieve so," Pa said. "I think that old witch done you a favor, if you'd like to know. Helped you find the courage to come here, just as you should. But we'll know it all tomorrow when we go to your aunt and uncle's place, which you allow as how you now wish to do. And it'll turn out just what I'm thinking. You wait and see!"

How Emily would have loved to believe what Pa said as she lay in a cot later in the cozy room that served as parlor, dining room, kitchen, and Piper's bedroom, while Piper bunked that night in Pa's tiny room. How she would have loved to fall asleep thinking only of that lovely fishiness that filled the room, reminding her so much of an earlier, happier time. As it was, all she could think of was "we'll know it all tomorrow." Tomorrow! Never had that word filled her with so much dread.

18

Something Even Fishier

It was decided that they had better wait until late in the day when Uncle Twice should have returned from his work on the docks, before Pa and Piper walked Emily and Willa to the address given by Uncle Twice. Pa thought it would not be wise to surprise Aunt Twice when she was alone, her condition being what it was. Whether it would be a pleasant or an unpleasant surprise remained to be seen, but in either case, Emily's sudden appearance might be a shock. So it was late afternoon before they set out, going on foot because, as Uncle Twice had said, they did not live far from Coddy's Fish Shop.

Although Pa and Piper attempted to carry on a cheery conversation the whole way, they failed miserably, and were largely silent when they arrived at their destination. Emily was finding it difficult to breathe as Pa lifted a hand to knock on the door. It was Uncle Twice who answered the knock, and, of course, the first person he saw standing before him was Pa.

"Don't know if you remember me, Mr. Luccock," he said. "But I'm Caleb Coddy of Coddy's Fish Shop, where you stopped by the other day. Said I'd send my boy 'round with nice fresh fish for Mrs. Luccock to choose from."

"Of course I remember, Mr. Coddy," said Uncle Twice at once. "But I never expected you to be so kind as to take the trouble to come yourself."

"Well," said Pa, "I came on account o' I got something real important to deliver, something what ain't fish!" With that, he stepped aside to reveal Emily standing directly behind him.

Before she even had time to think what was happening, she felt two powerful arms wrapped around her, lifting her off the ground and hugging her so tightly she could not even breathe.

And then Emily knew! She knew even before a word was spoken! The horror was over. She was home again at last!

"What is it, William? What is it?" came Aunt Twice's anxious voice from across the little room.

"It's Emily, Fanny! It's our Emily!" Uncle Twice's voice was choked with tears.

"Emily!" cried Aunt Twice. "Oh, William, you know I can hardly rise from this chair. Bring her to me! Bring her to me!"

Then Emily was carried across the room as if she weighed no more than a feather, and set down on the small settee beside Aunt Twice. Tears were already streaming down Aunt Twice's cheeks, mingling with Emily's own, as she wrapped her arms around her niece. "Our dearest Emily! Our darling child!" she said again and yet again.

Uncle Twice now turned back to Pa and Piper, still standing at the open doorway. "How? Why?" he asked, throwing out his hands in a gesture of helplessness. "But I beg your pardon for leaving you standing at the door. Please do come in!"

"Gladly, Mr. Luccock, but my son Piper and me got a big dog here with us what belongs to your Emily," Pa said. "Gentle as a kitten, but we don't rightly know what we should do 'bout her."

Still wiping away tears, Uncle Twice could not help laughing. "Bring her in then, man," he said. "The room is small, but I'm sure we can squeeze in a dog."

As Pa, Piper, and Willa entered the room, Uncle Twice said, "You've met my wife, Mr. Coddy, but let me introduce our visitor, Captain Seaforth. Captain, allow me to introduce Mr. Coddy, who is the owner of a very excellent fish shop nearby, and his son, Piper."

So overcome by all else happening, Emily had not even noticed the man in the captain's uniform, nearly as tall and strapping as Uncle Twice, although with steel gray hair, who had been standing quietly in a corner of the room. Now he came forward with outstretched hand to shake the hands of Mr. Coddy and Piper.

"Perhaps, William and Fanny," he said, "with you having so much to talk over with Mr. Coddy, I should put off my visit until another evening."

"No reason at all for you not to stay, Captain," said Uncle Twice.

"None whatsoever, Samuel," echoed Aunt Twice. "Please do stay!"

"Besides," said Uncle Twice, "as I'm to be working for you, nothing says you should be kept from knowing all that goes on with us. I'm afraid Piper will have to share a place on the floor with Willa, but there's a chair for you, Mr. Coddy. We anxiously await the answers to my questions as to why and how this all came about, that you should suddenly appear on our doorstep with the most wonderful gift imaginable."

However, before Pa could begin to answer the questions, Uncle Twice first needed to go over to Emily and provide her with another hug. This was followed by a hug from Aunt Twice, and then yet another from Uncle Twice. So several minutes passed before the excitement, if not the joy, had subsided. But at last, Pa, now seated comfortably in the proffered chair, could begin his story.

"Well," he said, "it all come about on account o' you handing me your name and address for Piper here to be bringing fish 'round. Happened so I never looked at it for two days, but when I did, you could o' flapped me with a flounder if it weren't a name I knowed well . . . William Luccock. You see, happens you met up with someone name o' Abner Coddy, who has a fish shop and son name o' Kipper, way th' other side o' this continent. And happens Abner is my brother Ab!"

"You don't say!" exclaimed Uncle Twice in astonishment.

"Do, indeed!" said Pa, going on to tell how even

before Aunt and Uncle Twice had appeared in Coddy's Fish Shop, he had had a letter from his brother Ab passing on news from Kipper of Sugar Hill Hall being dead empty with no one living in it. What with Kipper thinking this mighty strange, and thinking his friend Emily might like to know about it, Pa said, he nosed around until he found her whereabouts. Then away went Piper offering fish for sale cheap so he could get in to see her and pass on Kipper's news.

"After that, along comes your name put right into my hand!" said Pa. "I was in a puzzlement thinking what to do, what with the child telling Piper her aunt and uncle were off to India and didn't want her living with them anymore. Anyways, I sent Piper back to her with the news that you were here, being certain there were some mistake made. And I was likewise certain you ought to be told as how she got made a servant at that school, and—"

"Whoa! Whoa, Mr. Coddy!" Uncle Twice interrupted, throwing his hands in the air. "Emily believing her aunt and uncle don't want her living with them anymore is indeed the biggest mistake in the world, and we will absolutely prove it to her. You were entirely right in thinking what you did. But what's this about Emily being made a servant at the school? Could it possibly be true? Or could it possibly be that the school provides a course in home management for genteel young ladies, and this might be taken as being a servant, quite in error? Emily, is that it?"

At this, the already-tearful Emily burst into sobs and threw herself on Aunt Twice's shoulder. "No! No! I was made a servant, just as I was at Sugar Hill Hall. Oh, Aunt Twice, I was! I *was*! And Mrs. Spilking's Select Academy is a terrible place where we were fed the most dreadful food day in and day out because she is a pinchpenny, just like Mrs. Meeching was. And we never had any proper studies at all, so I could just as well have gone to India or any other place. All we did all day was sew and read over and over again dull books so old the covers were falling off.

"For exercise, we just walked 'round and 'round and 'round in the dirt in a tiny yard that I don't believe ever had anything growing in it. And we weren't allowed to whisper to one another. All we did was listen to Wolf barking. Only it turned out Wolf was poor Willa. Mrs. Spilking just called her that to scare us and make us believe Wolf, who was not Wolf at all, would rip us to shreds if we did things she didn't like."

This all came tumbling out and ended with Emily sobbing uncontrollably in Aunt Twice's arms.

"I don't understand," said Uncle Twice, looking bewildered. "Emily darling, why did you write to tell us how much you loved the school and how happy you were to be there? Besides the one from Josiah Slyde welcoming us and wishing me well in the new business, we received two positively glowing letters from you before we left India."

"I *had* to write them!" Emily explained, sobbing. "Everything we wrote was read by Mrs. Spilking, checking for spelling and grammar, she said. Then she mailed our letters herself. But everyone knew that if you said one bad thing about the school, the letter would never be mailed."

"Oh, William!" said Aunt Twice in dismay. "How could we have let this happen?"

Uncle Twice shook his head. "How were we to know it was such a place? Josiah told us a member of a royal family actually attended Mrs. Spilking's Select Academy, which is what persuaded us of its excellence. Was there no such person there, Emily?"

"No!" said Emily, with a long, miserable sniff.

"There's only Princess Delilla, except she isn't a princess at all. I learned of it by accident when I overheard her and Mrs. Spilking having an argument. She was calling Mrs. Spilking 'Ma,' and Mrs. Spilking was calling her 'Dolly.' Bella, who is the maid there and is my friend, found out about it as well. Princess Delilla is really only Dolly Spilking, Mrs. Spilking's daughter! And she got me in dreadful trouble, making me go on an errand for her that I shouldn't have, and I got put in the Cupboard for punishment."

"The Cupboard? What is that, Emily dearest?" Aunt Twice asked. "It sounds dreadful."

"It is, Aunt Twice!" cried Emily. "It's like the Remembrance Room in Sugar Hill Hall, only Wolf was stationed outside the door to rip me to shreds if I tried to escape. But that's when I learned Wolf, who is really Willa, would no more have done such a thing than Clarabelle, the kitten!"

"Threatening young girls with being ripped to shreds!" exclaimed Aunt Twice. "Oh, William, how could Josiah have been so misled in recommending this horror of a place? And to think we left Emily in that—that woman's hands!"

"Well," said Uncle Twice, "he must have been

misled in turn by his friend Mr. Crawstone, who'd heard the school praised by so many of *his* friends. Perhaps they've all been misled."

Emily hesitated. "I—I believe Mr. Crawstone just told Mr. Slyde about the school because he's good friends with Mrs. Spilking himself. I had to sit outside the door of Mrs. Spilking's parlor the night Mr. Crawstone took me to the school. She was serving him tea and calling him 'Ichabod,' and he was calling her 'Sophronia.'"

Upon hearing this, Captain Seaforth broke in. "You know," he said thoughtfully, "I pray you don't mind my offering an opinion, but I believe your niece may be right. New York is a big city, and there could be another with the name of Ichabod Crawstone, but I strongly doubt it. And if he's the man I believe he is, I've heard of him, a lawyer with a very unsavory reputation. I wouldn't be surprised to know that he's steering students into Mrs. Spilking's Academy on his own and concocting that tale about a resident princess."

"Then we've all been badly misled," said Uncle Twice, "and at our darling niece's expense! What a terrible, terrible thing we have done to her. But, Emily, with all of this, you have yet to explain what you meant in saying you are now a servant at the school. What did you mean by that?"

"Uncle Twice," said Emily, "didn't you get the letter your friend Mr. Slyde wrote telling that all the money that was my fortune was lost, and asking what was to be done with me? Mrs. Spilking had me read the letter he wrote to her about it. He said he knew her academy wasn't a charity school, and he threw me upon her mercy. So she made me a servant. That's when I accidentally spilled the peppermints, and she found me when I was putting them back. So I was sentenced to the Cupboard again, only then she said I must live in the cellar ever afterward. So last night I ran away and came to Mr. Coddy and Piper."

"Peppermints again!" said Aunt Twice in despair, for she, too, knew of the peppermints always kept as a temptation in Sugar Hill Hall. "Is it a universally accepted idea that anything so delightful should be misused in such a dreadful way?"

Needless to say, no one present even attempted to answer that question.

"But did I hear you correctly, Emily?" Uncle Twice asked. "Did you say Mr. Slyde wrote that your fortune was lost?"

Emily nodded.

Uncle Twice then threw his face in his hands. "Yet another terrible blunder. Three in all . . . India, our precious niece left in the hands of that monstrous woman, and now this, losing her fortune. And all due to me!"

"Come now, William," said Captain Seaforth. "When we were fortunate enough to have met when you were working on one of my ships, I was convinced that you were many cuts above the average dockworker, with your intelligence and knowledge of seafaring. And recognizing you for the gentleman you are, I never hesitated in asking you to come and work for me in the management of my shipping company. I've had no reason to regret my decision, nor do I now. When you confided in me the so-called mistakes you've made, I believed you to be a victim of some very unfortunate circumstances, and I continue to believe it."

"But losing my beloved niece's fortune entrusted to me by my brother in his will! How could I have made such bad judgments as to lose it all?" said Uncle Twice. "But why have I never heard of this from Josiah himself? Well, I suppose considering the length of time it takes to reach India, the letter may still be on its way there, on its way back, or even lost."

"But, Uncle Twice, why didn't you and Aunt Twice come to see me at once when you returned, even if you *did* think I was happy at Mrs. Spilking's Select Academy?" asked Emily tearfully.

"Because, my sweet Emily," replied Uncle Twice, "it was exactly because we thought you were so happy that we didn't come to see you. We didn't want to distress you with how badly things had turned out for us. But we were going to come to you as soon as I started working for Captain Seaforth, and we could promise a better life for you. In only a day or so, we would have written Mrs. Spilking, informing her that we would be coming to see you."

"But why did things turn out badly for you and Aunt Twice?" Emily asked. "Did—did your business fail?"

Uncle Twice shook his head. "There *was* no business, Emily," he said sadly. And then he went on to relate the grim tale of what had befallen them in India.

They had arrived after a treacherous sea journey to find that the owners of the business purportedly purchased by Uncle Twice knew nothing of any sale. They had, in truth, never had any intentions of selling it. Further, they did not even know why letters addressed to Uncle and Aunt Twice had been sent to them. They only kept the letters in case someone named William Luccock should appear. That, of course, is how they received the letters from Emily and Josiah Slyde.

Fortunately, Uncle Twice had enough money to provide for lodgings for himself and Aunt Twice. With his seagoing experience, and asking for no pay but a berth for Aunt Twice, he was able to hire on to a ship in ten days. During that time, Emily's second letter came.

As soon as they returned to New York, Uncle Twice wrote Josiah Slyde, and had received a reply. It appears that he had had no doubts that the documents making Uncle Twice owner of the business were genuine. But he must have been duped, he said, and would do everything in his power to rectify the situation and see that Uncle Twice's losses were made up to him.

After Uncle Twice had finished telling this terrible tale, a long and deep silence fell over the small room. Then, at last, Pa spoke.

"Begging your pardon, Mr. Luccock," he said, "but in the letter you got *here,* which must o' been writ after Emily got word from the same party that her fortune were gone, shouldn't he o' said something on that matter to *you*?"

Uncle Twice looked startled. "I believe you're quite right, Mr. Coddy. No apologies necessary. He most certainly should have said something, at least mentioning a letter he sent me to that effect that went to India."

"What exactly *did* he say, William?" asked Captain Seaforth. "I mean to say, beyond speaking of the business?"

"Why," replied Uncle Twice, "he simply said that Mrs. Spilking had written him when he made Emily's tuition payment, telling him how well she was doing and how happy she was. He assured me that he was taking care to see that payments to the school were made promptly, and I had nothing to worry about on that score."

"Begging your pardon again," said Pa. "But when Emily said as how she believed she wasn't wanted on account o' you not coming to see her, I said something 'bout that sounding mighty fishy to me. Well, all this 'bout what your friend is or ain't writing you sounds fishier'n that. And I ain't talking fresh fish, neither!"

"Mr. Coddy," said Captain Seaforth, "I agree with you wholeheartedly. 'Fishy' is definitely the word for it! And I tell you what I'd like to do, William, if it's all right with you. I'm certain my attorney has connections out on the West Coast who can find out something about your Mr. Slyde. I realize you consider him a friend, but it sounds to me as if you haven't known him very long, and it can't hurt to look into it quietly. What law firm might he be with?"

"Screwitch, Chizzle, and Slyde," replied Uncle Twice. "And it's certainly all right with me, as long as it's done discreetly. If he turns out to be what I've believed, and this is all some misunderstanding, I wouldn't want him thinking I'd been investigating him."

"You may trust me on that score, William," said Captain Seaforth. "If nothing else is accomplished, I'd like to see Mrs. Spilking's Academy put out of business. Why, if I thought for one moment that my granddaughter Lucy were in a place like that, I'd be down there this minute tearing the place apart with my bare hands. Then I might do the same to my son-in-law Marcus Goodbody for putting her there!"

"B-B-But one of my roommates was Lucy

Goodbody," stammered Emily. "And—and she did say she had a grandpapa who'd been at sea since her mama died. She said one day she intended to run away and go to him, if she could find him."

At this, Captain Seaforth jumped to his feet. "Lucy Goodbody? Are you certain, child?"

"Oh, yes!" declared Emily. "She has the prettiest red curls, and—"

"By all that's holy!" said Captain Seaforth furiously. "That is indeed my granddaughter. But what is she doing in a place like that? Did she ever tell you, child, how she came to be there?"

Emily, overwhelmed with all that had transpired, had to take a few moments to collect herself. She knew that Captain Seaforth was very angry, but she knew he would want the truth, and that is what she intended to tell him.

So she related how all the girls at Mrs. Spilking's Academy truly believed they were sent there because they were not wanted at home. That is why, said Emily, it was easy for her to believe that she was no longer wanted by Aunt and Uncle Twice.

But Sarah, her other roommate, Emily said, had a pretty stepmama who considered Sarah so plain, she could not bear to have anyone think she was Sarah's mama. When she learned she was to present Sarah's papa with a new addition to the family, she easily persuaded him to send Sarah off to boarding school.

Lucy's stepmama, continued Emily, was not only pretty but also very, very young. She did not wish anyone believing she had a daughter as old as Lucy. She was also to present Lucy's papa with a new addition to the family. Lucy did not think her stepmama was very happy about that, either, only she could not very well send the baby away. But Lucy could be sent to boarding school. So she was.

"This is intolerable!" exclaimed Captain Seaforth. "And I beg the pardon of all present for saying this, but my son-in-law will live to regret marrying that bubbleheaded, vain little creature. Yet I have only myself to blame for what's happened to my poor Lucy. For when my beloved daughter Lucille was no more, I found it too painful to look at Lucy, who was so much like her. So I simply went to sea and stayed there. What I did was far worse than what you did, William and Fanny, for your motives were the highest. But I won't let another moment pass without making this right. Will you all pardon me if I leave at once to take her away from that miserable place?"

Permission instantly granted by Aunt and Uncle Twice, Captain Seaforth started for the door, but then came to a sudden stop. "Stay!" he said. "My storming over there to pull Lucy away a day after Emily disappears from the school may very well raise suspicions on the part of Mrs. Spilking. I don't want to do that in case there is even the remotest chance that there is some unwholesome connection between Crawstone, Slyde, and Mrs. Spilking. Emily, I trust in your judgment. Do you truly believe Lucy is quite safe at this school?"

"Yes," Emily said. "And Lucy will never be punished as I was. She and Sarah have never done anything to earn a single demerit."

"Then we'll wait the several days until my attorney can write and get word back," said Captain Seaforth.

"Begging your pardon again," said Mr. Coddy. "But my feelings ain't been wrong 'bout some other things, and now they're telling me waiting ain't the way to go. Ain't there anybody 'round here what can be found to give you what you might be needing to know?"

"We certainly can't be talking to Mrs. Spilking, Mr. Coddy," said Uncle Twice. "Bella, the maid known to Emily, could probably be of no help. Is there no one else at the school we could get to, Emily, someone who might not be in Mrs. Spilking's control?"

Emily hesitated. "There's—there's Mrs. Crumble," she said. "She's Mrs. Spilking's sister, who is in charge of the girls when they do sewing and knitting and other things. She's not like Mrs. Spilking, though. The girls think she's nice and that she's just as afraid of Mrs. Spilking as they are. But, oh, Aunt Twice, she does remind me so of Mrs. Plumly that I've never trusted her. Not long ago, she pulled me aside and said if I ever thought of fleeing the school, I could come to her. She put a slip of paper in my coat pocket with her address on it. I just thought it was a trick, though, so Mrs. Spilking could catch and punish me. But . . . but what if it wasn't? What if she really did believe something terrible was going to happen to me, for soon after was when Mrs. Spilking made me a servant."

Captain Seaforth and Uncle Twice exchanged questioning glances, and Uncle Twice nodded.

"Emily, is it too much to hope that you might have kept that address?" Captain Seaforth asked.

Emily reached into the pocket of her coat lying

on the settee beside her. Although she did not remember ever taking the slip of paper out, she was not at all certain it was still there. But her fingers found it, crumpled down into the corner of her pocket where it had laid since Mrs. Crumble put it there. Quickly, she handed it to Captain Seaforth.

"William," he said, "I suggest we pay a visit to Mrs. Crumble. Whether the visit will bear fruit, we have no way of knowing. But something tells me that our good friend Mr. Coddy is absolutely right. We should lose no time in finding out all we can."

"Agreed!" said Uncle Twice. "And, Mr. Coddy, you may be certain we shall keep you apprised of all that happens. For now, if Mrs. Luccock and I went on thanking you forever, we could never thank you enough for what you have done for us this evening. Why, if it were not for you . . ." Quite overcome, Uncle Twice could not go on.

But Captain Seaforth was now beckoning him from the open door, and moments later they were gone. To find out what? It could be the answer to everything. Or the hopeless answer to . . . nothing! There was little else for those of us left behind to do but wait.

19

Trapped!

It was five hours before Uncle Twice returned, and Pa and Piper had long since left for Coddy's Fish Shop. Captain Seaforth was not with Uncle Twice, who was clearly in a great state of excitement when he arrived. After very nearly being knocked over by Willa welcoming him at the front door, he found Emily and Aunt Twice on the settee, eagerly awaiting his arrival.

"I'm happy to see Willa's here," was the first thing he said. "I feared Mr. Coddy and Piper might have taken her back to the shop for the night. I'm happier knowing she's here with you, Fanny, for I'm afraid I shall have to take Emily away with me for a while."

"And I can't come with you, I suppose?" asked Aunt Twice.

"It wouldn't be wise, all things considered," replied Uncle Twice.

"Oh, William!" cried Aunt Twice, "this isn't something dangerous, is it, having to do with what you learned from Mrs. Crumble?"

"I confess to you, Fanny, it does have a great deal to do with that, but I promise you, Emily and I will be quite safe," Uncle Twice said. "You have nothing to fear!"

But it was not until they had climbed into the cab Uncle Twice had awaiting them on the street in front of the house, and he had given the cab-driver their destination, did he say anything to Emily of what lay before them.

Turning to her, he took her hand and said, "Emily, what I promised Aunt Twice is quite true. You may be frightened by what is about to transpire, but I guarantee you will come to no harm."

"But—but what about you, Uncle Twice?" asked Emily. "Might you be harmed?"

"No more than you," replied Uncle Twice. "I promised Aunt Twice that as well."

"What is to happen that might frighten me, Uncle Twice?" Emily asked, in truth, being frightened already.

"Well," said Uncle Twice, "you've heard, I'm certain, that rats often come aboard a ship when it's docked in port, haven't you?"

Emily nodded, for that was something she had often heard from Kipper. His descriptions of some had been enough to make her skin creep.

"All right, then," said Uncle Twice. "What we're about to do is trap some very large ones. But we're going to be well protected doing it. You'll see."

"Wh–Why do I have to be there?" she asked. Protected or not, she did not like this prospect at all. Kipper's descriptions of rats had been very colorful, indeed!

"It's better not to frighten you any more than you need to be, child. You'll find out everything soon. Try to be patient. And who knows, little Emily, you might even enjoy this when you look back on it!" Uncle Twice said, squeezing her hand and managing a smile. But it was a grim smile after all.

Enjoy catching very large rats? Emily could not imagine it. Was Uncle Twice joking to make her feel better? But he would say no more about it, so Emily had no choice but to be patient and try to dispel the knot that had developed in the middle of her stomach. For despite all of Uncle Twice's assurances, she *was* frightened. And she became more so when they arrived at the wharf where the ship on which they were to do their rat catching was docked. Awaiting them off in one dark corner of the cavernous building were Captain Seaforth and another sea captain.

"Poor mite!" Captain Seaforth said, which did not make Emily feel much improved. "It's too bad she had to be brought, but it will soon be over. William, allow me to present my very good friend Captain Dockard of the good ship *Ocean Star.* If it weren't for him, we couldn't have arranged this so easily. Daniel, this is William Luccock."

"You certainly have our gratitude, Captain," said Uncle Twice as the two men shook hands.

"Samuel Seaforth would do the same for me," replied Captain Dockard.

"Is everything ready aboard?" asked Captain Seaforth.

"All men stationed at their posts," replied Captain Dockard. "Your men, six of mine, and at least five of New York's finest!"

"And what of the rats?" asked Captain Seaforth.

"I told them they could take over the lounge,"

said Captain Dockard. "They're busy in there raising glasses to one another. You've made quite a haul, Samuel, you and William Luccock here!"

"We hope so," said Captain Seaforth. "But if we're all set, then let's get going!"

Emily by now understood that it was not really rats they were after. But who? She could not even guess. All she knew was that Uncle Twice was holding her hand very, very tightly as they treaded quietly up the gangplank. There were men, some in seamen's garb, some in policemen's uniforms, stationed at every door leading from the deck. And as soon as Uncle Twice, Captain Seaforth, Captain Dockard, and Emily stepped from the gangplank onto the deck, two policemen immediately closed in behind them, standing guard over the gangplank.

The four of them soundlessly entered through a door. Then they went down a short passage to another door. But before opening it, Captain Dockard put out his hand, holding back Uncle Twice and Emily.

"Stay behind for a moment," he said. "Allow Captain Seaforth and me to enter first." Then he opened the door, and the two men went through it.

Although all but hidden behind them, Emily could still see in the room beyond that six people, four women and two men, were gathered. They were all dressed in the most elegant clothes, as if they were off to dine in a fancy restaurant or attend a play at a theater. One of the six, the youngest woman, looked as if she actually *were* in a play, for she was wearing a brilliant red dress overflowing with lace and black velvet ribbons, and an outrageous scarf of pink boa feathers that reached almost to the floor.

All six in the room were in a high state of merriment, having no doubt sampled liberally of the bubbling liquid in the stemmed glasses they held. The two men were prancing about, kicking their legs up in the air, and causing even more merriment on the part of the ladies.

Upon catching sight of Captain Dockard, one of the men immediately raised his glass to him. "Here's to the good captain!" he shouted. "Let's give him three cheers!"

"Huzzah! Huzzah! Huzzah!" All six nearly rocked the ship with their cheers.

"And here's my good friend Captain Seaforth with me," said Captain Dockard jovially.

"Then three cheers for him, too!" shouted the second man.

"Huzzah! Huzzah! Huzzah!" They once again all enthusiastically obliged.

"Captain Seaforth, you will be pleased to know," said Captain Dockard, "has brought you all a very nice surprise!"

"Then let's have it!" called out the first man. "We all like surprises!"

With that, Captain Seaforth stood aside and motioned to Uncle Twice, still holding tightly to Emily's hand. As the two of them entered the room, a glass dropped to the floor, the sound of it splintering like a clap of thunder in the room that suddenly fell silent as a tomb. The faces of the six revelers went deathly white, as if all their blood had drained right out of their elegant shoes. They stood like marble statues, their eyes fixed, staring.

"Ah, I see that some of you recognize me," said Uncle Twice, calm and unruffled as a windless day at sea. "And most of you recognize my niece, Emily Luccock, whom I strongly suspect you had hoped would be lost in the big city, never to be seen or heard from again. But she happens to be a young person who was resourceful enough to survive, find us, and enlighten us on a great many things. A great many, indeed! It grieves me to have to disappoint all of you, but as you see, she is alive and well, brought here tonight so you can have no doubt of it!"

This said, Uncle Twice passed Emily's hand to Captain Seaforth, who took it and held it as tightly as Uncle Twice had. So tightly and safely, in truth, that Emily soon found herself no longer trembling.

"Now, I am sure you are all anxiously awaiting personal greetings from me," Uncle Twice continued smoothly. "So here you are, Theodosia Sly Meeching and Prunella Blossom Plumly, released from prison, it appears. How very nice to see you once more!

"And Mr. Crawstone, who so kindly transported my niece to Mrs. Spilking's splendid Select Academy for Young Ladies, as recommended to him by his many dear friends. It's a pleasure to be meeting you again, sir!

"As for you, my great good friend Josiah Slyde, what can I say to you, you who have done so much for me and my family? It is simply beyond my powers of speech to tell you how happy I am to see you again!

"And now, if you will pardon me for a moment, I must consult with my niece," Uncle Twice said, bowing to his audience of six, then leaning over and whispering something in Emily's ear. She, in turn, whispered back.

"Ah, yes," he continued, "I believe I am also now addressing the fabled Mrs. Spilking and—and the member of a royal family who graces her fine establishment, Princess Delilla."

Uncle Twice now paused, as if to give any one of the six the opportunity to say something about how pleased they were to see and meet *him*. But, in truth, they all appeared too paralyzed to say anything at all.

"Well," Uncle Twice continued, sighing deeply, "it grieves me to announce to you, my good friends, that all doors and exits from this ship are being guarded, and several members of the police force stand ready to escort you from the ship. Is there anything you now wish to say, or would you rather wait to explain yourselves from your jail cells?"

This brought one of the six to life at last. It was Mrs. Spilking. "How dare you come barging in here with this announcement?" she snapped, her eyes flaring in the usual manner. "We are all here to escort Princess Delilla back to her country. This is a gross insult, and her country will be deeply offended."

"Oh, come, Mrs. Spilking," said Uncle Twice. "This ship carries you all to a South American country that knows no royalty, to begin with. To end with, Princess Delilla is no more a princess than my niece or anyone else at your school. She is Dolly Spilking, your daughter, as my niece inadvertently discovered. Have you anything further to say to that?"

"Simply that your niece lies, Mr. Luccock," said Mrs. Spilking coldly. "She has even been punished for doing so."

"So I understand," said Uncle Twice, making no effort to hide his amusement, "with a dog posted outside her door who would rip her to shreds, I believe."

"I'm sure she deserved it!" snarled Mrs. Meeching. "She lied at Sugar Hill Hall as well, did she not, Plumly?"

"She is an accomplished liar," said Mrs. Plumly, an accomplished actress who somehow managed to have her rouged cheeks turn quite purple with outrage.

"Oh, that's right. I apologize. I forgot all about that," said Uncle Twice, further amused. For, after all, it was these two ladies who had assigned him to purgatory by accusing him of a crime they themselves had committed. Lying was a subject they were both quite familiar with, being past masters of the art!

"But none of us wishes to stand here and continue to be insulted," said Mrs. Spilking, drawing herself up in righteous indignation. "We shall gather our bags from our cabins and leave the ship. And we shall go on our own. We hardly need to be escorted."

"Oh, but we think you do," Captain Seaforth broke in. "Perhaps you didn't note that Mr. Luccock said *you* would be escorted from the ship . . . nothing about your bags. We have obtained a warrant to search your cabins, and have information that leaves no doubt as to what will be found in those bags."

"Information that you have learned from where?" inquired Mrs. Spilking, flaring her eyes directly at Emily. "From Mr. Luccock's lying niece, I presume?"

"You presume quite wrongly," said Uncle

Twice. "What we learned was from your sister, Bedelia Crumble, whom Captain Seaforth and I called upon this evening. Of course, she also happens to be cousin to Mrs. Meeching, as you are."

"That sniveling little creature," snarled Mrs. Meeching. "She was always afraid of her own shadow, and a big tattletale when we were growing up together. Might have made something of herself if she'd listened to my advice as her sister Sophronia did."

"Yes, such advice as to keeping peppermints in a bowl to entice the unwary, as you did the poor old people in your care, Mrs. Meeching!" Uncle Twice said angrily. "Heaven keep us from such wonderful advice!"

"So what exactly did Bedelia have to say to you?" asked Mrs. Spilking icily. "And how do you know *she* wasn't lying?"

"Simply because she chose to stay where she was and not be with you here tonight! That speaks as loudly and clearly as anything could," replied Uncle Twice, just as icily.

Now Mr. Slyde finally stepped forward, a broad smile on his face. "Come, come, William, I can explain everything to your satisfaction if you'll only let me. I trust you will, for our friendship's sake."

"Josiah," said Uncle Twice, "we *have* no friendship. I ask that you no longer continue to insult my intelligence by pretending that we do. As for your explanations, they are apparently not worth the paper you use to write them on. But, if you will pardon me, I now intend to tell you what will be found in your bags, and why.

"First, there will be gold and jewels worth many times the value of our old home, Sugar Hill Hall, hidden there behind the paneled walls of the former ballroom by Madams Meeching and Plumly. Jailed for blackmail, smuggling, murder, and intentions to murder my wife and niece, the ladies secured the services of one Josiah Slyde, of the firm of Screwitch, Chizzle, and Slyde, to plead their case. They soon recognized that here was someone as unscrupulous as they were, who might be persuaded to participate in a very interesting scheme devised by them. As it turned out, Mr. Slyde was easily persuaded, as they suspected he would be.

"After we left for India, Mr. Slyde was able to have the ladies proved innocent of murder by claiming the charge was based only on the words of a dying old man. He had the accusations of intentions to murder and charges of blackmail dismissed for the same reason. As for the smuggling, Meeching and Plumly claimed that it was all done without their knowledge, and Mr. Slyde managed to persuade the courts of that as well.

"In the meantime, their scheme was put in place. Knowing that I was in dire straits and needed to sell Sugar Hill Hall, and knowing what was still hidden behind the walls, they had Mr. Slyde purchase it without revealing who the purchasers were.

"Wanting to get me out of the way lest I raise any questions in the future, not to mention getting the money paid for Sugar Hill Hall, it was decided that Mr. Slyde should convince me of a wonderful opportunity to purchase a business in India. There was indeed a business there, but it was never for sale, as you knew all along, Josiah. So I'm sure you can see why your explanations now would mean nothing, because your word is worth nothing.

"It is my belief that my murder was to take place in India, as in the few days I was there, I was twice attacked on the streets. I presume if I *had* been murdered, my wife would have been left to die on her own. And, of course, as this would have all taken place in a far-off foreign country where we knew no one and no one knew us, none would have been the wiser for either of these deaths.

"To ensure that there would never be any questions raised by our niece in later years, not to mention wanting to lay your hands on her vast fortune, arrangements were made to imprison Emily in Mrs. Spilking's Select Academy until the right time should come for disposing of her as well. Being persuaded of your honesty and competence, Josiah, I entrusted the management of her fortune to you while I was overseas. That fortune was all soundly invested by me, and all sold by you. There never was any catastrophic failure of any of it. So much for your explanations!

"So, ladies and gentlemen, what we expect to find in your bags will be all the gold and jewels from the walls of Sugar Hill Hall, money that was to go toward the purchase of the company in India, and the proceeds of the investments I made representing our niece's fortune. Had all your plans worked out for my demise, I suppose you would not have had to be on this ship tonight planning an escape to South America. I must offer my sincere apologies for the inconvenience to you of my niece's courageous escape from your splendid academy, Mrs. Spilking, and for my managing so quickly to arrange for the return to this country of Mrs. Luccock and myself.

"But now, unless one of you has something to add to what I have just revealed to you, I believe it is time to have you all removed to jail, where you belong!"

Uncle Twice had no sooner finished this speech, however, than the young woman in the red dress, Princess Delilla, otherwise Dolly Spilking, threw her face into the pink boa feathers draped around her neck, and began to howl.

"Am I going to have to go to jail, too? You said you had prospects for me. Is going to jail prospects, Ma? Is that your idea of prospects? Well, it ain't mine!" she bawled, and then dropped to her knees, shrieking.

"You're sounding common, my girl," said Mrs. Spilking crossly. "Get up and stop your caterwauling. It won't do you a bit of good. You're not at the school anymore."

"But she will be, Mrs. Spilking," said Uncle

Twice. "There's no reason an innocent young woman should have to pay for her mother's crimes. Mrs. Crumble is waiting for her at the school, where she will be escorted by Captain Seaforth. Her future will be decided later."

"See what you've done for me, Ma?" her daughter pointed out, sobbing.

"Oh, do be still, Dolly!" was all Mrs. Spilking had to say to her.

Now at last, Uncle Twice reached for Emily's hand. "Come along," he said. "You've been a brave girl, Emily. Now we must hurry home to tell your Aunt Twice all!"

"All"! But for Emily, what a different meaning that word now had at last!

20

Sugar Hill Hall

"Felicity Emily Luccock!" whispered Emily, looking down at the bundle she cradled so very carefully in her arms as she sat in a rocking chair beside the fireplace in Captain Seaforth's cozy parlor.

The parlor was filled with remembrances of his years at sea. Paintings of ships hung on almost every bare space on the pine-paneled walls. A rusted anchor rescued from the sea leaned solidly in a corner. Enormous pink-lined tropical seashells stood on the mantelpiece over the great stone fireplace. There was even a brass porthole, giving anyone looking through it the feeling they should be seeing the ocean instead of Captain Seaforth's prize rose garden.

But Emily at the moment was concentrating only on the important job she was performing.

And someone kneeling beside her rocking chair was seeing to it that she did. This was Felicity's anxious nursemaid, Tilly. Yes, Tilly!

Tilly, who had come all the way across the continent because Aunt Twice said she would have no other nursemaid to help with the most important task in the whole world. Tilly, who had had to stay behind when Aunt and Uncle Twice left for India. Tilly, who had gone around with such a long face when told she could not be spared that her new employers finally gave up and agreed to let her go. Tilly, who was delirious with happiness now that she was not only back with Aunt and Uncle Twice, but with the only friend she had ever had, Emily. But it was also, unfortunately, Tilly, having had the care of a baby at her recent place of employment, who was an absolute tyrant when it came to deciding the proper care for Felicity. Why, even Aunt Twice had to bow to her authority!

But Emily and Tilly were not the only guests in Captain Seaforth's parlor. For happily assembled were also Aunt and Uncle Twice, Mr. Coddy and Piper, Mrs. Crumble, who had enlisted the aid of a friend to watch over the school for that evening, and Bella, Lucy, and Sarah, who had been invited to come live with Lucy and her grandpapa, Captain Seaforth. It perhaps might be mentioned here, as well, that Aunt Twice thought Lucy and Sarah two of the most delightful girls ever, and she won Sarah's undying devotion by remarking that she thought Sarah had the most beautiful eyes she had ever seen in her life!

By now, they had all enjoyed a delicious supper of roast chicken and baked ham, all manner of vegetables, and a very rich chocolate cake, all prepared by the excellent cook whom Captain Seaforth claimed to have "borrowed" for this event from one of his ships. But the first course for the meal was an outstanding fish chowder, brought from his shop in a great black iron pot by Mr. Coddy!

As Emily rocked Felicity, she was not only being closely watched by Tilly, but by Bella as well, seated on the floor beside them. To no one's surprise, Bella and Tilly had struck up an instant friendship, and had already made grand plans to "do the shops" together every chance they had.

Across the room, at a table that was once a ship's hatch, Lucy, Sarah, and Piper had gathered, and were enjoying a rousing game of cards. Piper, if anyone had been observing, would have been seen to be blushing furiously as his red curls were compared favorably to Lucy's and his blue eyes to Sarah's, but it might have also been observed that he was enjoying himself immensely.

Across from Emily, Tilly, and Bella sat Aunt Twice and Mrs. Crumble, between whom a friendship had been struck up to the degree that they were already addressing each other as Fanny and Bedelia. Both ladies were thoroughly enjoying a conversation in which the worthy Mrs. Crumble was shocking Aunt Twice to death with tales of the horrors of her sister's Select Academy for Young Ladies.

Directly in front of the fireplace stood the three men of the party, Captain Seaforth, Uncle Twice, and Mr. Coddy. At the moment, Uncle Twice had just turned from looking somberly in the embers snapping and crackling in the fireplace. He gave a deep sigh.

"You know," he said, "it still grieves me that Fanny and I put off for one moment going to see Emily when we first arrived."

"And if you had, William," said Captain Seaforth, "weren't you intending to send Mrs.

Spilking a note announcing your impending visit? I believe that's what I heard you say."

"Yes, I did, Captain, and we would have done just that," said Uncle Twice. "Good manners would have required it."

"Then I believe that by not going, you may have saved her life," said Captain Seaforth.

"How so?" asked Uncle Twice.

"Well, the way I see it is that if you had arrived at the school only to find Emily as a servant there, Mrs. Spilking would have had to give an explanation for it. Of course, she could have instantly turned Emily back into a student for your benefit, but how could she depend on Emily not to reveal that?

"You may well then have begun investigating the reasons for Josiah's announcement that all your investments on Emily's behalf had failed, which, as we all now know, they had not. That may have effectively ended all plans of that criminal lot escaping to South America with their ill-gained millions.

"So it stands to reason that Mrs. Spilking would have done everything in her power to keep you from meeting up with Emily at this critical time.

Would you agree with my thinking?" Captain Seaforth concluded, addressing the question to Mr. Coddy.

"I most definitely do, Cap'n!" that worthy gentleman said wholeheartedly.

"I do as well," said Uncle Twice. "And I thank you inexpressibly for pointing it all out to me, Captain. It removes a great deal of my guilt."

"And well it should!" said Captain Seaforth. "Of course, you realize I have some guilt of my own to deal with, but we'll talk of that later. What I've been wondering at the moment, William, is this. You're a wealthy man now, for you'll not only be regaining all you were paid for Sugar Hill Hall, but because it was your home, all the riches stored in its walls will be yours as well, as there are no claims on it. That being said, much as it would disappoint me to lose you, for I intend to retire soon and need someone like you to run my company, I would understand if you decided not to come aboard."

"Captain," said Uncle Twice without hesitating a moment, "I most definitely *do* want to come aboard, as you put it. I feel honored to have been asked. I intend to be at work every day, and to see to it that you never regret your decision to hire me!"

"And you don't think you'll ever want to return some day to Sugar Hill Hall, which I believe you have learned from Caleb's brother still stands empty?" asked Captain Seaforth.

"Never!" said Uncle Twice. "*Never!* If for no other reason, and there are, of course, many others, I don't care to revisit the scene of all my past mistakes!"

"I can't tell you how happy I am to hear all this, William," said Captain Seaforth. Then he added with a rueful smile, "As for mistakes, we've all made them. But as long as we learn from them, well . . . But tell me, aren't there some benefits, in the end, that have come about for you as a result of your mistakes?"

"Oh, yes!" said Uncle Twice. "I had that time aboard a ship learning about the sea when I was being blackmailed by Meeching and Plumly into believing I was a murderer. The sea experience is what led to our acquaintance and your offering me the position with your company. Then, I learned a great deal about money matters in handling Emily's inheritance from her father. He, of course, had built up his part of the inheritance we both had from our own father, while I was busy squandering mine. I believe I have done quite well for Emily, though Josiah Slyde attempted to persuade everyone otherwise. But most of all, had I not made those early mistakes, I wouldn't be standing here with all of you, my very good friends!"

"Hear! Hear!" said Captain Seaforth.

"Amen to it!" said Mr. Coddy.

"There are, sadly, two people missing who would make this party complete," Uncle Twice said. "They are Mr. Coddy's brother, Abner, and Emily's good friend Kipper. If only wishes were horses . . ."

At this, Mr. Coddy beamed. "Perhaps they may be in this case! See, it's this way. Ab and me, growing up, always figgered as how we'd some day go into the fish business together, living close to the docks like we did, and our pa being a fisherman besides. But Kipper's ma wanted to try the other ocean, so off they went, and ended up staying.

"Now with Kipper's ma long gone, Ab allows as how he'd like to come back here, to visit leastways, if not more. But my thinking is he'll be wanting to stay once he gets here so we can be Coddy and Coddy like we always planned, and o' course he'll be bringing Kipper 'long with him!"

Kipper coming! Emily, having heard bits and snatches of the men's conversation taking place in front of the fireplace, had pricked up her ears upon hearing Kipper's name mentioned. Now she let out a squeal of delight. Tilly was on her feet in an instant.

"Ain't you got no sense, shrieking like that, Emily?" she whispered crossly. "Here, you just give the little precious to me, an' you're excused from the job. I ain't never in all my borned days!"

Emily gently handed Felicity to Tilly, who then immediately usurped Emily's place in the rocker. Emily lost not a moment going up to Pa.

"Is it really true that Kipper and Pa will be coming here?" she asked. "Oh, then everything would be perfect!"

"I ain't got a doubt in the world 'bout it!" said Pa. "Only thing is, it 'pears to me there's a problem we got to consider. What with you calling Ab 'Pa' and calling *me* 'Pa' likewise, well, supposing we're in the same room, who's got to answer?"

Emily must have looked so taken aback at the

question that it brought a burst of laughter from Captain Seaforth and Uncle Twice. This, in turn, earned them all glowering looks from Tilly and her good friend Bella.

"Does Piper know about Kipper coming?" asked Emily.

"Not yet, but you got my permission to run and tell him," said Pa, winking at Captain Seaforth and Uncle Twice.

Now, Emily, in truth, had been happy to be relieved of her job in the rocker. Her arm had gone to sleep, and she was envying all the merriment taking place at the ship's hatch over the card game. She flew over there now and had the great pleasure of being the first to announce to Piper the astonishing news of Kipper's almost certain forthcoming arrival!

But as the evening wore on, with Felicity having been fed and now soundly asleep in her basket, everyone gathered around the fireplace. The conversation then turned to the matter of what was to become of Mrs. Spilking's Select Academy for Young Ladies. And this appeared to be the exact right time to announce to Mrs. Crumble what, with her permission, might happen to it.

It had been Emily's idea to start with. After she had spoken to Uncle Twice about it, and he had enthusiastically agreed that it was indeed a splendid idea, they had been in consultation with Mr. Dewright, Captain Seaforth's attorney at the firm of Thinkwell, Thinkwell, and Dewright. Mr. Dewright could see no reason why the plan could not be carried out. It had to do, of course, with the fact that Uncle Twice and Emily were now wealthy. Very wealthy. Very, *very* wealthy!

They were both so wealthy, in truth, that they could take all the money needed for the purpose Emily had suggested, and still have enough left over to last them several lifetimes. And what Emily had suggested was this, that the two buildings now occupied by Mrs. Spilking's Select Academy be sold. Emily and Uncle Twice would then add whatever money was necessary to buy a much, much larger and nicer building in a much more pleasant neighborhood. And it so happened that Captain Seaforth already knew of just such a building for sale on his very own street!

Uncle Twice had directed their cabdriver to pass by it on their way to Captain Seaforth's house that afternoon, and Emily had been so excited upon seeing it, she could hardly bear it. Besides a great double-oak front door that would open onto a portico with tall white columns, there were windows, windows, and more windows that would bring light and sunshine into every room of the magnificent redbrick house. Every window, moreover, boasted shutters painted a cheerful garden green.

As for the garden itself, Emily could hardly believe what she saw. For surrounded by beautiful wrought-iron panels joined by tall brick columns were handsome, well-tended evergreen shrubs and tall oak, maple, and pine trees. But what was even more important than this was what Captain Seaforth had told them was behind the house, although that could barely be seen as they bowled by in the cab. It was a lawn—a lawn where lawn tennis and croquet could be played by the girls, and where they could have lovely outdoor picnics. There was even a brick path circling the lawn for pleasant walks. And, of course, there were flower beds everywhere, for what would a true garden be without flowers?

Emily was naturally quite ready to burst out with all this news the moment she walked into

Captain Seaforth's house, but Uncle Twice advised that they should wait for a quiet moment. And at last that quiet moment had arrived!

Emily had agreed that Uncle Twice should be the one to present the plan. This he did as soon as there was a lull in the cheerful hum of conversation of those gathered around the fireplace. While describing the building and garden, however, he made no mention of his real purpose in doing so, and made it seem that this was a house he and Aunt Twice contemplated buying for their own home. But he finally made the suggestion in the most offhand manner that he believed this house would make a splendid school, so splendid, in truth, that he would like to invest in it. Yet he would consider doing so only if Mrs. Crumble, now acting headmistress of Mrs. Spilking's Academy, would agree to be headmistress of the new school.

At this point, Mrs. Crumble, who had been listening with only polite interest, sat looking stunned for a few moments, and then burst into tears! For a while, it seemed that she would never regain her powers of speech. But when she did, she could hardly stop talking, what with thanking both Uncle Twice and Emily over and over again. She was, of course, immediately apprised by Uncle Twice of Emily's part in the plan. Then Mrs. Crumble entered into excited conversation with Emily, Lucy, and Sarah, not only putting forth her own ideas for the school, but eagerly listening to those of the three girls as well.

To begin with, there would be proper classes with proper teachers in such things as geography and history. There would be music lessons and real painting lessons and reading from interesting books that were not old and dilapidated. There would, of course, be all the wonderful outdoor activities thought of by Emily, and then there must be lots and lots of washrooms, so lining up to use one would never be heard of again. At last came the subject of food. Was there to be a new cook?

Well, here Emily felt the need to express a firm opinion. She had grown truly fond of Mrs. Slump and believed she should stay. And, as she pointed out to Mrs. Crumble, they should remember the delicious fish stew, Slump's Supreme Surprise, prepared by her when she actually was given something better than potatoes and turnips with which to work. In a word, Mrs. Slump actually was able to provide "goormette" cooking, and Emily believed she should be given the opportunity to do so. As it turned out, Mrs. Crumble shared Emily's feelings and was easily persuaded that Mrs. Slump should remain.

Bella declared that she most certainly wished to stay as well, and so she should, declared Mrs. Crumble. She would, however, no longer be the servant of all work, or "donkey of all work" as she described herself, but would be promoted to head housekeeper with at least two maids under her. She would have a special dress and wear a belt with a grand bunch of keys dangling from it, just as Mrs. Spilking had. And she would never, ever again be residing in a cellar, but would have her own sunny room upstairs. Needless to say, upon hearing this from the very lips of the new headmistress, Bella herself burst into tears!

Then there was the matter of the former Princess Delilla, now reduced to being plain Dolly Spilking. When this subject came up, Mrs. Crumble could not help sighing deeply and shaking her head in despair. Dolly, of course, would soon be old enough to determine her own future, which might include marrying the grocer's boy. Whether this would be a greater disaster for him or for her was the only question, should this unfortunate event take place.

But she was, after all, Mrs. Crumble's niece, and so, despite all, she wanted only the best for Dolly. Now that her ma was no longer around to "spoil her to death" and there was no more of "all that princess nonsense," Mrs. Crumble would make every effort to try to persuade her to avail herself of the education now to be offered at the school. She felt she might even succeed, for when Captain Seaforth, accompanied by his young aide, took Dolly back to the school from the ship that memorable night, Dolly had remarked to her aunt Bedelia that the aide had cast an approving eye in her direction. *She* apparently had likewise cast an approving eye back at him. But Mrs. Crumble had assured her that no one but a grocer's boy would look twice at her if she did not improve her mind. Dolly did not argue the point, so Mrs. Crumble felt there might be some hope in that direction after all.

As for the other girls still at Mrs. Spilking's Select Academy, they would no doubt be quite thrilled with the new prospects. But then there were the two older girls who had been there "longer than they ought," as Bella had once said to Emily. "And such lovely girls, too," said Mrs. Crumble. "What is to become of them?"

It was at this juncture that Captain Seaforth entered the conversation. He would host some balls, he said, to which the girls would be invited. He would be a whale's tail, he said, if that didn't add some spark to their lives, especially as he would also be inviting several handsome young naval officers from his ships. Captain Seaforth, always used to doing everything with great dispatch, had managed to take care of this matter with great dispatch as well. With a very satisfied look on his face, he now sat back to listen to further matters. There turned out to be three.

One was Willa. The only problem there, of course, was that everyone wanted her. But there was no question that she should now be in a home where she could have all the freedom denied her for so long, not to mention the attention she deserved. Those requirements, all concluded, would be met in the home of Aunt and Uncle Twice and the overjoyed Emily!

The second matter to be talked over was a name

for the new school, for all agreed that Mrs. Spilking's name connected to it could not be tolerated. Did Mrs. Crumble wish the school possibly to be called Mrs. Crumble's Select Academy? "No indeed," was the indignant reply to the question when it was posed to her. They would have to come up with something else. Other names were suggested, including Luccock School, which Uncle Twice, Emily, and even Aunt Twice positively opposed. What, then?

In the end, Emily timidly made a suggestion that came to her when she had seen the entry to the proposed school. Persuaded that her suggestion would be thoroughly rejected, if not actually laughed at, she had not dared to mention it. But in the end, she mumbled the words, "Sugar Hill Hall." For a few moments, there was silence. But then to her amazement, everyone began to clap, and her idea was unanimously approved. And so Sugar Hill Hall it was to be!

That decided, there was but one matter left, and that was what Emily, Lucy, and Sarah wished to do regarding the new school, having such unpleasant memories of the old one. But Mrs. Crumble, although saying again and again how grateful she was for all that was being done for her, went on to say she could only be truly happy if the three girls were to return to the school when it became the new and wonderful Sugar Hill Hall. She intended to have day students as well as boarders, so they could even choose to be either one. And though, as she said, she hesitated to use the term, she promised them that they would indeed be "royally" welcomed!

A decision on that score, needless to say, was then easily reached. But considering all that poor Mrs. Crumble had had to suffer with Dolly and "all that princess nonsense," it was just as well that, in the course of time, it was not Princess Everbold, Princess Lionheart, and Princess Strongspirit, but just plain Emily Luccock, Lucy Goodbody, and Sarah Tibbits who happily entered the great double-oak doors of Sugar Hill Hall on the very day that it opened!

Epilogue

Kipper did, in very fact, come to stay in New York, and so was able to take part with his cousin Piper in the grand opening of Coddy & Coddy Fish Shop, begun at long last by the two bothers, Abner and Caleb Coddy. But both Piper and Kipper constantly expressed wishes to Emily that *they* could have a school as nice as Sugar Hill Hall to attend. By dint of Emily pleading and pleading, Mrs. Crumble thought about this, and thought about it some more, and then made her decision. If both boys would pay particular attention to improving their speech, she might allow them, and a few other boys, into the school as day students. And so it was that when Emily, Lucy, and Sarah finally graduated from Sugar Hill Hall, Piper and Kipper proudly graduated right along with them!

the history
of Ireland
f.j.m. madden

For over 60 years, more than 40 million people have learnt over 750 subjects the **teach yourself** way, with impressive results.

be where you want to be with **teach yourself**

For UK order enquiries: please contact Bookpoint Ltd, 130 Milton Park, Abingdon, Oxon OX14 4SB. Telephone: +44 (0) 1235 827720. Fax: +44 (0) 1235 400454. Lines are open 09.00–18.00, Monday to Saturday, with a 24-hour message answering service. Details about our titles and how to order are available at www.teachyourself.co.uk

For USA order enquiries: please contact McGraw-Hill Customer Services, PO Box 545, Blacklick, OH 43004-0545, USA. Telephone: 1-800-722-4726. Fax: 1-614-755-5645.

For Canada order enquiries: please contact McGraw-Hill Ryerson Ltd, 300 Water St, Whitby, Ontario L1N 9B6, Canada. Telephone: 905 430 5000. Fax: 905 430 5020.

Long renowned as the authoritative source for self-guided learning – with more than 40 million copies sold worldwide – the **teach yourself** series includes over 300 titles in the fields of languages, crafts, hobbies, business, computing and education.

British Library Cataloguing in Publication Data: a catalogue record for this title is available from the British Library.

Library of Congress Catalog Card Number: on file.

First published in UK 2005 by Hodder Education, 338 Euston Road, London, NW1 3BH.

First published in US 2005 by Contemporary Books, a Division of the McGraw-Hill Companies, 1 Prudential Plaza, 130 East Randolph Street, Chicago, IL 60601 USA.

This edition published 2005.

The **teach yourself** name is a registered trade mark of Hodder Headline.

Typeset by Transet Limited, Coventry, England.
Printed in Great Britain for Hodder Education, a division of Hodder Headline, 338 Euston Road, London NW1 3BH, by Cox & Wyman Ltd, Reading, Berkshire.

Hodder Headline's policy is to use papers that are natural, renewable and recyclable products and made from wood grown in sustainable forests. The logging and manufacturing processes are expected to conform to the environmental regulations of the country of origin.

Impression number 10 9 8 7 6 5 4 3 2 1
Year   2010 2009 2008 2007 2006 2005

contents

introduction

Where does one begin to tell the story of Ireland? There is a school of thought that suggests that to understand Ireland's present one must understand its past, because when speaking of Irish history it is sometimes difficult to tell where one ends and the other begins. Can the recent 'Troubles' be understood without the context of the Act of Union? Can the Act of Union be understood without the context of the plantations? Can the plantations be understood without the context of the Reformation? Can the Reformation be understood without the context of English involvement in Ireland? Can English involvement in Ireland be understood without the context of the Norman invasion?

How do we understand that invasion? Do we not need to look at the political and social structures that existed in pre-Norman Ireland? Can we understand the Vikings without the Celts?

Can we comprehend anything in the present without going back to the beginning?

Therefore it is back to the beginning – or as close to it as we can get – that we will go.

01

Ireland before 1500: a land of saints and scholars

This chapter will cover:
- Ireland's earliest inhabitants
- the Celts
- the coming of Christianity
- the Vikings
- the Norman Conquest
- medieval Ireland
- the House of Kildare.

The earliest inhabitants

Modern archaeological research would tend to suggest that some of the earliest inhabitants on the island of Ireland were based around the Mountsandel area of Co. Derry, on the outskirts of the modern town of Coleraine and close to the mouth of the River Bann. Similar evidence of contemporaneous human settlements has also materialized close to Tullamore in Co. Offaly.

Living somewhere about 7000–6500 BC, it would appear that these early inhabitants were an itinerant people who were ignorant of farming methods, thus falling into the category of hunter-gatherers. Moreover, the heavily forested nature of the Irish landscape at that time meant that they seldom ventured inland. Instead they remained close to the coastline of seas and rivers.

The first Neolithic farmers emerged in Ireland perhaps close to 3,000 years later. These people were breeders of animals – cattle, sheep and goats – and, having cleared some of the dense forest, also began to cultivate crops such as wheat and barley. Evidence of the cultivation of the former – dating back to 2500 BC – has been found in the Newgrange area of Co. Meath.

Although their wattle and daub dwellings have long since disappeared, these Neolithic inhabitants have left us plentiful evidence of their more spiritual architecture. Great megalithic (made of stone) monuments including cairns, dolmens and passage graves were constructed across the island. Of particular note in the case of the latter is the monument at Newgrange, which occupies about 0.4 hectares (1 acre) of land. One of the earliest recorded buildings in the whole of Europe, this tomb was specifically designed to allow a ray of light to penetrate to its innermost chamber every winter solstice.

Over the course of the next few thousand years copper and bronze appeared in Ireland, allowing an impressive range of weaponry and jewellery to be produced. More modern methods of farming were also introduced, including the use of a basic form of ox-drawn plough.

The arrival of the Celts

It was somewhere about 600–500 BC that the race perhaps most associated with early Irish history first appeared on the scene. The Celts – as they were known – had been living in central and western Europe, prospering as both farmers and fighters. From these locations they had begun to fan out across the continent and beyond, eventually ending up in Ireland.

These iron users were soon to become the dominant people on the island. They spoke a form of Gaelic and, although they had no written language, they developed a system of writing that we know as *Ogham*. This was made up of a series of straight and angled lines of varying lengths which were carved onto large standing stones.

Initially the Celts were pagan and celebrated the great festivals of *Imbolg, Bealtaine, Lughnasa* and *Samhain*. By about AD 400, however, they had begun to accept Christianity. That said, many of the deeper pagan practices were slow to die out.

Political and social structures

Under the Celts Ireland developed a recognizable political structure. Historians estimate that by the start of the eighth century AD there were in excess of 150 small kingdoms in Ireland. These kingdoms, known as *tuatha* (singular *tuath*), governed a mainly agricultural population of about 500,000 people.

Each small kingdom was presided over by a king – a *rí tuatha* – whose successor or *tánaiste* (a term still used today to apply to the Irish deputy prime minister) was elected during the incumbent's lifetime. Not surprisingly, the holding of such a contest inevitably resulted in a high level of competition among those eligible within the king's family unit, the *derbfine*. Interestingly the *rí* did not own the land within the *tuath*; instead it belonged to the freemen of the kingdom.

A group of small kingdoms was governed by an over-king or *rí ruire*. Finally there was the king of the province of which there were five by about AD 300. At this time there was no recognition in law of the fabled position of High King, however by the seventh century the Uí Néill Kings of Tara were probably the most powerful family in the land.

For protection such groups lived in easily defendable enclosures such as raths, ring-forts or promontory forts. Archaeologists have identified the sites of over 40,000 of the former across the island. Some tribes even created artificial islands in the middle of lakes; about 200 of these have come to light. These structures are known as *crannogs*.

While the king was supported by a number of nobles the majority of the population were peasants. A few of these were freemen, a privilege that enabled them to move from place to place, seeking employment. The vast majority, however, were unfree and remained in the same *tuath*, working whatever sliver of land had been allotted to them by the nobles and providing some of the produce they made to their master. The Celts were mixed farmers who grew a wide range of crops and, for reasons that shall be explained, cattle rearing was also an important element of their work. Within these *tuatha* there also dwelt slaves, often captured in raids on neighbouring kingdoms.

The final significant group in Celtic society was the *Aos Dána*. This consisted of those individuals within the *tuath* possessed of particular skills. It included lawyers, doctors, druids, musicians, historians and poets. From among this group two categories stand out as having been of particular significance. The first was the lawyer or *breitheamh* (which translates as judge). From this title the law of the land became known as *Brehon Law*.

Brehon Law differed significantly from the kind of justice that we are familiar with. Rather than imprisonment or corporal punishment the system relied – at least in the majority of cases – on a structure of fines. Each man was given a value or honour price, which was the value put on the victim of a crime. This value was always measured in terms of cattle. Not surprisingly, therefore, possession of cattle was an indication of wealth and cattle raiding was a common occurrence in Celtic Ireland. A system of other fines was also in existence for punishing those found guilty of committing lesser crimes.

However it was the poet or *file* that was the most important member of the *Aos Dána*. His task was basically to act as a spin-doctor for the king, recording his heroic deeds – in verse of course – so that they could be recounted throughout the land. If the particular monarch demonstrated a lack of generosity to the *file* he would be rewarded with a satire. Evidence would suggest that this was not the most pleasant of experiences for those so 'honoured'.

The coming of Christianity

Many assume – wrongly as it happens – that it was St Patrick who introduced Christianity to the Irish. However the religion existed – in some shape or form – on the island before Patrick's mission. Indeed Patrick wasn't even the first significant missionary figure to come to Ireland. He was preceded by another missionary, Palladius, who, according to Prosper of Aquitaine, was dispatched to the island in 431 by Pope Celestine I (422–32). His task was to instruct the Christians already living there, however little else about him or his mission is known.

The following year is traditionally commemorated as the year of Patrick's arrival, however modern scholarship tends to be more guarded about accepting this date, placing the actual date roughly 30 years later. Of course, according to legend he had previously been in Ireland as a slave, captured on a raid in Britain by Niall of the Nine Hostages, and condemned to a life of herding pigs on the slopes of Slemish Mountain in Co. Antrim. Patrick herded for six years before escaping and training to be a priest and missionary. Eventually he returned to Ireland to take on the work begun by Palladius and, if legend is to be believed, had a jolly old time casting out snakes and teaching the mysteries of the Trinity with the aid of the three-leaved shamrock.

Whatever the case, in the wake of Patrick's mission Christianity took root and began to flourish, albeit with some degree of resistance from the pagan druids who saw their positions coming under threat. Patrick wasn't the only bishop to come to Ireland – others such as Auxilius and Secundus come to mind – but he is the best known, mainly due to his writings, particularly his *Confession*.

The following centuries marked the golden age of Irish Christianity, resulting in the island becoming known as 'the land of saints and scholars'. Of particular note amongst a pantheon of missionary luminaries was Colum Cille, revered as the founder of Derry, who also founded the monastery of Iona off the west coast of Scotland and Columbanus, and who established several notable monasteries in mainland Europe. At home too, famous monasteries sprang up in places such as Bangor, Armagh and Clonmacnoise and offshore on seemingly inhospitable islands such as Sceilig Mhichíl.

Vikings!

Still dotted around Ireland in places such as Devinish, Glendalough and Monasterboice are the remains – many still complete – of round towers. These buildings – about 27 to 30 metres (90 to 100 feet) in height, with their doorways 4.5 to 6 metres (15 to 20 feet) above ground level – were erected in or near monasteries to allow the monks to protect themselves and their valuables from the Viking raids that began at the very end of the eighth century (the earliest recorded raid was on Lambay Island in AD 795). These valuables included artefacts such as the great illuminated manuscripts that had been created to pass on the scriptures – for example the *Cathach* (extracts from the Psalms) and the Books of Kells and Durrow – as well as valuable gold and silver fashioned into striking creations such as the Ardagh and Derrynaflan Chalices.

Over the course of the next few years a series of raids took place against the monastic settlements that were dotted all around the Irish coast. It would appear that for about the first 40 years the Vikings were simply raiders, taking what they could find and leaving after their attacks; however, from about AD 830 this began to change and the Vikings started to establish settlements on the island. Within a generation a series of significant Norse settlements had sprung up in the southern parts of the island. Dublin (where significant Viking archaeological remains have been and continue to be found) was a Viking settlement and the modern conurbations of Cork, Limerick, Waterford and Wexford were also tenth-century Norse establishments.

By the end of the ninth century the Vikings were becoming – as the saying goes – more Irish than the Irish themselves; intermarrying was taking place while the Norse were also beginning to embrace Christianity. Sitric Silkenbeard, the Viking King of Dublin, converted to Christianity in AD 1000 and within a generation Dublin's Vikings were constructing a cathedral on the site of the current Christ Church Cathedral.

Despite their growing influence, however, their power was eventually destroyed. One of the main actors in this development was the legendary Brian Boru.

High Kings?

In the recent past many nationalist singsongs have included the ditty 'A nation once again'. The implication behind this song is the aspiration that British involvement in the running of the island would cease, thus allowing Ireland to be ruled as a single entity by the Irish themselves. Of course this simplistic interpretation is fatally flawed; as already mentioned, the Irish political system was not homogenous, rendering fond recollections of a golden age of Irish self-government as rose tinted at best. In reality the only time that Ireland was ever successfully governed by a single political entity was when it was under British rule.

That didn't stop people trying, however. It is probably fair to say that the closest that Ireland ever came to a native form of single party government was possibly during the time of Brian Bóruma or Boru, who became King of Munster at the end of the tenth century. Initially Brian was King of the Dál Cais in Co. Clare. In an attempt to increase his power, Brian began to build up alliances with other local kings while also strengthening his military resources. While this soon resulted in him gaining the kingship of Munster, Brian's ambition was greater; he wanted to rule the whole island. Achieving this feat would mean obtaining the acquiescence of the Uí Néills of Meath who claimed that title for themselves. In 1002 Brian received that acquiescence – somewhat reluctantly it must be said – and peace reigned for a time.

It did not last, however, and before long Brian was involved in what would become his greatest victory, the 1014 Battle of Clontarf. The occasion was an attempt by Maol Morda, King of Leinster to challenge Brian's position as High King. At Clontarf – which lay close to Dublin – Brian faced a coalition of Gaelic and Norse allies. Brian was victorious but unfortunately for him the fruits of victory were not to be savoured: the same battle also cost him his own life. In the words of the contemporary Viking sagas 'Brian fell but saved his kingdom'.

In the vacuum caused by his death an extended period of conflict broke out between rival kings, each attempting to obtain the coveted high kingship. No one king was ever able to claim the title effectively and those that claimed it were usually known as High King with opposition. In 1166 Rory O'Connor, King of Connaught, was crowned High King of Ireland. He might have thought that he could see off any challenges from within the island, and in that context he might have been right. However his opposition would come elsewhere, from a new and hitherto unknown quarter – the Normans.

1167 and all that!

The individual most associated with the arrival of the Normans in Ireland is Dermot MacMurrough, who from the 1130s was King of Leinster. According to Gerald of Wales (Giraldus Cambrensis) who penned a tome entitled *The Conquest of Ireland* Dermot 'preferred to be feared rather than loved...He was inimical towards his own people and hated by others'.

One of these others was Rory O'Connor and in 1166 O'Connor defeated MacMurrough in battle. The fight took place for two reasons; first, MacMurrough had refused to submit to O'Connor as the new High King, and second, over a decade previously MacMurrough had kidnapped Dervorgilla, who just happened to be O'Connor's daughter as well as being the wife of O'Connor's ally Tigernán Ua Ruairc, King of Bréifne.

In the aftermath of his defeat MacMurrough was forced to flee from Ireland. He ended up in Bristol with the intention of seeking help from the Normans. It became clear, however, that none would provide assistance without the permission of their king and so from Bristol Dermot headed for France in search of help from King Henry II (1154–89). Having tracked him down to Aquitaine, MacMurrough begged Henry to help him regain his throne and in return promised to become his 'liegeman'. Henry gave MacMurrough permission to go to Wales and approach the Normans there for help.

Why, however, did Henry care about Ireland? Like many previous rulers of England – perhaps even dating back to Roman times – Henry had considered an invasion of the neighbouring island but had never actually got round to it. Furthermore, over a decade previously the English Pope, Hadrian IV (1154–9), had penned *Laudabiliter*, a document conferring on Henry the title 'Lord of Ireland' and allowing him to take control of Ireland and reform its church.

Many of the Normans based in Wales had less land than their compatriots in England and so they were more than interested in helping Dermot. In 1169, therefore, a Norman force landed at Bannow Bay, Co. Wexford. MacMurrough and his followers joined the invaders and together they attacked and captured the town of Wexford. Shortly after, MacMurrough was restored to the kingship of Leinster. Because of the help he had received he became known as 'Dermot of the Foreigners'.

Over succeeding years increasing numbers of Normans arrived in Ireland. Most prominent among these was Richard de Clare, Earl of Pembroke, better known to us as Strongbow, who landed in 1170. It was to Strongbow that MacMurrough had offered his daughter Aoífe's hand in marriage, as well as the prospect of succeeding him as King of Leinster if he helped him regain his throne.

Led by Strongbow, the Normans captured Dublin by the end of the year and when MacMurrough died unexpectedly in May 1171 Strongbow succeeded him as king. However, despite having a strong new leader, it is probably fair to say that the kingdom remained far from stabilized.

The arrival of Henry II

Henry II was none too pleased when he heard of Strongbow's success in Ireland and so in October 1171 he landed at Waterford accompanied by a large army. Thus he became the first Norman monarch to set foot on Irish soil.

Ostensibly Henry had arrived because of his concern that Strongbow was becoming too powerful and might eventually challenge Henry's own influence. While that was undoubtedly true he had other – more pressing – reasons to escape from his regular haunts. Just ten months earlier three of his knights had executed Thomas Beckett, Archbishop of Canterbury, in the belief that Henry wanted rid of 'this turbulent priest'. Henry was also keen to continue the process of church reform in Ireland. This had begun earlier in the twelfth century – overseen by prelates such as Anselm of Canterbury and Malachy of Armagh – and had resulted in the holding of great reforming Synods at Cashel and Ráthbresail. In this way, Henry reasoned, he might be able to get back into the Pope's good books again.

The king returned to England in April of the following year. By the time of his departure all of Ireland's significant political leaders – including Strongbow – had submitted to him save for a handful of monarchs including Rory O'Connor. The leaders of the Irish church also submitted to the Norman king, wisely regarding him as a more likely supporter of ecclesiastical reform than any of the local leaders.

Those who had submitted to Henry had their territories regranted to them. In 1175 Rory O'Connor also submitted and – by the terms of the Treaty of Windsor – was permitted to rule the lands outside Norman control as *Ard rí*.

In the decades following Henry's visit, the Norman conquest continued – in defiance of the terms of the Treaty of Windsor – until about three quarters of the island had come under Norman control. Despite the superiority in numbers of the native Irish, superior military experience and tactics usually saw the invaders emerge victorious whenever and wherever battle commenced. Norman magnates such as John de Courcy gained influence in areas such as the Kingdom of Ulidia in North East Ulster while Connaught came under the influence of Richard de Burgo. Meath was controlled by Hugh de Lacy and Munster by a number of different Norman families.

Once control had been gained it was defended by the building of castle strongholds. Initially these were motte and bailey structures, erected because of their speed of construction, but before long they were being replaced by more permanent stone buildings. Many of these still survive, albeit in different states of repair. Of particular note one can point to the impressive castles at places such as Carrickfergus, Dundrum and Carlingford.

Beyond the Pale: establishing English control

It was during the reign of King John (1199–1216) that elements of the type of administrative system previously introduced in Norman England began to appear. Chief among these was the jury system, but it also included a structure of sheriffs whose job it was to collect fines and taxes and enforce the Norman's system of law which was called Common Law. There were other innovations too: the feudal system made its Irish debut, whilst coinage bearing the harp symbol began to be minted. Finally, under Norman influence, elements of the county system began to emerge. Dublin was the first county to be created, first appearing in records in 1200.

As the thirteenth century progressed more and more evidence emerged of the colonists' efforts to cement their control over Ireland. As new territories were conquered in Munster, North-West Ulster and Connaught, castles, cathedrals, monasteries and towns (including Athlone, Drogheda, Dundalk, Kilkenny and Galway) were built, many with some form of defensive walls. At the same time more sophisticated forms of trade and commerce were developed, whilst introducing more intensive forms of agricultural production became a major preoccupation.

Increasing control?

By the middle of the thirteenth century the greater part of the island had come under Norman control. The Normans' superior weaponry, their skills at building easily defensible fortifications and their tactical nous made them irresistible – in a negative sense – to the native forces. At the same time the latter groups were often engaged in debilitating internecine struggles leaving them capable of offering little or no genuine resistance.

The monarchy was clearly keen to demonstrate the extent of its influence by this time. In 1254 Henry III (1216–72) gave Ireland (along with other areas) to his heir, the future Edward I

(1272–1307), declaring them to be inalienably annexed to the crown. It was clear that the Normans wanted their control to be consolidated. There is plenty of evidence that they were well on the way to achieving this. By the middle of the century there were eight counties in Ireland.

Of course for most of the time the king was not there. In his absence a Justiciar (later to be known as the Lord Deputy or Viceroy) was in charge of running the colony and protecting the king's interests. One of the Justiciar's main tasks became the summoning of great meetings or parliaments, the first clearly documented one being held in June 1264 at Castledermot. A Council made up of other senior office-holders such as the Treasurer, Chancellor and Escheator supported the Justiciar in his work.

The decline of the colony

For all of their impressive systems and structures, however, the Normans were never able to conquer the Irish completely. By about 1250 three quarters of Ireland was under Norman control, yet they simply were not able to finish the job. One key reason for this strange state of affairs was that English monarchs began to pay less and less attention to what was going on in Ireland, while those left in charge were often more interested in increasing their own particular position, to the detriment of the monarchy's.

On top of that there just weren't enough of them in Ireland; the Norman population was concentrated in Leinster and parts of Munster and thinly spread elsewhere. Moreover – as with previous invaders – they began to intermingle with the Irish way of life, particularly outside Dublin. Although forbidden to do so, many Normans made use of Brehon Law, as its penalties were less severe than their own system.

Most significant of all, however, was the emergence of a fight back by the native Irish after the middle years of the thirteenth century. Over the next century and a quarter some form of 'Gaelic recovery' took place. It was never a united campaign but bit by bit conquered territory was recovered. This was mainly achieved by using Norman weaponry and tactics and by employing Scottish mercenaries called Gallowglasses.

By the start of the fourteenth century, therefore, much of the land was back in the hands of the Gaelic chieftains; however, a strong ruler was needed to finish off the Normans. The man chosen was Edward Bruce, brother of Robert Bruce, King of Scotland.

Land held by the Native Irish

Land held by the Anglo-Normans

■ Towns founded by the Vikings

• Towns founded by the Anglo-Normans

Coleraine

Sligo

Dundalk

Tuam
Drogheda
Athlone
Galway
Athenry
Loughrea
DUBLIN

Roscrea
Nenagh
Carlow
LIMERICK
Thurles
Kilkenny
Tipperary
Cashel
Tralee
Clonmel
New Ross
Carrick on Suir
WEXFORD
Dungarvan
CORK
Youghal
WATERFORD

Kinsale

figure 1 The extent of Norman control over Ireland by the start of the fourteenth century.

Edward Bruce

Edward Bruce arrived in Ulster in 1315 having been invited by a number of local Gaelic chiefs to lead an expedition to drive out the Normans. Initially Bruce was successful – in 1316 he was crowned as King of Ireland – but before long his luck began to change and at the 1318 Battle of Faughart the Normans finally defeated him. During this encounter Bruce was killed and his head was sent to King Edward II (1307–27). In spite of having been invited in, many of the Irish were pleased by this defeat since Bruce had not exactly endeared himself to the locals with his harsh tactics. Of his demise it was written, 'There was not done from the beginning of the world a better deed for the men of Erin than that deed' (*Irish Annals*).

In spite of the Gaelic resurgence, over the remainder of the middle ages no further serious attempt was made to overthrow the Norman colony or to unite the disparate elements that made up Gaelic Ireland. Yet the native population didn't need to do much in any case. The Norman colony had been further weakened by the physical and material damage caused by these events and by the middle of the fourteenth century it had been banished from Ulster.

In 1360 the colonists sent a desperate message to the king, warning that their situation was dire. They listed the problems that were weakening their position and made clear their fear that the Irish were going to reconquer the whole country. Their plea was taken seriously and Edward III's (1327–77) son Lionel, Duke of Clarence, was appointed Viceroy in Ireland.

The Statutes of Kilkenny

Clarence arrived in Dublin in the autumn of 1361 and immediately started a campaign to regain control. However military success was not forthcoming. Indeed, the Duke's time in Ireland is best remembered for the series of laws enacted in an attempt to stop the Norman assimilation into the native population. At a parliament held in Kilkenny in 1366 the 'Statutes of Kilkenny' were enacted. These aimed to achieve their purpose by prohibiting, amongst other things, marriage between the races, the Norman use of the Irish language and Irish names within the colony, riding horses bare backed, the playing of hurling and so on.

However things did not really improve and mixing between the races went on. It looked more and more likely that unless decisive military action was taken the colony would cease to exist. Therefore in 1394 Richard II (1377–99) landed in Ireland with a force of about 10,000 men, the largest army so far sent to the country and a good indication of the seriousness with which he took his task. He was the first monarch to visit Ireland in nearly 200 years. His aim, he said, was to 'establish good government and just rule'.

The king remained in Ireland until the following year and in this time obtained the submission of many significant Gaelic chieftains. However he was forced to return within four years as hostilities had broken out again. This time his visit was considerably shorter. Politically Richard was having problems back at home with challenges to his position from the Lancastrians. Upon learning that Henry Bolingbroke had seized the throne (as Henry IV, 1399–1413), the king was forced to turn for home where he was overthrown and murdered. His attempts to settle Ireland had lost him both his throne and, ultimately, his life.

Richard was the last English monarch to come to Ireland for over 300 years. The early Lancastrian monarchs were not particularly interested in events across the Irish Sea and without strong English involvement the Norman colony was left to its own devices and continued to decline even more rapidly than before. Indeed, the area it covered continued to recede until it covered only the region surrounding Dublin, later known as the Pale (from the Latin *pallus* denoting the stakes used to mark the borders of the area).

Yet it wasn't all doom and gloom for the colonists. Outside this area three Norman families still retained power. Particularly important were the Fitzgeralds of Kildare. Although nominally loyal to the monarchy in England they continued to flout the guidelines laid down by the Statutes of Kilkenny. By the latter years of the fifteenth century they had become the most powerful rulers in the land.

Ireland and the Wars of the Roses

As the fifteenth century progressed, Ireland began to play an increasingly significant role in the continuing unrest within English political circles better known to us as the Wars of the Roses. In 1447 Richard, Duke of York, became heir to the English throne. In the same year the Lancastrian King, Henry VI (1422–61), appointed him Viceroy to Ireland. Richard's visit to the colony in 1449–50 resulted in the creation of strong links between Ireland and the Yorkist cause. In the sure knowledge of this support Richard turned for home. Five years later the Wars of the Roses began.

For a time York was in the ascendancy but then the tide began to turn against him. Following his defeat at Ludford Bridge in 1459, he returned to Ireland once more. In the following year the Irish parliament – demonstrating its loyalty to the Yorkist cause – declared that it was treasonable to oppose York. It decreed that Ireland would be bound only by laws passed by its own parliament and stated that English writs were invalid. In a final flash of autonomy it also established a separate coinage for the island.

To all intents and purposes the colony was using the opportunity provided by events in England to declare its independence from London. It would not be the last time that it would be claimed by dissatisfied natives that 'England's difficulty was Ireland's opportunity'.

In the same year – 1660 – York was killed in battle, but within 12 months his son had been crowned as Edward IV (1461–83). The question now was how the great Norman lords of Ireland would make use of the domestic power that they had gained as a result of the decisions of the 1460 parliament.

The answer was not in a manner that was pleasing to London in spite of the loyalty that those in power in Ireland had shown the Yorkist cause. By the end of the decade the English monarchy was becoming less and less enamoured with the behaviour of the Gaelic Irish and with the overly close links to them of the Anglo-Irish magnates such as the Earl of Kildare. However, attempts by Edward IV to restore some form of order only resulted in the outbreak of rebellion and in 1468 the crown was forced to agree to appoint Thomas, Earl of Kildare, as Lord Deputy even though it feared the consequences of such a move.

But why do this? Put simply, the crown did not possess the resources to conquer Ireland fully.

The power of the Kildares

The Lancastrians regained the throne after the defeat of the Yorkist Richard III (1483–5), on Bosworth Field in 1485. Although Kildare was a supporter of the Yorkist cause the new king, Henry VII (1485–1509), left him in place as Viceroy. However the dangers to England of a semi-independent Ireland ruled by a man who was all but king were obvious and became even clearer in 1487 when Lambert Simnel – a Yorkist pretender to the English throne – was brought to Ireland.

The majority of the Anglo-Irish magnates, including the Earl of Kildare (now Garrett Mór), accepted Simnel's claim and he was crowned King of England (as Edward VI) in Christ Church Cathedral, Dublin. However on his return to England Simnel, accompanied by several Anglo-Irish noble supporters, was defeated in Nottinghamshire. In 1489 Henry VII summoned the Irish nobles to England, and had Simnel – now working as a kitchen hand – wait on them at a banquet.

Not surprisingly these developments increased Henry's suspicions of Kildare but he was still not secure enough to move against him. Nor were the king's problems over at least as far as Irish involvement in challenges for his throne were concerned. In 1491 Perkin Warbeck – another Yorkist pretender – was received in Ireland as Prince Richard (the younger of the two princes supposedly murdered in the Tower of London about

1483). Kildare was more circumspect this time and Warbeck did not enjoy the same levels of support as Simnel had four years earlier. The pretender was executed later on at Tyburn in London. Henry was unimpressed by the Irish support for this second effort and was heard to remark 'they will crown apes next'.

Poynings' Law

Joking aside, Ireland was clearly proving to be something of a concern to the Lancastrian monarchy. Put simply, the Lord Deputy had done little or nothing to stop these challenges against his master the king. In 1494 Henry VII finally took action. He sent Sir Edward Poynings to Ireland as Lord Deputy. His instructions were to reduce the country to 'whole and perfect obedience' and thus to prevent Yorkist pretenders from using it as a base.

Poynings summoned a parliament, which enacted a range of significant legislation in terms of the future relationship between England and Ireland. Of particular note was 'Poynings' Law' which decreed that parliament could meet in Ireland only after royal permission had been granted and the 'King and Council' in England had approved the laws that it proposed to pass. This legislation was clearly intended to curb the ability of the Kildares to act in a manner damaging to the Lancastrian monarchy, however it had a much longer life. Having found it a useful method of enforcing control, it remained on the statute books – increasingly resented – until its amendment in 1782.

In 1495 Kildare was summoned to London and sent to the Tower. However, Poynings advised Henry that the Kildares were still necessary to keep Ireland in order in the absence of any attempt to conquer the whole island, something that simply wasn't on the cards. The Earl was therefore released and returned to Ireland as Lord Deputy. Henry ruefully remarked, to the Bishop of Meath, who had bitterly complained that 'all Ireland cannot rule yonder gentleman,' that 'he is fit to rule all Ireland seeing that all Ireland cannot rule him' (*Book of Howth*). Whether or not he was now to be trusted was, however, another matter.

Garrett Mór ruled as Ireland's 'all-but-king' until his death in 1513 when he was replaced by his son Garrett Óg, who had been brought up at the English court. Four years previously Henry VIII (1509–47) had come to the throne in England; he would be a much more secure and powerful ruler than his father and less tolerant of dissenters like Kildare. Under his rule the relationship between England and Ireland would change utterly.

02

reformation and rebellion

This chapter will cover:
- Henry VIII, King of Ireland
- the Reformation
- the Munster Rebellion
- the Nine Years' War
- the Ulster Plantation
- the 1641 Rebellion
- Cromwell in Ireland.

The fall of the House of Kildare

Initially Henry allowed Garrett Óg to continue as his Lord Deputy but Kildare was significantly less secure in his position than his father had been, while concomitantly Henry was considerably more so. Although there was a number of differences between the king and his deputy, the issue really came to a head after 1533, the year in which Henry married Anne Boleyn and broke with Rome. Soon after, Garrett Óg was summoned to London to answer charges of treason. The origin of these charges could be traced to the jealousy of other Irish families who had complained to Henry about Garrett Óg. One of these families, the Butlers, just happened to be related to Henry's new wife.

Kildare set off for London in early 1534, entrusting the government of Ireland to his son, Thomas, Lord Offaly. The Butlers continued to stir things by spreading false rumours to the effect that Garrett Óg had been executed. To begin with Offaly did not know these rumours were not true and in response he led a group of armed men (each with their jacket edged in silk, hence Offaly's nickname of 'Silken' Thomas) to St Mary's Abbey in Dublin where he hurled the sword of state to the floor of the Council Chamber.

Having declared that 'I am none of Henry's Deputy; I am his foe', Offaly returned to his base at Maynooth Castle and started to raise an army. His intention was to persuade the king that he couldn't afford to dispense with the Earls of Kildare as his deputies in Ireland. There is some evidence that his father knew and approved of his plans which leads one to surmise that Offaly would have rebelled, rumours or not.

Henry was not overly impressed with this sequence of events. Kildare Senior was dispatched to the Tower of London, where he died in September. A month later Sir William Skeffington arrived in Ireland with an army in excess of 2,000 men. In the meantime Offaly was doing his utmost to rally support for a 'Catholic crusade' by making contact with English and Welsh Catholics, the Pope and continental rulers including Charles V (1519–58), the Holy Roman Emperor. It seemed that the religious issue was making its debut on the stage of Irish politics.

In 1535 the Fitzgerald castle at Maynooth was besieged and overrun by Skeffington. The survivors were all put to the sword despite having received the – obviously worthless – 'Pardon of Maynooth'. Two years later Offaly and five of his uncles were executed in London. With their deaths the influence of the most powerful of the Irish families had been destroyed. Henceforth Ireland would be governed by English officials and controlled by an English garrison. Moreover, settling the key political issue of who ran Ireland now left the way clear for Henry to introduce his religious reforms.

The Reformation

The early sixteenth century echoed strongly with the calls for reform of the abuses that had sprung up in the Catholic Church. Interestingly none of these calls had ever come from Ireland, in spite of a marked decline there in the quality of religion. Yet this lack of native-sourced protest wasn't to stop the Reformation spreading to Ireland, wanted or not. In 1536 the Irish parliament – with a considerable degree of reluctance – passed an act making Henry 'the only supreme head on earth of the whole church of Ireland'. Under the terms of this Act of Supremacy, the Church of Ireland became the established church with the English monarch as its supreme head. No other churches were to exist and the population was to pay a tax or tithe to support the church's existence.

Initially these changes spread no further than the Pale, which, as indicated previously, by this time didn't extend very far. Although the state's policy of surrender and regrant (see below) required the renunciation of the Pope's authority for the maintenance of property title, those Gaelic chieftains who embraced it saw it as little more than a form of words and retained their traditional religious affiliations. Equally, many of the clergy paid no more than lip service to the liturgical modifications that were implemented. The only element of genuine change that did occur was with the attempted dissolution of the monasteries but even then many of them survived.

Henry, King of Ireland

In 1541 the Irish parliament declared Henry King of Ireland. He therefore became the first monarch to bear this title, if one excludes the aforementioned Edward Bruce, who never really reigned. In the same year Henry introduced the policy of surrender and regrant as a method of controlling Ireland that was cheaper than all-out warfare. By this, many of the main Gaelic Irish chiefs submitted to Henry and in return received titles of nobility from him. The policy also demanded that they should abandon the Gaelic language and traditions and their loyalty to Rome. Like many of his predecessors Henry seemed determined to enforce some sort of uniformity of language and dress – one that was acceptable to the English of course!

One of the most notable subjects of the policy was Conn O'Neill, Ulster's most powerful chieftain. In 1542 he travelled to Court in London to submit to Henry and was rewarded – amidst great fanfare and a healthy dose of propaganda – with the title of Earl of Tyrone.

Surrender and regrant was relatively successful as a method of control. By the time of Henry's death in 1547, no fewer than 40 Gaelic rulers had submitted to him.

Over the next decade the English administration built on this success by introducing an assortment of policies intended to tighten its grip on Ireland. This work was undertaken by a new generation of bureaucrats – such as Skeffington – who brought their own followers with them. This new generation of administrators became known as the New English (to distinguish them from the Old English – those who could trace their lineage back to the earliest Norman settlers). The fact that such a distinction was now being made, however, suggested that the Old English were regarded by their successors as something of a different, less reliable race.

One of the new policies introduced was that of plantation. First attempted during the reign of Henry's son, Edward VI (1547–53), it had a number of attractions for the New English, not least the issue of cost. Like surrender and regrant it was seen as a cheap and possibly even more effective way of gaining control of hostile areas. The first opportunity came after the defeat by crown forces of a rebellion in Laois and Offaly in 1547. In 1549 the plantation of Laois and Offaly (which were henceforth to be known as Queen's County and King's County) was begun.

The organization of the plantation was well set out in theory but the reality turned out to be somewhat more complicated. It proved less than easy to deprive the natives of their land in favour of English settlers and to ensure that they were able to hold on to it. Time and again the settlers came under attack yet the settlement was ultimately able to maintain some sort of precarious hold. Although it wasn't a raging success, it suggested that as a strategy, plantation could work. Indeed in later – and perhaps more sophisticated – guises this scheme would turn out to be one of the most far-reaching initiatives introduced into Ireland by the crown.

The Reformation after Henry

As already suggested, most of Henry's Reformation changes did not impinge greatly on Ireland, with the possible exception of the dissolution of the monasteries and even then the results were fitful. This situation changed radically after his death and particularly during the reign of Edward VI. However Edward's changes – which went far beyond Henry's structural adjustments and included doctrinal and sacramental alterations – were not well received in Ireland and the government was still not powerful enough to enforce them fully.

During Mary I's reign (1553–8) some efforts were made to re-Catholicize the country and in 1557 the Irish parliament revoked the Act of Supremacy. However with Mary's death and her replacement by her Protestant half-sister Elizabeth (1558–1603), a more Protestant form of religion was again introduced. In 1560 the Irish parliament passed a second Act of Supremacy, making Elizabeth Supreme Governor (rather than Head since she was a woman) of the Church of Ireland. All clergy and government officials were obliged to swear an oath accepting Elizabeth's supremacy and renouncing foreign jurisdictions.

As before – and despite the best efforts of the administration – the Irish population, including the Old English, resisted the great majority of these changes. Furthermore, when Pope Pius V (1566–72) declared Elizabeth a heretic and excommunicated her in 1570 it theoretically freed up the Old English Catholics from having to accept her form of religion. Unfortunately the Pope's action also had a major downside. By commanding 'all noblemen and subjects not to obey her or her orders and laws', it made the crown suspect the loyalty of the Old English and resulted in it treating them in a manner that would eventually drive them into union with the Gaelic Irish.

Hugh O'Neill

Catholic Ireland's reluctance to adhere to Elizabeth's religious policy concerned the crown. The fact that there were many cultural and trading links between Ireland and Catholic Europe was a further source of worry. Yet the queen was happy to rule by persuasion as opposed to force. That is, of course, if she was allowed to do so. In the case of the O'Neills of Tyrone this proved not to be possible.

The earldom of Tyrone proved to be one of the most intractable problems of Elizabeth's reign. As we have seen the title had been conferred on Conn O'Neill by Elizabeth's father. In 1558 Matthew O'Neill (whom the crown had recognized as heir to his natural father Conn) was assassinated on the instructions of his rival and half-brother Shane, better known as Shane the Proud. When Conn died in the following year, Elizabeth accepted Shane as the rightful Earl of Tyrone.

Within two years however Shane had rebelled in his efforts to extend his power and as a result was proclaimed a traitor. In the course of the following year Shane submitted to Elizabeth yet within a few months he was again in rebellion. By this stage he was plotting with Elizabeth's Catholic cousin, Mary Stuart (Queen of Scotland, 1542–87), whilst also seeking help from the King of France.

Shane was killed by the O'Donnells in 1567 and was succeeded by Turlough Luineach O'Neill. At the same time Hugh O'Neill, son of Matthew (Conn's original heir), was installed as Baron of Dungannon in the southern part of the O'Neill territory to act as a counterweight to the Earl. This policy seemed to work and for a time peace reigned in the north.

Rebellion in Munster

Peace didn't reign in the south however. Shortly after, trouble broke out at the other extreme of the country with the Desmond rebellion in Munster, led by James Fitzmaurice Fitzgerald. The rebels turned to Catholic Europe for assistance but none was forthcoming and the rebellion was put down. Elizabeth – perhaps somewhat foolishly – pardoned the rebels. The crown also set up what were christened the Presidencies of Munster and Connaught as a method of extending English rule in the south and west. Not surprisingly this innovation didn't go down too well with the locals.

Fitzmaurice wasn't particularly grateful for his pardon. In 1575 he travelled to France and Spain to seek assistance for the liberation of Ireland. Pius V's excommunication of Elizabeth in 1570 had made him hopeful that this time he would obtain help from Catholic Europe. He wasn't wrong; four years later he returned to Ireland with a small military force supplied by the Pope and proclaimed holy war. In this way Fitzmaurice was different from other rebels, including Shane O'Neill, who were simply interested in extending their own power.

Fitzmaurice was killed but others among the Old English including the Earl of Desmond (Gerald Fitzgerald) decided to take up the cause in defence of Catholicism. In 1580 a small force – again supplied by the Pope – arrived in Kerry to support the rebellion but before long they were captured and put to the sword. The rebellion was over by 1583 with Desmond dead and the province laid waste. The condition of the people was atrocious. An English official wrote, 'out of every corner of the woods they came, creeping forth on their hands for their legs would not bear them. They looked like skeletons; they ate corpses. If they found a plot of shamrocks, they flocked there as a feast'.

The Munster Plantation

English law decreed that the land of rebels was forfeit and so in the aftermath of the Desmond rebellion a plantation of Munster was organized by the crown as a way of further increasing its control over far-flung regions. About 202,000 hectare (0.5 million acres) of land, both good and bad, was made available. A survey of the land was undertaken and it was divided up into vast estates. The crown then concentrated on the difficult task of getting suitable men to undertake the plantation of these lands.

These undertakers – as they became known – included some of the most prominent Elizabethans of the age and included the poet Edmund Spenser, who wrote his *Faerie Queen* whilst in Ireland and the explorer Sir Walter Raleigh, who got around 17,000 hectares (42,000 acres) at a peppercorn rent. In return for paying these low rents the landlords pledged to introduce English methods of farming and to settle a certain number of English families on their estates. The terms of the plantation also decreed that the native population be removed from the land while defensive measures were also required to shield the new settlers from almost inevitable attack.

As with Laois and Offaly it all seemed fairly straightforward on paper but again in reality it turned out to be not quite as simple. The land in question was desolate; indeed it was in such bad condition that there weren't enough settlers *in situ* to bring it under cultivation. For that reason alone there was no option but to keep the Irish working on the land – in contravention to the express terms of the plantation.

So did it work? Yes and no; although some settlers established themselves quickly and prospered, cost cutting meant that the appropriate defensive measures were not introduced. Thus, when the hostile natives struck back – as they did in 1598 as part of the Nine Years' War (see below) – the plantation was fatally exposed and laid waste.

When the war ended the province was replanted, but this time many of the great landlords did not return. Instead they became absentees or sold their land cheaply to their compatriots who were already in Ireland, a group that became known as adventurers. This time the planters learned from their mistakes and the settlements became much better defended with walled towns being built in places such as Killarney, Tralee and Bandon.

The Nine Years' War

In 1587 Hugh O'Neill succeeded to the earldom of Tyrone. Although loyal to the crown and anxious to bear the title of an English nobleman, he also hoped to be allowed to rule his possessions in the traditions of his forbearers. Basically he wanted to have his cake and eat it. Of course this would not be possible. To make matters worse Tyrone had enemies at Court and he came to realize that the only way that he could guarantee his independence would be to fight for it. After extensive preparations – which included the forging of an alliance with Red Hugh O'Donnell – O'Neill's allies struck out in 1593 (although he himself did not join in until 1595). Thus began what became known as the Nine Years' War.

As part of his preparations O'Neill appealed for help from Philip II of Spain (1556–98-he of the Armada) 'to restore the faith of the Church'. This crusading element was also used within Ireland as a method of gaining help from the Catholic Old English; however for the most part they continued to regard the Ulster Irish with suspicion and remained loyal to the crown. Only in Munster – the scene of recent religious-based rebellions – did the Old English join common cause with O'Neill. However lacking a strong leader their localized campaign soon petered out.

For over five years O'Neill was able to hold Elizabeth's forces at bay. In fact he was able to do more than that. In 1598 he defeated the English forces at the Yellow Ford, near Armagh, undoubtedly the high point of his campaign. However, if Tyrone thought that this would mark a turning point he was to be sorely disappointed; thereafter he would face a stronger English leadership in the shape of Lord Mountjoy who was appointed in 1600 as Lord Deputy and commander of the queen's forces. Under Mountjoy's leadership the tide of the campaign began to turn in favour of the crown.

O'Neill desperately needed help from the continent and while it finally came it did not arrive until 1601. Worse still, when it did arrive, it landed on the wrong part of the island. Stormy conditions meant that the Spanish forces put ashore at Kinsale on the coast of Co. Cork and a long way from Ulster. Before long Mountjoy's forces were besieging the town. O'Neill and his allies set off to relieve the relief but they were heavily defeated by Mountjoy at Kinsale on Christmas Eve. O'Neill then withdrew to Ulster and continued his fight but without foreign help his position was helpless. Eventually he accepted that he was going to have to sue for peace.

The Treaty of Mellifont

Elizabeth died on 24 March 1603 to be succeeded as monarch by James Stuart, the son of Mary Queen of Scots. Six days later O'Neill surrendered and was pardoned; the resulting Treaty of Mellifont ended the Nine Years' War. By its terms O'Neill again agreed to rule his lands according to English law and custom. All told it seemed a pretty good deal, especially given what had happened in Munster following the Desmond Rebellions; however James I was anxious to restore peace to the land.

Not everyone was happy with the deal. Many of the New English were enraged at the perceived leniency of the Treaty's terms and local officials began a rigorous enforcement of the English system of government in O'Neill's territories. Their actions caused the former rebels some degree of inconvenience whilst they were also finding themselves increasingly discontented at having to live as subjects to the crown. To make things worse a whispering campaign against O'Neill and his allies was going on in London. In 1607 O'Neill was summoned by the king to answer charges of treason.

O'Neill took to sea but not for London. In September 1607 the Earl of Tyrone, along with Rory O'Donnell and others set sail secretly for the continent from Lough Swilly, the so-called 'Flight of the Earls'. Tyrone finally ended up in Rome where, in the church of San Pietro in Montorio on the Janiculum Hill, his tomb can still be seen today.

The fugitives were subsequently charged with high treason, and their lands declared forfeit. The last of the Gaelic strength was gone, Ireland was now finally under a single ruler and the crown now possessed the blank canvas it needed for its next great scheme – the plantation of Ulster – to begin.

The Ulster Plantation

During the following year preparations began for the plantation of six of Ulster's counties (Armagh, Cavan, Coleraine [later Derry], Donegal, Fermanagh and Tyrone). However this was not the first step taken with regard to the plantation of the island's most northern province. A few years previously inhabitants of the lowlands of Scotland – many of whom were Presbyterians – had been encouraged to settle in counties Antrim and Down. (Ultimately this private enterprise would prove to be the more successful of the two endeavours.) Now in the aftermath of the 'Flight of the Earls' and a subsequent rebellion by Sir Cahir O'Doherty roughly another 1.6 million hectares (4 million acres) was to be made available.

A Commission of Inquiry travelled through the province in 1609 and decided that all land except that owned by the established church was up for grabs. With this decided, various types of estate were identified and categories of owner sought. These were categorized as undertakers (gentlemen), servitors (former soldiers and government officials) and 'deserving Irish'. Undertakers weren't allowed to have any Gaelic tenants but servitors and the 'deserving Irish' were permitted some. As with previous plantations, all classes were instructed to erect suitable defensive edifices.

Undertakers employed a variety of methods to attract tenants to their land. One such individual, Thomas Blenerhasset, advertised in a 1610 pamphlet for various types of tenant including tradesmen, farmers, gentlemen taking pleasure in the hunt and even religious ministers, stating (in the case of the latter) 'Make speed, the harvest is great. Thou shalt see the poor ignorant untaught people worship stones and bricks'.

Initially not enough undertakers expressed an interest in the scheme and so in 1610 the Irish Society of London (a group of City companies) agreed to carry out the plantation of the town of Derry, Coleraine and part of Tyrone. In the same year settlers from England and Scotland began to arrive in Ulster. However because of the perceived dangers of the region it was not found possible to attract in enough non-native labourers and so Irish tenants were allowed to remain on the land, which was against the conditions of the plantation. In this way while the ownership of the land changed hands, there was no great change in terms of the religious makeup of the province's overall population.

That said, in a general sense the Ulster Plantation was the most successful of the three that had been implemented since the 1540s. Historians believe that within three decades upwards of 40,000 settlers were resident in the province. It is further estimated that about one third of this number was made up of men capable of bearing weapons.

Such men were not a luxury. As with previous plantations the settlers lived in constant danger of attack by the dispossessed Irish population, including those who had been allowed to remain on the land as tenants. The existence of fortified buildings provided some degree of protection but life remained dangerous. The large number of towns that sprang up in the planted territories also provided some degree of security. Many of these were built on or near earlier foundations and a common theme among them was the layout with a central square and streets running off. This system can still be seen today in so-called 'planter' towns including Derry, Coleraine, Strabane, Dungannon and Enniskillen.

Charles I

In 1625 James I died to be succeeded by his son Charles (1625–49). The new king found himself facing an increasingly agitated Old English class, disconcerted because they were losing their political power to an increasingly Protestant Irish parliament and were in fear of losing their land to further crown plantation schemes.

In the short term their concerns were alleviated. Charles needed money and the Old English still had plenty and so in 1627 the king offered 'graces' or concessions to his Irish subjects in return for money to maintain his army. In total 51 'graces' were promised covering highly contentious issues such as religion and land. It was also agreed that a parliament would be summoned to confirm these concessions in law but this was never met, even though the Old English fulfilled their part of the bargain and Charles received the money promised.

Wentworth

In 1633 Charles appointed Thomas Wentworth as Lord Deputy of Ireland. Wentworth's aim was to increase his master's income and authority in Ireland at a time when Charles was refusing to co-operate with parliament in England. Wentworth went about his task with gusto, trying to improve the economy, but his most successful – although ultimately self-defeating – policy was to raise money through fines.

Wentworth imposed all manner of charges on undertakers for perceived breaches of the conditions of plantations. Whether it was for taking over church lands or employing native Irish tenants the money came in thick and fast. Finally – in spite of what Charles had conceded in the 'graces' – the Lord Deputy also began to consider a plantation of Connaught. Of course it would be the Old English who would stand to lose the most by the introduction of such a scheme.

In his efforts to raise money for the king, Wentworth was, therefore, annoying a considerable cross-section of the population in Ireland. He irritated even more with his religious policies, particularly the Presbyterians who had become a significant element in the Irish population in the aftermath of the Ulster Plantation. Just as Charles was attempting to do in Scotland, Wentworth wanted to impose an episcopal church on this group. When the Scottish Presbyterians rebelled against Charles' religious policies in 1638 the unrest quickly spread to Ireland.

Charles summoned the English parliament in an effort to gain help against these rebellions. However in 1640 the king fell out with parliament, further increasing his difficulties. While all of this was going on Wentworth was attempting to raise an army in Ireland that Charles could use against his enemies in Scotland. Catholics were recruited as part of this force. Wentworth also summoned a parliament to raise revenue for Charles but at this he came up against a previously unlikely alliance of Old and New English. They – with encouragement from the English Commons – protested to Westminster at Wentworth's despotic rule. Westminster used this as an excuse to impeach Wentworth and as a result he was put to death in 1641.

The Old and New English alliance against Wentworth had emerged for negative rather than positive reasons and with the common enemy gone it began to disintegrate. Moreover, the developing crisis in England convinced many Irish leaders that the opportune time had come to strike for the restoration of their lost territories.

The 1641 rebellion

By 1641 the relationship between king and parliament in England had broken down completely. This chaotic state of affairs was just the opportunity for which the dispossessed landowners in Ulster had been waiting and in October 1641 rebellion broke out. Yet again it could be said that 'England's difficulty was Ireland's opportunity'. A plan to capture Dublin Castle fell through meaning that the rebellion's initial concentration was in Ulster. In taking up arms the Irish were at pains to point out that their quarrel was with parliament and not against the monarchy. Indeed Sir Phelim O'Neill stated that, 'The rising is in noe wayes intended against our soveraine Lord the King, nor the hurt of any of his subjects, eyther of the Inglish or Schotish nation, but only for the defence and liberty of our selves and the natives of this kingdome.' Normally this would have been a 'nice' distinction, but in the context of contemporary English politics it worked.

As part of the rising the dwellings of settlers throughout Ulster were attacked. Evidence would suggest that at least 4,000 Protestants were killed in these attacks. Many Catholics were also massacred as a result of reprisals carried out by the settlers. Some of the settlers fled to the relative safety of the walled towns of Ulster. Others went back across the Irish Sea, carrying florid tales of the hardships that they had faced. There, whatever atrocities had taken place were magnified further still through anti-Irish and anti-Catholic propaganda to the point that, not for the last time, fiction replaced fact as reality.

It didn't take long for the conflict to spread south into Leinster. At this point the Old English formed an alliance with the rebels, leading to a general Catholic rising across the country. This had been a hard choice for the Old English, but they decided that their future lay with their fellow Catholics rather than with a government to which they wanted to be loyal, but which refused to trust them and which they feared would punish them afterwards, no matter what. 'You are marked forth for destruction as well as we', the Irish warned them. The Old English decided to believe their co-religionists.

The Scottish parliament responded to events in Ireland by sending over a large army under the command of General Robert Monro. Westminster's response was somewhat hampered by the ongoing dispute between it and the monarchy which soon flared up into civil war. However a military expedition was planned, to be funded by the proceeds of the

Driuinge Men Women & children by hund reds vpon Briges & casting them into Riuers, who drowned not were killed with poles & shot with muskets

A contemporary propagandist illustration of the 1641 massacre of Protestants, which took place at Portadown.

Adventurers Act (1642). By this clever piece of legislation 'adventurers' were invited to contribute funds towards the defeat of the Irish. In return they would be granted the forfeited lands of the defeated rebels. Over 1 million hectares (2.5 million acres) were set aside for this purpose.

The Confederation of Kilkenny

In 1642 the Catholics established a Confederacy at their Kilkenny headquarters. As part of this a General Assembly was established to operate in the manner of a parliament. Its purpose was to administer Catholic-controlled parts of the country pending a final settlement. However although the Catholics were nominally united, there were clear differences between them over their ultimate aims. The Old English would have been satisfied to declare their loyalty to the king (whom they saw as a better ruler than parliament) in return for freedom of religion and security of possession of their lands.

This was not enough for the Gaelic Irish who sought much more. In many ways they wanted a return to the situation pertaining before the religious and territorial changes introduced almost a century earlier by the Tudor monarchs. Moreover they were not so keen to accept Charles as their rightful monarch. In this they had the support of Giovanni Rinuccini, who arrived as papal nuncio in Ireland in 1645. Unfortunately his self-interested policies – based solely on the desire to restore Catholicism – did little to improve relations between the two groups. These differences, along with the debilitating effect of petty jealousies amongst the military leadership of the two factions, meant that the effectiveness of the Confederacy was fatally compromised.

To hell or Connaught: Cromwell in Ireland

The conflict dragged on inconclusively for much of the 1640s. Then things changed; the execution of Charles I by parliament in January 1649 was swiftly followed by the arrival in Ireland of Oliver Cromwell as Commander-in-Chief and Lord Lieutenant. With him he brought an army of about 12,000 (although the numbers given vary). His aim was to defeat those loyal to the Stuart monarchy, to avenge the events of 1641, to prepare the ground (literally!) for the implementation of the Adventurers Act and to provide a method of occupying and paying the wages of the now-redundant parliamentarian army. He was determined to achieve all of his objectives!

Cromwell's first target was the town of Drogheda, which covered the natural route into Ulster. However the town's inhabitants refused to surrender and – after a prolonged shelling of the walls – the town was entered and its garrison executed. While this might seem somewhat excessive and has certainly gone down in nationalist folklore as evidence of British brutality, contemporary military laws permitted such actions when a garrison refused to surrender an impossible position. Cromwell described his actions (in a report to the House of Commons) as 'a righteous judgement of God upon these barbarous wretches, who have imbrued their hands in innocent blood'. The massacre also provided Cromwell with useful propaganda that he hoped his enemies would heed. It certainly worked; shortly after, the garrisons of Dundalk and Trim fled without even bothering to take their munitions.

Cromwell then turned his attention southwards, specifically upon the town of Wexford. Betrayed by one of its garrison, it suffered a fate worse than that of Drogheda in that the ordinary townspeople were also put to the sword. Over the next number of months Cromwell moved through the province of Munster. By the time he left for England in May 1650 the majority of Irish resistance had been snuffed out. That said, a lengthy siege of Limerick was required before the last maor stand of the combined Irish and royalist forces was ended.

A few pockets of resistance remained but with the surrender of Galway in May 1653 the conflict came to an end and Catholic Ireland had been defeated. After over a decade of intense warfare the country yet again lay in ruins. Once more it presented a blank canvas for the English government to paint.

Ireland under the Republic

The first thing that the new administration attempted to do was to rid itself of the many 'undesirable' people who were now roaming the land. Irish soldiers – over 30,000 of them – were permitted to enlist in foreign armies that were not at war with the Commonwealth. Beggars, any remaining soldiers and Catholic clergy were transported to such far-flung places as the West Indies.

In 1652 parliament passed an Act for the Settling of Ireland, which was designed to deal with the land situation. As a way of paying off debts and honouring the Adventurers Act, Irish land was to be handed out. A survey – covering a massive 22 counties – was carried out by Sir William Petty and land was taken off all who had actively opposed parliament in or after 1641.

For the first time this meant that land was being taken off the Old English as opposed to the Gaelic Irish who were well used to such losses by this stage. Those deemed to have been involved to a lesser degree lost reduced amounts. These terms were to cover both Catholic and Protestant opponents but in practice Protestants were able to get off with a heavy fine. Those Catholics allowed to retain some land were to be set up in Connaught or Clare, cut off from the rest of the country and surrounded with a 'mile-line' of soldiers' settlements.

As with previous plantations the intention was to leave no Irish on the land. However, as had happened previously this was easier said than done and significant numbers of Catholics remained *in situ*. Even in the case of the English settlers many did not stay and those that did often ended up intermarrying with the native population. Yet there was significant change to the land-holding pattern after the Cromwellian settlement. The Catholic population lost out on huge amounts of land and was excluded from living in towns or from involvement in the administration of the island. Ireland's wealth and political power had been lost to a new system of rulers who were Protestant in faith and English in attitude.

03 from restoration to revolution

This chapter will cover:
- the War of the Three Kings
- the Penal Era
- colonial nationalism
- the American War of Independence
- legislative independence
- the French Revolution
- the 1798 Rebellion
- Union.

Charles II

Following Cromwell's death in 1658 the quality of government deteriorated rapidly and the republican experience ended with the restoration of Charles II in 1660 (he reigned until 1685). His reinstatement led many in Ireland to believe – having remained loyal to his cause – that they too would experience a restoration, in their case of lost lands. Charles however was anxious not to annoy either side and somewhat ambiguously promised he would not punish those who had rebelled against his father. In a typically Irish fashion both sides took this to mean that they would either get back what had been lost or keep what they had.

Of course satisfying both sides was going to be impossible and in 1662 the Irish parliament passed the Act of Settlement. This confirmed the Adventurers Act whilst putting the onus on those seeking restitution by stating that any party who could prove their innocence of involvement in rebellion could get their lands back.

This compromise proved to be a disaster with many more able to prove innocence than the government had anticipated and much less land available than was needed. As the Viceroy, the Earl of Ormond remarked, 'There must be new discoveries of a new Ireland for the old will not serve to satisfy these engagements.' A further compromise was therefore presented in the 1665 Act of Explanation. This stated that there would be no more claims and that the Cromwellian settlers were to forfeit one third of their land to provide land for those already proved innocent and certain named others.

The 'Popish Plot'

Charles did not overturn the anti-Catholic legislation passed by earlier Tudor and Stuart monarchs, however for much of his reign it was not enforced. In a climate of relative peace the Irish Catholic Church began to reorganize itself. However the possibility of anti-Catholic persecution remained, particularly in England, and in 1678 a 'Popish plot' was 'discovered' there.

This was supposedly an attempt to replace Charles as king by his brother James, Duke of York, who was a Catholic. In reality it was an invention of Titus Oates, a disgraced Anglican minister. The resulting hysteria led indirectly to the death in 1680 of Peter Talbot, Catholic Archbishop of Dublin (who died while imprisoned in Dublin Castle). It also led directly to the death of the Catholic Archbishop of Armagh, Oliver Plunkett, who was hanged, drawn and quartered in London in 1681 after being found guilty on the perjured evidence of two Franciscan priests. Plunkett has the distinction of being the last Catholic martyred for his faith in England and became, in 1975, the first Irish-born saint for almost seven centuries.

James II and the War of the Three Kings

Charles died in 1685 and was succeeded by James (1685–9). Not surprisingly Protestants viewed this development with concern but since James' heir, Mary, was a Protestant, they were prepared to allow the succession to take place.

James was keen to provide his Catholic subjects with some greater degree of freedom and appointed the Catholic Richard Talbot, Earl of Tyrconnell and brother of the recently deceased Archbishop of Dublin, to head the Irish Army. Almost immediately Tyrconnell began to install Catholic soldiers and officers in the army in place of Protestants. Then, after he became Lord Lieutenant in 1687, Tyrconnell began appointing Catholics to key government positions. During the following year James issued the Declaration of Indulgence in England which revoked the anti-Catholic and anti-Presbyterian laws in place. The king's aims may have been laudable in a pluralistic kind of way, but the haste with which he attempted to implement them caused considerable unease and was a significant element in his eventual undoing.

Although increasingly concerned, Protestants remained reassured by the inevitability of the Protestant succession. Unfortunately from their perspective events took a change for the worse in July 1688. In that year James' second wife, Mary of Modena, gave birth to a son who was baptized a Catholic. The prospect now of a Catholic succession combined with the gauche manner of James' government led leading Protestants to invite James' daughter Mary and her husband William of Orange to become joint monarchs albeit under the strict limitations of a Bill of Rights (William ruled until his death in 1702; Mary died in 1694). In November 1688 William and Mary landed in England. In December James fled to France. The revolution had been bloodless and had transferred the majority of power to parliament, a tradition that has continued ever since. For these reasons it became known as 'Glorious'.

The Siege of Derry

Back in Ireland Tyrconnell declared that the island would remain loyal to James. This announcement was accepted everywhere save Ulster where the Protestants declared their loyalty to William. The crisis in Ireland came to a head in December 1688 when 13 'Apprentice Boys' refused to allow a Catholic army into Derry. The town of Enniskillen also defied James II.

While on the throne James had been an ally of King Louis XIV of France (1643–1715), the Sun King. The French monarch was now determined to help his ally regain his crown. With William and Mary having declared their loyalty to the coalition of European rulers opposing Louis, the scene was set for some type of conflict, which would have Europe-wide ramifications. It just happened that this conflict took place in Ireland. It became known as the 'War of the Three Kings'.

Louis provided James with an army to hold Ireland. It landed at Kinsale in March 1689. A month later it began a siege of Derry. The city's Governor, Lieutenant Colonel Robert Lundy, wanted to surrender (hence the tradition of his effigy being burnt each year on the eve of the Twelfth of July celebrations) but the citizenry refused and – under the redoubtable leadership of Revd George Walker – held out for 105 days until a ship, the *Mountjoy*, broke through the boom which the Jacobites had placed across the Foyle.

The successful defence of Derry was a real blow to the Jacobite cause but it reflected the military reality, at least in the northern part of the island. Bit by bit most of Ulster came under the control of the Williamite forces. Meanwhile a Jacobite parliament was meeting in Dublin. It removed all restrictions on Catholics and restored property to the Catholic landowners. It was clear that the stakes were now very high.

In June 1690 William himself arrived in Ireland. The forces representing the two kings met at the Battle of the Boyne on 1 July (according to the dating used by the pre-Gregorian calendar – now 12 July). William commanded an army of close to 36,000 men while James' force numbered some 11,000 fewer.

The eventual Williamite victory at the Boyne was viewed as a defeat for Louis XIV. As such it was welcomed by his enemies all over Europe, including the Pope, Alexander VIII (1689–91). In the aftermath of the defeat James II again left for France and permanent exile, leaving command of his forces in the hands of Patrick Sarsfield (later Earl of Lucan).

After overcoming dogged Jacobite resistance at Cork, Athlone, Aughrim and Limerick the Williamites were eventually victorious. The conclusion of hostilities was marked with the signing of the Treaty of Limerick in October 1691.

The post-war settlement

Under the terms of the Treaty Jacobite forces were given the choice of returning home, joining the Williamites or going abroad. The Treaty promised Ireland's Catholics 'such privileges in the exercise of their religion as are consistent with the laws of Ireland or as they did enjoy in the reign of Charles II'. William was more than happy to accept these terms, however for many on his own side they were far too lenient even if they did further reduce the amount of land in Catholic hands. This additional territory came through confiscation from those who had fallen during the war, those who had surrendered before the Treaty of Limerick had been signed or those who had already fled to the continent.

The Protestant population might have won but they feared the reoccurrence of a similar crisis in the future. Not surprisingly they were afraid that Irish Catholics remained desirous of restoring a Catholic monarchy. It was imperative, therefore, that laws be enacted that would totally destroy Catholic political power. While William did not agree, he needed parliament on his side and so acquiesced in their demands. In 1695, therefore, a series of these 'penal laws' were enacted. They restricted the rights of Catholics to teach or run schools, to be educated abroad, to bear arms, or to own a horse worth more than five pounds. As Edmund Burke commented nearly a century later, these laws were 'a machine of wise and elaborate contrivance, and as well fitted for the oppression and impoverishment and degradation of a people and the debasement, in them, of human nature itself as ever proceeded from the perverted ingenuity of man'.

Measures were also introduced with the aim of restricting the influence of the Catholic Church. The 1697 Banishment Act required most Catholic clergy to leave the kingdom by 1 May 1698, and prohibited Catholic clergy from entering it. In 1704 the Registration Act demanded that each and every Catholic priest be registered and that there was to be no more than one per parish. It further stipulated that these clergymen were not to be replaced upon their death. In this way – it was hoped – Catholicism would die out naturally.

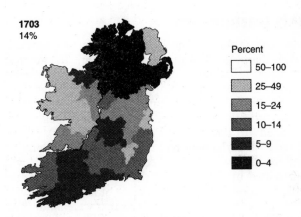

1703
14%

Percent

☐	50–100
☐	25–49
☐	15–24
☐	10–14
☐	5–9
☐	0–4

figure 2 A people dispossessed: the changing face of Catholic land ownership during the seventeenth century.

The 1700s: a century of peace?

The events of the 1690s copperfastened the changes that had been taking place in Ireland since the time of the Tudor monarchs. The New English were now confirmed in their political, territorial and religious ascendancy. The past distinctions between the Old English and Gaelic Irish no longer existed: like it or not now they were all simply the Catholic Irish.

The seeming finality of their respective positions meant that a long period of peace broke out, lasting for the greater part of the eighteenth century. Yet although politics were relatively pacific within Ireland, there were times during the century when relations between Ireland and Britain became fraught. These tensions were caused by the attempts of some in the ruling Ascendancy class to achieve a greater degree of legislative independence from London.

In many ways the Ascendancy class found themselves in a catch-22 situation. As a small minority among a potentially hostile majority the Ascendancy was totally reliant on the political and military might of the English government. At the same time, however, the members of the ruling class were frustrated at the lack of political influence that they had over the running of the country and fought against the dominance of the English administration. This frustration would increase throughout the course of the eighteenth century.

The Irish parliament

So what was their problem? The Dublin parliament was much less powerful than its Westminster equivalent. Its greatest weakness was that it had no control over the Irish government, which was made up of individuals appointed by and answerable to London. Moreover, for the greater part of the eighteenth century these officials were English born. Parliament was further restricted by Poynings' Law (see Chapter 1), which stated that the Irish parliament had to get London's permission to meet, and for the laws it wanted to enact. After 1720 it was further constrained by the terms of the Declaratory Act (also known as the Sixth of George I). This piece of legislation stated that Westminster had the right to pass laws that were binding on Ireland even if the Irish parliament did not agree.

Yet London could not totally ride roughshod over Dublin. The Irish parliament had the power to raise revenue through taxation and, as the administration was often short of cash, this meant that it had to ensure that a majority of members voted as it wanted. Such an outcome was usually guaranteed by the liberal use of patronage, and later on by the work of a group of parliamentary managers, who became known as 'undertakers'. This title was the same as that which had been given to the men who had been charged with managing the plantations, however the purpose was now markedly different.

The penal laws

As previously suggested the penal legislation had been introduced as a way of ensuring the political subjugation of the Catholic majority. Yet for significant periods of the eighteenth century, many of these laws were allowed to fall into abeyance. Put simply the legislation was enforced when the colony felt under threat and ignored when it felt more secure.

It was the laws restricting religious practice that were enforced most fitfully. If the statutes against the Catholic Church had been rigorously enforced then it is likely that its strength would have been significantly compromised; yet for most of the 1700s priests and prelates were able to exercise their ministry with a fair degree of freedom.

If this suggests that the eighteenth century was a time of outright toleration then that would not be strictly true. For the majority of the century the laws that restricted Catholic political power were rigidly enforced. Apart from losing the franchise – in 1728 – and the right to serve in the military, the penal legislation also prevented Catholics from sitting on juries or indeed from any involvement in the professional practice of the law.

Not surprisingly, property ownership was a major preoccupation of penal legislation. Even if Catholics could not vote, landowners of large estates could still influence the voting of their Protestant tenants and so it was imperative that such estates be broken up. Catholics were restricted in the purchase and leasing of land and where they still held land it was to be divided down amongst sons so that the size of estates would gradually decrease. Most insidiously, if a son converted to Anglicanism he would be assured ownership of all the land. As a result of such conversions the percentage of land held by Catholics further shrank from 14 per cent to 5 per cent between 1700 and 1775.

By the middle of the eighteenth century an emerging Catholic middle class was lobbying the government to relax aspects of the penal legislation. Around the same time Catholic landowners established the Catholic Committee as a lobby group for their cause. Their task was helped when, in 1766, Pope Clement XIII (1758–69) refused to continue to recognize the Stuart succession, instead recognizing George III (1760–1820) as England's legitimate ruler. It now became easier for Catholics to convince others of their loyalty to the English monarchy. Elsewhere, too, the British expectation of Catholic disloyalty seemed to be changing, albeit in far-flung parts of their Empire. In 1774 the Quebec Act granted Canadian Catholics religious and civil rights. Such legislation gave the Irish Catholics something to aim towards.

It wasn't just the Catholic population that was affected by the penal laws. The legislation also impacted on the Presbyterian population's civil and religious freedoms. Although they could vote they could only hold public office if they took the 'Sacramental Test', which required them to attend services in the Anglican Church. In addition, their marriages were not recognized as legal which meant that their children could not inherit their father's property. As with the Catholic population, Presbyterians were compelled to pay a tithe towards the upkeep of the Established Church.

Again, as was the case with Catholics, much of the anti-Presbyterian legislation was not rigorously enforced. The 1719 Toleration Act permitted their services to be held openly. It also opened the way for meeting houses to be built. Yet it was clear that many within the Presbyterian community were unhappy with their lot. Between 1730 and 1770 over 50,000 Presbyterians emigrated to America; the first real influx to what would become Irish America.

The origins of Irish Nationalism

The dissatisfaction felt by some in the Ascendancy with the amount of power they held has already been noted. The year 1698 witnessed the first shots in a struggle for legislative supremacy between the Irish and English parliaments that lasted for most of the eighteenth century and was only ended with the passage of the Act of Union in 1800.

In 1697 Westminster had threatened to place a ban on the export from Ireland of woollen cloth (the ban was finally enforced in 1699). In response William Molyneux published *The Case of Ireland's being Bound by Acts of Parliament in England Stated*. In this pithily titled tract he argued that Ireland should be governed by her own king and parliament. The pamphlet caused such an outcry that tradition suggests it was ordered to be burned by the hangman. The dispute was deepened in 1720 with the passage through Westminster of the inflammatory Declaratory Act (see above).

Within a few decades this nascent Irish nationalism had found a new hero in the shape of the Dean of St Patrick's Cathedral,

Jonathan Swift. Swift is perhaps better known to us as the author of *A Tale of a Tub*, *Gulliver's Travels* and other notable works of satire, such as *A Modest Proposal*. In the latter volume he 'suggested' that the Irish unburden themselves of their numerous children and break the cycle of poverty as well by selling them to the rich as food! In 1724 Swift re-echoed Molyneux's demand in his famous *Drapier's Letters*. In these he argued that 'government without the consent of the governed is the very definition of slavery'. He went on to remind them that 'by the laws of God, of nature, of nations and of your own country, you are and ought to be as free a people as your brethren in England'.

The demand for reforms which would at least allow the Protestant middle classes to take up seats in parliament continued and intensified in the second half of the eighteenth century. Within parliament itself the cause was taken up by a small group of MPs (usually no more than 50 strong) who became known as 'Patriots'. This group included such men as Henry Flood, MP for Kilkenny, and Lord Charlemont. Outside parliament Edmund Burke was a supporter of the Patriot cause and the grouping also had the backing of the Whig Party in Westminster. However they did not have the support of most Irish MPs who were content with the *status quo*. Indeed so poor were the prospects for reform that in 1775 Henry Flood took up a government position and was replaced as Patriot leader by Henry Grattan. In the context of parochial Irish politics this was a seismic enough event, but across the Atlantic Ocean other changes were taking place that would have an even greater impact on Ireland.

The American War of Independence

The events unfolding in the 13 American colonies were watched with great interest in Ireland, since many in the Patriot camp saw a similarity in the political positions of the two colonies. Yet the Patriot view that the American Revolution was a positive development was perhaps still a minority one and towards the end of 1775 the Irish parliament voted to send 4,000 troops to help the British fight the colonists. Perhaps its decision was based on the fear that if Britain lost the colonies it would seek to make up the lost revenues with increased Irish taxation.

Many in Ireland felt that the country had been left exposed defensively with the departure of so many troops. Their sense of fear increased markedly in 1778 when Spain and France demonstrated their support for the American cause by declaring war on Britain. With the spectre of invasion raised and with no more troops available, Protestants began to form themselves into armed groups of Volunteers. It is estimated that by the close of the year about 40,000 had enrolled in the new movement.

Because of the penal legislation's ban on Catholics bearing arms, members of the majority population were not able to join the Volunteers. For some Catholics this was a matter of regret, but others viewed the group with some degree of suspicion. In any case at such a time of tension it was felt appropriate to remind the king of his Catholic subjects' loyalty and so an address to this effect was made to George III. It was clearly a worthwhile venture; the London government responded in 1778 and again in 1782 by relaxing many of the penal laws. In this way – the British reasoned – the Catholics' loyalty at a time of crisis could be ensured.

The Catholic question was also a thorny one for the Volunteers. Initially there was suspicion of Catholic support but over time the views of some of the senior Volunteers modified; they came to realize that for their campaign to be successful force of numbers was vital and since the majority of the population were Catholic the movement began to advocate the removal of religious restrictions.

Free trade

Apart from their security role the Volunteers also took a keen interest in contemporary political developments. It comes as little surprise, therefore, that they began to express their opposition to the limits that Westminster had placed on Irish exports as a result of the American War. They began to press for the removal of such restrictions, seeing them as little more than legislative manifestations of the jealousies and insecurities of English manufacturers.

The campaign for 'free trade', as it became known, caught the public imagination and before long many were advocating the need to buy Irish goods as a way of showing their opposition. The Volunteers took to the streets of Dublin in an effort to show the government the depth of their opposition. Just in case the executive remained in any doubt about their position, a November 1779 rally in front of the Irish parliament included a cannon with the epitaph 'Free trade or this' hanging beneath its barrel!

In the context of a difficult international situation the British government did not need any additional problems with Ireland and so in 1780 many of the restrictions on Irish trade were removed. The Volunteers were cock-a-hoop; they were confirmed in their belief in the power of their influence as a pressure group. They decided, therefore, to use this influence to push for other reforms. The chosen area this time was legislative independence.

In search of legislative independence

The Volunteers – along with Patriot leaders such as Grattan – argued that the continued existence of Poynings' Law and the Declaratory Act would allow Westminster to reintroduce measures restricting Irish trade whenever it saw fit. Not surprisingly the issue raised political temperatures throughout the land. Outside parliament many were in favour of the removal of these restrictions; however, within parliament, opinion remained more circumspect. There, many MPs resented the growing influence of the Volunteer movement and feared the implications of a removal of the existing legislative restrictions on the potential power of the Catholic majority.

In early 1782 the Volunteers organized a huge convention in Dungannon to press home their demands. A series of declarations was passed which Grattan agreed to place before the Irish parliament. However, before he had the opportunity to do so, the Tory government in London fell and was replaced by a Whig ministry. Given that the Whigs were supporters of the Patriots they quickly acceded to their allies' demands and provided the Irish parliament with legislative independence.

Grattan summed up the import of the moment in a passionate and oft-quoted speech delivered in the Commons Chamber of the Irish parliament. 'I found Ireland on her knees', he proclaimed, 'I watched over her with eternal solicitude; I have traced her progress from injuries to arms and from arms to liberty.' Indeed it must have seemed like the dawning of a brave new world.

A year later the British government copperfastened the changes of 1782 by passing the Renunciation Act. As its name suggests this renounced forever Westminster's right to make laws for Ireland. However, while its passage might have had some significance in terms of the constitutional position of the Irish parliament, its genesis had more to do with a somewhat petulant attempt by Henry Flood to regain the adulation of the Patriots' supporters currently being enjoyed by Grattan.

Grattan's parliament: independence achieved?

So what had changed? In many ways not an awful lot. The repeal of the Declaratory Act and the changes made to Poynings' Law meant that London could no longer suppress or alter Irish bills. Yet the chief ministers of the government in Dublin remained appointed by and answerable to London and the Irish parliament was as corrupt as ever. That said, in the aftermath of the 1782 settlement the government began to appoint Irishmen to some of the most senior positions in the administration as a way of helping them to control the newly independent parliament. The truth remained, however, that for real change to take place parliament itself would have to be reformed.

The Volunteers were not slow in stepping up for the task. They began to urge the reform of various aspects of the Irish parliamentary system – particularly its system of elections with its 'pocket' and 'rotten' boroughs ('pocket boroughs' were boroughs within large estates that returned the members that the landlord wanted, while 'rotten' boroughs returned MPs for areas where there were no inhabitants). The Volunteers also called for the extension of the franchise, albeit still limited to those of the Protestant faith.

A second Volunteer convention was held in Dublin in November 1783. At this meeting a detailed reform plan was drawn up and was then presented to parliament. Unsurprisingly the Irish House of Commons rejected the plan. Too many of the MPs had too much to lose from a change to the *status quo*. In any case they were not prepared to be dictated to by an extra-parliamentary force such as the Volunteers. Likewise the Volunteer leadership was not prepared to act against parliament. Having received such a slap in the face after having had so much influence, the Volunteers' influence waned rapidly. Within a short period the group had lost its aristocratic control and had become a much more populist movement.

Pitt the Younger

In 1784 William Pitt the Younger became British Prime Minister. At only 24 years of age he was – and remains – the youngest ever holder of this office. Pitt was keen to ensure that Ireland did not go the same way as the 13 American colonies had done, however in 1788 it seemed as if that very fear might come to pass.

In that year King George III became insane. Whilst quick to sympathize with the monarch's predicament, both the British and Irish parliaments were equally quick to assert that they had the right to nominate a regent to rule in the king's place until his faculties returned. In addition both asserted their right to enumerate the powers that this regent should enjoy. It became clear that a serious conflict of interests might potentially arise if the Irish parliament – as seemed likely – decided to choose a different regent from the one appointed by Westminster.

Thankfully – at least from the British point of view – the king's recovery ended the so called Regency Crisis before it became too serious. However there was no hiding from the fact that a very serious crisis had narrowly been averted. The entire episode had demonstrated just how weak the link between Britain and Ireland now was. From this point on Pitt began to consider the possibility of a union between the two parliaments as the only way of avoiding such conflict in the future.

The French Revolution

Events elsewhere were to create a context that made such a conflict increasingly likely if not inevitable. The storming of the Bastille in July 1789 marked the beginning of the French Revolution. More than any other event this would prove to be an inspiration to Irish radicals.

The Irish public followed events in France with great interest. Two years after the fall of the Bastille the event was still being commemorated by Belfast's Volunteer Corps. Not surprisingly, the more radical members of the Irish body politic – including the Catholic middle class – were invigorated by the calls for *liberté, egalité, fraternité*.

However the French example did not win wholesale approval in Ireland. The Irish Ascendancy saw events in France as evidence of what might happen if parliament was not reformed. Similarly the Catholic aristocracy was shocked at the treatment meted out to the French monarchy and nobility, not to mention to the Church itself.

Apart from being able to read about it in the press, a number of highly influential books was published which helped inform the arguments in favour or against the revolution. In 1790 Edmund

Burke published his *Reflections on the Revolution in France*. A year later Thomas Paine issued his *The Rights of Man* (Part I) as a rejoinder to Burke's work.

Paine's book proved to be a major influence on Irish radicals. In particular it exercised a significant influence on a young Dublin lawyer, Theobald Wolfe Tone. Tone had reached the conclusion that the religious divisions existing within the country were fatally undermining the search for reform in Ireland. He wrote later of the need to 'forget past differences and replace the words "Protestant" and "Catholic" with the one name of "Irishman"'.

Therefore, in August 1791 Tone published (albeit anonymously) *An Argument on behalf of the Catholics of Ireland*. This pamphlet condemned the incompleteness of the 'changes' introduced in 1782, urged parliament's reform and advocated extending the franchise to Catholics.

Tone's arguments hit their target with Belfast's Presbyterians in particular and in October 1791 he, along with local radicals Henry Joy McCracken, Thomas Russell and Samuel Neilson, established the Society of United Irishmen. In its original form the Society sought the reform of the Irish parliament. It stated that such reform must include Irishmen of all religious persuasions if it was to be 'practicable, efficacious or just'. A few weeks later, under the influence of Napper Tandy, the new Society was also inaugurated in Dublin.

The Catholic Committee was also climbing on board the reform bandwagon. The increasing radicalism of its middle-class members had recently resulted in the more conservative members seceding from it, thus increasing its militancy. These members had been equally impressed with Tone's arguments and so appointed him as their Secretary in early 1792. This created an important link between the two organizations, which was further strengthened when a number of Catholic Committee luminaries joined the United Irish Society.

Further reform

All this radicalism had a negative impact on the most senior members of the Irish administration. They feared that the British government would grant further reform – reform that they simply didn't want – if faced with a combination of

Catholic and Radical pressure, particularly at a time when war with France was on the cards. They weren't that far off the mark; in 1792 and again in 1793 Pitt's administration forced through two important Relief Acts, which granted Catholics the right to serve in the army and vote (although not the right to sit in parliament), hold government jobs or serve on the bench.

Pitt hoped that such concessions would prevent the emergence of a full-blown Catholic–Radical alliance. He also hoped that this would be the end of the matter and so the government also passed a Convention Act. This piece of legislation banned representative bodies – such as the Volunteers – being set up to campaign for further changes to the law.

War with France

Revolutionary France's declaration of war on Britain in February 1793 transformed the political situation completely. In particular, organizations that had shown sympathy with revolutionary views – such as the United Irishmen – were automatically highly suspect. It came as no great surprise, therefore, when in 1795 the Dublin Society of United Irishmen was suppressed. Tone meanwhile was allowed to go to America.

The United Irish Society was swiftly reconstituted, this time as an underground revolutionary movement. However, although strenuous efforts were made to ensure that its deliberations remained secret, the Society was riddled with spies who kept the government fully informed about what was going on.

Initially it appeared as if the Society might not be needed to press for reform as for a short time it seemed as if such reform was going to be granted. In January 1795 Earl Fitzwilliam arrived in Ireland as Lord Lieutenant. Fitzwilliam had previously made it clear that he was in favour of reform and proved his *bona fides* by dismissing some of the most reactionary members of the Dublin administration. However, within seven weeks Fitzwilliam was gone, recalled by Pitt under pressure from the same Irish conservatives that he had so recently dismissed.

Catholic and Radical hopes had been raised high and then cruelly dashed again. It appeared clear to them that no further reform was going to be granted voluntarily. Any further change would only come at the point of a gun.

Countdown to revolution

The United Irishmen now set about preparing themselves for a revolution. Links were made with other groups, in particular the Defenders. This group had emerged in Ulster as a riposte to the Protestant Peep o' Day Boys. Both movements specialized in terrorizing members of the opposite religion, usually as a result of competition over land. Their most infamous encounter came in the 1795 Battle of the Diamond near Loughgall, Co. Armagh, which resulted in the Peep o' Day Boys reconstituting themselves as the Orange Society (later Order). Its aim was 'to defend the king and his heirs as long as they shall maintain the Protestant ascendancy'.

As a consequence of these developments many Catholics were driven out of Ulster and as a result Catholic membership of the United Irishmen grew, particularly from the ranks of Defenders who saw it as a vehicle for addressing their particular concerns. While this certainly increased the numbers in the movement, it also introduced an unfortunate sectarian context to it, which would make a revolution based on religious unity that much harder to achieve.

From his exile in America Tone travelled to revolutionary France. There he found a welcome for his idea for a French invasion of Ireland and in December 1796 a fleet carrying over 14,000 troops set sail from Brest for Ireland. However inclement weather conditions meant that only a portion of the fleet arrived off the coast of Co. Cork and the same conditions prevented these ships from landing their cargo of troops. After waiting around for better conditions for a few days, the French fleet was forced to turn for home. The best chance – because of the element of surprise – for revolutionary success had come and gone.

Not surprisingly the realization of just how close the French had come to invading Ireland gave the government a hefty jolt. Before the attempted landing it had already been taking action – passing laws forbidding the importation and distribution of guns and ammunition; allowing magistrates draconian powers in their efforts to maintain law and order; establishing a militia and a yeomanry to support the already stretched army and suspending *Habeas Corpus*. However, in light of recent events, the response became more uncompromising still.

The decision was taken to disarm the United Irishmen so that they would be of no use to a French force if one ever did arrive.

Ulster was seen as being the most seditious province and it was there in 1797 that General Lake's army first searched for weapons and then engaged in a campaign of terror in an effort to annihilate the revolutionary movement. The campaign proved successful in that many members of the United Irishmen ended their involvement with the movement; now there remained only a dedicated core.

The 1798 Rising

The action taken by the government in Ulster was extremely effective and in light of its likely impact if it was extended elsewhere in the island, the revolution was pushed forward to May 1798 even though there was no guarantee of further French assistance. Of course the government's spy network had kept it informed of developments and in March 1798 many of the Society's leading members were arrested. One of the most senior figures to escape, Lord Edward FitzGerald, was captured just days before the revolution began, being fatally wounded in the process.

FitzGerald, a son of the Duke of Leinster, might seem at first glance to be an odd bedfellow for such a motley crew of revolutionaries. Born in 1763 he fought for the British during the American War of Independence and enjoyed several other adventures in the North Americas including sailing down the Mississippi River. On his return to Ireland, via a spell in revolutionary France, he became closely identified with the Patriot cause and demonstrated his green credentials by wearing a cravat of that colour and refusing to burn English coal. Ironically his resting place – St Werburgh's Church in Dublin – also holds the grave of the man who shot and arrested him, Major Henry Sirr.

The revolution that broke out on 23 May 1798 was – not surprisingly – not the nationwide experience once hoped for. Without the input of the most prominent leaders, plans to launch an attack on the administration's strongholds were cancelled. Instead a series of mini rebellions broke out in different parts of the country. All but two of them – those in the north and in Wexford – were easily dealt with.

In the end the risings in Antrim and Down were put down without any great difficulty after engagements in Antrim and Ballinahinch. At one stage Ulster had been the most radical part of the country but the actions of General Lake in 1797 coupled with increasing sectarian tensions and fears of the type of rule to which they would be subjected by the French had significantly reduced the temperature of revolution.

However it is the rebellion in Wexford that has gained most notoriety, even if in its character it was more a reaction to local pressures than a true interpretation of the original United Irish blueprint. After early successes the rebels were routed at Vinegar Hill near Enniscorthy. The rising's notoriety came from the previous massacre at Oulart of Viscount Kingsborough's militiamen and yeomanry and of over 100, mostly protestant, civilians at Scullabogue (given the massive propaganda value, numbers here vary depending on the account read). These atrocities had, in turn, been encouraged by the earlier actions of government forces in search of weapons and the impact of the ever-prevalent misinformed propaganda, be it deliberate or otherwise. The events at Oulart and Scullabogue in their turn also informed the harsh measures implemented by the government forces after the rising had ended.

The French forces turned up after the main event. An expedition landed in Co. Mayo in August 1798 but after initial success at Castlebar surrendered at Ballinamuck in September. At the end of the same month another French fleet was intercepted by the British Navy and was escorted into Lough Swilly. On board one of the vessels, the *Hoche*, was a certain Theobald Wolfe Tone.

figure 3 The events of 1798.

After his arrest Tone was sent to Dublin where – because he was to be denied a soldier's death – he died by his own hand albeit more painfully than strictly necessary. Having cut his windpipe rather than his jugular vein he lingered for a number of days, informing the surgeon attending him, 'I find I am but a bad anatomist'. In many ways the mess Tone made of his suicide provides a useful metaphor for the defeat of his political ambitions. He had failed spectacularly in his attempts to forge a union of Catholic, Protestant and Dissenter (with a bit of help from Revolutionary France) that would wrest Ireland away from British control and establish an independent republic.

The Act of Union

Tone might have failed, but Britain's Prime Minister, Pitt the Younger, wasn't prepared to take any more chances with Ireland, given the fragile context of European politics. Mindful perhaps of the adage 'keep your friends close but your enemies closer', Pitt decided that Ireland would be less wilful and less of a security nightmare if ruled directly from Westminster.

As we have already seen, Pitt had been in favour of a union between Ireland and Britain since the Regency Crisis had revealed the ambiguities of the 1782 settlement. In truth there was never any genuine likelihood of the Irish parliament going its own way, but the events of the 1790s had confirmed to him just how vulnerable Britain was with a continuation of the current constitutional arrangement. His problem had always been how to get support for his ideas from within Ireland. The 1798 rebellion provided him with the persuasion that he needed.

Pitt believed that for a union to be successful it would have to be supported by as great a number of the population of Ireland as possible. Of course in the case of Ireland this meant the Catholics. To make this possible Pitt decided that an Act of Union would have to be followed by a law giving Catholics the right to sit in parliament. Providing them with this concession within the context of a much larger United Kingdom context would reduce the danger to continued Protestant control and thus reduce their fears.

While there was support for a union from among the aristocracy, the idea was vehemently opposed by the Patriots and some of the individuals whose wealth and influence was guaranteed by the continued existence of a parliament in Dublin. These included office-holders such as John Foster,

Speaker of the Commons, and the large landowners who controlled pocket boroughs. Members of the business classes argued that the Irish economy would be fatally undermined by untrammelled competition from the larger island while those in the legal profession feared the reduction in their workload if the Dublin parliament was lost. Interestingly enough, union was also opposed by the Orange Society – probably because of the prospects of Catholic emancipation – and by a group of Catholic lawyers including the then unknown Daniel O'Connell (see below).

Pitt began to construct a coalition of support for his plans. In this he was assisted by the sterling efforts of the Chief Secretary, Viscount Castlereagh. The prospect of full emancipation was sufficient to ensure public support from the Catholic hierarchy while Presbyterians were promised an increase in the *Regium Donum*, an annual grant that had been initiated by Charles II. Meanwhile to those in the business classes, the prospect of increased investment and greater wealth was held out.

The measure was first introduced into the Irish Commons in January 1799. However it was defeated by 111 votes to 106. Pitt was not perturbed and now set about ensuring victory using all possible methods. Against those within the government an early form of collective responsibility was employed, to the extent that Sir John Parnell, Chancellor of the Exchequer was dismissed for his continued opposition.

For the remainder, liberal amounts of persuasion or compensation were employed, both financial and in terms of ennoblement. All told it is believed £1.25 million was spent by Pitt's administration. Ireland's independence, William Drennan ruefully observed, had been 'Lost! By the chosen children sold, And conquered – not by steel but gold.' While Young Irelander (see Chapter 4) John O'Hagan later added that the Union was passed 'By perjury and fraud; By slaves who sold their land for gold as Judas sold his God.' That said, the government's approach – although it might appear mercenary to a twenty-first century audience – was common enough practice in eighteenth-century political circles.

In February 1800 the measure came before the Irish parliament again. This time, despite the appearance within the ranks of opposition of the legendary Henry Grattan, replete in Volunteer uniform, the government had a majority of 43. It was a tense occasion; during the debate Grattan and another MP, Isaac

Corry, became involved in so heated an argument that they repaired outside and engaged in a duel with the latter ending up with a wound to his arm.

The Act of Union came into effect on 1 January 1801. Under its terms 100 MPs and 32 Lords (including four Anglican bishops) would represent Ireland's interests in the Westminster parliament. The government of Ireland would continue to be carried out by a Lord Lieutenant and his staff, particularly the Chief Secretary. Anglicanism would remain the official religion of the kingdom while there would be free trade between the two islands apart from some minor, temporary exclusions. In addition Ireland was to be responsible for providing the funding for just under 12 per cent of the United Kingdom's expenditure.

After centuries of existence the Irish parliament had voted itself out of existence. Just how the island would fare under the new dispensation remained to be seen. Whether or not the Westminster parliament would have the understanding of Irish affairs necessary to ensure good government would be a moot point. In the final analysis bad government by a parliament of Irishmen based in Dublin might be infinitely preferable to uninformed government overseen by a parliament dominated by English, Welsh and Scottish MPs.

04 nationalism and unionism

This chapter will cover:
- the struggle for emancipation
- repeal of the Union
- the Great Famine
- the Fenians
- Home Rule
- the 'land war'
- the fall of Parnell.

Emmet's rebellion

If Britain hoped that the Act of Union would herald a long period of stability in its relationship with Ireland it was to be sorely disappointed. The dying kicks of the United Irish movement were felt in Robert Emmet's abortive 1803 rebellion. The rebellion was risible both in its planning and in its execution, but it is remembered principally for the speech made by Emmet at his trial, an oration that some elements of republicanism still hold dear today: 'When my country takes her place among the nations of the earth, then, and only then, let my epitaph be written.' It was a challenge that would be taken up by many others over the course of the next two centuries.

The struggle for emancipation

As already mentioned, it had been Pitt's intention to introduce a measure for Catholic emancipation hard on the heels of the Act of Union. In the event the obdurate opposition of King George III made this impossible. In his view, agreeing to such a measure would be tantamount to breaking the oath to preserve the Protestant religion within his kingdom that he had sworn at his coronation. Many supported George in his opposition. In particular numerous members of the Irish Ascendancy still feared – in spite of the Union – that their position would come under threat if the Catholic majority in Ireland obtained full political freedoms.

Equally, many others were supporters of emancipation. They saw it as a way of ensuring Catholic loyalty to the new political dispensation. Chief among these were some senior Ascendancy figures, most of Ireland's 100 MPs and a fair smattering of Tories and, in particular, Whigs. However the administration was not planning to grant something for nothing. In return for this concession it wanted the British government to have a say over who was appointed to vacant Catholic bishoprics within the United Kingdom.

In 1813 a Bill was placed before parliament, which was drawn up along the lines outlined above. The Irish Catholics' response to it was divided, mainly because of the issue of the veto over episcopal appointments. Most strident amongst the voices opposing the measure was that of Daniel O'Connell, whom we met previously as a vehement opponent of the Act of Union. The measure was dropped and while further emancipation Bills were put forward in 1819 and again in 1821 no significant progress was made.

O'Connell was an interesting figure. In 1815 his name rose to prominence for reasons other than the political when he killed a certain John D'Esterre in a duel. It seems that O'Connell had refused to pay a toll to cross a bridge that was owned by D'Esterre, and was challenged to fight as a result. That said, other accounts suggest that O'Connell had severely criticized the Dublin Corporation of which D'Esterre was a member. After the duel, O'Connell vowed that he would never fight anyone again. Such antipathy to bloodshed fits in well with his later attitude to violence (see below). O'Connell is once reputed to have stated that the freedom of Ireland was not worth the spilling of one drop of blood.

The Catholic Association

The emancipation question was revived in 1823 when O'Connell – with the support of Richard Lalor Shiel – established the Catholic Association as a vehicle for a renewed emancipation campaign. Initially its high membership charge (one guinea) ensured that the membership was restricted and thus its influence limited. This changed completely in 1824 when O'Connell established an associate category of membership at a fee of just one shilling per annum. At once membership exploded and the movement rapidly organized across the island. Its spread and influence were materially assisted by the Catholic clergy. Out of nothing O'Connell had created a pressure group, which included the vast majority of the Irish population.

The government responded to this development by banning the Association and although it was soon relaunched as the New Catholic Association it seemed to have lost some of its initial drive. This energy was rediscovered, however, when a General Election was called in 1826.

The election resulted in a number of pro-emancipation candidates being returned for Irish constituencies. The government elected in London was also relatively sympathetic to the Catholic cause and repealed the Test Act (see Chapter 3) in 1828. O'Connell was hopeful that further concessions would follow, but soon after, the administration fell to be replaced by one led by the Duke of Wellington as Prime Minister and Sir Robert Peel as Home Secretary. Both men were hostile to emancipation; indeed the Home Secretary's earlier opposition to the emancipation movement when he had served as Chief Secretary in Ireland had led O'Connell to christen him 'Orange Peel'.

O'Connell's election

Faced with such obduracy the Catholic Association cranked up its campaign once more. Meetings were held across Ireland in support of the campaign, but the real challenge to the government materialized in Co. Clare where a by-election was scheduled to take place. Although the local candidate was pro-emancipation, the Association wanted to lay down a challenge to the administration. It therefore nominated O'Connell as its candidate. Although a Catholic could not sit in parliament, a Catholic candidacy was not forbidden by the legislation. O'Connell was successful by a considerable margin – 2,057 votes to 982.

The question now was how the government would react. It was clear that the Catholic masses had been politically energized by the emancipation campaign and Wellington and Peel realized that there was a real chance of rebellion breaking out if the situation was not handled appropriately. Reluctantly, therefore, they agreed to introduce a measure for Catholic relief, which reached the statute book as the 1829 Emancipation Act. This removed the anti-Catholic oaths that MPs and other office-holders were expected to take, replacing them with an uncontentious Oath of Allegiance. O'Connell finally entered the House of Commons in 1830, having been forced to stand for election for the same seat again.

The reforms of the 1830s

O'Connell's success earned him the title of 'Great Liberator' but it is interesting to consider just who had been liberated. At the same time as it passed the Emancipation Act the government emasculated the potential power of the Catholic electorate in Ireland by raising the qualification for voting from 40 shillings (£2) to £10. Most of those who had previously held the vote lost it and for the overwhelming majority of the poor people of Ireland life remained as harsh as ever it had been. Emancipation might have removed a long-standing grievance of the Catholic population, but in the short term it did little or nothing materially for the majority of those who had campaigned for it.

Having sorted out the emancipation issue, O'Connell now turned his attention to the small matter of the repeal of the Act of Union. O'Connell argued that Ireland would best be ruled by Irishmen in a parliament based in Dublin. Yet, unlike Tone,

O'Connell was not a republican and did not seek separation; rather he envisaged the re-establishment of a local parliament that would look after Ireland's internal affairs. At the same time Ireland would remain part of the United Kingdom.

However repeal proved to be a no-goer in the context of the Westminster parliament of the 1830s and O'Connell had to content himself in pushing for a series of lesser – though no less significant – reforms. Chief among these was the abolition of the tithe, the tax that all Irish landholders, irrespective of religion, had to pay for the upkeep of the established church. Sustained opposition to continuing to pay the tax emerged in 1830 and soon developed into widespread and severe agrarian unrest. The government countered this with a draconian Coercion Act but also reduced the amount of tithe in 1838 and – rather subtly if somewhat disingenuously – included it within the rent paid for land.

The government introduced reforms in a number of other areas during the same decade. To oversee improvements to the educational system a Commission on National Education was established. This established a successful compulsory but free education system throughout the island, although it was not quite as non-denominational as the legislators had intended. It did, however, have a major impact on the continued prevalence of the Irish language as all lessons were delivered in English.

Likewise reforms were needed to counter the widespread problem of poverty. A huge percentage of the population lived at subsistence level, kept going solely by the annual potato harvest. As the population continued to increase, the pressure on the available land was reaching saturation point. At the same time, unemployment was increasing in urban areas as Irish industry found it impossible to cope with the competition from British industries, newly mechanized by the inventions of the industrial revolution.

Westminster's solution to this social and economic crisis was the introduction of a Poor Law in 1838. This established 130 unions across the country controlled by Boards of Guardians elected locally by landlords and prosperous farmers. These bodies used the proceeds of a property-based tax known as the 'Poor Rate' to build workhouses and provide for the local underprivileged. So that workhouses would not be seen as an easy option, conditions within were kept less than comfortable. Despite this – and in spite of a natural resistance within the population to avail of what was described as a 'poor man's gaol'

– 40,000 places were filled by 1845, close to half the number available.

Political reform had been a key demand of the eighteenth-century Patriots and it remained a key aim of O'Connell and his supporters in the nineteenth century. The 1830s saw a number of changes in the political arena which would have pleased both groups to some extent. The 1832 Reform Act increased the number of Irish MPs to 105 and removed the right of the majority of town corporations to elect MPs. Town government itself was overhauled with many existing corporations abolished. Such reforms enabled O'Connell to stand successfully for the Lord Mayorship of Dublin in 1841. Thus he became the first Catholic to hold the position since the brief reign of the Catholic James II. Catholics also found themselves obtaining appointments to other public positions, situations that had been closed to them since the introduction of the penal legislation in the aftermath of the War of the Three Kings.

Repeal of the Union

The Whigs fell from power in 1841 to be replaced by the Tories who were traditionally less amenable to reform in Ireland. O'Connell was of the opinion that there was a significant amount of reform still necessary but realized that the achievement of this was now highly unlikely. For this reason, therefore, O'Connell decided that he would relaunch his campaign for repeal of the Union.

Remembering how effective the Catholic Association had been in helping to achieve emancipation, O'Connell began by setting up a Repeal Association. Initially the new movement enjoyed only limited support: many middle-class Catholics were happy with what had already been achieved whilst Protestants feared that a parliament in Dublin would result in a Catholic ascendancy. The first stirrings of Ulster as a special case were also murmured, her economic development since Union being cited as a reason to maintain the *status quo*.

O'Connell was undeterred, however, and continued with his efforts to build up support for the movement. To this end he was materially assisted by the establishment of the *Nation* newspaper by Charles Gavan Duffy. Duffy, along with his friends John Blake Dillon and Thomas Davis – they became known as Young Irelanders – was of the opinion that for O'Connell's campaign to succeed, appropriate propaganda was essential. Published under the banner of 'Educate that you may be free', this weekly newspaper, with its articles about the 'glorious' past and its vision for the future, did much to educate public opinion within Ireland and to increase support for the repeal campaign.

Initially the government paid little or no attention to this new movement. This changed in 1843, however, when the repeal campaign really began to gather steam. The main reason for its change in fortunes was the success of a new tactic recently introduced by O'Connell – the mass rally. These were held across Ireland in locations – such as Tara – designed to create stirring associations with significant romantic episodes in Irish history. This early form of pressure group activity attracted crowds as big as 1 million – if contemporary accounts are to be believed!

Size wasn't everything, however, and the British government – supported by the majority of opinion within parliament – remained unmoved by O'Connell's arguments. However, it was becoming somewhat uneasy about the increasingly violent tone being adopted by O'Connell, even though he had undertaken never to use coercion to achieve his aims. For this reason a monster meeting planned for Clontarf in October 1843 was banned by the administration. Having pledged so publicly not to fight, O'Connell had little option but to back down.

The government wanted more, however, and O'Connell and other prominent repealers were arrested. They were charged with conspiracy to overthrow the government, tried and found guilty. Although the convictions were overturned on appeal, the lessons of this episode were not lost on O'Connell. While he remained firmly wedded to the achievement of repeal, he decided that he would wait and work with the Whig Party – once they were back in government – towards reform rather than begin another campaign.

O'Connell had stuck resolutely to his belief in the primacy of politics, even when peaceful protests seemed to achieve little. Others were not so convinced however, particularly the leading members of the Young Ireland movement. Initially strong supporters of O'Connell, they were appalled by his change of policy. The final break between the two groups resulted from the demand – made by O'Connell in 1846 – that the movement would never subscribe to the use of force. The Young Irelanders could not agree to rule out this possibility and as a result the repeal movement was split asunder.

O'Connell's campaign ultimately petered out against the horrific backdrop of the Great Irish Famine of 1845–9 (see below). During those hellish years people had more important things than national self-determination to worry about – survival for instance. The 'Liberator' himself died in 1847 on his way to Rome, prematurely worn out by his Herculean efforts on Ireland's behalf. His remains (minus his heart which still resides in the Irish College, Rome) were interred in Dublin's Glasnevin Cemetery. Today a massive round tower stands sentinel over the 'Liberator's' grave, dwarfing all other headstones. A monument perhaps intended to honour O'Connell as the greatest of all Irishmen.

The Great Famine

By the start of the 1840s there were well over 8 million people living in Ireland. A significant proportion of this number lived off the land but as the population had continued to increase the slivers of land available had been continually subdivided amongst families to the extent that many people were living off slivers of land that were simply not sufficient to guarantee health and well-being. In addition to these there were many thousands of others who possessed no land at all.

For all of these people the potato was their earthly salvation. Its relatively high yield meant that it could supply the dietary needs of a significant number of people, even if grown on relatively small plots. For as long as the potato crop remained healthy the population would be fine; if it wasn't then real problems would emerge. This was what happened in 1845.

In the summer of that year a new fungal disease *phytophthora infestans* – better known to us as potato blight – attacked the Irish potato crop, destroying about a third of it. There had been many such partial failures already in the course of the nineteenth century and so there was not undue worry at this development. In any case Peel made £100,000 worth of Indian maize available to the Relief Committees that sprang up across the country. While few ate it for its gourmet qualities, it did keep famine at bay. At the same time public work schemes were initiated to provide some employment for the poor and needy.

Unfortunately the disease returned with interest in 1846 and the whole crop was destroyed. By this stage Peel's government had fallen, to be replaced by a Whig administration headed by Lord John Russell. Russell's government was a proponent of the *laissez-faire* economic theory. This meant that it believed governments should not interfere in the area of economics. For this reason it refused to buy food to help the Irish in the way that Peel had done. Instead the administration argued that whatever food was required could be sourced locally. Unfortunately, in this theory it was wrong.

The starving population was forced to turn to public work schemes and to the workhouses for survival. Regrettably, the resulting overcrowding in the latter made the spread of disease all the more likely and many succumbed to its effects. Indeed, more people died of such diseases than died of starvation. At the same time some help was forthcoming from private charity, with soup kitchens being established and funding being made available by groups such as the Quakers. Many Irish landlords also did their utmost to assist their tenants, but there remained many more who did little or nothing to provide relief.

Emigration

In 1847 the government realized that *laissez-faire* was not working and so it, too, opened soup kitchens. The number of Poor Law Unions was also increased as a way of assisting the population and for many these provided some degree of relief. However for many others the only solution was seen to be emigration.

The vast majority of those who fled the country did so in vessels that were so overcrowded and disease-ridden that they became known as 'coffin ships'. Despite the obvious dangers of long voyages to places such as North America, hundreds of thousands of people set sail. With them they brought not an understanding of the limitations of the prevalent economic theories, but a burning belief that the landlords and the British government had abandoned them.

A census of the population taken in 1851 revealed that there were 2 million fewer people living in Ireland than there had been in 1845. However this was not the only change wrought by the events of the late 1840s. The reluctance of farmers to subdivide their land as in the past meant that those without land had to emigrate. Likewise the emergence of new landowners in place of the old landlords ruined by the famine brought further change. They removed many of the smallholders from their land as a way of creating bigger farms and thus greater profits. Again these now landless people had nowhere to go but abroad. Such changes, combined with a falling birth rate meant that the Irish population continued to decrease even after the famine had ended.

The 1848 Rebellion

As mentioned already the Young Irelander movement split from O'Connell over the question of whether or not force should be employed if necessary. Renaming themselves the Irish Confederation in 1847, the group came more and more under the influence of John Mitchel who had taken Davis' place on The *Nation* after the latter's death. Mitchel's language was much more revolutionary than his colleagues, advocating that tenants refuse to pay rent and fight for the establishment of an independent republic. He went even further and stated, 'Let the man among you who has no gun, sell his garment and buy one.' For his pains he was arrested in 1848 and transported to Van Diemen's Land, better known to us now as Tasmania.

The year of 1848 was one of revolution throughout Europe, and Ireland was no exception. Mitchel's treatment convinced many within the movement that actions would speak louder than words. Unfortunately for them the government's spy network had kept Dublin Castle fully informed of what was being planned and, deciding that attack was the best means of defence, the government closed down the *Nation* and arrested senior Confederation figures.

Although it was clearly going to be little more than tokenism, the Confederation went ahead with an event that could only be very loosely described as a rebellion. Indeed it was so ill conceived that it became known as the 'Battle of Widow McCormack's Cabbage Patch', named in honour of a brief affray within view of that same lady's residence in Co. Tipperary. Indeed the only point of note about the whole affair was that it marked the first widespread use of the green, white and orange Tricolour (the colours representing the two main traditions on the island bonded by peace) that would in the next century become the flag of an independent Ireland.

The 1848 Rebellion – along with most of its contemporaries throughout Europe – might have failed, however, it successfully revived the idea of physical force within Irish politics. This development was to cast a long and bloody shadow over Ireland's future political development.

The Fenians

Ireland didn't have long to wait before the next physical force movement came knocking on the door. This time the protagonists were the Fenians or more properly the Irish Republican Brotherhood (IRB). The movement was founded in 1858 – in both the United States and Ireland – by some of those who had been involved in the 1848 debacle, including a certain James Stephens. The latter had only escaped capture by the authorities in 1848 because his friends had persuaded them that he had died – they even buried a coffin filled with rocks to prove their point. The IRB believed that Britain would only concede independence to Ireland through physical force. That, of course, left just one course of action open to it.

The IRB was a secret society and to maintain the degree of secrecy that had been sadly lacking in earlier revolutionary movements it was organized into groups or circles. However laudable the aim, in its execution it was a disaster; some circles had many hundreds of members and so were laughably easy for Castle spies to infiltrate. Very little that the movement planned went unreported to the authorities.

Stephens was the IRB leader and under his direction the movement began to organize across the southern parts of Ireland. However, as the movement grew it began to attract the enmity of followers of constitutional nationalism and of the Catholic hierarchy. In particular the Archbishop of Dublin, Paul Cullen, was vehement in his opposition and was instrumental in having membership of the Fenians declared a mortal sin. Cullen wasn't the only episcopal opponent. One of his colleagues on the bench of bishops – David Moriarty of Kerry – is reputed to have gone so far as to declare that 'hell is not hot enough nor eternity long enough' to punish members of the movement. Strong sentiments indeed!

Stephens was very sure of his abilities as a leader but despite growing membership he seemed unable to actually start the promised rebellion. At the same time he was badly hampered by divisions within the American movement over which tactics to employ. The longer the delays went on, the more the movement began to disintegrate. Eventually Stephens was removed as leader by elements in the American movement and the rising – such as it was – took place in 1867. It was over in a matter of hours.

The failure of the Fenian insurrection – as with the 1848 shambles due to remarkably inept planning – relegated physical force politics to the lower divisions of Irish political options for nearly 50 years. In its place the constitutional push for some form of self-government was resurrected and given fresh impetus.

Gladstone and the Irish Question

Arguably the most significant outcome of the Fenian rising was that it focused the formidable attention of one of nineteenth-century Britain's greatest statesmen on conditions in Ireland. After 1867 the Liberal leader William Ewart Gladstone became convinced that Britain was doing Irish nationhood a grave injustice. Following his Party's victory in the 1868 General Election he announced 'My mission is to pacify Ireland'. Clearly he enjoyed a challenge!

This was a highly significant development. O'Connell's fruitless repeal crusade had proved that no political campaign in Ireland, no matter how popular, could force the British government to alter the determined course of its Irish policy. What was needed for Home Rule – as it would become known – to be granted would be the support of the British government. For decades such support had seemed highly unlikely, but now it appeared as if it might be forthcoming.

Gladstone's first steps were to disestablish the Church of Ireland and to attempt some reform of the country's chaotic land situation. With regard to the former, the Prime Minister had come to the conclusion that it was a nonsense that a church of less than 700,000 members should be the established faith in a land where nearly 90 per cent of the population were Catholics. In 1869, therefore, an Act of Parliament disestablished the Anglican Church in Ireland (as from 1871). At the same time long-standing government grants to the Catholic and Presbyterian Churches were also withdrawn.

Finding a solution to the land question was significantly more problematic. The vast majority of Irish farmers were known as 'tenants-at-will'. This meant that they could be evicted with little notice and no compensation even after a lifetime of toil on the land. Naturally this situation led to a great deal of insecurity within farming circles and many campaigned for a reassessment of this situation. Equally many did not. Many of Gladstone's own Party maintained a more *laissez-faire* attitude to interfering in the internal running of landed estates.

Gladstone's solution was the 1870 Land Act. While undoubtedly well-intentioned it nevertheless fell well short of granting the demands for fair rent, fixity of tenure and free sale (the three Fs). These had been the goal of Irish politicians and agrarian pressure groups such as the Tenant League since the immediate post-Famine period. Instead the Act simply provided for increased compensation for unjust evictions.

The 1870 Land Act proved to be nowhere near enough to eliminate the serious problems that existed within the Irish agricultural landholding system. However the industry happened to be enjoying a degree of prosperity at the time and so initially the legislation's weaknesses did not become apparent. Gladstone was content that he had 'pacified' Ireland and so his attention was refocused elsewhere.

The Home Rule movement emerges

Gladstone's sense of contentment was not widely shared within Ireland. Some began to consider – as O'Connell had done – that the most satisfactory solutions to Ireland's problems would be found by a parliament based in Dublin, not by a fitfully interested London administration. Thus the demand for some form of self-government or Home Rule – not heard of for a generation – again showed its face.

In Ireland it was a successful Protestant lawyer, Isaac Butt, who initially picked up the baton for Home Rule. He had previously come to national prominence through his defence of some of those charged with crimes in relation to the 1848 debacle. Earlier in his career Butt had been a supporter of the Union, however he had come to the conclusion – in light of the events of the Famine years – that Ireland would be better served by her own parliament.

He gave the nascent movement some structure by founding the Home Government Association (after 1873 the Home Rule League) in 1870. A motley collection of Protestants and Catholics, tenants and landowners, Conservatives and Liberals and even a few Fenians gave it their support.

An important development in terms of the movement's prospects for electoral success came in 1872 with the introduction of the secret ballot. This changed decades of electoral bullying by freeing up tenants from voting as their landlord wished. The reform undoubtedly benefited the new party and in the 1874 General Election 59 Home Rule MPs were returned to the Westminster parliament. The Party pledged to follow an independent line at Westminster, working with whichever party offered the best deal for Ireland. It seemed as if a real breakthrough had been made in the struggle to achieve Home Rule.

However things were not as straightforward as they might have seemed. Many of the new MPs only paid lip service to the ideals of the movement. Moreover the new Tory administration – headed by Benjamin Disraeli – was not minded to give Ireland further concessions. Most importantly Butt was too much of a gentleman and parliamentarian to make an effective impression on Westminster in these unpropitious circumstances. Each and every time matters relating to Ireland came before the Commons they were voted down by the majority of members. Time and time again, however, Butt would simply begin the same process all over again. That, of course, was when he was there. Often Butt was away because of work commitments – resulting from his need to keep on top of spiralling debts. This only served to provide a bad example to his followers – when the leader was absent many of the Party faithful didn't bother to turn up either.

Parnell

Eventually frustration boiled over within the Party even if it didn't reach the leader. A group of MPs decided that they would have to play fast and loose with Standing Orders (the rules of parliament) if they were ever to get the Commons to take notice of Ireland's problems. They decided to follow a policy of obstructionism, holding up the business of the Commons so that nothing got done. One of the earliest of the Home Rule MPs to obstruct the work of parliament was Belfast IRB man Joseph Biggar, but the real star of the campaign was the recently elected MP for Meath, Charles Stewart Parnell.

Parnell was a Wicklow landowner, another Protestant, with the (in Irish terms) slightly exotic parentage of an Irish father and an American mother from whom he had inherited a strong dislike of the English people. She was Delia Stewart, a daughter of the American naval hero, Commodore Charles Stewart who was himself the stepson of one of George Washington's bodyguards. Parnell had studied at Cambridge but had left that venerable institution under something of a cloud after being involved in a drunken altercation.

Although not renowned for his oratorical skills, Parnell did possess a remarkable degree of self-assurance, which served to attract people to him. Not many British MPs were attracted by the obstructionist policy Parnell and others adopted and yet it began to get the Home Rule issue noticed. It also got Parnell noticed within the Party and before long his influence was such that he had become leader in all but name. It also got him noticed by the Fenians who soon began co-operating with Parnell with regard to the re-emerging land question.

The Land League

As already mentioned, the period following Gladstone's first Land Act had been one of prosperity within the agricultural sector and this had effectively masked the legislation's inadequacies. However in the middle 1870s agricultural prices began to fall as a result of increased foreign competition and a reduction in demand from the rest of the UK. This, coupled with poor weather between 1877 and 1879, meant that farmers were close to destitution and unable to pay the inflated rents that had been introduced in the years of prosperity. If a farmer were evicted for failure to pay rent then he would not benefit from the compensation for unjust eviction included in the 1870 Land Act.

The developing crisis came to the attention of a certain Michael Davitt, a man whose approach to the land problem reputedly inspired Mahatma Gandhi several decades later. Davitt was originally a Fenian who had been convicted of arms trafficking and had spent seven years in Dartmoor Prison. He knew from at least vicarious experience the traumas being suffered by Irish farmers. His family had emigrated to northern England after having been evicted from their farm in 1850. There he had been employed as a child labourer, working from the age of nine up to 12 hours per day. He had been forced out of this 'career' when he lost his arm in an accident. Now able to return to education he got a job as a printer and from thence became involved in politics.

Davitt headed for Co. Mayo, his home county and one of the most affected areas. Once there he organized a protest against the unfair rents that were being charged. The demonstration was successful in that it persuaded the local landowner to reduce his rents and Davitt organized others. In June 1879 he invited Parnell to address a rally in the Co. Mayo town of Westport. Parnell agreed and at the meeting urged farmers to maintain 'a firm grip on your homesteads and lands'.

But why did Parnell, a member of the landowning class get involved in this issue? Quite simply he had come to the conclusion that land mattered more to ordinary people than politics and that if he could help solve their agrarian problems they would in turn provide the Home Rule movement with the public support that it required to get noticed. Therefore, when in October 1879 Davitt established the Land League as an engine to drive the farmers' campaign, Parnell accepted the position of President. Their co-operation was christened the 'New Departure'.

There was also, it must be admitted, a very sizeable Fenian influence within the organization. For a movement hitherto involved in only extra constitutional methods, their co-operation with Parnell might seem somewhat strange. Indeed as recently as 1876 the IRB leadership had condemned co-operation with representatives of constitutional nationalism. Suffice to say an element of the movement had decided that more progress towards independence, even independence itself, could be achieved by pursuing such a strategy.

The League aimed to achieve its objectives of reductions in rent and an end to evictions through peaceful protests. When attempting to prevent an eviction a mass demonstration was organized. Often these proved successful, but when they did not, provision was made for the victims while non-violent strategies were introduced to discourage anyone else from taking over the evictee's land. In particular, tenants were encouraged by Parnell to shun anyone who took over the land of an evictee. 'Boycotting' entered the English language following the success of this tactic of ostracization when used against a certain Captain Charles Boycott, a Co. Mayo land agent.

It will come as no great surprise to report that the government was greatly concerned at the Land League campaign. Gladstone – back in power since 1880 – responded by introducing two pieces of legislation: a Coercion Act to enable a crackdown on the growth in disorder, and a second Land Act, in 1881, which introduced mechanisms for establishing fair rents. This Land Act went some way to meeting the League's demands, however, like its 1870 predecessor it was still full of flaws. As a result, the League was divided over whether to accept it or not.

Parnell's solution was to try a few test cases to see if the mechanisms established worked. Such ambivalence did not impress Gladstone, and Parnell – along with other League leaders – was arrested, accused of attempting to prevent the Land Act from working, and placed in Kilmainham Gaol. The

League responded by calling for a rent strike in its No Rent Manifesto. The government responded by banning it for its troubles.

While in existence the League had been successful in keeping violence off the agenda, but with its influence gone, chaos resulted. Indeed Parnell had warned that without his moderating influence 'Captain Moonlight (a rather catchy euphemism for anarchy) would ride again'. Realizing that Parnell was the key to stability, the government agreed the Kilmainham Treaty with him in May 1882. This undertook to free any jailed League leaders and promised assistance to those who had fallen behind with their rent.

Peace was short-lived. Less than a week after the signing of the Treaty the Chief and Under Secretaries for Ireland were assassinated while walking in Dublin's Phoenix Park, close to their official residence. Later in the year Parnell used this opportunity to make a break with the Fenian-dominated Land League and establish a new movement, the Irish National League. Its primary aim was no longer land reform (although that remained a secondary objective) but the achievement of Home Rule for Ireland.

Home Rule?

The last time we encountered Parnell wearing his Home Rule hat he was acknowledged to be the most influential figure within the Party even though he was not its leader. He succeeded to the leadership in 1880 and instituted a restructuring of the Party throughout the country – through the offices of the National League – and a reinvigoration of it in parliament through the introduction of a party pledge. The reforms introduced paid off and in the aftermath of the 1885 General Election Parnell found himself the undisputed head of a disciplined 86-strong party in Westminster.

It was during that election campaign that Parnell made what is perhaps his most famous speech, one that adorns the statue of him that stands at the opposite end of O'Connell Street from that of the eponymous Liberator. Speaking in Cork, Parnell stated, 'No man has the right to fix the boundary to the march of a nation. No man has the right to say to his country, "Thus far shall you go and no further"'. It was a message that his audience was keen to hear, but what about the London administration?

Parnell's political career would ultimately prove to be an abject failure in many ways, but for a time he came closer than anyone before to achieving the Holy Grail of self-government for Ireland. That this was possible was due to the support of Gladstone who, in 1886, finally introduced a Home Rule Bill.

Success was not forthcoming, however, as the Bill fell in the House of Commons. A significant number of Gladstone's own Party – henceforth known as Liberal Unionists – agreed with the Conservative opposition that such a measure would be the first step in the disintegration of the British Empire. In Ireland, too, opposition was vociferous from certain quarters. Protestants feared that a Catholic-dominated parliament in Dublin would enact sectarian laws. Landlords feared that the same body would attempt to reverse centuries of Protestant land control.

However the opposition was strongest in the north-eastern corner of the island in the province of Ulster. Here the Protestant majority felt themselves to be inextricably linked to the British system and so were vehemently opposed to a Dublin parliament, which they feared would ruin the prosperity that had followed the successful industrialization of that region. In particular, industries such as linen, shipbuilding and engineering had flourished to the extent that Belfast had more in common with the industrialized towns of North-East England than it had with towns in other parts of Ireland. Unionists believed that the continuation of this prosperity was dependent upon the maintenance of existing links with Britain.

In 1886 this opposition coalesced to form the Unionist Party. It was also strengthened by support from the Conservative Party, which, in the person of Lord Randolph Churchill – father of Winston – told them, 'Ulster will fight and Ulster will be right!' The two parties joined forces and the Conservative Party became 'Conservative and Unionist' in both name and nature.

In the end the Bill's defeat meant that there was no need for fighting (although the issue did lead to rioting on the streets of Belfast). In the shadow of its defeat Gladstone's Party fractured and his administration collapsed. The Tories returned to power and remained there for the next six years. By the time the Liberal leader introduced a second Home Rule Bill in 1893 Parnell was dead, his career having been destroyed by a sex scandal.

Kitty O'Shea

In November 1890 Captain W. H. (Willie) O'Shea (an erstwhile member of the Home Rule Party) brought divorce proceedings against his wife Kitty. The petition named Parnell as co-respondent. Evidence suggests that O'Shea had long known about the dalliance – the two had been lovers since 1880 and Kitty O'Shea had borne Parnell at least two children – but had kept quiet in the hope of sharing in his wife's expected inheritance. When the inheritance came it did so in a manner that meant that O'Shea would enjoy none of it and at that point he sued for divorce. When the case came to court Parnell did not contest it and thus was presented in a very unfavourable light during the ensuing proceedings.

Immediately Ireland was split and with it the Home Rule Party. However, the main pressure on Parnell came from the Liberals. It is more than likely that Gladstone had also long known about the affair, but while it had been acceptable for as long as it had been a 'secret', it was a different matter now that it was public knowledge. Public opinion in Britain – particularly that which supported the Liberals – would not tolerate Gladstone working with Parnell in such circumstances.

Fearing a reduction in his own support, therefore, the Liberal leader urged Parnell's temporary resignation as Party Leader until the scandal had passed. Gladstone made it clear to the Irish Nationalists that they could have their leader or they could have another shot at self-government but as things stood they could not have both. Parnell received similar advice from Cecil Rhodes who sent him a rather terse telegram stating he should 'Resign – marry – return'.

In hindsight it would have been good advice to follow, however Parnell refused to stand aside, even temporarily. At a tense gathering held in Westminster's Committee Room 15, the majority of Parnell's Party abandoned him by walking out of the meeting, albeit after several days of acrimonious debate. An example of the height (or indeed depth) to which tensions were running is apparent from an exchange between Parnell and a senior party member, T. M. Healy, during the meeting. When Parnell challenged Gladstone's ultimatum with the question, 'Who is the leader of the Party?' Healy responded '[The question should instead be] who is the mistress of the Party?'

Parnell told the minority who remained after the walkout, 'Gentlemen, we have won today.' Of course this was spin *par excellence*. No one had won; certainly not Parnell and the real loser would be the campaign for Irish self-government.

Back home in Ireland Parnell was also roundly condemned, particularly by the Catholic bishops whose opinions held great sway. Parnell went on a publicity tour of Ireland to whip up support, but in three successive by-elections his candidates were defeated. Already in poor health, during this campaign he fell victim to a humble cold and died on 6 October 1891 at the age of 45. With him at the end was his wife, Katherine, whom he had married in June 1891. His burial in Dublin's Glasnevin Cemetery was witness by 200,000 people.

With Parnell's demise Ireland had lost its 'uncrowned king'. Without the leadership of the man described by Gladstone as 'the most remarkable man I ever met', the Home Rule Party was left bereft. Now bitterly divided, it took almost a decade to reunite – some contend that it never really recovered.

The second Home Rule Bill, 1893

Gladstone proved that his conversion to Irish self-government was not transitory when he introduced another Home Rule Bill in 1893. This time the Bill negotiated all its Commons stages successfully. However it was not so fortunate in the Upper Chamber, the House of Lords. The unelected Lords had a permanent Conservative majority that was implacably opposed to Irish self-government for the reasons outlined already. More importantly, at that time it enjoyed a permanent veto over all legislation. For a second time a Home Rule Bill was lost. Shortly after, Gladstone, now in his mid-80s, resigned as Liberal Leader.

The situation in the Lords was an important element in terms of the future prospects for Home Rule. For as long as the Tory majority in the Upper House remained, Ireland would never have self-government. A solution to this conundrum did not seem readily apparent; indeed it did not present itself until the early years of the next century.

Killing Home Rule with kindness

Between 1895 and 1905 the Conservative Party was continuously in power. During this period it introduced a series of reforms aimed at reconciling the Irish to rule from London through addressing the issues that concerned them most. The government's policy became known as 'constructive unionism' or, more popularly, as 'killing Home Rule with kindness'.

Significant reforms were introduced in a range of areas. In agriculture the highly successful Wyndham Land Act of 1903 followed on from the previous less successful legislation already highlighted and provided the finance necessary to enable tenants to buy their land from the landlords. This money would then be repaid in annuities over the next half-century or so. A Department of Agriculture was established in 1899 to help disseminate improved farming methods. Congested Districts Boards were set up to help the poorest inhabitants by encouraging the development of cottage industries, while tourism and transport were enhanced through a range of improvements to both road and rail networks. Last and by no means least, the quality of local government was greatly improved by the introduction of the 1898 Local Government Act, which established a system of locally accountable county and district councils.

Did the Tories' policies work? In one sense they did in that the reforms introduced were long overdue and highly beneficial. However in terms of achieving their ultimate aim they were a failure. The fact that close to four fifths of the MPs elected for Irish constituencies continued to support the introduction of Home Rule would lead one to conclude that – despite the Tories' best efforts – kindness had not done for Home Rule.

05

culture, society and politics

This chapter will cover:
- cultural renaissance
- republican revival
- social unrest
- Home Rule and civil war
- the First World War.

Cultural renaissance

The twentieth century dawned against a backdrop of rediscovery of Ireland's rich cultural heritage. The dislocation caused by tragedies such as the Great Famine, coupled with the realization among many that command of the English language was an indispensable element of modern living, had meant that the Irish language had begun to die away. Towards the end of the 1800s however, a number of organizations emerged with the aim of ensuring that Ireland's Gaelic heritage was not totally eroded. This movement became known as cultural nationalism. It would play a significant part in the country's political development in the new century.

The Gaelic Athletic Association

Chief amongst the emerging groups was the Gaelic Athletic Association (GAA). Founded in 1884 by a group of individuals who feared the increasing influence of games such as rugby and soccer, the GAA provided a countrywide structure for the playing of football and hurling. Rules were adopted and a championship structure was established. As evidence of the movement's desire to preserve a unique culture, members were forbidden from playing 'foreign' games. (Later on a ban on members of the police and British Army joining the GAA was introduced.) Of course this would restrict its appeal to those of a nationalist background. Nevertheless the Association spread quickly throughout Ireland and the first All-Ireland finals took place in 1888 (although the competition of which these matches were the culmination took place in the previous year).

New beginnings in literature

The baton for preserving linguistics was taken up by the Gaelic League, established in 1893 by Irish scholars Douglas Hyde (later first President of Ireland) and Eoin MacNeill. Its aim was to revive Irish as a spoken language while also encouraging its use as a literary medium. Hyde was quite stringent in his viewpoint, particularly regarding Ireland's English-speaking separatists. Speaking in 1894, he argued that he would like to 'call attention to the illogical position of men who drop their own language to speak English...of men who read English books and know nothing about Gaelic literature, nevertheless protesting…that they hate the country which at every hand's turn they rush to imitate'.

Although its initial growth was slow, by the turn of the century the movement was prospering and within a few years it could boast of hundreds of clubs across the country. The League also had its own newspaper, *An Claidheamh Soluis*, which was edited for a number of years by Padraig Pearse.

Elsewhere literature was experiencing a revival through the work of figures such as W. B. Yeats who, along with others, set up what became known as the Abbey Theatre in Dublin. Here work by playwrights such as J. M. Synge attempted to educate audiences in the richness of Irish traditions and experiences. Sometimes they were less than successful. When Synge showed *The Playboy of the Western World* to Dublin audiences for the first time in 1907 there was rioting in the auditorium. Many felt that rather than illuminating the richness of Gaelic culture it portrayed it and Irish people in a highly negative light.

Revival and division

Individually all of these groups played a significant part in reviving awareness of Ireland's rich – and distinctive – cultural heritage. Collectively they also performed a much more significant political task. Through their work and influence the nationalist cause was kept alive at a time when the darkness surrounding Parnell's death and the internecine struggles of his Party threatened to snuff it out. Republicans were active within the ranks of the GAA while the literary revival convinced many of the need for Ireland to be Gaelic as well as free.

However in their efforts to create a homogenous culture these movements might also be accused of having sowed the seeds of broader discontent. Yet how could it be otherwise when a quarter of the population did not see their historical experiences or their political ambitions being reflected in the mirror of Gaelic cultural revival that was being held up?

Such division, coupled with the revival of the prospects of success for Home Rule, resulted in something of a decline in the impact of cultural nationalism after 1910. However, its impact on the thinking of future political leaders such as Padraig Pearse, Michael Collins and Éamon deValera cannot be over-emphasized.

Republicanism rejuvenated

The ongoing cultural revival coincided with and perhaps influenced the celebrations to mark the centenary of the 1798 rebellion. This occasion provided the opportunity for the writings and speeches of men such as Wolfe Tone to receive a public airing. In this heady atmosphere of republican recollection a number of new movements sprang up which were to have a significant impact on twentieth-century Irish history. One such grouping was Sinn Féin.

Sinn Féin was established in 1905 by Dubliner Arthur Griffith. Although a republican at heart – he was a member of the IRB – Griffith realized that most of the Irish population did not share his views. Yet neither was he overly impressed with the prospect of Home Rule, believing that it would leave too much English influence in Ireland. As a way forward Griffith suggested a form of dual monarchy for Ireland such as had existed in Hungary for the previous four decades. Before 1866 Hungarian representatives had sat in the Austrian parliament. After they withdrew from that body a separate Hungarian parliament was set up and the Austrian Emperor was separately titled King of Hungary.

Griffith believed that this model could work in Ireland. In such a system Ireland and Britain would have separate parliaments with the King of Great Britain also serving separately as King of Ireland. However before it could happen Ireland's MPs would have to withdraw from or abstain from attending Westminster and set up their own legislative assembly in Ireland. Griffith believed that with the King of Great Britain also serving as King of Ireland unionists could be encouraged to support the changes.

Sinn Féin's ideas generated a degree of popular interest but no significant levels of support. Although it initially enjoyed some political success at the micro level it fell into decline after the prospects for Home Rule improved in 1910. For that reason it remained on the peripheries of Irish politics until 1916, more a name than a fully-fledged political organization.

The IRB

The new dawn also witnessed the revival of the IRB. After years of decline a new generation of enthusiasts, stimulated by the contemporaneous cultural revival, joined up and reinvigorated the movement. Men such as Bulmer Hobson and Denis McCullough from Belfast joined up with individuals such as

Leitrim-born Sean MacDermott in an effort to create a tightly-knit movement capable of exercising greater influence in key areas of society. These men were aided in their aim by the support of Thomas Clarke, an old-generation Fenian who had done time for his involvement in republicanism. Clarke's reputation provided this new departure with an injection of gravitas and helped substitute a more cautious older generation with dedicated younger men. By 1912 the IRB had been revitalized and its leadership was ready to strike once more for Ireland's freedom.

Industrial unrest

Yet such developments and ambitions remained somewhat esoteric for most of Ireland's population, and in particular for the citizens of Dublin, who had more pressing concerns to worry about. In this context other political viewpoints had an opportunity to develop. One such philosophy was socialism. On first inspection it would seem that such a philosophy had plenty of potential for development. Living conditions for the working class in the city were abysmal and disease, social dislocation and death were rife. Indeed Dublin's mortality levels gave it the unwanted distinction of having the highest death rate of any European city.

Into this situation came two men, James Larkin and James Connolly. The Edinburgh-born Connolly came to Ireland in 1896 and attempted – without great success – to develop a socialist movement. Because of his lack of success he emigrated to the United States in 1903. Like Connolly, Larkin was not Irish-born. He hailed from Liverpool and had arrived in Dublin in 1907 via a stint in Belfast as a union representative.

What he saw in terms of the living and working conditions of the workers did not impress him and Larkin resolved to bring some sort of organization to them that would enable them to act as an effective pressure group. As a result he set up the Irish Transport and General Workers' Union (ITGWU) in 1908. Before long it had established itself in most of Ireland's industrial or port centres.

Connolly returned to Ireland in 1910 and became involved in the ITGWU. By that stage the union was enjoying some success in its aim of improving workers' conditions, however in 1913 a group of some 40 employers – led by press magnate William Martin Murphy – decided to break the power of the ITGWU.

After failing to persuade their workers to leave the union, the workers were locked out of work.

By September 1913 the number locked out numbered more than 24,000. Tensions increased to the extent that Connolly set up a small paramilitary force, the Irish Citizen Army, to help protect the workers. The strikers and their families were initially supported financially by contributions from British unions but when Larkin fell out with their leadership the funds dried up. Gradually, the workforce was left with no option but to return to work, although not before having to renounce their membership of the ITGWU.

The union's power had been broken (although it survived and later prospered), but the problems that had led to the crisis still had to be dealt with. To many it seemed that only a native-based parliament could achieve this goal. Connolly himself argued that 'The cause of labour is the cause of Ireland, the cause of Ireland is the cause of labour.' The urgent need for a Home Rule administration seemed clear.

Home Rule achieved?

By the time of the Dublin lockout such an eventuality – a parliament in Dublin – had changed from being a pipe dream to almost a reality. Yet for this to happen there would have had to be considerable alterations to the veto powers of the House of Lords. As we saw previously, it was their intractable opposition to the 1893 Home Rule Bill that had led to its failure. With a permanent Conservative majority in the Upper House it was difficult to see how this situation could ever change.

Ironically it was the actions of the Conservatives, the party most opposed to Irish Home Rule, which finally allowed the removal of the permanent House of Lords veto. The Tories had been in power uninterrupted from 1895 until they lost the General Election in 1906. They viewed the Liberals' return to power with horror and vowed to use all means to make the life of the new government difficult. Their control of the Lords enabled them to make this threat a reality. In the years following the 1906 Election a number of lesser Bills were lost due to opposition from the Lords. Then in 1909 the Upper House did the unthinkable: it rejected the government's reforming Finance Bill, a budget that would have hit the wealthy particularly hard.

This unprecedented, almost revolutionary, act of defiance threw the British establishment into chaos. A General Election was called to allow the great British public – or at least those of its male members who had the vote – to decide the issue. Unfortunately this attempted sidestep didn't work; the Election left the two parties almost level on seats.

The Liberals were only able to remain in office with the support of the Home Rule Party, now reunited and led by John Redmond, a man wholly different in appearance and manner from his predecessor, Charles Stewart Parnell. Of course the Home Rulers were not supporting the Liberals out of the goodness of their hearts; they saw a very real chance of a *quid pro quo* which would result in a third Home Rule Bill being introduced.

The 1911 Parliament Act

Of course there remained one small problem for both the Liberals and the Home Rulers – the Lords' veto. Another election was called which, because of an even closer result, again left the Irish Party as kingmakers. Then, with the threat by King George V (1910–36) to create enough new Liberal peers (250) to leave that Party controlling the Lords in perpetuity, the Tories backed down and reluctantly accepted the passage of the 1911 Parliament Act.

By the terms of this piece of legislation the power of the Upper House was emasculated. From now on a Bill passed by the Commons in three successive sessions (each roughly equivalent to a year) would become law even without the Lords' approval.

The way for Home Rule now seemed clear. The Liberal government therefore introduced a third Home Rule Bill for Ireland in 1912. Even with opposition from the Lords it would become law in 1914. Although the powers under offer were extremely limited (see below) it would still mean that there would be, once more, a parliament and government in Dublin. It seemed that after nearly a century of trying, Ireland's nationalists were about to taste a long anticipated victory.

As suggested above, the measure that the Liberals intended to introduce was fairly anodyne. It proposed an Irish parliament with relatively limited powers. Control over areas such as health and education would be devolved, but more significant powers over areas such as security, trade and taxation would be reserved for Westminster.

Unionist opposition

Of course not everyone in Ireland was delighted by the very real prospect of Ireland having its own parliament, even if it wasn't going to be much more than a glorified local authority. Significant parts of the population of the northern province of Ulster still wanted to maintain the Union with Great Britain. In the past they had been able to rest confident in the knowledge that the House of Lords would protect them. In the aftermath of the 1911 Parliament Act a very different and less certain future seemed to beckon.

So what was the unionists' *raison d'être*? If truth be told it was pretty much as it had been in 1886 and 1893. Fundamentally they believed that the Irish just weren't up to the job of running the country – at least to the standards that unionists expected. To support this view they pointed to the highly industrialized nature of the city of Belfast – where the ill-fated *Titanic* was just being built – and the advanced agricultural economy of the rural hinterlands. They argued that these compared more than favourably with the backward industrial and agricultural economy of the remainder of the island.

SECOND THOUGHTS.

Mr. John Redmond. "FULL SHTEAM AHEAD! (*Aside*) I WONDHER WILL I LAVE THIS CONTRAIRY LITTLE DIVIL LOOSE, THE WAY HE'D COME BACK BY HIMSELF AFTHERWARDS?"

The one that got away? Herding the provinces (almost) through the 'Home Rule Gate'.

Yet there was more to this opposition than just economic reasoning. In particular, the unionists were afraid that a parliament in Dublin would come under what they deemed to be the perfidious influence of the Catholic Church and its insidious doctrines. As evidence of the intolerant nature of the Catholic Church they pointed to the *Ne Temere* Decree of 1907 whereby Pope Pius X (1903–14) had stated that Catholics could only marry Protestants if the Catholic partner promised to bring up any children as Catholics. In addition unionists (particularly Conservative ones) feared that Home Rule would be the start of a slippery slope that would result in an independent Ireland and the break-up of the British Empire. They were determined, therefore, that Ireland should not and would not have its own parliament.

'Ulster will fight'

At this time unionists were blessed with an intelligent and resourceful, albeit psychosomatic, leader in Sir Edward Carson. Leader of the Unionist Party since 1910, the Dublin-born barrister, the first Irish QC to take silk in England, was perhaps better known to many for his literary connections. He had been the prosecuting barrister in the libel case taken by Oscar Wilde (with whom he had been at Trinity College, Dublin) against the Marquis of Queensbury that ultimately resulted in Wilde being charged with the committing of indecent acts and carted off to Reading Gaol. Upon hearing that Carson was to lead the prosecution case, Wilde is reputed to have said, 'No doubt he will pursue his case with all the added bitterness of an old friend.' In addition Carson was the defence counsel in the Archer–Shee theft case, later dramatized by Terence Rattigan in *The Winslow Boy*.

Carson believed that if Ulster's opposition to Home Rule was strong enough, the government would give up the idea completely rather than divide the island. He also believed that nationalists would give up on achieving Home Rule if they were faced with the prospect of the top part of the island being lopped off in a political sense. In organizing his campaign of opposition Carson was ably assisted by James Craig. Craig had been born near Belfast in 1871, the son of a self-made millionaire whiskey distiller. He had attended school in Scotland before working as a stockbroker and serving in the second Boer War. He had entered Westminster in 1906. Although significantly less charismatic than his leader, Craig was a first-rate organizer. Moreover, in the campaign against Home Rule the Ulsterman differed from Carson in one key respect. If push came to shove he, like his fellow provincials, would accept the partitioning of the island.

Yet resourceful leaders or not, how could unionists, a minority in the context of Ireland never mind the entire population of the UK, stop the will of the government of the land to which they had given their allegiance? More importantly, how could they justify opposing the government of the monarch to whom they professed loyalty? This was a seemingly insoluble conundrum to which the unionists found a neat response: they decided that if the king's government was acting disloyally this would give them the right to oppose its will even to the extent of taking up arms to prevent the government from imposing its will. It was a new twist on Locke's contract theory.

Petitions, plans and private armies

The unionists' first step was to establish a provisional government, which would come into operation in Ulster if Westminster pressed ahead with the introduction of Home Rule. At the same time a well-organized propaganda campaign was implemented. In Britain unionists who hailed from the southern provinces of Ireland used their influential positions in the military and in politics to raise awareness of the potential dangers of the legislation.

Meanwhile, in a series of speeches across the province Carson whipped up opposition to the planned parliament in Dublin. Clearly he was successful in his oratory; on 'Ulster Day', 28 September 1912, over 400,000 men signed the *Solemn League and Covenant* by which they promised to 'use all means which may be found necessary to defeat the present conspiracy'. A less high profile women's version was also highly subscribed to, with roughly a quarter of a million signing it.

The leadership of the Conservative Party also encouraged the unionists' opposition. The Party's leader, Andrew Bonar Law, had ancestral connections to the province. Yet his support threatened to go far beyond the boundaries of blood being thicker than water. Speaking in Blenheim in 1912 he announced that 'there are things stronger than parliamentary majorities' and added that he could 'imagine no length of resistance to which Ulster can go in which I would not be prepared to support them'. The Tory leader could be accused either of having a very poor imagination or of fomenting revolution among part of the population of the United Kingdom. The stakes were being raised very high.

Given that they might need to resist the introduction of Home Rule by force, the unionists also decided that they would form a private army. This army, the Ulster Volunteer Force (UVF) was established in January 1913. Under the command of retired soldiers this group, which numbered in excess of 100,000, soon achieved a high degree of military competence. Yet competence was not much use without firepower and of this the UVF had little.

Nationalist reactions

There were two significantly different reactions from within nationalism to what was happening in the North. Like many senior Liberal politicians, the Home Rule Party leadership initially dismissed the unionist opposition as little more than blustering and posturing, which would come to little in the final analysis.

As time went on, however, it was clear that this head in the sand approach simply would not work and so some talk of compromise and concession began to emerge. The problem was what the solution to the crisis should be. Carson (still hoping to destroy the whole scheme) sought the permanent exclusion of six of Ulster's nine counties (Antrim, Armagh, Derry, Down, Fermanagh and Tyrone), knowing that the large Catholic majorities in the remaining Ulster counties of Cavan, Donegal and Monaghan meant that they were pretty much off limits. Redmond would accept nothing more than the temporary exclusion of the four counties with the greatest numbers of unionists living within (Antrim, Armagh, Derry and Down). Even then the nationalism majorities in areas within these counties would have to be considered. Because of the extreme differences in both side's minimum demands, discussions on a solution were getting nowhere.

Others, however, were more active in their response to events in the North. Not to be outdone by unionists, a group of more advanced nationalists decided to set up their own force. Encouraged by the ideas of Gaelic League founder Eoin MacNeill and of Padraig Pearse, who would lead the 1916 Rising, the Irish Volunteers came into being in November 1913. MacNeill had argued that to ensure that self-government was introduced as parliament willed, the nationalists should also have their own army. Pearse meanwhile had famously observed that the only thing more ridiculous than a unionist with a weapon was a nationalist without one. Of course one group that such a development would particularly interest would be the IRB.

The IRB's interest and influence within the Volunteers is not hard to measure. A dozen members of the Volunteers' Committee were IRB members. Their influence would be crucial in future developments but in the shorter term the Volunteers came under the influence of the Home Rule Party which feared the existence of such an influential nationalist force outside its control. In May 1914 Redmond demanded – and achieved – control over the movement.

Gunrunning!

By that stage the question of weapons for both armies had been settled to some degree. Soon after their formation both forces were able to boast of a membership in excess of 100,000 men, yet an army is not very frightening without weapons and at their inception all that both forces could muster (despite Pearse's views) were broom handles and wooden rifles. The question was – where did one go to arm a force of 100,000 plus? Of course the answer was simple – Germany – the country that by this stage was more than likely to go to war with Britain in the near future. In the early months of 1914 both forces successfully smuggled German weapons into Ireland, the unionists at Larne and Donaghadee and the nationalists at Howth. However, the UVF brought in 35,000 rifles and 5 million rounds of ammunition, while the nationalist haul was significantly less than that.

Civil war?

By mid-1914 both sides were armed and the Home Rule Bill was close to completing its final passage through parliament. With no obvious solution in sight it seemed as if civil war was about to break out between the two groups.

In such a situation the government would naturally have turned to the Army as the best way of maintaining law and order within Ireland. Unfortunately things were not quite that simple. In March 1914 a number of officers based at the Curragh in Co. Kildare had let it be known that they would resign from the

Army rather than enforce Home Rule on an unwilling Ulster population.

Now seriously concerned, the government called a conference of unionist and nationalist leaders to meet at Buckingham Palace. At this meeting the prospect of the exclusion of a number of counties from the terms of the Home Rule Bill was again raised. In the end the plans came to naught: Carson would still only negotiate on the basis of a permanent exclusion of six counties while Redmond was equally insistent that any exclusion be for – at worst – an unspecified length of time. This in itself was something of an advance on his earlier position but it was still not enough for the unionist side.

Just when it seemed as if things could not get any worse, they did in one sense – and didn't in another. Fate intervened in the shape of Gavrilo Princip, Franz Ferdinand's teenage assassin and (unwitting?) instigator of the chain of events that led inexorably to the First World War. It seemed as if the nightmare scenario of war in Europe would serve to postpone the nightmare scenario of war in Ireland.

With the outbreak of war in August 1914 it was agreed to postpone the introduction of Home Rule until the conflict had ended, even though the Bill actually became law in September 1914. At the same time it was recognized that there would also have to be some reconsideration of the Ulster question. In this context the UVF and the majority of the Irish Volunteers were sent off by their respective leaderships to fight 'For King and Country'. Of course each side hoped that their sacrifice would result either in Home Rule being granted or being stopped forever.

Initially it was expected that the war would be over by Christmas 1914. As it turned out, this was ever so slightly optimistic. Furthermore, by the time that the Great War (as it became known) did grind to a halt in November 1918, Home Rule would no longer be enough for the majority of Ireland's nationalists.

Ireland's war experience

In common with many other countries in Europe, the war was initially popular in Ireland. It is estimated that in total somewhere around 200,000 Irishmen volunteered to fight. Interestingly – if not wholly surprisingly – the recruits from the two sides were treated somewhat differently by the British military. Despite Redmond's requests Irish soldiers were not brought together into a distinctive Irish Brigade. At the same time the UVF volunteers were formed into the 36th Ulster Division.

Out of those that volunteered, something approaching 60,000 were killed. Of that number a significant proportion lost their lives at the Battle of the Somme of July 1916, an event that became and has remained an integral part of unionist folklore.

The same cannot be said for the sacrifice of the tens of thousands from the nationalist side who fought and in many cases paid the ultimate sacrifice of their lives. In the changed political situation resulting from the events of 1916–18 (see Chapter 6), those who returned home after the war had ended found that their contribution was being ignored at best, denigrated at worst. Unfortunately such reactions remained the case for many decades thereafter.

Home by Christmas?

As the war continued on into 1915 the Home Rule Party also found itself in something of a no-man's-land. Home Rule was the law of the land but it was not in operation. This created something of a political vacuum with the Party having little or nothing to do. At the same time it seemed as if the influence of the key unionist leaders was growing. In June 1915 they were invited to become ministers, and thus influential, in a newly formed coalition government. Redmond was also invited to join but declined the opportunity, losing out on the chance of equal influence.

At the time, perhaps, this did not seem to matter. The war would soon be over, Home Rule was on the way and the population was waiting quietly in anticipation of its chance at self-government. Well, at least most of them were.

06 making the break

This chapter will cover:
- planning the Rising
- Easter 1916
- the aftermath of rebellion
- the rise of Sinn Féin
- the 1918 General Election
- the establishment of Dáil Éireann
- the War of Independence
- the Government of Ireland Act.

The Volunteer split

The overwhelming majority of the Irish Volunteers answered Redmond's call to go and fight in defence of the freedom that was being threatened by the actions of the Central Powers (Germany and Austria-Hungary). They adopted the name of National Volunteers. A minority of the movement – perhaps close to 11,000 – refused to fight 'For King and Country'. Taking their lead from Eoin MacNeill, the Gaelic scholar who had been instrumental in the Volunteers' establishment, they decided to remain in Ireland. They retained the title of Irish Volunteers.

By the close of the year the movement had reorganized itself with MacNeill operating as Chief of Staff, Joseph Plunkett as Director of Military Operations, Thomas MacDonagh as Director of Training and Padraig Pearse as Director of Organization.

MacNeill's aim for the Irish Volunteers was very simple. In his opinion the movement's *raison d'être* was to ensure that the British government did not renege on its commitment to introduce Home Rule at the war's conclusion. However, that was as far as it went; he argued that there was absolutely no evidence that the Irish people were desirous of a rebellion. The only circumstances in which the Volunteers should take up arms would be to resist the introduction of conscription to Ireland, or if the government ever attempted to disarm the movement.

England's difficulty is Ireland's opportunity

Within this Volunteer minority, however, there was another minority who believed that the Kaiser's ambitions for European domination had created a situation of which they would be fools not to take advantage. The majority of the Volunteer leadership were also IRB members and they believed that with the British military's attention focused elsewhere, a rebellion in Ireland might have a chance of success. Even if it did not, Pearse argued, the example that the laying down of their lives would give would inspire many others to take up the struggle. Pearse called this idea the 'blood sacrifice' and explained it most succinctly in an oration he gave in 1915 at the funeral of a veteran Fenian, Jeremiah O'Donovan Rossa. He suggested that 'Life springs from death, and from the graves of patriot men and women spring living nations.'

Padraig Pearse

So who was this republican philosopher? Pearse was a Dubliner, born in 1879, the son of an English stonemason father. A great admirer of Gaelic culture, even though his first vocation had been the law, Pearse established an Irish-medium school called St Enda's on the outskirts of the capital. A somewhat vain man – he was almost always photographed in profile so as to disguise a cast in one eye – Pearse had become convinced that the only way to solve Ireland's problems was through violence. This was why he had found the example provided by the UVF's establishment so inspiring.

James Connolly

Another key figure in the events of 1916 was James Connolly whom we have already met through his attempts to nurture socialism in Ireland and his involvement in the 1913 Dublin Lockout. During that crisis he had founded the Irish Citizen Army, although with a tiny membership of perhaps 300 men, the name army might seem a little grandiose. Connolly had also come to the conclusion that the time was ripe for a rebellion. Like Pearse, he too had developed ideas of some form of martyrdom in respect of a greater cause.

Connolly was in the midst of planning his own uprising when the IRB learned of his plans. Knowing that such a small force had absolutely no chance of success and fearing that a military clampdown in the aftermath of such an attempt would scupper their own plans, Connolly was brought on board by the IRB and involved in the bigger planning.

Planning the rising

By 1916 the Military Council of the IRB, which was planning the rising, was seven strong. Apart from Pearse and MacDermott the Council included Thomas Clarke, Joseph Mary Plunkett, Eamonn Ceannt, Thomas MacDonagh and James Connolly.

This group knew that they would need some help if their planned rising was to have any chance of success. Although they were intending to make use of the Irish Volunteers in the rebellion they needed these men to be better armed. To this end they turned to Sir Roger Casement. Born in Co. Dublin in 1864, Casement had worked in Africa for the British colonial service and had been awarded a knighthood for his work in exposing maltreatment of natives in various countries, including the Congo and Peru. He had joined the Volunteers in 1913.

Casement went to Germany to seek arms and men. Of the latter, he obtained few (a handful of prisoners of war); in terms of arms he did not do much better. All the Germans would commit to supply was a boatload of weapons. This was to arrive in time for a rising during Easter weekend 1916.

Overall the IRB's plans were not overly complicated, an indication perhaps of their inexperience as military strategists. On the arrival of the German weapons a general rising was to take place. Specific details were few and far between. In Dublin a range of 'strategic' buildings were to be seized. Holding these, it was reasoned, would enable the insurgents to hold the centre of the city.

Disaster strikes!

The rising was planned for Easter Sunday, by which stage the German guns would have arrived. If there was to be any chance of getting the rank-and-file Volunteers to take part MacNeill would have to give the order for action. For that to happen the Chief of Staff would have to be convinced that a rebellion was justified. As we have seen already there was a very limited range of circumstances in which he was prepared to do so.

One such circumstance was a government move against the Volunteers, but there seemed to be little prospect of this happening. The authorities did not seem to think that the movement posed any great threat, and rather than antagonize them let them march around the place to their hearts' content. Yet in the end MacNeill was persuaded to order the Volunteers to muster. This was achieved by informing him of the imminent arrival of German weapons and by showing him a forged document, which indicated that the authorities were on the verge of arresting the Volunteer leadership.

Then just as it must have seemed that it was all going to work, everything began to unravel. On Good Friday a Royal Navy vessel intercepted the *Aud*, the German vessel that was bringing in the weapons. The boat then proceeded to scuttle herself and her cargo. On Holy Saturday Casement was arrested in Co. Kerry moments after disembarking from a German submarine.

Upon learning of these setbacks, MacNeill issued a countermanding order, telling the Volunteers to stay at home on Easter Sunday. So that no one would miss his message it was printed in the *Sunday Independent*.

The Easter Rising

It was a deflated Military Council that gathered in Dublin's Liberty Hall early on Easter Sunday. It was clear to them that all hope of military victory – if indeed there ever had been any – was now lost. It was a day that symbolized the beginning of new life in the Christian calendar; in their case, however, all it seemed to herald was the death of months of carefully laid planning.

Yet they decided to go ahead with the rising, albeit a day later than had originally been anticipated. Why did they make this choice? Quite simply Pearse's idea of 'blood sacrifice' had now come to the fore; the rising might be doomed even before it had begun and the lives of those involved would more than likely be forfeit, but from that very sacrifice might flow the example that would lead generations of others to take up the struggle for freedom.

Dublin was quiet on Easter Monday. Apart from it being a holiday many Dubliners were out at Fairyhouse watching the horseracing. A small crowd on Sackville Street (later O'Connell Street) watched as a detachment of Volunteers marched into the city's General Post Office (GPO) . Other units moved to take up position in the buildings, which had been identified as strategically important. The Irish Tricolour appeared on the GPO's flagpole. Shortly after, some of the same crowd listened in bemusement as Pearse stepped out and read what has become known as the *Proclamation of the Republic*.

Pearse informed his puzzled audience that 'Ireland, through us, summons her children to her flag and strikes for her freedom.' He added:

> We declare the right of the people of Ireland to the ownership of Ireland, and to the unfettered control of Irish destinies, to be sovereign and indefeasible…We hereby proclaim the Irish Republic as a Sovereign Independent State, and we pledge our lives and the lives of our comrades-in-arms to the cause of its freedom, of its welfare, and of its exaltation among the nations.

The seven members of the Military Council had signed the Proclamation. They now described themselves as the Provisional Government of the Irish Republic. Their intention, as described in the Proclamation, was to run the Irish government until 'Our arms have brought the opportune moment for the establishment of a Permanent National government, representative of the whole people of Ireland and elected by the suffrage of all her men and women'.

Military matters

All told, about 1,600 rebels had taken up positions in various locations around Dublin. The College of Surgeons on St Stephen's Green was held, as were Boland's Mills, the South Dublin Union, the Four Courts and Jacob's factory. A somewhat desultory effort was made to take control of Dublin Castle, the seat of British government and therefore symbolically important for the rebels. However the approaching party was fired upon by one of the few men on duty and believing that there were many more men inside, the rebels retreated. By the close of the same day the Castle was full of British soldiers.

Even though their military tactics were suspect at best the rebels were able to hold out for the best part of a week. By the time the end came, on Saturday 29 April, there were probably in excess of 30,000 Crown troops in Dublin. The British had even brought a gunboat, the *Helga*, up the Liffey from where it was able to shell the GPO with deadly effectiveness.

All changed, changed utterly

The damage caused was considerable. Close to 450 people – the majority of whom were innocent civilians – had lost their lives and a further 2,500 and more had suffered injuries in some shape or form. Nor had the city escaped; as much as £2 million worth of damage had been caused, particularly by the sustained shelling of rebel positions on Sackville Street. Little wonder, then, that as they were led away the rebels were jeered at and even physically attacked by some Dubliners.

However that initial reaction of angry contempt soon changed to one of sympathy and support. In the words of the poet W. B. Yeats all 'changed, changed utterly' (*Easter 1916*). The reason for this sea change was arguably the incredibly inept way in which the British administration handled the fallout from the rising.

The British government had been caught totally off guard by the events of Easter 1916. They had heard some last minute whispers of a planned rising but had assumed that the capture of the *Aud*, the arrest of Casement and the countermanding order issued by MacNeill had put an end to whatever had been planned. However, they were wrong.

At a time of national emergency there was a feeling abroad within government circles that citizens of an integral part of the United Kingdom had stabbed them in the back. Not surprisingly, Ireland's unionist population echoed these sentiments. For this reason the military establishment in Ireland, commanded by Sir John Maxwell, was given *carte blanche* to handle the response as it saw fit. Despite warnings from the Home Rule Party's leadership that precipitate reactions could backfire on the British, that is exactly what Maxwell did.

Thousands of suspects, many of whom had had nothing to do with the planning or execution of the events of Easter week, were rounded up and shipped off to internment camps in Britain. The individuals identified as the ringleaders were tried by military court martial and sentenced to death by firing squad. Over 90 were to be dealt with in this manner although in the end 'only' 15 were executed.

Nor was Pearse unaware of the potential of what was going on. During his court martial he attempted to vocalize not only his own emotions now that he was facing certain death, but also his understanding of the current mood of antipathy towards the rebels and how this would ultimately change. He proclaimed that the rebels...

> are ready to die and shall die cheerfully and proudly...You must not grieve for all of this. We have preserved Ireland's honour and our own. Our deeds of last week are the most splendid in Ireland's history. People will say hard things of us now, but we shall be remembered by posterity and blessed by unborn generations.

Pearse wasn't wrong, but he was relying on the British to achieve, by their reaction, what he hadn't been able to achieve militarily. They didn't let him down. Between 3 and 12 May, 15 individuals were led out to the stonebreakers' yard in Kilmainham Gaol and shot by firing squad. The last to die, James Connolly, was unable to stand due to injuries received while in the GPO and so was shot tied to a chair.

As Pearse had hoped, the manner of the British crackdown began to shift public opinion in favour of the rebels. Bit by bit, through a veil of military secrecy, news of what was happening leaked out to an increasingly appalled public. In particular the ten-day duration of the executions and the terse notifications of the names of that day's dead – posted on the prison gates – had a profound impact. Speaking in the House of Commons on 11 May, John Dillon, the Deputy Leader of the Home Rule Party, summed up concisely just what was at stake if the executions were to continue. He told the government that it was 'washing our whole life work in a sea of blood'. He added 'it is not murderers who are being executed; it is insurgents who have fought a clean fight, a brave fight, however misguided'. On the following day the last executions took place.

The government had started out with a significant amount of public opinion more or less behind it; by the time of Connolly's death this support had been completely squandered. In many ways the prophecy so recently uttered by playwright George Bernard Shaw was already proving correct. In a letter to the *Daily News* (10 May 1916) he had suggested that 'The shot Irishmen will now take their places beside Emmet and the Manchester Martyrs (a group of Fenians executed in 1867 for their alleged involvement in the death of a policeman) in Ireland, and beside the heroes of Poland and Serbia and Belgium in Europe; and nothing in heaven or earth can prevent it.'

But what of Casement? He too was executed, his death coming at the end of a hangman's noose. Initially after his sentence had been pronounced there had been a spirited campaign to obtain a reprieve for him, given his sterling service on behalf of the British Crown. This campaign petered out, however, in the aftermath of the publication of the so-called *Black Diaries*. Supposedly written by Casement, these volumes revealed that he had been a practising homosexual. Their authenticity has been a matter for violent conjecture ever since.

The emergence of Sinn Féin

The IRB had been so successful in keeping its involvement in the rising secret that the government blamed Sinn Féin for planning the insurrection. Although its leader Arthur Griffith – incidentally one of those shipped off to a prison camp in Britain – was a republican, the Party had never been involved in this form of political action. Nevertheless, this mistaken association meant that as the rebellion began to grow in popularity, Sinn Féin's popularity began to increase concomitantly.

Of course an increase in support for Sinn Féin had to come from somewhere. In this case the likely losers would be the Home Rule Party. They had the continuing ineptitude of the British government to thank for helping to make them less popular and Sinn Féin more so. The occasion was the talks organized to try and find a political solution to the events of Easter 1916.

The Lloyd George talks

Having dealt with the immediate military problems, the government's next step was to hold a series of meetings with the main players within nationalism and unionism to see what steps could be taken politically to improve the situation.

These meetings, which involved Redmond and Carson, were chaired by David Lloyd George, soon to replace H. H. Asquith as British Prime Minister. Negotiating with each leader separately he managed to get Redmond to agree to what he understood to be the temporary exclusion of six counties of Ulster. At the same time Lloyd George provided Carson with a written guarantee that the exclusion would be permanent. Such a piece of typical Lloyd George chicanery could not work and when Redmond realized what had happened he repudiated the agreement.

However, damage had been done to the Home Rule Party. For many, granting all-Ireland Home Rule now would have been a little like shutting the stable door after the horse had bolted! However to add in to that mix an agreement to partition Ireland, whether it be temporarily or not, did Redmond and his Party no good at all. What was particularly damaging was the fact that Redmond had agreed to the exclusion of counties with nationalist majorities. The winds of political change were starting to blow strongly; there was no telling what might be swept away.

A changing political climate

Another reason for the changing political climate was the release of most of those who had been imprisoned in Britain in the immediate aftermath of the Easter Rising. The new Prime Minister, David Lloyd George, intended this as an act of conciliation. The problem was that many of those who returned were now firm in their republican convictions even if they hadn't been before. Among those released were men such as

Michael Collins and Cathal Brugha. They and others like them would go on to play an important part in the developing campaign for Irish political freedom.

Clear evidence of the decline in support for the Home Rule Party came with the North Roscommon by-election of January 1917. Here George Noble, Count (a papal title) Plunkett, the father of the executed Joseph Mary Plunkett, easily defeated the Home Rule Party candidate with the support of a number of groups including Sinn Féin.

However Sinn Féin was not the only nationalist grouping on the go by this time. Indeed the fact that there was a myriad of groups all claiming to offer the best way forward meant that a coherent opposition to the Home Rule Party was lacking. Such a situation could not be allowed to continue and came to an end at the Sinn Féin *Ard Fheis* (party conference) in October 1917. At this meeting Éamon deValera was elected President of Sinn Féin.

Éamon deValera

Born in New York in 1882 to an Irish mother and Spanish father, deValera was now the senior surviving commandant from the Easter Rising, having been in command of the garrison at Boland's Mills (during which time, rumour has it, he suffered some sort of nervous collapse). Given his seniority he had been sentenced to death by court martial, but this sentence had been commuted to life imprisonment as a result of his American birth. Along with other lifers he was released in June 1917 as the government made another attempt to make amends for the mess it was making of the situation in Ireland. In the same month, he successfully stood as the Sinn Féin candidate in the East Clare by-election.

The position of Sinn Féin President belonged rightfully to Arthur Griffith; however, in the interests of creating a unified movement he stood down in favour of deValera. The Party also developed a single strategy, which attempted to provide a common direction to the motley crew of advanced republicans and dual monarchists which now made up the rank-and-file membership. Put simply, this was to work towards the achievement of a Republic, which, once achieved, would allow the people to choose the form of government they most desired.

Clearly the new Party was a coalition of different interests, all of which preferred various and different methods to achieve their chosen goals. What made the compromise work, however, was the existence of a common enemy in the shape of the British government. For as long as that enemy remained, the coalition would survive. If it ever disappeared then it was inevitable that the old differences would re-emerge.

Soon after his elevation within Sinn Féin, deValera also became leader of the Irish Volunteers. This meant that all those groups and individuals who were striving towards an independent Irish Republic were now co-ordinated under a single leadership system. Thus their effectiveness would be greatly increased. Any success, however, would come at the expense of the Home Rule Party.

The Irish Convention

The emergence of Sinn Féin as a major player was obvious when the British government invited them to attend the 1917 Irish Convention. This conference was set up by Lloyd George in another effort to find a solution to the continuing crisis in Ireland. However, right from the start the Convention's chances of success were significantly weakened by Sinn Féin's refusal to attend, and by Carson's insistence that there should be no Home Rule at all.

True to his beliefs, Redmond used the opportunity to make yet another attempt to find a way to make Home Rule a reality. Talks held with the southern unionists seemed to hold out some prospect of success, but before his Party could discuss them properly, Redmond died. His successor, John Dillon, did not like the plans, as they included an even weaker form of Home Rule, and the Convention broke up without reaching a solution.

It might have been expected that this failure would further weaken support for the Home Rule Party while increasing it for Sinn Féin, which had refused to attend the Convention and could not, therefore, be associated with its failure. Interestingly, however, in the winter of 1917 support for the Home Rule Party seemed to rise and it won three by-elections on the trot. Whether or not this was due to Dillon's new and more hard-line leadership or because of a lack of initiative on the part of Sinn Féin is hard to say. In the event it was only a temporary setback; in 1918 Sinn Féin's support rocketed. Again they had British government policy to thank.

The conscription crisis

The growth in support for Sinn Féin had become a matter of some concern to the British government. However, it seemed that each and every step that they took to counter the movement's growth only served to increase its support further. In 1917 a number of prominent Party members were arrested as part of a government crackdown; when one of them, Thomas Ashe, died while on hunger strike, support for the Party shot up.

The speech that Michael Collins delivered at Ashe's funeral makes interesting comparison with that delivered by Pearse at O'Donovan Rossa's a few years before. The rapidly rising Collins stepped forward just after a volley of shots had been fired over the coffin and announced, 'Nothing additional remains to be said. The volley which we have just heard is the only speech which it is proper to make over the grave of a dead Fenian.' Times had changed somewhat!

However what really boosted Sinn Féin's popularity was the government's decision – in April 1918 – in the face of strong German advances on the Western Front, to extend conscription to Ireland. The Home Rule Party withdrew from Westminster in protest and along with Sinn Féin organized a nationwide campaign opposing this plan. Across Ireland opponents of conscription spoke out. From Catholic and Protestant bishops to members of trade unions came widespread opposition to the plan. The Volunteers, which had been revived by Cathal Brugha (or to give him his proper name, Charles William St John Burgess) announced that if necessary they would oppose the introduction of conscription by force. Before long the Volunteers could again boast of a membership of 100,000.

Faced with such widespread and determined opposition the government withdrew the plan. However, while the campaign was ultimately successful because of the combined opposition, it was Sinn Féin who gained all the credit. Moreover, the very fact that the Home Rule Party had withdrawn from Westminster seemed to be a tacit acceptance of the correctness of one of Sinn Féin's main policies, that of abstention. It looked as if the old Party couldn't win.

The 'German Plot'

In the middle of scoring this own goal the government notched up an even bigger one in the shape of the 'German Plot'. In May 1918 the authorities declared that they had 'discovered' a plot by Germany to land more weapons in Ireland and encourage another rising. In light of this intelligence the government arrested scores of prominent republicans, such as deValera, and proscribed Sinn Féin. Few in Ireland believed the veracity of Dublin Castle's claims.

Sinn Féin simply went underground and, with deValera offside, came more and more under the influence of more radical men such as Brugha, Collins, Richard Mulcahy, Harry Boland and Rory O'Connor. Their influence thus established would last long after the immediate crisis had passed.

The 1918 General Election

The Great War finally ended in November 1918. A month later the first General Election since December 1910 was held. This would be a crucial election in a number of ways. Not only would it enable the first real test of public opinion in Ireland since the events of 1916, it would also involve a greatly augmented electorate as the voting age for men had been reduced to 21 while women over the age of 30 had also been enfranchised for the first time. All told, the numbers that could vote had been increased by 150 per cent.

The manifestos of the two main nationalist parties could hardly have been more different. While the Home Rule Party promised nothing more than a continuation of their campaign for self-government, Sinn Féin offered the prospect of the establishment of a parliament in Dublin, Dáil Éireann, a campaign to gain recognition for Ireland's claims to nationhood at the forthcoming Peace Conference in Paris and a promise to make the continuation of British rule more difficult than previously.

It wasn't just the two parties' manifestos that were like chalk and cheese. In terms of energy and organization, too, there was little or nothing that enabled effective comparison between the two. The Home Rule Party was as old and tired as its leadership; indeed it did not even put forward candidates in nearly a quarter of the constituencies. In contrast Sinn Féin was, like its leaders, young and energetic.

The voting revealed that the majority of the electorate had indicated their preference for Sinn Féin. When the votes were counted there were 26 unionists (up from 18); six Home Rulers (down from 78 and including four seats guaranteed from a pact with Sinn Féin so as not to split the nationalist vote in Ulster) and 73 Sinn Féiners (up from seven). Quite clearly all had 'changed, changed utterly'; the question now was how would the supporters of the *status quo* react?

The establishment of Dáil Éireann

True to Griffith's long-standing opposition to sending representatives from Ireland to the Westminster parliament and fulfilling one of the promises in their election manifesto, the newly elected Sinn Féin MPs refused to cross the Irish Sea and instead set about forming their own assembly. Dáil Éireann, as it was called, met for the first time on 21 January 1919 in Dublin's Mansion House.

Although there had been 73 successful Sinn Féin candidates, nowhere near that number turned up on 21 January. First, some had been elected for more than one constituency, as was then permissible. More significantly a large number of the MPs were in prison, arrested as part of the 'German Plot'. Two others – Michael Collins and Harry Boland – were in England in an effort to beak Éamon deValera out of Lincoln Gaol. This was achieved with the help of a key smuggled into the jail in a cake. Invitations were also sent out to the non-Sinn Féin MPs but not surprisingly the Unionist Party and Home Rule Party representatives chose not to attend. In total 27 members turned up.

The first meeting of the first Dáil concluded its business relatively quickly. In the space of two hours it restated the existence of the Republic as first proclaimed by Pearse in 1916. It then proceeded to appoint representatives (to be led by Seán T. O'Kelly) to attend the Peace Conference that was just about to meet in Paris. In light of US President Woodrow Wilson's Fourteen Points Sinn Féin hoped that the Conference might recognize the right of the Irish people to self-determination.

However the most notable action was the adoption of what was called the *Democratic Programme*. This was an agenda of social ideals, setting out the predominance of 'public rights and welfare' that should exist within the new state.

The Dáil met again on the following day. Its main work was to establish the key positions within the new government. The Head of government was going to be known as Priomh-Aire or President. His ministerial team would be collectively known as the Executive Council.

The Dáil next met in April 1919. By this stage most of the main protagonists had been released from prison and so the attendance list was much fuller. As leader of Sinn Féin, deValera was appointed as Priomh-Aire. Arthur Griffith became his deputy and was also to be Minister for Home Affairs. Other cabinet positions filled included Cathal Brugha as Minister for

Defence, Michael Collins as Minister for Finance, Eoin MacNeill as Minister for Industries, William T. Cosgrave as Minister for Local Government and Constance, Countess Markievicz as Minister for Labour.

Markievicz was an interesting case. Born Constance Gore-Booth in 1868, she had married a Polish Count hence the exotic name. Her involvement in the republican movement came early and she was in command of the rebel detachment in the College of Surgeons on St Stephen's Green in 1916. As such a senior figure she was sentenced to death by military tribunal but had her sentence commuted to imprisonment because she was a woman. Markievicz was elected MP for a Dublin constituency in December 1918 and thus became the first woman elected to the House of Commons in its history. However because she did not take her seat that accolade is usually reserved for Nancy Astor (elected November 1919) who did sit in Westminster.

It had been Griffith's intention that if parallel ministries were set up they would receive the allegiance of the people and the British versions would wither away. Although the latter aim was never likely to happen, the Dáil institutions did make significant progress in a number of areas. What is most remarkable is that this happened in the context of the unstable Irish situation, and despite the fact that most of the ministers were inexperienced, operating with little administrative support and, most tellingly, frequently on the run.

As Sinn Féin controlled most of the councils outside Ulster these soon declared their allegiance to the Dáil. In addition the system of Courts established by the Dáil in June 1920 to administer law and order was a notable success. An elaborate court system was established and a mark of its reputation was that it was soon overwhelmed with petitioners. Meanwhile, under the guidance of Michael Collins the Finance Ministry attempted to fund the administration through the collection of taxes. This had mixed results; however, much more successful was its introduction of a loan in the form of Dáil Bonds which raised in excess of £350,000. Legend has it that Russia's Communist leader Vladimir Illych Ullyanov, better known to us as Lenin, heard about Collins' loan, and sent a representative to Dublin to borrow some money to help fund the establishment of what became the USSR. It would appear that the emmisary offered some of the Russian Crown Jewels as collateral. The story goes on that the jewels remained in a Dublin safe, forgotten by all, until the 1930s, when they were again discovered.

Whatever the truth of such stories it is fair to say that the success of these aspects of unofficial self-government was one of the main reasons for the growth in support for the Dáil system.

DeValera in America

A few weeks after his appointment as Priomh-Aire, deValera travelled to the United States (as a stowaway) in an attempt to get political recognition of Sinn Féin's cause and to raise funds to augment the work that Collins was doing at home. In a mission lasting 18 months deValera probably had more downs than ups. On a positive note he raised $6 million through a loan scheme; however, he was unable to convince either of the main US parties to come out in favour of Sinn Féin's struggle.

Mission to Paris

Another area where Sinn Féin's hopes came to naught was the appeal to the Peace Conference. In reality the Party's leadership should have realized that this action was a complete waste of time. Before the end of the war Sinn Féin had declared its support for the German cause and with their defeat there was little or no reason why Wilson, Clemenceau (the French Prime Minister) or Lloyd George should entertain Sinn Féin's pleas. In any case, Wilson was hardly likely to go against the wishes of his closest ally and support Sinn Féin's demands.

The War of Independence

On the same day that the Dáil first met the first shots in what would be christened the Anglo-Irish War of Independence (or 'the Troubles') were fired. A small detachment of Volunteers (fully reorganized by Brugha and now known as the Irish Republican Army or IRA) attacked a police convoy in Co. Tipperary in search of weapons and explosives.

It should be noted that this operation was not sanctioned by the Dáil. Indeed, although the IRA and Sinn Féin had a significant number of key leadership figures in common, the former was an independent operation with a purely military agenda. Indeed it was not until April 1921, over two years into the conflict, that the Dáil accepted responsibility for the contemporaneous military campaign.

In particular parts of the country, chiefly Munster, the IRA was extremely active. Its speciality was attacks on isolated police barracks. As a result the police were forced to withdraw into urban areas for protection. In consequence the IRA was left in control of large swathes of the countryside. Bit by bit recruitment to the Royal Irish Constabulary (RIC) began to decline. It was in an effort to address this decline that the British government began to take a much more active line.

Michael Collins

Much of the credit for the IRA's success must go to Michael Collins. Collins combined his position as Minister of Finance with that of IRA Director of Intelligence and (after 1919) head of the IRB. Born in Co. Cork in 1890, Collins had spent some time working in London before returning to Ireland. There he became involved in the republican struggle in and after 1916, serving in the GPO during the Easter Rising and being rewarded with a spell in a Welsh prison camp for his efforts.

Collins believed that earlier attempts at overthrowing the British had failed because of the government's superior intelligence. He therefore based his campaign on the basis of being better informed than the enemy. His extensive network of spies and informers, built up since 1916 and including government employees, kept him acquainted with exactly what was being planned by the British. At the same time his own assassins, known as 'the Squad' clinically dispatched those with too much information and influence on the other side. Legend has it that one of these men, Vinny Byrne, reputedly prefaced every assassination with the phrase 'May the Lord have mercy on your soul.'

The British were more than a little keen to make Collins' acquaintance and to that end a bounty of £10,000, a huge amount of money at that time, was put on his head. However, in some ways similar to an earlier Pimpernel, Collins travelled undisguised around Dublin with impunity. Despite what was described as a striking physical appearance, no one on the British side was really sure what he looked like. Stories of Collins stopping and joking with unsuspecting policemen and soldiers when the occasion required or when the fancy took him are legion.

The government's response

The British government at first responded slowly to events in Ireland, but from 1920 it became much more active in its opposition to the IRA campaign. The administrative system in Dublin Castle, which could not exactly have been described as a model of efficiency, was reinvigorated by the introduction of new blood.

A much tougher line was also taken militarily. Curfews were introduced and the military presence was augmented by the introduction of two new forces, the Black and Tans and the Auxiliaries. At the same time the intelligence network in Dublin Castle was also given new strength.

The Black and Tans – so called because of the mixed colour of their uniforms – were mainly recruited from demobilized soldiers in Britain. Their function was to provide back-up for the police force, the Royal Irish Constabulary (RIC), which was finding it increasingly difficult to attract members in light of the ongoing IRA attacks. The Tans took to their task with gusto and a considerable degree of ruthlessness. Their particular speciality became the night-time raid in search of suspects, and many parts of Ireland soon echoed to the sound of their approaching vehicles and their insistent knocking for admittance.

The Black and Tans were not the only new force on the scene at this time. Later in the war they were augmented by another force, this time recruited from ex-Army officers. This group was known as the 'Auxies' as they were officially an Auxiliary Division of the RIC.

Atrocities

The IRA could not hope to take on these forces in a straight fight and so they began to stage a series of guerrilla attacks. Small detachments, known as 'flying columns' moved around the country and set up ambushes against the Black and Tan forces with devastating effect. The British forces responded with terror tactics that particularly focused on the harassment of individuals and the burning of property. Of particular note was the murder of the Lord Mayor of Cork, Tomás MacCurtain, at his home by members of the police.

It is fair to say that both sides bear the responsibility for a range of atrocities that brought the Anglo-Irish conflict to the attention of the wider world. The long lingering death in Brixton Prison of another Lord Mayor of Cork, Terence MacSwiney, brought the passions and commitment of the conflict home to a British audience. MacSwiney had been imprisoned because of his membership of the IRA. Indeed, by his own actions he had already brought into reality the words he had spoken on his appointment as Mayor. Then he had argued that, 'The contest on our side is not one of rivalry or vengeance, but of endurance. It is not those who can inflict the most, but those who can suffer the most who will conquer.'

Similarly the death by hanging of medical student Kevin Barry attracted the attention of the world's media. Barry was only 18 at the time of his execution for involvement in an IRA ambush in which six British soldiers died. His youthfulness resulted in him being raised high in the pantheon of republican martyrs, to the extent that a rebel song was composed in his memory.

However it was the earlier of two events both known in Irish history as Bloody Sunday, which perhaps best encapsulated the horror and pointlessness of much that went on in Ireland in these years. On Sunday 21 November 1920 Collins' Squad, augmented by other IRA men, assassinated 14 men, believed to be members of the so-called 'Cairo Gang', undercover intelligence agents that had been sent to Ireland with the express purpose of destroying the IRA's campaign.

That afternoon, the Black and Tans entered Croke Park – Dublin's main GAA stadium – and opened fire on the crowd. A dozen died and over 60 were injured in an attack that could most charitably be described as indiscriminate. The government justified the event by claiming that the assassins were believed to be among the crowd watching the match. Later on the same night three IRA men were shot dead while trying to escape from custody in Dublin Castle. That, at least, was the story being told by the authorities.

In December 1920 the Tans and 'Auxies' went so far as to torch the city of Cork in reprisal for a successful IRA attack led by Tom Barry in which all but one member of an 'Auxie' patrol had been killed. The same IRA attack had led Lloyd George to impose martial law on parts of the island and make greater use of the Army against the enemy. Up to this point the British Prime Minister had refused to recognize the IRA as an army and had thus insisted that the fight against them be handled by the police and their supporters.

Dealing with Ulster

Such events only served to harden the resolve of both sides and in the case of the IRA probably did a great deal to encourage further recruitment. At the same time public opinion in Britain and abroad was putting Lloyd George under increasing pressure to reach some kind of settlement that would end 'the Troubles'. Of course Home Rule had been on the statute book since 1914 but with the proviso that it could not be implemented until some form of resolution to the Ulster Question was reached.

But what should it be? Politically, Lloyd George was himself in a difficult position. The coalition government that he headed was made up largely of Conservative MPs and their traditional sympathies had lain with the Ulster unionists and the preservation of the British Empire. Both of these issues would also be of considerable interest to the Sinn Féin leadership at some future point, albeit with a different resolution in mind from that of the British.

Lloyd George decided that it would be easier to deal with the republican politicians if the Ulster question was, in some way, off the agenda. Therefore in 1920 his government introduced and passed the Government of Ireland Act. This brought into legislation something that the Ulster unionists had long sought and many others long opposed – the partitioning of Ireland into two parts.

The unionists were able to have a greater influence on the shape of this Act for two main reasons. First, and as already indicated, their staunch allies, the Conservatives, were a significant force in Lloyd George's administration. More important, the 26 unionist MPs were at Westminster while the Act was going through its parliamentary stages, ensuring that their requirements were being met; the abstentionist Sinn Féiners were nowhere to be seen.

The unionists did indeed have an input. The Act originally called for a nine-county Northern Ireland but realizing that this would create a population that was almost equally divided the unionist leadership decided to jettison Cavan, Monaghan and Donegal in spite of the existence of significant unionist populations in each.

The Government of Ireland Act 1920

Under the terms of the Act there would be two parliaments in Ireland. One in Dublin, which would administer the affairs of the 26 counties that would henceforth be known as Southern Ireland. One in Belfast that would run the government of the remaining six counties that would constitute Northern Ireland. Each part would have powers similar to those that had been passed into law in the 1914 Home Rule Act.

The Act also established a Council of Ireland as a mechanism for achieving a reunited Ireland at some future point. Members from both Southern and Northern parliaments would serve on this body and would impose policies on areas of common concern such as fishing and trade. If both parliaments saw fit they could increase the powers available to the Council and thus bring about reunification.

Reaction to the Act was predictable within Ireland. Sinn Féin rejected the legislation as insufficient although they used the electoral mechanisms it established to elect a second Dáil. Ulster's unionists accepted the parliament that would be established in Belfast as the best way of protecting their interests because it would place government within their own hands. As a result, elections were held within the six counties that made up Northern Ireland in May 1921 and King George V opened the resulting parliament with great pomp in the following month.

In his address on that day the king made use of the opportunity to hold out an olive branch to those fighting his government in the rest of the country. The question was, would it be grapsed by the republican leadership?

07

the freedom to achieve freedom?

This chapter will cover:
- agreeing a truce
- negotiating a settlement
- the Anglo–Irish Treaty
- the breakdown of consensus
- the search for agreement
- civil war.

A truce

With the Northern Ireland part of the Irish conundrum seemingly settled and certainly something of a *fait accompli* in Britain's eyes, Lloyd George turned his attention to ending conflict in the rest of the island. All other factors aside, public opinion was growing increasingly vociferous in its opposition to a continuation of the conflict.

Over a period of six months tentative contacts were made with republican leaders, in particular Éamon deValera who had returned from the United States in December 1920. Lloyd George insisted that, notwithstanding his position, deValera should not be arrested so as to facilitate contact. However, despite this concession, the Prime Minister's initial preconditions for talks – IRA disarmament and the handing over of Collins and other military protagonists – meant that no progress was made.

The final catalyst turned out to be the king's aforementioned address at the opening of the Northern Ireland parliament in June 1921. In his speech George V made a heartfelt plea for peace between the peoples of the two islands. On the back of this initiative Lloyd George issued an invitation for deValera and Craig (who had replaced Carson as the unionist leader) to meet to explore the possibilities for a settlement.

DeValera was equally keen on an end to hostilities. The IRA was finding it increasingly difficult to maintain its guerrilla campaign; indeed Collins was of the opinion it had only a few weeks' worth of ammunition left if the struggle continued. More importantly perhaps (and certainly in terms of continued support for the IRA) the Irish population was suffering from war weariness. After a period of preliminary negotiating skirmishing both sides agreed to an unconditional ceasefire. It came into effect on 11 July 1921.

Background negotiations

Difficult through agreeing an armistice was, it would pale in comparison with the difficulties in achieving a settlement that would not mean a return to conflict. The basic negotiating positions of both sides were poles apart. Sinn Féin was demanding a 32-county sovereign independent state; Britain was still thinking along the lines of a 26-county government with strong ties to the Crown and the British Empire.

Yet each side had already made some concessions. The Irish knew – or should have known – that talks without having defeated the British would mean that they would never achieve all of their aims. At the same time Lloyd George was having to negotiate with the Irish as equals, even though he had just been conducting a war against people he had described as murderers.

The first substantive meeting between the two sides took place in London where deValera went to meet Lloyd George. This conference gave both sides a chance to set out their stalls; deValera putting in a bid for an all-Ireland Republic, Lloyd George countering with an offer of 26 counties with the same degree of freedom as other Commonwealth – as the Empire was now more frequently referred to – states such as Australia and Canada. This level of autonomy was known as dominion status.

DeValera was not impressed by Lloyd George's offer. He felt that dominion status, which left the king as Head of State, would place limitations on the legislative competence of the Irish parliament. Moreover the British requirement of an oath of loyalty from members of parliament would be a far cry from the utopian Republic of the 1916 Proclamation. With little or no progress made the meeting broke up and deValera returned to Dublin.

Over the following months painstaking efforts were made to come up with a formula that would allow negotiations to begin with the minimum level of concession being implied by the simple fact of agreeing to take part. Eventually the British suggested a form of words that the Irish felt they could accept. They were to go to London 'with a view to ascertaining how the association of Ireland with the community of nations known as the British Empire may be reconciled with Irish national aspirations'.

The Irish team

Negotiations began in earnest in October 1921 when the Irish plenipotentiaries – as the delegates were titled – headed to London to discuss a settlement. The make-up of this delegation was extremely interesting and has exercised generations of historians ever since. Contrary to what might have been expected deValera – in spite of his position as Head of government – did not lead the Irish side; instead the group was led by Arthur Griffith and included Collins, Robert Barton,

Eamonn Duggan and George Gavan Duffy. Erskine Childers, author of *The Riddle of the Sands*, accompanied the group as non-voting secretary.

So why did deValera not attend the negotiations? The simple answer is that no one – apart from deValera – really knows. He himself argued that by remaining in Dublin he would be able to keep an eye on the extremist republican elements, people such as Brugha. He added that as all proposals agreed would have to be referred back to him for ultimate confirmation, this would provide the Irish delegation with a break from the pressure of the hothouse atmosphere that the more experienced British negotiators might try to create around them.

Should he have gone? As with all historical controversies the position one takes depends on one's attitude to deValera. In the aftermath of the split that followed the Treaty he was accused of not going because he knew that a Republic was never going to be an option. Others argued that if the delegation had referred the Treaty back to him before signing a different outcome could have been possible. Certainly it seemed strange that the Head of government of one delegation was not there when the vastly more experienced Head of government of the other side was.

That was not the only weakness that the Irish delegates brought with them. It would be an understatement to say that not all members of the team were bosom buddies. Both Collins and Griffith were less than happy with Childers' inclusion, suspecting – probably correctly – that he had been placed there as an informant for deValera. More importantly, the Cabinet hardliners such as Brugha and Austin Stack – both of whom refused to take part in the negotiations – were more unrealistic in their expectations of what could be achieved. Those who went, particularly Collins and Griffith, were more pragmatic about what was possible and ultimately more inclined to negotiate what they felt to be the best possible settlement. The problem was that that might not necessarily be a Republic and that would not go down well with those left behind in Dublin

Another problem was the lack of clarity in what was expected from the negotiations. The delegation was given the impression that Irish unity mattered more than the achievement of a Republic and that if necessary there should be some movement on the latter to achieve the former. Just how much movement there should be was not really clarified. Again this meant that different interpretations could be arrived at by those holding different viewpoints about the same agreement – all validly held.

Britain's negotiators

As already mentioned, Lloyd George headed the British team. He was assisted by Colonial Secretary Winston Churchill, Austin Chamberlain, soon to be Conservative Party leader and Lord Birkenhead, Lord Chancellor and in a former life – as F. E. Smith – a darling of the unionist cause. It was a delegation with formidable experience both in a general sense, but particularly in terms of experience of negotiations. In this area in particular the Prime Minister was hugely experienced, having recently concluded the Byzantine negotiations that resulted in the Paris Peace Settlement. This was the sort of experience that the Irish simply did not have.

Yet within a maelstrom of change it is interesting to note the repetitive familiarity of the Irish Question for these British politicians and the resigned sense of *plus ça change, plus c'est la même chose*. Speaking in the House of Commons, Churchill spoke of the dislocation caused by the Great War and went on to bemoan that 'as the deluge [of the war] subsides and the waters fall short, we see the dreary steeples of Fermanagh and Tyrone emerging once again. The integrity of their quarrel is one of the few institutions that has been unaltered in the cataclysm which has swept the world.'

Just like the Irish delegation, the British had an absolute minimum with which they wanted to leave the negotiations. While they were keen to protect the concept if not the current size of Northern Ireland, they were principally concerned with protecting the security of the United Kingdom and the unity of the British Empire. As had been the case for centuries, the British feared the prospect of an independent Ireland being used as a launching pad for an attack on Britain. The best way to prevent this, they reasoned, was to tie Ireland into the Commonwealth.

Talking

The negotiations dragged on over the course of the next eight weeks. Non-contentious issues such as trade and defence were dealt with relatively quickly and without any great drama. The difficulties began to arise when the conference began to focus on the more substantive issues.

The Irish delegation put their proposals for Ulster on the table. These were that individual counties be allowed to decide whether to be part of the Dublin or Belfast parliaments. Those that remained with Belfast would ultimately be under the control of the Dublin parliament. Not surprisingly the British rejected this, but their counter-offer showed just how far they were prepared to go to maintain the Empire. It was for an Irish parliament that would have ultimate control over Northern Ireland.

At the start of November Lloyd George attempted to move things along by persuading Griffith to commit to paper his promise that if there was a guarantee of the 'essential unity' of Ireland, he would recommend that Ireland be involved in a 'free partnership' with the Commonwealth and consent to 'a recognition of the Crown as head of the proposed association of states'. For his part the Prime Minister undertook to convince Northern Ireland to come under Dublin's control.

A Boundary Commission

It should come as no great shock to report that Craig was not in favour of such an arrangement. As an alternative Lloyd George came up with the idea of a Boundary Commission that would judge whether and in what ways the border between north and south should be redrawn. He convinced the Irish that such a Commission would alter the border in such a way as to leave Northern Ireland too small to survive. The Irish delegation accepted the idea, as did the remainder of the cabinet in Dublin, albeit with some reluctance. Significantly, Griffith also undertook not to break off negotiations on this issue.

On the issue of Commonwealth membership, however there was to be no compromise. The British rejected out of hand deValera's *via media* of 'External Association'. This, for its time, radical concept envisaged a fully independent Ireland freely forming a link with the Commonwealth.

Finally in early December the talks came to a head when Lloyd George made what he described as his final offer. Ireland would become known as the Irish Free State and would have dominion status within the British Commonwealth of Nations. A Governor General would represent the King of Great Britain in Ireland and all Irish parliamentarians would swear an oath of loyalty to him. Britain agreed to remove all military forces from the 26 counties save for three ports – which became known as Treaty Ports – in which she would maintain a presence.

With regard to the already-existing Northern Ireland it was agreed that the north could opt out of the settlement. If she did so – and of that there was little doubt – a Boundary Commission would be held to adjudicate on what parts of the north would be given to the south and vice versa.

Decision time!

The Irish delegation returned to Dublin to enable the cabinet to discuss the proposals. The hardliners were not prepared to accept dominion status and the delegation returned to London with the understanding that nothing would be signed until it had previously been seen and approved by the Dáil.

On their return the Irish again tried to float the idea of External Association, however Lloyd George was having none of it. On the following day Lloyd George began playing a game of brinkmanship. He demanded to know if the Irish were prepared to accept the Boundary Commission and when they prevaricated he reminded Griffith of his promise not to break on the issue. From that point on there was no possibility of the negotiations falling over Ulster. Indeed for his principled stand on this issue, Griffith earned high praise from one of the British delegates who later said of him, 'A braver man than Arthur Griffith, I never met.'

Lloyd George offered some further concessions regarding trade and proposed a new version of the Oath that allowed loyalty to be sworn first to the constitution and then to the Crown. Again the Prime Minister demanded that the Irish agree and when they stated that they were required to refer the deal to Dublin he warned them that a refusal of the terms would mean an immediate recommencement of hostilities.

Finally, early on the morning of the 6 December 1921 the Irish put their names to the agreement. If they were hopeful for its chances of success they were keeping it well hidden. Collins wrote to a friend that same day, musing somewhat morbidly about what had so recently taken place. He wrote:

> Think what I have got for Ireland? Something which she has wanted this past seven hundred years. Will anyone be satisfied with the bargain? Will anyone? I tell you this – early this morning I signed my death warrant. I thought at the time how odd, how ridiculous – a bullet may just as well have done the job five years ago.

Debate and division

On hearing the news of what had transpired deValera was incandescent with rage. He could not believe that the delegation had signed the document without first consulting him. His anger had not abated by the time the cabinet met two days later. The three cabinet members who had negotiated the Treaty wanted to submit it to the Dáil while the three hardliners – Brugha, Stack and deValera – wanted to rip it up there and then. The seventh member, William T. Cosgrave sided with the delegates and so the Treaty went to the Dáil.

The Dáil debate began just over a week later. It was obvious from the off that the Chamber was deeply divided over the agreement in general and in particular the issue of the Free State's inclusion within the Commonwealth and the Oath of Allegiance to the Crown.

It was to these issues that deValera turned first. In a session behind closed doors he argued that rather than achieving the Republic which had been proclaimed by Pearse in 1916, reaffirmed by the Dáil in 1919 and fought for ever since, the delegates had settled for considerably less. In his view the agreement 'gives away Irish Independence; it brings us into the British Empire; it acknowledges the head of the British Empire not merely as the head of an association, but as the direct monarch of Ireland'. He added, 'Does this assembly think the Irish people have changed so much within the past year or two that they now want to get into the British Empire after seven centuries of fighting?' Of course he himself knew; speaking in early January 1922 deValera stated 'Whenever I wanted to know what the Irish people wanted, I only had to examine my own heart and it told me straight off what the Irish people wanted.'

On this basis he offered the Dáil an alternative to the Treaty known as *Document No. 2*. In all but one respect this was basically the same as the Treaty, down to the inclusion of a Boundary Commission, which leads one to conclude that the border was not a significant issue for the President. The difference was with regard to the Oath, membership of the Commonwealth and the Governor General; deValera had replaced these elements with an association with the Empire.

As the pro-Treaty side pointed out this was pretty much a rehash of proposals that had already been rejected by the British so there was never going to be much mileage with them. Neither were the more republican elements particularly impressed. Hardliners like Brugha were prepared to accept nothing short of full independence and called for a renewal of hostilities with the British. As a result deValera withdrew the proposals.

Nothing more productive than the destruction of the Treaty was offered by the other anti-Treatyites who spoke during the debate. The more moderate elements accepted that there had to be some sort of compromise with the British but felt that this document just wasn't it, mainly because of the Oath and the link to the Commonwealth. The hardliners – particularly populated by the female TDs (*Teachta Dála* – Dáil Deputies) – could not get their heads around the idea of the only solution being the implementation of the republican utopia as declared by Pearse on the steps of the GPO in 1916. Anyone who accepted a jot less than that idea was a traitor to the Republic and would have to be dealt with as such.

Those who had signed the agreement knew that there was no point in pretending it was something that quite clearly it was not. Instead they attempted to convince the Dáil that they had achieved something that was a pipe dream only a few years ago. As Griffith argued 'we have brought back the evacuation of Ireland after seven hundred years by British troops...we have brought back to Ireland equality with England; equality with all the nations which form the Commonwealth'. Collins tried to take a longer-term view in his contribution. He asked the assembly to see the agreement as 'not the ultimate freedom that all nations aspire and develop to, but the freedom to achieve it'. Richard Mulcahy, IRA Commander-in-Chief made it clear that the IRA was not in a position to engage in renewed conflict. He added that in any case they could never achieve a Republic militarily.

The debate was exhausting and became increasingly bitter as time went on. The Christmas recess gave TDs the opportunity to take soundings from their localities and when the Dáil reassembled in January the vote was taken. As might have been expected it was close but the agreement was endorsed by 64 votes to 57.

The split was not long coming. Immediately deValera resigned as President and led his supporters from the Chamber. Griffith replaced him and appointed a new cabinet, but despite his best efforts the deep cracks that had appeared in an organization bound together by common opposition to the British were now appearing. With both sides now seeing different enemies the prospects of renewed warfare in Ireland were clear. This time, however, it would be conflict between Irishmen, a civil war.

A Provisional government

The Treaty stipulated that the final transfer of power from London to Dublin would occur on 6 December 1922. In the intervening period power was to be handed over incrementally to a newly established Provisional Government. All of this was taking place against a background of increasing tension and hostility. Kevin O'Higgins, later Vice President of the Executive Council (as the new state's government was called), provided a real sense of the difficulties facing the new leadership when he spoke of the Provisional Government as 'simply eight young men in the City Hall standing amidst the ruins of one administration, with the foundations of another not yet laid, and with wild men screaming through the keyhole'.

On 14 January Collins was elected as Chairman of this Provisional Government. As such he had the responsibility of taking over from the British both politically and militarily. This required him to oversee the drafting of a Constitution and the establishment of the various organs and services that were required to support a state. At the same time the fissures that had appeared in the Dáil were beginning to widen.

In the short term there were some, albeit fleeting, pleasures to be gained. One of Collins' first duties was to take possession of Dublin Castle from the British. The story goes that on the appointed day Collins arrived for the ceremony seven minutes late. When chided by a British representative for his tardiness Collins is reputed to have replied 'You've kept us waiting 700 years. You can have your seven minutes.'

Countdown to conflict

Civil war did not break out immediately though; strenuous efforts were made to try and find some form of compromise that would avoid a debilitating internecine conflict. However, a split in the IRA made this possibility more and more likely. The majority of those working at IRA HQ accepted the Treaty, but senior figures such as Liam Mellows and Rory O'Connor rejected the deal. Across the movement as a whole, most local commanders in the south were anti-Treaty. In general the men in their commands tended to follow a similar line. All in all the anti-Treaty side were probably numerically superior to those in the IRA who supported the Treaty.

On 26 March the IRA formally split over the Treaty and the anti-Treaty forces set up their own Executive. Just under three weeks later a group of anti-Treaty soldiers seized control of Dublin's Four Courts. For a time Collins was content to let them stay, still unwilling to begin fighting his former colleagues despite significant pressure from the British to take decisive action. Apart from wanting to explore each and every political avenue to avoid civil war, Collins also wanted time to build up his own forces.

In attempting to reach an accommodation with his opponents Collins quite frequently sailed close to the wind in terms of not fulfilling the expectations of the British. In February he agreed with deValera to delay elections until June. In the interim he wanted to draw up a Constitution that would win the anti-Treatyites over to his side.

In May the two leaders also agreed a pact that would have allowed them to fight the forthcoming elections on the same ticket. In this way the voters would not have been able to choose between the two positions. Collins' own colleagues were none too pleased with such semantics but his response ws that he was trying every means possible to avoid conflict breaking out.

Churchill denounced the election pact and urged Collins to act against the men holding the Four Courts. Yet if he was angry at what had gone before, he was angrier still when the draft Constitution was published in June. It made absolutely no mention of the Oath of Allegiance or indeed of the king. The British response was swift; they threatened to tear up the Treaty unless the omissions were corrected.

With little other option the changes were made. Collins then rejected the electoral pact that he had previously made just two days before the polls opened. On the day of the election the revised Constitution was published. DeValera claimed that this meant that the voters could not exercise their choice in an informed manner.

The results revealed the election of 58 pro-Treaty TDs, 35 anti-Treaty and 35 others. This latter group included a fair number of TDs who were also pro-Treaty, including the representatives of the Irish Labour Party. This gave the pro-Treaty side a significant majority in the Dáil. It seemed that the people had come down clearly in support of the Treaty.

As June progressed events came to a head. The assassination in London of the pro-unionist Army leader, Sir Henry Wilson, by two IRA gunmen, was an important development. Wilson, who was also acting as an adviser to the Belfast government, was returning home from unveiling a war memorial when he was gunned down. Evidence reveals that he attempted to draw his sword in a vain effort to defend himself. One of the assassins had only one leg, having lost the other one at the Battle of Ypres. Not surprisingly this hampered his escape and both men were apprehended and later hanged.

The assassination resulted in Churchill again urging Collins to move against the anti-Treaty forces that he believed were responsible. Historians believe that in actuality Collins probably ordered the assassination. Yet Collins still hesitated; then when some of the Four Courts troops captured one of his generals he finally had the justification that he needed to act. On 28 June the Four Courts was bombarded, ironically with guns borrowed from the British. The Civil War had started.

For his part, Churchill was over the moon. He telegrammed Collins stating that 'If I refrain from congratulating you it is only because I do not want to embarrass you.' No doubt Collins was delighted!

Civil War

The outbreak of conflict now forced people to take sides. Having prophesied about Volunteers having to wade 'through the blood' of their opponents, deValera supported the anti-Treatyites or Irregulars as they were known. However for much of the Civil War's duration his influence was eclipsed by the authority of the military leaders who were prosecuting the Irregular campaign. Collins meanwhile temporarily gave up his position as Head of the Provisional Government to assume command of the pro-Treaty forces.

There was never a great amount of doubt about which side would be ultimately victorious. Despite the anti-Treaty forces being stronger initially, rapid recruitment meant that before long numbers heavily favoured the pro-Treaty forces. Pro-Treaty soldiers were soon in control of the anti-Treaty strongholds in Munster.

The conflict then degenerated into the same kind of guerrilla conflict that had taken place between the IRA and the British forces so recently. As was the case during that earlier conflict, harsh legislative measures were passed, this time by a Dublin government. The executions of close to 80 former comrades were carried out by government forces. Those put to death included O'Connor (who had been best man at Kevin O'Higgins' wedding), Mellows and Childers. In addition, laws permitting internment were introduced resulting in the imprisonment of over 11,000 opponents by the middle of 1923.

By that stage it was quite clear to the anti-Treaty leadership that continued opposition was pointless and in May 1923 their forces were ordered to lay down their arms. The physical and economic damage that had been caused was huge, but buildings would be much easier to repair than the bitter divisions which had emerged between former comrades and even within families.

Even more irreplaceable were the leaders who had fallen during the conflict. Cathal Brugha, strongly anti-Treaty, was killed in action early in the Civil War. Arthur Griffith succumbed to a stroke, worn out by the intense pressures of leadership. Perhaps most cruel of all – in terms of the successful future development of the new state – was the death of Michael Collins just over a week after he had buried Griffith. He was just 32 years old when he was ambushed by anti-Treaty forces at Béal na mBláth (which translates as the Mouth of Flowers) in Co. Cork on 12 August 1922.

The loss of both Griffith and Collins would be keenly felt. Speaking in the Dáil shortly after their respective deaths, Richard Mulcahy stated that Ireland had 'lost two people who were the leaders, and to whom we looked as the leaders of the future, one of them the sower who lived in Ireland, and the other the greatest reaper the country has ever had'.

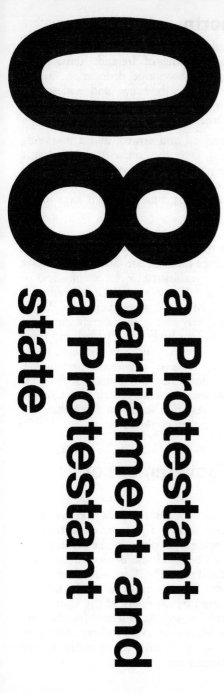

08 a Protestant parliament and a Protestant state

This chapter will cover:
- establishing a government in Belfast
- nationalists' reactions
- unionist suspicions
- the Boundary Commission
- economic problems.

Violence in the north

The IRA detachments based in the north had begun to stage attacks even before the partitioning of Ireland. Tensions in Belfast, resulting from ongoing economic dislocation, added further pressure to an already heady brew, and widespread sectarian violence erupted in the north in the aftermath of the annual July 1920 Orange Order commemorations.

As a result the UVF was revived and armed, and a markedly sectarian conflict commenced. Over the course of the next year thousands of Catholics were driven from their places of employment, and Catholic businesses and dwellings were torched. All told, several hundred people lost their lives in the period 1920–2.

The British responded by setting up the infrastructure of a government in Belfast even though the Government of Ireland Act had still to finish its passage through parliament and receive the Royal Assent. It also established a force of 'Special Constables' (more properly the Ulster Special Constabulary – USC) to deal with the unrest. Most of its members were drawn from the UVF, which immediately and unfortunately implied a partial application of the law. This body was divided into three sections, A, B and C Classes. The A Class was full time; the C Class consisted of reservists. However it was the part-time B Specials, which became most notorious. Long after the A and C Classes had been disbanded, the B Specials remained active and were viewed, in nationalist eyes, as a sectarian force that was only employed against the minority community.

Establishing the government of Northern Ireland

The unionists might not have sought their own Home Rule parliament initially, but once it was a *fait accompli* they set about making it work. The powers devolved by the Government of Ireland Act allowed for a 52-seat House of Commons and a Senate made up of 26 individuals. The Commons was to be elected using Proportional Representation (PR). Of the Senators, 24 were to be elected by members of the Commons. The remaining two seats were, *ex officio*, reserved for the Lord Mayor of Belfast and the Mayor of Londonderry. Northern Ireland was to continue to elect 13 MPs to sit in the United Kingdom parliament at Westminster.

The Act allowed the parliament in Belfast to control most of the everyday affairs of the new state. There was, however, a considerable assortment of what were called reserved powers. Westminster retained responsibility for matters concerning the Crown, foreign policy, defence and taxation. It also retained the power to overrule any law made by the Northern Ireland parliament.

The elections for the new parliament were held in May 1921. The results indicated a more than healthy majority for the unionists in tune with the majority they enjoyed across the six counties that made up the new state. They won 40 out of the 52 available seats. With such a majority it was going to be easy for the unionists to dominate the political institutions. Indeed Sir James Craig, the unionist leader, later remarked (in a 1934 Parliamentary speech) 'All I boast of is that we have a Protestant parliament and a Protestant State.'

The remaining 12 seats were shared equally between Sinn Féin and the Home Rule Party. However neither party actually recognized the legitimacy of the new state, thus rendering their minority position even more irrelevant within parliament.

Sir James Craig became the first Prime Minister of Northern Ireland. Carson had decided on the passage of the Government of Ireland Act that he was too old to serve as Northern Ireland's leader. Instead he was appointed to the Lords as Baron Carson of Duncairn and took up the post of one of the Lords of Appeal, more popularly known as Law Lords. Indeed there is some evidence of a change in Carson's outlook in the latter years of his life. He struck up an unlikely friendship with some nationalist politicians including Kevin O'Higgins, and is reputed to have stated that he was 'only a puppet, and so was Ulster, and so was Ireland, in the political game to get the Conservative Party into power'.

Nationalists and the new state

While the unionist population might have speedily reconciled itself to the prospect of its own parliament, the nationalists' reaction was less sanguine. The vast majority felt bitter about becoming citizens of a state in which they made up only one third of the population and to which they had not given their consent. The signing of the Treaty in December 1921 further emphasized their sense of isolation. Their opposition was demonstrated in two main ways, one violent, the other passive.

The agreement of the Treaty resulted in an increase in the levels of violence in the north. Indeed the violence that developed was particularly vicious. IRA units launched attacks on a wide range of targets not all of which were military. The unionist response meant that the death toll rose while Catholics also continued to be driven from their places of employment. In the first six months of 1922 over 250 people died; just under two thirds of whom were Catholics. Given such figures many Catholics concluded that Northern Ireland was never going to be their utopia.

The spiralling levels of violence eventually resulted in an interesting and unlikely (if temporary) union between Michael Collins and James Craig. The two leaders met three times in the first three months of 1922. In return for Craig agreeing to do more to protect Catholics, Collins undertook to bring the Belfast Boycott to an end. This boycott of all goods emanating from Belfast had been initiated by the Dublin government in response to the spiralling sectarian violence in Belfast.

While hopes were high, the results were meagre in Collins' opinion. In the aftermath of the Belfast government's introduction of draconian security measures that had a particularly anti-Catholic focus, he changed his approach. Co-operation with Belfast decreased and Collins arranged for IRA opponents of the Treaty to provide weapons to northern IRA detachments.

However this was not the only visible evidence of nationalist opposition to the creation of the new state. Violence aside, there was, in the eyes of unionists, a less tangible but equally insidious nationalist reaction to Northern Ireland that did not make use of violence but which still implied a lack of loyalty. Put simply, since they expected partition to be temporary, nationalists refused to recognize the existence of Northern Ireland.

Their refusal manifested itself in a number of ways: Sinn Féin and Nationalist Party (as the old Home Rule Party became) MPs refused to fill their 12 seats in the new Northern Ireland parliament; teachers in Catholic schools refused recognition to the new Ministry of Education and were instead paid by Dublin, at least until Collins died; finally Catholics did not join the Royal Ulster Constabulary (RUC) formed in 1922, despite the fact that a quota was set aside for them, evidence that Craig was at least initially keen to create some form of pluralism.

The government's reaction

The government responded to the violence with a range of draconian actions. Its crackdown was given the legislative teeth that it needed through the passage of the Civil Authorities (Special Powers) Act in 1922. This allowed the government, through the person of the Home Affairs Minister, 'to take all such steps and issue all such orders as may be necessary for preserving peace'. In practice this mainly translated into enabling the authorities to arrest and detain people without any trial although it also permitted the imposition of curfews. In the aftermath of the government's proscribing of the IRA in June 1922 over 500 suspects were arrested and detained on a ship moored in Belfast Lough.

As already suggested, the security forces were also reconstituted in the aftermath of partition. The RIC ceased to exist to be replaced by the RUC. Like its predecessor the RUC was an armed police force. The USC also came under the microscope, being brought under the direction of the Home Affairs Ministry. All told, the Belfast government could call upon close to 50,000 policemen by the middle of 1922. In addition, there were also the 13 British Army battalions based in the area, although they came under the control of the London government.

In spite of their substantial majority, the more than supportive police force and the possibilities of the security legislation, the unionist population remained highly suspicious of the potential motives and ambitions of the nationalist population, almost to the point of paranoia. The highly negative reaction to Northern Ireland emanating from nationalists did nothing to ease these fears and many unionists came to believe that nationalists were out to undermine the new state, perhaps with the support of the large nationalist majority in the rest of the island. For this reason they regarded them as disloyal and not to be trusted with any form of political power.

PR and gerrymandering

What political power was there, however, given the unionists' total domination of central government? One area of potential influence remained at the local level and a number of nationalist authorities had initially attempted to remain loyal to Dáil Éireann. These bodies were finally suspended in 1922.

The government then moved to reduce the potential of electorates returning nationalist local councils by abolishing PR and by gerrymandering electoral boundaries to ensure unionist control of local authorities where Catholics were in a majority. This form of discrimination was particularly obvious in the city of Derry where, despite a clear nationalist majority, the electorate always produced a unionist majority. In addition, the right to vote was limited to property holders, again favouring Protestants more than Catholics.

The resulting unionist-dominated local authorities did little to prevent Catholic claims of discrimination in jobs and housing. It was an injustice that would become particularly significant in the 1960s.

In 1929 PR was also abolished for General Elections to the Northern Ireland parliament. Interestingly this was due less to a fear of nationalists than to concerns over the fragmentation of the unionist vote. Given the numerical impotence of the nationalist politicians, Northern Ireland was essentially a one-party state and the (now renamed) Ulster Unionist Party (UUP) the only party of government. However, before long, some degree of dissention had begun to emerge from within unionist ranks, usually concerning poor economic conditions. This first occurred at the time of the 1925 General Election and also embraced an emerging number of Labour politicians; taken together they won seven seats.

The abolition of PR in 1929 more or less shut the door on the possibility of a repeat of the 1925 result. As a result, a large percentage of seats were never contested, as there was only ever the possibility of one side or the other winning them. This was not good for politics or for the need to permit healthy debate on the key issues of the day.

The Boundary Commission

Under the terms of the 1921 Treaty the unity of Ireland was recognized. Article XI stated that the Free State was to take over the powers reserved to London by the 1920 Government of Ireland Act unless the Belfast parliament asked to be excluded from its terms. Article XII laid down what would happen in the more than likely event of Northern Ireland opting out. There would be a Commission established with three members, one nominated by Dublin, one by Belfast and the Chair, appointed by London. Its task would be to 'determine, in accordance with the wishes of the inhabitants, so far as may be compatible with economic and geographical conditions, the boundaries between Northern Ireland and the rest of Ireland'.

During the Treaty negotiations Lloyd George had led each side to believe that the Boundary Commission would provide an outcome pleasing to them. Of course that simply was not going to be possible.

Not surprisingly Craig refused to have anything to do with a body that might emasculate his government's territory. His catchphrase became 'What we have we hold.' For a time the Free State government was preoccupied with winning the Civil War and establishing the new state on firm foundations. It was 1923, therefore, before the Dublin government turned to the issue again, appointing Eoin MacNeill as its Commission nominee.

Craig refused to nominate a representative. In the end the British government nominated Belfast unionist J. R. Fisher as the Northern Ireland representative. They also appointed the Commission's Chairman, South African Supreme Court judge Richard Feetham.

The Commission took evidence beginning in November 1924. Almost exactly a year later a British newspaper, the *Morning Post*, leaked – with remarkable accuracy – the main recommendations of the Commission. Under Feetham's influence it had placed significant weight on its interpretation of the phrase 'so far as may be compatible with economic and geographical conditions' with regard to moving the border. Its decision was basically to give a little of the north to the south and a little of the south to the north.

There was an outcry in Dublin when the newspaper was published. Never in their wildest dreams had the Irish ever expected to lose land never mind not gain what Lloyd George had led them to believe would be huge chunks of Northern Ireland. This expectation had been one of the main reasons why the issue of partition had exercised so little influence during the Dáil debates on the Treaty. MacNeill was forced to resign as Minister for Education in the face of a less than understanding public reaction.

The Irish leader, William T. Cosgrave moved swiftly to repair some of the damage and met with Craig and the British Prime Minister, Stanley Baldwin, in London. It was agreed to shelve the Commission Report in favour of an Anglo-Irish Agreement. This stated that the border would remain unchanged from that fixed by the 1920 Government of Ireland Act. It added that the powers of the Council of Ireland, established by the same Act, would pass to the Belfast government. At the same time the Free State was relieved of its Treaty obligations to pay part of the

British national debt while Northern Ireland was let off paying any further land annuities.

Politics after the Boundary Commission

The failure of the Boundary Commission to alter the border copperfastened partition. Nationalist politicians differed on what strategies to employ after the Commission debacle. The more moderate element led by Joseph Devlin decided that as Northern Ireland was clearly not going to go away the time was right to enter the Northern Ireland parliament. However the more republican element continued in their refusal to recognize the Northern Ireland State. Of course this did nothing to convince the already suspicious unionists of the minority's *bona fides*.

States within a state?

In many ways the two communities lived as strangers even though they shared the same, relatively small piece of land. Few Catholics were involved in helping to run the institutions of state and in an agricultural and commercial sense both communities exercised a form of religious apartheid. Jobs stayed within communities; as future Prime Minister Basil Brooke stated on 12 July 1933, 'I would appeal to loyalists wherever possible to employ good Protestant lads and lassies.' Education of the young, an ideal opportunity to dispel myths, was delivered along sectarian lines and triumphalism was delivered through either the activities of the Orange Order or the Ancient Order of Hibernians.

The Northern Ireland economy

One of the main reasons for unionist opposition to rule by an Irish parliament was their fear that the Ulster economy would have been damaged if not destroyed by Dublin rule. Throughout the nineteenth century the northern economy had developed at a much higher level than the remainder of the country. While most of Ireland retained an agricultural economy, Belfast and its hinterland had developed highly successful shipbuilding and engineering industries. Agriculture had also remained important and in particular the linen industry had played a significant element in economic success.

However by the 1920s cracks were beginning to appear in the province's previously prosperous economic façade. The agricultural industry was labouring under the weight of small, inefficient farms while shipbuilding, engineering and linen were suffering the effects of an economic downturn in the aftermath of the Great War. Unemployment began to rise inexorably.

In its attempts to do anything about such weaknesses the Belfast government was always going to be severely limited. The administration had very little control over the raising of taxes locally. In addition the main decisions about how whatever money was available could be spent remained with the British government.

Concerning agriculture the government responded by establishing the Agriculture Faculty at Queen's University Belfast. It also introduced an improved standards system for both meat and dairy produce. As a result the value of agricultural exports increased by close to 50 per cent in the period 1926–39.

Improving the industrial sector was not as easy and became markedly more difficult in the aftermath of the 1929 Wall Street Crash and the resulting world depression. Unemployment levels shot even higher to the extent that during the 1930s over a quarter of the male workforce was without a job.

The Stormont (after 1932 this Belfast suburb was the location of the Northern Ireland parliament) government's response was limited, not because of some form of Dickensian indifference, but because of its own financial situation. As already indicated the financial settlement drawn up at the time of partition did the Belfast administration no favours. It was unable to raise significant amounts of additional revenue through taxation and the money it was receiving from Westminster was simply not sufficient. For this reason the conditions endured by the poorest levels of society were harsh and unremitting.

The depression was ecumenical in its impact. Protestants as well as Catholics felt its bite and in the early 1930s both sides actually joined together – albeit exceedingly briefly – to protest at the conditions they were forced to endure. The Belfast government's response was to encourage the employment of Protestants to the exclusion of Catholics and before long the union was broken. It was soon back to the way things had been and in 1935 sectarian tensions erupted once again in Belfast.

09

breaking the links: the Irish Free State, 1922–39

This chapter will cover:

- establishing a state
- seeking stability: social and economic
- Ireland within the Commonwealth
- DeValera in power
- the Blueshirts
- undoing the Treaty
- a new Constitution
- economic war.

State-building

With the Civil War over, the challenges facing the Free State government changed, yet the ones it now faced were no less difficult. With Collins and Griffith gone and with deValera on the 'wrong' side, the initial question centred on appointing a new leader. Eventually William T. Cosgrave, a Dubliner who had fought with Cathal Brugha during the 1916 Easter Rising and who subsequently served as Minister for Local Government from 1919–22, was given the task not only of heading the new regime, but of establishing a state with little or no precedent to call upon. Although not a charismatic figure in the mould of Collins, Cosgrave provided the steadiness of hand that helped guide the Free State through its early difficult years.

Setting up a new system would be a challenge at the best of times, but in the context of Ireland in 1923 it was a daunting task. The country had been physically ravaged by four years of conflict of one kind or another. Added to this was the legacy of bitterness that the Civil War had left. Politics was not really able to develop along what might be seen as a traditional left–right continuum. Instead it would be a question of whether one was 'for' or 'against' the Treaty.

Parliamentary structures

Under the terms of the Constitution drawn up by Collins' Provisional government the Irish parliament, or Oireachtas, was, like Britain's, to comprise of two chambers. The members of the lower house or Dáil, known as TDs, were to be elected using the PR system. All adults over the age of 21 were enfranchised. The government and the Dáil would then select the 60 members of the second Chamber, the Seanad or Senate. It would contain a number of ex-unionists in an attempt to ensure that a genuine pluralism existed in the new state. Senators would serve a three-year term before having to submit themselves for re-election. As with the American Senate these elections would be staggered.

All members of the Oireachtas were required to swear an oath of loyalty to the Constitution and to the British monarch. The latter's representative in Ireland was styled the Governor General. The first holder of this office was T. M. Healy, a former member of the Home Rule Party. As befitting the status of the position, the Governor General's residence was the former home of the Viceroy, located in Dublin's Phoenix Park.

The government or Executive Council was to be headed by a President and he in turn would be assisted by a team of 11 ministers, each heading a discrete department. If the Dáil rejected a piece of legislation proposed by the Executive Council a General Election would result. If a similar rejection emanated from the Seanad the measure would be subject to a delay lasting 270 days.

The institutions of state

In a great many areas the various institutions created to support the machinery of government were not very far removed from those that had existed under British rule, mainly because that was the system with which the Irish were most familiar. The system of Dáil Courts was abolished in 1924 and replaced by a legal structure which looked different but was in reality pretty much the same as had gone before. Admittedly there were minor structural changes to make the legal system more accessible, however much of the day-to-day working of the court system remained unchanged, even to the extent of the main actors wearing gowns and wigs. The one significant difference was the creation of a Supreme Court, which, despite what its name might imply, was not the ultimate legal authority in the land. Rather, the Judicial Committee of the Privy Council in London was the highest legal authority in Ireland, even if use of it would mean recourse to a Commonwealth institution.

Likewise, thousands of civil servants transferred from serving the British administration to serving the Irish one, which itself was developed by men trained in the British model. While this provided much-needed continuity it also ensured that a great deal of the conservatism that had been prevalent within the old system was retained. This was particularly true in terms of the influence exercised by the Department of Finance.

There was slightly more change when it came to local administration. The British had left a legacy of what might politely be described as confusion in this area, with a plethora of competing and overlapping institutions. The new government restructured the system, establishing new institutions while reassigning existing responsibilities.

Security

One of the most pressing requirements for the new regime was establishing law and order on a firm basis, particularly in the aftermath of a sustained period during which both had broken down. The Army, which had its origins in the pro-Treaty IRA, had, at close to 60,000 men, become far too large for peacetime duties and so had to be reduced in size. It also needed to be reduced in terms of its own influence, emerging as it was out of a period when conditions dictated that military leaders exercise a huge influence over the government of the state.

This reduction, which was overseen by Richard Mulcahy as Minister for Defence, led to one of the new state's first crises. By the start of 1924 the Army had been reduced to a quarter of its 1923 size. A further reduction of 1,000 was planned and this was when the problems began. In March 1924 a mutiny broke out amongst a group of officers unwilling to accept the continuing reduction. They demanded that demobilization cease forthwith and that more effort be made to move towards the republic that Collins had argued could still result from the Treaty.

As a former Commander in Chief of the IRA Mulcahy had some sympathy with the mutineers' concerns. He went so far as to revive the IRB – a movement to which many of the commissioned soldiers belonged – as a way of dealing with the growing unrest. However, he was too much of a democrat to have ever considered bowing to their demands, especially given the manner in which they were being made.

Unfortunately his military background and association with both the IRB and the legacy of Michael Collins had made him suspect to a number of cabinet colleagues, in particular the Minister for Home Affairs, Kevin O'Higgins. O'Higgins used the opportunity to bring the crisis to a head and force Mulcahy's resignation from the government.

In the end O'Higgins' actions helped create a tradition in Ireland of the civil authority no longer being dictated to by the military. In the meantime, the episode damaged relations within the government unnecessarily and could have lost it power if Sinn Féin had not been absent from the Dáil.

There was also the need to establish a police force appropriate to the new system. A new force, the Garda Síochána, was set up in 1923. Unlike its predecessor, the RIC, or indeed the new northern police force, the RUC, the Garda Síochána was from day one an unarmed force. Under the leadership of Eoin O'Duffy it quickly won acceptance by and respect from the Irish population.

New parties

The political split that resulted from the signing of the Treaty meant that at least one party was going to have to change its name. At the start of 1923 the government party adopted the name Cumann na nGaedheal. However, although they had established a new party, the Cumann na nGaedheal leadership never really took the time to develop a party structure throughout the country. This failure would return to haunt them at a later date when faced with deValera's highly organized political machine.

Meanwhile the anti-Treatyites continued to use the name Sinn Féin. Led by deValera they refused to take their seats in the post-Treaty Dáil because of the Oath of Allegiance. Given the basis of their opposition to the Treaty and the Civil War that resulted from it, they could do little else. However their lack of success in creating a parliament to rival the Dáil soon led deValera to the conclusion that he would have to enter the Dáil sooner or later.

Because Sinn Féin refused to enter the Dáil, the job of opposing the government fell to the smaller parties. The largest of these was the Labour Party which had been founded by Larkin and Connolly in 1912. It had deliberately remained on the peripheries of Irish party politics in the years of struggle with the British, but had begun to emerge again after the establishment of the new state. Between the years 1922 and 1927 it served admirably as the Official Opposition, berating the government over its conservative policies while constantly reminding it of its duties and responsibilities to the less fortunate members of Irish society.

However, despite their significant contribution to the establishment of the new state the Labour Party was never really able to make the electoral breakthrough that would have enabled it to compete with the other parties on an even footing. There were a number of reasons for this; the main political focus remained on the Treaty while the Party itself suffered from a number of internal disputes and from the impact of the post-war depression. Finally, due to the relatively small working class in Ireland and to the natural suspicion within a conservative

Catholic country of left-wing politics, the Labour Party was never able to make a significant breakthrough. Indeed the Party was never able to make a significant breakthrough. Indeed the Party was never able to gain more than 19 seats at election time during the pre-war period.

It was the failure of the Boundary Commission (see Chapter 8) to settle the border issue in a manner satisfactory to the Free State that started the chain of events that resulted in deValera entering the Dáil. By agreeing to retain the border as it stood and to the powers of the reunification-biased Council of Ireland being handed over to Northern Ireland, Cosgrave had basically accepted the permanence of partition. Moreover he had failed to have the Free State freed from its obligation to pay Britain land annuities (see below), something that Craig had managed to do.

DeValera recognized that the government had forfeited huge amounts of popularity over the issue. However, he also realized that for as long as his Party remained outside the Dáil, he could do little that was constructive. Significantly, recent local election results had indicated a lack of support for his Party, due mainly, he suspected, to its abstentionist policy. As a result deValera recommended to his Party that they should take up their seats in the Dáil if the Oath were removed.

The majority of his Party did not agree with deValera and so he left Sinn Féin and established a new movement, Fianna Fáil (the Republican Party) in May 1926. The Party rapidly developed a nationwide organization and a coherent political and economic strategy, and in the following year's General Election won just three seats less than the government (44 to 47). The government's support had decreased markedly due to the impact of its overly conservative economic policies, its continued payment of land annuities and the introduction of internment to deal with increased IRA activities.

This result was a clear indication that much of the support that had previously gone to Sinn Féin was now being transferred to Fianna Fáil (the government's erstwhile support had gone largely to Labour). It also revealed how tenuous the government's hold on power would be, particularly if the Fianna Fáil TDs attempted to enter the Dáil. However, when the new TDs turned up at the Dáil to take their seats they were barred because of their refusal to sign the ledger that contained the Oath.

DeValera enters the Dáil

A solution to the crisis was not immediately apparent and when it arrived it was not the solution that people might have expected or indeed wanted. On 10 July the Minister for Home Affairs, Kevin O'Higgins, was assassinated while walking to Sunday Mass by a gang of speculative republican assassins. Cosgrave's government swung immediately into action and, apart from introducing new security measures, passed a law that allowed the government to remove the right to sit in the Dáil from any TD who refused to take the Oath.

Fianna Fáil now decided that the Oath was no more than an 'empty formula' and soon after deValera led his new Party into the Dáil for a second time. This time when presented with the Oath he signed it and entered the Chamber. Before placing his signature on the register the Fianna Fáil leader announced that he was not 'taking any oath nor giving any promise of faithfulness to the King of England…I am putting my name here merely as a formality…and I want you to know that no other meaning is to be attached to what I am doing'.

Cumann na nGaedheal had brought Fianna Fáil into constitutional politics. From that point onwards any war over the 1921 settlement would be more than likely a war of words. Somewhat ironically, the eventual reward for this act of political selflessness would be defeat in the 1932 General Election. In the short term Cosgrave called another election and with an improved mandate was able to hang onto power for a while longer with the support of smaller parties.

Now that they were in the Dáil and acting as the Official Opposition, the Fianna Fáil TDs lost no time attacking the government on what they perceived to be its two main areas of weakness: the condition of the economy and the Free State's continued relationship with the British Commonwealth of Nations.

Society and economy

The government had swiftly moved to Gaelicize the educational system in the Free State, although in other areas there was more continuity than change. The study of Irish was made compulsory, as indeed was attendance at school up to the age of 14, although evidence suggests many still departed before reaching that age. There were some efforts at rationalization of existing elements, whilst a new examination system was introduced for secondary education. To provide training for those wishing to be taught a trade a system of vocational schools was established. While these were important developments, for most children in the Irish Free State, education still finished after the primary stage and in many areas the educational infrastructure remained woefully inadequate.

A green paintbrush was used – literally and metaphorically – to obliterate evidence of British rule. Red pillar-boxes got a fresh coat of emerald green while place names were also de-Anglicized wherever possible. However in their efforts to create a uniquely Gaelic cultural identity, some changes were introduced that were not so positive. In the mid-1920s a Censor and a Censorship Board were established to keep an eye on elements of culture which might infect and weaken Ireland's unique traditions. It is fair to say that not all of the material that came under the censor's ban could be regarded as poor examples of their particular medium.

With regard to the economy the simplistic nationalist view was that an Irish government would be able to achieve economic independence and make the Irish economy successful. This viewpoint did not really take into account the realities of the position in which the Free State found itself. Economically Ireland was starting from a relatively low base. The country was predominantly agricultural and the physical dislocation of the domestic war years, coupled with the economic fallout from the Great War, had a significant impact. Most important, the Irish economy was inextricably linked to Britain's; any attempt at separation would be fraught with difficulties.

The main focus of the Dublin government's policy was on agriculture. It was felt that improving this area would provide the kick-start to overall improvement. The man faced with dealing with this state of affairs was Patrick Hogan. By the end of the decade he had succeeded in greatly improving the conditions and prospects of Irish agriculture through overseeing the introduction of a range of reforms. Compulsory land purchase was completed, smallholdings were amalgamated (to some degree) and high standards for all types of produce were implemented. In addition an Agricultural Credit Corporation was established to enable farmers to purchase machinery. Previously such an opportunity would have been beyond all but the wealthiest farmers.

While there were some improvements in export figures by the end of the decade, they were due mainly to improvements in the cattle industry. In any case, whatever improvements had been made were wiped out by the wave of depression that rippled out inexorably from the Wall Street Crash. Meanwhile, despite the innovative nature of the Agricultural Credit Corporation, few took advantage of the possibilities on offer.

The government cut income tax and reduced its spending in an effort to ease the burden on farmers, however it is likely that only the better-off minority benefited. The majority of smaller farmers – along with those who suffered from wage cuts and reductions in social welfare – enjoyed no real benefit. Not surprisingly, none of this increased the government's popularity at election time.

If agriculture was badly off, heavy industry was almost non-existent. Most of what had passed for industry in the island of Ireland was now on the northern side of the border. Before new large-scale industries could be established the state had to do something about the poor provision of electricity supply. The establishment of the Electricity Supply Board (ESB) in 1927 was a huge advance. Much of the current being distributed emanated from the huge hydroelectric power stations that were erected on the River Shannon.

Although the government introduced tariffs on smaller scale imports it was not until the effects of the Great Depression kicked in that this policy was extended. Even then their actions came nowhere close to what Fianna Fáil was suggesting. By now it was advocating full-scale protectionism, in line with the economic ideas expounded by Griffith almost a quarter of a century earlier.

The 'Restless Dominion'

Historian D. W. Harkness entitled his seminal study of the Free State's relationship with the British Commonwealth *The Restless Dominion*. This title appropriately sums up the way in which the Free State government began to challenge its relationship with Britain by trying to show that they could do the same kind of things as other independent countries. In this way they were proving, as Collins had suggested, that the Treaty gave them 'the freedom to achieve freedom'.

In 1923 the Free State joined the League of Nations, the first

Commonwealth member so to do. In the following year they notched up another first when they appointed their own ambassador to the USA, as opposed to operating through the British representative. In 1924 they successfully registered the 1921 Treaty at the League as an international agreement. This was to counter British claims that the Agreement was not a treaty as that could only be agreed by two sovereign nations. Instead Britain regarded it as an act of the Westminster parliament.

These were important initial steps but what Cumann na nGaedheal really wanted to achieve was a declaration that Commonwealth member states were not bound by any legislation passed by the Westminster parliament.

Such a declaration was slow in coming. At the regular conferences held among members of the Commonwealth the Free State tried to persuade other dominions to demand equality with Britain. This pressure finally resulted in the British parliament passing the 1931 Statute of Westminster. It stated that Westminster could not pass a law that was binding on Commonwealth states. Equally important, it added that any laws that Westminster had previously enacted did not bind member states. This meant that if it wanted to, the Dublin government could repeal the 1921 Treaty. It was a major achievement.

Groundbreaking though these measures were, the Free State government did not gain a great deal of political kudos from those successes back home. There were a number of reasons for this: partly the issues involved were too complicated for those not *au fait* with constitutional theory to understand; partly also because working within the Commonwealth, even if it was to gain more freedom, was still not popular. But it was mainly because ordinary people had, perhaps, more mundane concerns.

Countdown to election

It was in to the more prosaic issues that Fianna Fáil began to tap. The Great Depression had an impact on Ireland as elsewhere and, as privation kicked in, support for the government began to suffer. Fianna Fáil pointed to things like the continued payment of land annuities – money for pre-partition government loans for land purchase – which was being collected by the Cumann na nGaedheal government and handed over to London. It promised to halt these while also protecting

Ireland's hard-pressed industries with a tariff system. Such ideas won Fianna Fáil popularity at a time when the government's support was further on the wane.

By the early 1930s republican violence was again on the increase. The government clamped down hard on the movement by passing the Constitution (Amendment) Act in 1931. This allowed it to proscribe organizations and establish a military tribunal to try political offences. Immediately the IRA was declared illegal, however, these actions lost the administration precious support. The government also tried to tar the IRA with the red brush of communism and enlisted the support of the Catholic hierarchy as part of its campaign.

Nevertheless, when the General Election was called in 1932 Cumann na nGaedheal's luck ran out. It stood on the basis of what it had done, but seemed to offer little new as people faced a future of economic uncertainty. On the contrary, Fianna Fáil's manifesto placed particular emphasis on its socio-economic agenda, promising to abolish the land annuities, introduce protectionism and improve social security payments. Its republicanism was played down, although it did commit itself to deal with the Oath and the position of Governor General.

In the event the opposition's manifesto proved the more attractive and Cumann na nGaedheal was replaced in office by a coalition of Fianna Fáil and the Labour Party. DeValera had finally been given the chance to dismantle the Treaty.

DeValera takes over

Given the recent history of violent enmity between the forefathers of the Free State's two main parties there was initially some concern over the forthcoming transition of power. Would Cumann na nGaedheal surrender authority peacefully and gracefully? The fears of trouble were certainly not unfounded; on the day that the new Dáil was to meet, a number of deValera's colleagues arrived at Leinster House – seat of the Irish parliament – carrying weapons.

In the event there was no reason for apprehension; Cosgrave approached the handover of power in the highest traditions of democracy. Moreover he made sure that those in authority over the institutions of state did the same. The Free State had come through a difficult birth and a contentious infancy. The question now was how it would fare in the future with different, less accommodating, perhaps even less loving, guardians.

The Blueshirts and the IRA

While the actual handover of power was smooth, there was a maelstrom of tension bubbling below the surface. The new administration revoked some of the coercive security measures so recently passed by Cumann na nGaedheal and lifted the ban on the IRA. It now regained some of its confidence with deValera in power and began to make threatening noises against Cumann na nGaedheal.

In order to protect itself Cosgrave's Party sought support from the ex-military membership of the recently established Army Comrades Association (ACA). It seemed as if such protection was indeed necessary. In 1933 deValera called a snap General Election during which the IRA and ACA clashed on numerous occasions. Shortly after, Eoin O'Duffy, newly relieved of the command of the Garda by deValera, took command of the ACA, renamed it the National Guard and developed a programme based on vocationalism, a theory of government closely related to corporatism.

The new group was more popularly known, due to the colour of its recently adopted uniform, as the Blueshirts. However at a time of European tensions resulting from the actions of Germany's Brownshirts and Italy's Blackshirts it is not surprising that this new organization caused some concern to the Dublin administration. This fear reached its zenith when O'Duffy announced that there would be a Blueshirt parade in Dublin to commemorate the deaths of Cumann na nGaedheal's three icons, Griffith, Collins and O'Higgins. The government banned the march and the organization forthwith and the crisis abated swiftly.

Not long after this the National Guard coalesced with Cumann na nGaedheal and the minority National Centre Party to establish a new party, Fine Gael, with O'Duffy as leader. Its stated purpose was to oppose what they believed was deValera's dictatorial inclinations.

However O'Duffy's reign at the top didn't last long. Within a year he had been replaced as leader by Cosgrave; his removal was the consequence of a series of impolitic speeches. At a time of increasing economic dislocation he urged farmers not to pay rates. He had also speculated about the possibility of an invasion of the north to remove British rule. After his removal O'Duffy attempted to continue with the Blueshirts, but the movement soon sank into obscurity.

Before long deValera was having problems with another quasi-military organization. This time the culprit was the IRA. Although the Fianna Fáil government had acted in a conciliatory manner towards the organization in the months after its electoral success, the relationship had turned sour within a couple of years with the IRA feeling that it was taking Fianna Fáil far too long to achieve a republic. The IRA's continued refusal to disarm was followed by the resumption of violent activities in 1935 and 1936. Much as he might have wanted to tolerate his old comrades, the violence left deValera with no choice. In 1936 he banned the IRA.

Dismantling the Treaty

The new President wasted no time in starting to deal with the more distasteful elements of the Free State Constitution. Shortly after coming to power, he announced that the Oath would be abolished forthwith. Responding to British protests against his announcement he wrote to the London government condemning the Oath of Allegiance as an 'intolerable burden to the people of this state'. The Removal of the Oath Act of May 1933 eliminated one of the most contentious elements of the Treaty at a stroke.

DeValera then initiated a process to remove the remaining symbols of British power in the Free State. His first target was the office of Governor General, the king's representative in Ireland and a living symbol of its membership of the Commonwealth. DeValera began by instructing his ministers to ignore the Governor General, James MacNeill, brother of Eoin. They were further ordered to boycott any functions attended by the king's representative. Their campaign soon had an effect; in November 1932 MacNeill was recalled by the British government.

In his place deValera appointed a low-profile member of his own Party, Domhnall Ó Buachalla. He was given the title of *an seanasca* (Chief Steward) rather than the more imperial Governor General. In reality deValera would have preferred to abolish the position completely but the legal advice he received informed him that he required at least a figurehead to sign Bills into Law. Ó Buachalla fulfilled that remit perfectly. He never resided in the Governor General's official residence in Phoenix Park, but rather in a typical Dublin suburb. Moreover, during his time in office he carried out no official duties.

Bolstered by his success in the 1933 snap General Election – which he took to imply support for his policies – deValera continued with his campaign to rid the Free State of its constitutional links with Britain and the Commonwealth. He amended the Free State's Constitution so that Free State citizens could no longer appeal Irish court verdicts to the Judicial Committee of the Privy Council – the highest court in Britain. The British government was incensed by this unilateral action and went so far as to challenge the amendment before the very same Privy Council in 1935. However that court – somewhat ironically – ruled that all of deValera's actions were fully permissible under the terms of the 1931 Statute of Westminster.

Opposition to these policies was not totally external to the Free State. Cumann na nGaedheal was uneasy about many of the changes deValera introduced in this period although much of it was accomplished using freedoms they had helped achieve within the Commonweatlh. Their opposition in the Seanad, coupled with that of former unionist members, caused some of deValera's legislation to be delayed. DeValera would brook no opposition to his policies and for this reason the Seanad itself was abolished in May 1936.

However the most significant alteration to the Free State's relationship with both Britain and the Commonwealth came with the British abdication crisis of December 1936. DeValera took advantage of the general state of confusion within British politics to pass – within 24 hours – the Constitution Act and the External Relations Act. These laws removed the king's authority within the Free State and abolished the position of Governor General. At the same time the Free State continued, at least theoretically, to recognize the monarch as Head of the Commonwealth with which the Free State retained an association.

A new Constitution

All of these changes emasculated the 1922 pro-Treaty Constitution and rendered its continued existence somewhat meaningless. In 1937, therefore, deValera introduced a new Constitution. Starting anew, he reasoned, would permit him to fashion a nation that reflected his ideal of what Ireland should be. It seems fair to suggest, therefore, that the 1937 Constitution marked the culmination of deValera's strategy of eliminating whatever constitutional links with the United Kingdom still remained.

The new Constitution, or *Bunreacht na hÉireann*, altered a number of key elements within the Irish body politic. The name of the state became 'Éire' or in the English language, 'Ireland'. To replace the recently eliminated monarch, the Head of State was to be the President, elected on a seven-year cycle. While this position was meant to be mainly ceremonial, the President was given the power to refer Oireachtas legislation to the Supreme Court (see below) to check its constitutionality. This power would become particularly significant in the 1970s (see below).

The Head of government was titled Taoiseach. As previously – or at least until the Seanad had been abolished in 1936 – there was to be a bicameral legislature comprising the Dáil and Seanad. The former was still to be elected by PR. The latter's system of election was altered and its ability to delay legislation was reduced by two thirds to just 90 days. In addition, changes to the Constitution could only come about as the result of a referendum.

The Supreme Court that had been established by Cumann na nGaedheal was retained and was given the power of constitutional interpretation and judgement on the constitutionality of Acts of the Oireachtas. Of course, given that the right of appeal to the Privy Council had previously been removed, the Supreme Court was the ultimate legal authority in the land.

Somewhat controversially, although perhaps not all that unexpectedly, the new Constitution recognized the special position of the Catholic Church in Ireland. However, there was at least a nod to some form of religious pluralism in that 'Freedom of conscience and the free profession and practice of religion' was granted to all other faiths. That said, divorce, which was accepted by a number of other faiths, was made unconstitutional.

There were other areas of controversy, although they might be seen as more controversial now than they did at the time. Article XLI stated that a woman's place was 'in the home' and added that 'economic necessity' should not be allowed to drive women into employment where they would be neglecting 'their duties within the home'.

Most notoriously of all, however, particularly in the context of later political developments, Article II of the Constitution claimed political jurisdiction over the whole island. In addition, Article III stated that Éire's laws would only apply to the 26 counties that made up Éire until the time when partition came to an end.

The Constitution made Ireland a republic in all but name, yet there were severe contradictions existing within it. Although it made no mention of the British monarch, Ireland remained as a member of the Commonwealth. What possible reason was there for this seeming incongruity, particularly if one considers deValera's political philosophy and recent political actions? The answer is simple. DeValera believed that keeping this link with Britain might make it easier to end partition. If Ireland did not use the word 'republic' to define itself, unionists might find it easier to throw in their lot with their southern neighbours. It is hard, however, to see this as anything more than wishful thinking.

The Constitution was submitted to the verdict of the people in a referendum. The result was surprisingly close with over 685,000 voting in favour and nearly 527,000 voting against. Whatever the size of the majority, the Constitution had gained the support of the majority of voters and in 1938 Douglas Hyde, co-founder of the Gaelic League at the end of the nineteenth century, was inaugurated as Ireland's first President.

London's reaction

London had opposed all of the steps taken by deValera since 1932 to alter the Free State's relationship with Britain and the Commonwealth. How would it react now to such extreme unilateral actions? The answer was by doing very little at all. Although it was clear that the new Constitution had eliminated most remaining political links between the two islands, the British government treated the changes introduced as relatively inconsequential and not materially altering Ireland's Commonwealth membership. If truth be told, the British were uncertain whether or not Ireland was still a member of the Commonwealth, but to make things easier they were prepared to give their neighbours the benefit of the doubt.

The economic war

For the entire period during which the changes described above were taking place, and in no small part because of them, Ireland and Britain were engaged in a debilitating economic war. Debilitating in particular for the Free State (as it was styled when the war began) because it did not possess the depth of natural resources or the range of alternative markets that the British did.

The cause of the conflict was deValera's refusal – in line with his previously stated position – to continue to pay land annuities to the United Kingdom Exchequer. As part of his justification deValera argued that Northern Ireland's annuities had been cancelled by Westminster in the mid 1920s while the Free State's had not. Interestingly however, while the dispute progressed the £5 million involved was still collected, but instead found its way into Irish governmental coffers. It was clearly the principle rather than the payment itself to which deValera objected!

Shortly after, and in line with its protectionist agenda, Fianna Fáil introduced taxes on a range of imports, the majority of which just happened to be British. London responded by imposing a similar range of duties on Irish exports. This particularly impacted on the cattle export industry, since Britain was one of Ireland's main markets for that commodity. In turn the Dublin government placed tariffs on a range of British imports, particularly coal. A tit-for-tat style of economic war had begun.

Fianna Fáil had long wanted Ireland to increase its levels of self-sufficiency and so in many ways this situation suited them as they could introduce the types of policies they had always really wanted to while blaming the resulting hardships on the British. At the same time, the agricultural sector was encouraged to introduce a wider range of crops for home consumption while moves were also made to develop a range of indigenous industries – such as sugar beet – albeit with varying degrees of success due to the lack of experience.

The government provided the agricultural sector with subsidies but the money for these had to come from somewhere. The victim was the Irish taxpayer who was also suffering from having to pay higher prices for the goods that were being protected. It was a real double whammy!

Industry was the government's main area of interest and under the direction of Sean Lemass, Minister for Industry and Commerce, a significant amount was achieved against the difficult background of the depression and the impact of the economic war itself. Lemass argued 'We believe that Ireland can be made a self-contained unit.' The Industrial Credit Fund was established to provide capital for industrial ventures and a number of semi-state companies was also set up. The development of the ESB was speeded up so as to provide plentiful supplies to power industrial expansion.

Hand in hand with this industrial expansion, the government introduced a more generous range of social security payments while local authorities were encouraged to improve living conditions through the renovation or construction of new housing.

So did it all work? While the numbers in industrial employment did increase by close to 50 per cent, by the end of the 1930s emigration, which was a perennial concern, had not been halted. Moreover, the attempts to develop an industrial infrastructure resulted in a balance of payments deficit, which was not helped by the continued imposition of British tariffs on Irish agricultural exports. On top of this the standard of living was on a downward slope and self-sufficiency had not been achieved. It was clear that sooner or later some form of accommodation with the British was going to have to be found.

The Anglo-Irish Agreements, 1938

The first moves towards an accommodation came with the 1935 Coal–Cattle Pact. This eased the restrictions that had been imposed on the goods of the Pact's title. Then in 1938 – with Ireland's new constitutional position safe and sound – moves were made to try and bring the economic and political crises that were being played out across the Irish Sea to an end. Fortunately the new British Prime Minister, Neville Chamberlain, was also keen to set Anglo-Irish relations on a new footing, not least because of his preoccupation with the deteriorating international situation.

Negotiations started early in the year and resulted in the signing in April of the Anglo-Irish Agreements. These dealt with a range of issues, both economic and strategic. To bring the annuities question to an end Ireland agreed to pay the British a one-off lump sum of £10 million. Both sides also approved a three-year Trade Agreement. In turn Britain agreed to vacate the so-called Treaty Ports which she had retained control of as part of the 1921 Treaty.

Not everyone agreed with the decision to return the naval facilities. Individuals such as Winston Churchill vociferously opposed the return of what he described as 'the sentinel towers of the western approaches' and cast doubt on the friendship of the Irish government as it was led by individuals 'whose rise to power has been proportionate to the animosity with which they have acted against this country'. Chamberlain, however, seemed to believe that the sacrifice of strategically important ports that were being held against the will of the native population would be recognized by the Irish as an act of goodwill. As a consequence, Chamberlain believed, Britain would be amply compensated by the generous and freely given offer of Irish assistance during any future conflict.

However this must be seen as something of a pipe dream on Chamberlain's part. The return of the naval bases at Cobh, Berehaven and Lough Swilly would make it significantly easier for deValera to declare Ireland neutral in the event of a war, something that he was very keen to do. Therefore it should come as no surprise to us that when war broke out in Europe just over 16 months later, that is exactly what he did.

10

Ireland and the Second World War

This chapter will cover:
- the north's readiness for war
- the Belfast Blitz
- Ulster's wartime contribution
- Éire's neutrality
- neutrality in action
- British reactions.

Playing a full part? Northern Ireland's war effort

Are you ready?

Notwithstanding its much-lauded close relationship with the rest of the United Kingdom, Northern Ireland was not ready for hostilities when they finally arrived in September 1939. Regardless of the importance that Belfast was likely to have in terms of its contribution to Britain's war economy – thus rendering itself a likely target for enemy attack – the Stormont government had failed to agree to the introduction of measures that would have enabled the city to defend itself effectively. The furthest that Viscount Craigavon (as Craig had become in 1927) got to doing something practical was to inform his neighbours in a radio broadcast, 'we are king's men and we shall be with you to the end'.

The reason for this frankly unforgivable state of affairs was not difficult to work out. Again and again the Belfast government had spurned the opportunity to prepare itself for a conflict that had been on the horizon for some considerable time. Despite the huge advances that had been made in bomber aircraft flight capability, the administration had continued to delude itself into believing that Northern Ireland was still beyond the range of enemy aircraft.

Even after the war had begun the government remained slow to act. While it is true to say that by 1941 some steps had been taken to increase radar coverage, improve anti-aircraft defences and augment Royal Air Force (RAF) facilities, many felt that far too much remained undone. The fear remained that there were ways in which enemy planes could still approach Northern Ireland without detection and that there were still nowhere near enough anti-aircraft defences in place to discourage enemy attacks. In addition it was clear that the RAF still hadn't the resources necessary to enable it to protect the north effectively.

The public's reaction to the dangers of air attack was almost as blasé as the efforts of their political masters to protect their citizens. Although steps were taken to introduce appropriate civil defence measures, the Air Raid Protection (ARP) service remained voluntary unlike that in Britain. To make matters worse, ARP wardens were not taken seriously as they went about their duties. In spite of constant warnings to the contrary, the majority of people did not carry gas masks until after the 1941 blitz of Belfast.

The role of the Northern Ireland government

If apathy bred from complacency could be used to excuse public inaction, there was no excuse for the government's. No effort was made to plan for the evacuation of Belfast's citizens until close to the first anniversary of the war's outbreak. Even then, only a small proportion of Belfast's children were ever sent away. Nor did the situation improve much when it came to the provision of air-raid shelters. Again nearly a year after the declaration of war only 15 per cent of the Belfast households entitled to a shelter had received one.

Thereafter things began to improve a little, at least if one considers government action. In June 1940 John MacDermott was appointed to head the newly created Ministry of Public Security. His remit was to prepare the province against the possibility of Luftwaffe raids. The Minister acted quickly – as was required – however even though he effected some improvement it was too little too late and when, in April and May 1941, the Luftwaffe bombed Belfast (see below), the city still wasn't ready to deal with the consequences of the attack.

The Blitz

Why did the Germans care about Belfast? Quite simply, the Germans were aware of the key role that a number of Belfast's industries were playing in the war effort. Of particular note were the contributions of Harland and Wolff to shipbuilding and repairs, Short and Harland to aircraft manufacture and Mackies to the manufacture of ammunition. Added to this, a significant number of linen factories were involved in the production of uniforms and other material necessities. That said, there is some evidence that these industries were not quite as productive as the Germans suspected!

It wasn't just a matter of supplies. Northern Ireland was also fulfilling an important strategic role in the war, particularly as the remainder of the island had opted to remain neutral. Much of Britain's trade was forced to take the northern sea routes so as to keep a safe distance from the Nazi-controlled European mainland. The ports of Derry, Larne and Belfast provided valuable bases for the convoys protecting merchant shipping from the ever-present U-Boat menace. There was also a number of important RAF bases dotted around the province. They, too, played their part in helping to protect vital supply routes.

For reasons such as these the Luftwaffe visited Belfast four times in 1941. Collectively the raids – which took place in April and May – became known as the Belfast Blitz. If the damage caused by the initial reconnaissance raid was slight, this was certainly not the case with the other three. In total, close to 1,000 civilians lost their lives during the Belfast Blitz. To put the impact into some sort of perspective, the total of 745 civilians that officially died in the second raid was – with the exception of London – at that stage the highest death toll for a single attack anywhere in the UK. The scenes reported in the aftermath of the raids were heart-rending. One witness spoke of having seen a coffin containing the remains of a young mother clasping her dead children, one in each arm.

Nor was the damage confined to loss of life. Well over 50,000 homes were damaged or destroyed, leaving in excess of 100,000 people without a roof over their heads. Of course the Germans' main target had been Belfast's industrial infrastructure and this too suffered extensive damage. Indeed the damage caused to the shipyard and aircraft factories was so extensive that six months had passed before industrial production returned to normal levels.

Leadership changes

The death and devastation visited upon Belfast threw into sharp relief the less than impressive job that Stormont was making of running the Northern Ireland war effort. Upon his death in 1940 Craigavon had been replaced as Prime Minister by his Finance Minister, J. M. Andrews. Unfortunately, Andrews, brother of Thomas Andrews who had designed the ill-fated *Titanic*, was not up to the demands of the job, yet he obstinately refused to compensate for his inadequacies by bringing in younger, more able ministers.

Despite its loyalty to the UUP the voting public was not beyond sending a warning shot across the Party's bows. In 1941 two safe seats were sacrificed in Stormont by-elections. By 1943 the situation had deteriorated to the extent that discontent was bubbling just beneath the surface of the normally comatose Party itself. Faced with the threatened resignation of his two most able ministers – Basil Brooke and John MacDermott – Andrews bowed to the inevitable and fell on his sword. The new Prime Minister was one of the men who had threatened to resign, Basil Brooke. Born in June 1888 in Co. Fermanagh, he had been educated at Winchester College and at the Sandhurst military academy. Brooke had seen action during the First World War and for his service had been awarded the Military Cross. After some time as a farmer he had become involved in the Ulster Special Constabulary and thereafter in politics.

Conscription

As had been the case during the First World War, conscription was not extended to Northern Ireland at the time of its introduction across the Irish Sea in 1939. Again, similar to the experience during the Great War, the issue still proved to be divisive within Ireland.

The decision not to extend the policy to the north certainly was not the wish of the Stormont government. Indeed it had even demanded that conscription should be introduced. However, Westminster hesitated, mainly because of its concern over how nationalists would react. In the end the unionists also thought better of the issue, coming to the conclusion that giving nationalists guns and training them how to use them might not be such a good idea after all.

That was not the end of the matter however. In the aftermath of the 1941 Luftwaffe attacks on Belfast the British Labour Minister, Ernest Bevin, again raised the possibility of conscription. Again the nationalist reaction was predictable. Aside from deValera condemning the proposal as 'an act of oppression', thousands of nationalists took to the streets of Belfast in protest, supported by the local Catholic hierarchy and nationalist politicians.

As before, some unionists still believed that conscription was more trouble than it was worth. Perhaps, however, the most telling advice came from the RUC which informed the government of its fear that serious public disorder could result from any attempt to introduce the measure. The British government belatedly recognized the folly of Bevin's idea; they needed to get soldiers for the front, not to have to use them for peacekeeping duties in Northern Ireland. Soon after, London publicly declared that conscription would not be extended to the north.

Enlistment

The lack of conscription did not mean that the men and women of the north did not go off to fight. It is estimated that close to 40,000 people from the province joined one or other of the services. Just over 10 per cent of this number paid the ultimate sacrifice for their patriotism. One of those who volunteered was James Magennis. He had the honour of winning the only Victoria Cross (VC) issued to a citizen of Northern Ireland during the war. Using a miniature submarine he had attached six limpet mines to the hull of a Japanese cruiser off the coast of Borneo.

Nor was the call to arms heard solely on the northern side of the border. A similar number of Éire's citizens fought under the allied flags during the conflict. However the legacy of Anglo-Irish relations meant that their contribution was not recognized at home. As with the experience of Irish volunteers after the First World War, it became the sacrifice that dare not speak its name.

Agriculture

Of course much of the war effort took place at home and without doubt the best-performing section of the Northern Ireland wartime economy was agriculture. With increasing demand in Britain for food, the amount of land under tillage increased more than three-fold, supported by substantial improvements in mechanization. Likewise the numbers of cattle and poultry being reared increased significantly. Not surprisingly therefore, Ulster's farmers prospered during the war.

There were a number of reasons for this impressive performance. The continued availability of fertilizers coupled with the more than 100-fold increase in tractor numbers played a crucial part in what had been christened the 'Dig for Victory'. However a significant amount of credit can be laid at the door of the man who first used that phrase, the Minister for Agriculture, Basil Brooke. His success in this area played no small part in his selection, in May 1943, as Northern Ireland's new Prime Minister (see above).

Industry

Despite Brooke's best efforts within the agricultural sector, the fortunes of Northern Ireland's industrial economy were not quite as impressive. On the one hand, industrial production started to improve and unemployment fell from a high of 70,000 in 1941 to just 10,000 three years later. At the same time wages and the standard of living improved.

On the other hand, a number of factors including bad management and questionable working practices conspired to keep industrial productivity down. Nor was it helped by a series of strikes, even though they were meant to be illegal. That said, the industrial economy did play some part in the drive for victory. By the time the war ended much of the industrial unrest had dissipated and figures for industrial production had begun an upward climb.

All things considered, whatever the problems and limitations, Northern Ireland did contribute significantly to the allies' eventual victory. As we shall see, the British would not forget this contribution in the immediate post-war period.

Wartime conditions without a war: Éire, 1939–45

Declaration of neutrality

The day after Britain declared war on Germany deValera announced in the Dáil that Ireland would remain neutral for the duration of the conflict. For seasoned observers this came as no great surprise, particularly as the return of the Treaty Ports had recently removed the last remnants of British military presence in the 26 counties. Moreover, at the same time, deValera had declared that 'The aim of government policy is to keep the country out of war.'

Even if Ireland were not in the war in a military sense it would be impossible to pretend that 'the Emergency' – as it was euphemistically christened – would not have some impact on Irish life. The government's creation of two new departments – the Ministry of Supplies and the Department of the Co-ordination of Defensive Measures – was tacit acknowledgement of this likelihood.

DeValera was sure that the Irish population would support neutrality as the least divisive policy. He was correct in his assumption; while there was certainly no love for Nazi Germany amongst the Irish people, neither had there yet been enough passage of time for them to offer their support to Britain as an ally. Moreover, a declaration of neutrality was yet another unambiguous indication of Ireland's independence from her former Commonwealth partners, particularly Britain.

Daily Mail comment on the likely outcome of Éire's declaration of neutrality.

Yet just because Ireland declared its neutrality did not guarantee that it would be respected – as nations such as Norway and Belgium could ruefully attest. There remained the possibility – given the highly mobile nature of the Second World War – that Ireland might be invaded by Germany as precursor to an invasion of Britain. This scenario also held out the possibility of the British Army moving back into Ireland to secure its vulnerable western flanks.

Aware of this possibility, the Irish government swung into action, at least in so far as that was possible. An Emergency Powers Act permitted the administration extensive powers to use as it saw fit. Censorship was introduced and enforced with considerable strictness. The government also extended its defensive capabilities until there were close to a quarter of a million men in the Army (albeit most being members of the Local Defence Force), an extended navy and a newly established air force. Yet in spite of the growth in numbers the Irish armed forces remained poorly equipped. It is unlikely that they would have been able to prevent an invasion, from whatever source it came.

The realization of this weakness troubled deValera. As a consequence, shortly before the fall of France in 1940, he agreed that, in the event of a German invasion of Éire, the British Army would be invited in to help the Irish forces repel the invaders.

Britain's reaction to neutrality

Britain's concern about her vulnerability to an attack launched from Ireland manifested itself in the numerous attempts made to woo Éire to her side. This was particularly the case after Winston Churchill acceded to the premiership in May 1940. In June 1940 London presented proposals for the reunification of Ireland if the 26 counties entered the war on the allied side.

Tempting though the offer must have been, deValera rejected it on the strength of the negative impact it would have on Ireland's entire population and on the South's carefully nurtured independence. However that was not the end of the matter; shortly after the Japanese attack on Pearl Harbour, Churchill telegrammed deValera with an intriguing offer. The offer of 'Now or never "A nation once again"', was understood by de Valera to refer to the possibility of Irish unity if he joined in with the allies, but again he declined.

Neutrality in operation

Although deValera's principled stance against British temptations might seem to have implied an adherence to absolute neutrality, this was not strictly the case. Dublin's actions regularly suggested that their neutrality was biased in favour of the allies. German pilots who bailed out over Ireland were imprisoned; however, allied airmen in a similar position were allowed to cross the border into Northern Ireland. Moreover, during the Belfast Blitz, deValera authorized the dispatch of fire engines to help put out the fires. On that occasion he stated that 'We are one and the same people – their sorrows in the present instance are also our sorrows...any help that we can give them in the present time we will give them whole heartedly, believing that, were the circumstances reversed they would also give us their help whole heartedly.'

While these might have been dismissed as relatively minor concessions, Ireland also offered highly significant strategic concessions to the British and Americans. Allied airmen were permitted to fly over Irish territory through their use of the 'Donegal Air Corridor'. This saved them a 160-km (100-mile) detour during the course of their Atlantic missions. Furthermore, in the final months of the war, deValera allowed the RAF to establish a number of radar bases on Irish territory. Of course none of this ever came to the attention of the public; while the war lasted, censorship was enforced strictly.

DeValera also moved against the IRA in response to their rather inept efforts to make common cause with the Third Reich against the British, thus undermining neutrality. Using powers permitted by the Offences against the State Act, the government introduced internment without trial against suspected IRA members. Six IRA members ended up on the end of a hangman's noose and when a further three went on hunger strike they were allowed to die.

Were these actions against the IRA a case of overreaction? Possibly, however the organization had recently demonstrated its ability to poison Anglo-Irish relations. At the start of 1939 the IRA had issued an ultimatum to the British to leave Northern Ireland or face the consequences. The consequences happened to be a bombing campaign in Britain which, rather than encouraging the British to leave, whipped up anti-Irish hysteria across that island.

DeValera could not take the risk of the same thing happening again and thus he acted when he felt that neutrality might come under threat. In this the vast majority of the population supported him since neutrality was a popular policy. Of course, the fact that censorship kept the details of the crackdown and its consequences to a minimum did no harm whatsoever. In the event, the government's onslaught left the IRA broken.

On occasion deValera also went to quite extraordinary lengths – perhaps too far – in his efforts to display even-handedness. He outraged allied opinion when, in April 1945, he visited the German Ambassador to express sympathy over Hitler's death. Earlier the same month, however, he had carried out a similar visit to the American Ministry as a mark of respect to the late US President, Franklin Delano Roosevelt.

The impact of 'the Emergency'

Even though it wasn't directly involved, the war still impacted on Ireland in a number of ways. As already mentioned the Ministry of Supplies was set up and given to Lemass in an effort to ensure that Ireland was not left totally without essential materials. He established the Irish Shipping Company to carry supplies that had previously been brought by British ships, which were now otherwise engaged. However factories still had to close down because they could not get hold of sufficient raw materials and industrial machinery. Particularly in short supply were petrol and coal and as a result of the lack of the latter, the consumption of turf increased many times over.

As a result of its mainly agricultural economic base, Ireland benefited from a food surplus. However, the lack of available fertilizers damaged the productivity of the land, even if more of it was under tillage. In addition, other imported produce such as tea and sugar became scarce and had to be rationed. Attempts were made to increase wheat production to support the production of bread. Unfortunately the Irish climate was not best suited to this crop and so here, too, rationing had to be introduced.

Other goods to be rationed included butter, while fruit and chocolate became totally unavailable. At the same time the availability of most meat and dairy produce in addition to – of course – the humble potato meant that most people were able to survive 'the Emergency' without having to tighten their belts too much.

The closure of factories had an impact on employment levels. With few other options many Irish people began to seek their fortunes in Britain. It is estimated that between 1939 and 1945 about 200,000 Irish people crossed the Irish Sea. The leader of the Irish Catholic Church, Cardinal Joseph MacRory, condemned this, in a somewhat colourful phrase, as 'conscription by starvation'.

Despite the general support for the adoption of neutrality, the harsh economic situation meant that Fianna Fáil still lost ten seats in the 1943 General Election. Within a year all but one of these seats had been regained in another election. The reason for a second poll following on so quickly from the first was the allies' decision more or less to quarantine Ireland in the lead up to the D-Day landings. The explanation for this was deValera's refusal of an American request to shut down the German and Japanese Ministries in Dublin to prevent leaks of the allied invasion plans.

Neutrality from a British perspective

It is probably pertinent to reflect on the real reasons for Ireland's relatively successful maintenance of neutrality. First, the maintenance of neutrality was more than assisted by the sympathetic attitude displayed by the British and German ministers accredited to the Dublin government, and their recommendations to their respective governments not to do anything that would compromise that neutrality.

However, despite the benevolence of that neutrality towards the allies and the benefits that they received in terms of food supplies, it is probably fair to say that if the allies had found it strategically necessary to invade the south they would have done so, neutral or not. That they did not have to take such a step was due mainly to the significant strategic role that Northern Ireland played during the conflict.

This possibility was revealed in a speech delivered by Churchill on the war's conclusion when he condemned deValera's role in the conflict whilst praising the part played by Northern Ireland. The British Prime Minister attacked Ireland's neutrality and suggested that if push came to shove he would have been prepared to invade the south. The Prime Minister suggested that 'If it had not been for the loyalty and friendship of Northern Ireland we should have been forced to come to close quarters with Mr deValera or perish forever from the earth.'

DeValera's response was a model of dignity which he used to score a few palpable hits of his own. He argued that:

> It is indeed fortunate that Britain's necessity did not reach the point when Mr. Churchill would have [invaded Ireland]. All credit to him that he successfully resisted the temptation which, I have no doubt, many times assailed him in his difficulties and to which I freely admit many leaders might have easily succumbed. It is indeed hard for the strong to be just to the weak, but acting justly always has its rewards. By resisting his temptation in this instance, Mr. Churchill, instead of adding another horrid chapter to the already bloodstained record of the relations between England and this country, has advanced the cause of international morality an important step – one of the most important, indeed, that can be taken on the road to the establishment of any sure basis for peace.

DeValera concluded by asking Churchill if he could not 'find in his heart the generosity to acknowledge that there is a small nation that stood alone, not for one year or two, but for several hundred years against aggression?' It was – quite possibly – his finest hour.

11

Ireland in the post-war years

This chapter will cover:
- economic collapse
- the Inter-Party government
- declaring a Republic
- the Mother and Child Scheme
- the Republic of Ireland in the 1950s
- the Welfare State
- Northern Ireland in the 1950s.

Economic malaise

Although Ireland had not suffered significant material damage during the course of the Second World War, she became, nevertheless, one of the economic casualties of its aftermath. Whilst neutrality had been popular at home, it had not been – as we have seen – so well received across the Irish Sea. The result was that Ireland was forced to endure a period of economic dislocation not experienced since the time of the Famine or the agricultural crises of the 1870s.

The land was exhausted after years of increased production without the benefit of fertilizers. Meanwhile, continued industrial dislocation resulting from a shortage of resources meant that unemployment shot up. On top of this, wages were low despite rising prices while the rationing introduced during the war continued and was even extended during the harsh winter of 1947. In such conditions industrial unrest grew, most notably involving the Irish National Teachers' Organization, a union not known for its militancy.

All of this contrasted very unfavourably with the rapid economic and social changes that were already afoot in Britain and were just beginning to be introduced in the north (see below). Yet there was neither mention nor any prospect of the introduction of such a welfare state in the 26 counties. As a result, the popularity of the Fianna Fáil government – which had until recently seemed invincible – crumbled and in the 1948 General Election it was ousted by a motley coalition of other parties. After 16 continuous years deValera was out of office.

The Inter-Party government

The administration that replaced Fianna Fáil was christened the Inter-Party government. In total it comprised of five different parties as well as relying on the support of a dozen independent TDs. The largest party was Fine Gael, back in office for the first time since the defeat of its predecessor, Cumann na nGaedheal in 1932. It had spent most of the intervening period in the political doldrums and was nowhere near as well financed or organized as Fianna Fáil.

Fine Gael was joined by not one but two Labour Parties, their dual existence the outcome of a bitter internal dispute involving that perennial source of labour division, James Larkin. Joining these three was Clann na Talmhan, little more than a parochial and sectional movement representing the interests of part of Ireland's agricultural sector.

The final and most exotic coalition member was Clann na Poblachta. Established only two years previously, Clann na Poblachta was a heady mixture of republicanism and socialism whose policies attracted both constitutional republicans and voters from a younger generation disillusioned by economic stagnation and by the old, sterile Civil War cleavage.

Clann na Poblachta's leader was Seán MacBride whose own background was equally colourful. He was the son of Major John MacBride, who had been executed in the aftermath of the 1916 rising, and Maude Gonne, a republican supporter and the object of much of poet W. B. Yeats' affection. MacBride himself had served as Chief of Staff of the IRA from 1936 to 1938. The year after, he parted company with the movement when it embraced violence again. In the years until he founded Clann na Poblachta, MacBride plied his trade in the courtrooms, specializing in cases where the defendants were republicans.

Richard Mulcahy was the leader of Fine Gael. As such he had the right to expect that the post of Taoiseach was his. This was not to be, however. Mulcahy was unacceptable as Head of government to MacBride because of his involvement in the Irish Civil War. Magnanimously the Fine Gael leader stood aside and allowed his party colleague, John A. Costello, to be elected Taoiseach. Costello himself was not without executive experience. He had served as Attorney General in the Cumann na nGaedheal governments of the late 1920s and early 1930s.

Mulcahy served as Minister for Education. MacBride took over the External Affairs portfolio while his party colleague, Dr Noel Browne, was appointed as Minister for Health on his very first day as a member of the Dáil. It was an imaginative choice, which seemed to herald the advent of a new and more exciting period for Irish politics. This it turned out to be, although perhaps not quite in the way anticipated by the new administration.

The only glue that held the politically heterogeneous Inter-Party government together was its antipathy to deValera and Fianna Fáil. That said, the relatively relaxed attitude to leadership displayed by Costello – allowing ministers a considerable amount of latitude within their own departments – meant that for a time the government seemed to prosper in spite of the widely differing viewpoints of its constituent parts.

Economic developments

Under the new government's guidance the Irish economy began the slow process of recovery. Patrick McGilligan, the Minister for Finance, introduced the Keynesian concept of the capital budget to Irish economic planning. Ireland also joined the organization for European Economic Recovery and applied for funds from the recently established Marshall Plan. Here again, Ireland came up against the negative reaction of her years of neutrality during 'the Emergency'. The United States refused to gift Ireland money as was happening elsewhere. Money was forthcoming, but only as a loan.

Whatever the conditions of its award, the money received was put to good use. Huge land reclamation projects were initiated, electrification was extended and a massive programme of house building and improvement was begun. To support industrial expansion the Ministry of Finance established the Industrial Development Authority (IDA) in 1949.

All of this was a start, however the Irish economy had fallen years behind those of her competitors and a great deal more remained to be done. The population still voted with their feet when it came to judging what levels of improvement had taken place. Emigration continued and reached new heights with well over 20,000 boarding the boats to Britain and elsewhere each year.

Declaration of the Irish Republic, 1949

However, it is for the creation of two crises that the Inter-Party government is best remembered. The first was its decision to declare Ireland a Republic and finally sever all remaining links with the British Commonwealth.

The new government did not take the same view as deValera of the relationship that the 1937 Constitution had created between Ireland, Britain and the Commonwealth. Although his Constitution had created a republic in all but name, deValera had stopped short of declaring it as such and taking Ireland out of the British Commonwealth. DeValera argued that to go the whole way and declare a republic would make partition harder to end.

As a distinguished lawyer Costello had difficulties with such semantics. Moreover, he believed that clarifying Ireland's constitutional position would remove the ambiguities that allowed the potential for violence to remain. It would, he claimed, 'take the gun out of Irish politics'. It was a laudable but painfully premature aspiration.

Equally persuasive, however, were the views of Clann na Poblachta leader Seán MacBride. He wanted Ireland to declare itself a republic and his Party had campaigned on the issue during the recent General Election campaign.

Costello made the declaration in September 1948, not at home, as might have been expected, but on a visit to Canada. Rumour and innuendo swiftly grew up around the manner of the announcement, some rumours being more insidious than others. Particularly offensive was the accusation – peddled by some political opponents – that Costello had become inebriated at a dinner hosted by the Canadian Governor General, had taken offence at a model of 'Roaring Meg' (a cannon used by the supporters of the Protestant King William III in the Siege of Derry) being placed before his setting and had then rushed outside to announce that Ireland was leaving the Commonwealth.

While the model of 'Roaring Meg' was indeed on the table at dinner the reasons for the declaration being made were rather more prosaic. Records indicate that the issue had previously been discussed in cabinet although they also reveal that no firm decision had been reached. Rather, it should be suggested, they did not record that a decision had been made, an indication, perhaps, of the quality of record-keeping at this time. Costello's announcement, thousands of kilometres away from home, came in response to two separate issues and was made two days after the infamous dinner engagement. First was the general way in which he felt that the constitutional position of Ireland was being slighted during his Canadian visit. Second was the coincidental article that had appeared in the *Sunday Independent* under the headline of 'External Relations Act to go'. This had revealed that the Cabinet had discussed the issue. When journalists questioned the Taoiseach about the article, he made the announcement.

With the declaration made, the appropriate legislation was introduced into the Dáil. According to the terms of the Republic of Ireland Bill the President would be the Head of State while 'The description of the state shall be the Republic of Ireland.' The Republic of Ireland Act became law in December 1948, however, Éire's official transformation to a republic waited until Easter Monday 1949, exactly 33 years after Pearse's declaration of Easter 1916.

Reactions to the declaration

Ireland had become the first Commonwealth country to declare itself a Republic and break the Commonwealth connection. The question now was how Britain and the other Commonwealth members would respond. Almost immediately the new Republic found valuable allies in the shape of Australia and Canada. They cautioned against retaliatory acts by London arguing that Ireland's withdrawal from the Commonwealth should not be allowed to affect the development of friendly relations between all interested parties.

The British, however, came under a significant degree of pressure from Northern Ireland's unionists who feared that the newly declared Republic would go all-out in its efforts to end partition. An effort was indeed made by Costello's administration to end partition but Brooke rejected their proposals. Instead he declared 'Ulster is not for sale' and called a general election specifically as a referendum over the border issue.

Across the water the British Prime Minister, Clement Attlee, approached the whole affair with a good dose of political common sense. Although he regretted the Dublin government's decision he accepted that the declaration was consistent with the policy that deValera had pursued with regard to Britain since 1932. Taking into account their close links, economic and otherwise, Britain decided, through the terms of the Ireland Act, not to regard the Republic fully as a foreign state but rather as a neighbour with a special relationship. Unionists were outraged and damned this decision as a 'surrender to Éire'.

However, overall the unionists had little cause for complaint. Within the terms of the same Act a highly significant guarantee was given to the North. It stated that 'In no event will Northern Ireland...cease to be part of...the United Kingdom without the consent of the parliament of Northern Ireland.' The Stormont government had been handed what amounted to a veto over its political future. Not surprisingly the unionists were delighted.

Equally predictably the Dublin government was outraged. It was flabbergasted at the potency of the assurances that Northern Ireland had been given and made its displeasure clearly understood. However this opposition had no effect; Attlee was of the opinion that as his government had not been consulted by the Irish prior to their declaration, he could give whatever pledges he felt like to the unionists.

The Irish took their campaign against partition on the road. Whenever and wherever possible they raised the issue, hoping to put international pressure on the British to modify their position. Ireland even refused to join NATO on its establishment in 1949, arguing that to do so would involve the recognition of Northern Ireland. When it joined the United Nations in 1955 it was afforded a new platform for its anti-partition campaign. However nothing came of all these efforts and partition remained as contentious an issue as ever.

The Mother and Child Scheme

The second policy for which the Inter-Party government is remembered was its attempted introduction of the Mother and Child Scheme in 1951. Initially the whole issue of healthcare had been one of the government's successes. Under the leadership of the energetic Minister for Health, Dr Noel Browne, the Health Department had initiated a number of campaigns designed to improve the well-being of the Irish people. Strenuous efforts were made to eradicate TB, an insidious disease from which the minister himself had suffered. Millions raised through a Hospital Sweepstake were spent building new hospitals and these, thanks to their modern equipment, more or less destroyed this most serious affliction.

Browne then turned his attention to Ireland's maternity services, which were notorious for the high levels of infant and mother mortality. Based on an Act introduced by Fianna Fáil before it fell from power, he proposed the Mother and Child Scheme whereby all mothers and children up to the age of 16 would be eligible for free health care.

Browne's scheme was undone by the combined might of two of Ireland's most formidable pressure groups, the medical profession as represented by the Irish Medical Association (IMA) and the Catholic bishops. The doctors feared that their incomes would be reduced by the introduction of the scheme. They argued that it would also limit patient choice. The Catholic hierarchy, led by the formidable Archbishop of Dublin, John Charles McQuaid, regarded Browne's scheme as socialistic in nature. They also feared that it would result in advice on sexual health being imparted by the wrong individuals.

Their combined pressure was enough for the rest of the cabinet to disavow the scheme. Browne had already begun to fall out with his colleagues, particularly his party leader Seán MacBride.

When push came to shove, the Cabinet was more willing to listen to the concerns of the unelected hierarchy than to support their erstwhile colleague.

Shortly after this the Inter-Party government fell. Costello called an election in May 1951 in the aftermath of the Mother and Child crisis and a number of other difficulties. Although Fine Gael did well in the poll other coalition partners and especially Clann na Poblachta lost seats. With the support of a number of independent TDs, including Noel Browne, who had parted company with Clann na Poblachta, deValera formed a minority administration.

Browne had the final laugh however. In the aftermath of the Mother and Child debacle he published the key correspondence between McQuaid, Costello and himself. More clearly than anything else this seemed to reveal that Ireland did indeed have 'Rome Rule'. On the other hand, with only minor alterations, deValera was able to get the scheme accepted by the bishops soon after. This was achieved by a combination of behind-the-scenes negotiation and compromise which revealed Fianna Fáil to be much more adroit in its dealings with the hierarchy than the Inter-Party government had been.

Governing Ireland in the 1950s

Once again deValera was back in power and with him were pretty much the same people who had been there since the struggle for the foundation of the state. It is fair to say that, with the exception of Sean Lemass, the men in government were now past their best. What made their deficiencies even more obvious was their seeming inability to come to terms with the need to introduce a new type of policy to deal with an Ireland that was very different from that which had existed when they were at their political prime.

This conservatism was perhaps best exemplified by Sean MacEntee, deValera's Minister for Finance. In his efforts to counter a continuing industrial and economic decline and a growing balance of payments deficit MacEntee introduced extremely harsh economic measures. As a result the value of imports fell sharply and that fall was matched by a steep rise in unemployment levels. As levels kept on rising, the government's unpopularity rocketed and it was replaced by a second Inter-Party government in 1954.

The main difference between this coalition and its predecessor was the absence of Clann na Poblachta from the Cabinet table. As with the defeated Fianna Fáil administration, economic stagnation remained the main problem. Initially the government's response – directed by the Minister for Finance Gerard Sweetman – differed little from that which had led to the defeat of its predecessor. Economic growth slowed down even more and in this context the jobless figures continued to grow while standards of living declined further. As a result, the perennial problem of emigration reared its head once more.

Eventually the men with new ideas were given their chance. The Fianna Fáil government that returned to power in 1957 undertook much of this work; however, Sweetman had laid some important foundations during the second Inter-Party government's period in office.

Sweetman's most significant achievement was arguably the appointment of T. K. Whitaker as Secretary of the Finance Department. A radical theorist, Whitaker was prepared to think outside the box, unlike the vast majority of his economically conservative colleagues. His ambition for economic improvement was given free reign by Sean Lemass who finally persuaded deValera to take radical steps to salvage Ireland's economic position.

The first step was the publication of the 1958 *Programme for Economic Expansion*. This survey, aimed at radically improving the Irish economy, contained three key ideas: the expansion of agriculture as a central industry, a move towards free trade and the introduction of incentives to attract foreign industries to Ireland. Overarching all of these, however, was the clear need for significant levels of capital investment.

The attraction of foreign industries was the first element to take on steam and the resulting expansion of industry, helped by the efforts of the IDA, went some way to reducing the balance of payments deficit. At the same time, increases were recorded in GNP (Gross National Product) figures. The performance of the agricultural sector, however, was not quite as inspiring.

Nevertheless, a second *Programme for Economic Expansion* was introduced in 1963. It built on the modest successes of its predecessor and resulted in significant levels of growth over the next four years. With these improvements came growth in urban centres and increased spending on luxury goods. Slowly but surely Ireland seemed to be moving more into the mainstream of

European economic and social development. However, it must be recorded that the policies introduced also had the negative effect of creating a significant balance of payments deficit.

Northern Ireland

The economic and social contrasts between north and south were marked in the post-war years. The war had brought a good degree of economic prosperity to the province while the gratitude of the London government for Northern Ireland's wartime contribution was clear, as we have seen, from the praise bestowed by Churchill in his post-war victory broadcast when he spoke of the 'loyalty and friendship of Northern Ireland'.

Politically however it seemed as if little had or indeed would change. The 1945 General Election returned another unionist government, albeit with a slightly reduced majority. After several years of abstention the Nationalist Party returned to occupy the Opposition benches, but neither they nor the handful of Labour MPs ever had a realistic chance of disturbing the administration's serene progress.

However there were storms clouds on the horizon. The 1945 Westminster General Election had returned the first Labour government with an overall majority. Labour's sympathies were traditionally nationalist whilst the unionists had always enjoyed a special relationship with the Conservative Party. Would this change of government result in a change to Northern Ireland's constitutional position?

The Welfare State

One of the main reasons for Labour's victory in 1945 was its promise to introduce sweeping changes to the social and economic structure of post-war Britain. Many of the changes that were eventually introduced found their origins in the 1942 Beveridge Report, *The Report into Social Insurance and Allied Services*, which recommended a wholesale restructuring of the educational, health and social service sectors so as to benefit those on low incomes.

Although implementation of the Welfare State – as it became known – was initially limited to Britain, its introduction soon followed in the north. The unionist government initially greeted the prospect with no small measure of misgiving. It suspected Labour of attempting to introduce socialism by the back door, but, more importantly, it feared that it would not be able to afford the new system.

They needn't have worried. Grateful for the part played by the north during the war, the Labour government reached an understanding with Stormont, providing generous subsidies for the introduction of the Welfare State in return for parity of taxation levels between Belfast and London.

The net result of this was a considerable loss of control over the economy at the local level. However the compensations made this bitter pill easier to swallow. The amount of money flowing into the north from the rest of the UK multiplied seven-fold. In comparison the amount generated by higher taxation levels within Northern Ireland only doubled.

The compensations were indeed impressive. A new National Insurance scheme was introduced which enabled the payment of generous allowances to those in need. The archaic health structures were completely overhauled while the education system was revolutionized by the 1947 Education Act, which introduced a three-tiered education system with access to the secondary tier determined by an examination known as the 'Eleven Plus'.

Yet impressive as these changes were, their benefits were not necessarily enjoyed by every citizen of the state. The Catholic Mater Infirmorum Hospital in Belfast was forced to stay out of the health changes for fear of losing its particular ethos. The hospital had to be maintained from voluntary contributions from the minority community. Likewise there were problems with the education changes. As a result of their reluctance to join the state system, Catholic schools received only a percentage of the capital and maintenance grants available.

That said, there were significant benefits for Catholic children. For the first time they had the opportunity to engage in secondary and tertiary education. This resulted in the gradual emergence of an articulate and self-confident generation that, when it came of age, was no longer prepared to tolerate what it saw as the discriminatory nature of Northern Irish society. Its response would change utterly the face of Northern Ireland.

The economy

The economic prosperity that had accompanied involvement in the war continued after its conclusion. However, the profile of the Northern Ireland economy was facing a period of flux. The long-term decline within Northern Ireland's traditional industries – particularly shipbuilding and linen manufacture – had been temporarily halted by the requirements of war. With conflict now over it was clear that the economy would have to accommodate itself to the industrial requirements of the modern age.

The government attempted to counter the impact of industrial decline by providing loans and infrastructural support to new enterprises. Meanwhile the Northern Ireland Development Company made it its mission to attract inward investment. Improvements were made to the transport system while a major investment in housing provided a significant number of jobs as well as greatly improving the living conditions of the working class.

Unemployment, however, remained a problem although not in the agricultural sector. Here initial post-war demand was followed by a period of government subsidies aimed at protecting the sector from the impact of cheaper foreign imports.

Politics

As already mentioned, the constitutional changes that were taking place in the south caused no small levels of concern across the border. Brooke's response to the declaration of the Republic in 1948–9 was to call an election. His rallying cry of danger to the province was rendered more genuine in the eyes of unionists by the efforts of the nationalist Anti-Partition League to raise substantial amounts of money through church door collections to fund its campaign. The results of the so-called 'Chapel Gate election' were sweet, at least for the government Party, with the unionist majority increased. Sweeter still, however, was the seemingly watertight guarantee given to the north through the clauses of the 1949 Ireland Act (see above). It seemed as if the unionists had much to be grateful for to a government whose election they had so recently greeted with apprehension.

IRA activity

After years of inactivity the IRA resurrected its campaign against partition in 1956. The Stormont government responded quickly and decisively by using the powers permitted under the

1922 Special Powers Act to intern IRA suspects. Nor was there any refuge for the IRA south of the border. On his return to power in 1957, deValera also introduced internment.

These actions, along with the efforts of the B Specials, greatly incapacitated the IRA campaign and it was abandoned in 1962. In declaring its efforts at an end the IRA claimed that they had been influenced by 'the attitude of the general public whose minds have been deliberately distracted from the supreme issue facing the Irish people, the unity and freedom of Ireland'.

It could be argued that the lack of support provided conclusive proof of the northern Catholics' acceptance of the existence of Northern Ireland. Whether or not this was true is highly debatable; it was still the case that they were given little or no reason to believe that they were residing in a just and equal society. Catholics continued to suffer harassment at the hands of the forces of law and order while they were clearly discriminated against when it came to opportunities for employment. That unemployment, highest in the Catholic-dominated areas west of the River Bann, was not helped by the government's policy of investing most of its resources in the more Protestant east.

Catholics were also less likely to enjoy a fair share of the cake when it came to the allocation of council houses. The fact that property ownership was a prerequisite for voting in local elections made the ownership of houses more appropriate for Protestants. Moreover, in electoral terms, ownership of more than one property allowed extra votes up to a maximum of six. Since property ownership was mainly in Protestant hands, the contribution to continued unionist domination was obvious. Furthermore, the continued gerrymandering of local council electoral boundaries increased such imbalances.

12

transforming the face of Ulster? 1960s

This chapter will cover:
- Northern Ireland under O'Neill
- effecting change
- support and opposition: the emergence of Revd Ian Paisley
- the civil rights campaign
- the emergence of unrest
- O'Neill's fall.

A new premier

In March 1963 Viscount Brookeborough (as Brooke had become in 1952) resigned as Prime Minister of Northern Ireland. Increasing concerns about the state of the economy and the Prime Minister's inability or unwillingness to do very much about it led to his Party forcing him to step down. He had served in the position for two decades, longer even than the architect of the state, Lord Craigavon. His premiership, which had begun with the promise of action, had petered out with the reality of torpor. His replacement was the Minister of Finance, Captain Terence O'Neill, a former soldier whose father had the distinction of having been the first MP to be killed while serving in the British Army during the First World War.

However, right from the start the method of O'Neill's appointment only served to undermine his position. At that time the Party's leader was decided in a similar way to the contemporary Conservative Party. He or she 'emerged' after discussions among senior party members, not by election. Evidence suggests that the majority of the Unionist Party's MPs had wanted the Home Affairs Minister, Brian Faulkner, to succeed Brookeborough. There is no doubt that this lack of widespread support within his Party would undermine O'Neill throughout his premiership.

Improving the economy

Whatever the weaknesses in his longer-term position, initially O'Neill's appointment seemed to offer the prospect of change and progress in Northern Ireland after a long period of stagnation. The new leader believed that 'the face of Ulster' had to be transformed if it was to prosper. To achieve this goal O'Neill promised to bring in 'bold and imaginative measures'. The language was almost revolutionary in the context of Northern Ireland politics; would the actions match up to the words?

O'Neill's main concern lay with improving the economy. To this end a number of key economic measures were introduced during his period in office. Some of these were designed to improve the province's economic infrastructure and included the modernization of the railway system, the establishment of the new city of Craigavon, based upon the existing towns of Lurgan and Portadown, and the development of a second university in the market town of Coleraine.

Other initiatives revealed O'Neill's grasp of the need to plan for the longer term. These included an investment of £900 million in the economy, the establishment of an Economic Council under the direction of Brian Faulkner and, perhaps most significantly, the creation in January 1965 of a Ministry of Development (which included within its remit transport and local government) to drive forward Northern Ireland's economic revival.

Finally, in a move that perhaps served as a precursor for his own future political initiatives, O'Neill authorized co-operation with the Dublin-based Irish Trades Union Congress, a body whose support was important for the effective development of the economy.

These were bold initiatives and it was soon clear that they were having a positive impact. In total, over 35,000 new jobs were created during the 1960s, many as the result of government incentives which led to multinational companies such as Michelin, DuPont, Goodyear, ICI and Grundig setting up shop in the province. At the same time intra- and extra-provincial transport was boosted by the construction of a motorway system and the development of a new airport. Meanwhile tentative political contacts with the government south of the border (see below) resulted in the signing of an agreement on the supply of electricity from the Republic.

However the economic news wasn't all good. While new jobs were being created in one part of the economy they were being shed elsewhere. During the same period in excess of 20,000 jobs were lost as a result of the continued decline of the province's ailing traditional industries such as linen manufacture. Throughout the 1960s unemployment averaged between 7 and 8 per cent. Another traditional industry in trouble was shipbuilding. Between 1963 and 1969 financial assistance had to be given to shipbuilders Harland and Wolff to keep their company afloat.

There were also weaknesses in the government's policy of attempting to attract new industries into the north. A number of companies refused government grants to open factories west of the Bann, arguing that the area was too remote from their export markets. There might have been some justification for their concerns; there were no high-speed transport links, for example, between Belfast and Northern Ireland's second city, Derry. When the first motorway was built it went in a totally different direction and when the government eventually did build another motorway, ostensibly to link the two cities, it stopped over 64 km (40 miles) from its destination.

This last fact alone had significant implications, not only for unemployment in the west of the province (which stood at over 12.5 per cent) but also for feeding allegations of bias in government policy. Such suspicions gained some credibility from the fact that Derry was a mainly nationalist city. They were further fuelled by the unionist government's refusal to locate the new university in Derry, despite its citizens mounting a vigorous and far-sighted cross-community campaign.

Political changes

O'Neill understood that while his economic policies were an essential first step towards modernization, they would not change Northern Ireland on their own. He accepted that Northern Ireland's social and political structures would also have to be recast. There needed to be improvements in relations both within the province and within the island. However while he might have been able to grasp such truisms, not everyone within his Party or community was equally enlightened. Introducing such changes would greatly increase the chances of division within his Party and opposition from within the wider unionist family.

Extending the hand of friendship

O'Neill seemed prepared to take the risk. On 14 January 1965 the first face-to-face meeting of Ireland's main leaders since 1925 took place when O'Neill welcomed Taoiseach Sean Lemass to Stormont. That this was the first such meeting in 40 years was an indication of the tensions that had existed between the two parts of the island. It was also an indication of the seismic shifts that seemed to be taking place within unionist politics.

Speaking later on television, O'Neill defended the meeting by arguing that both political systems shared 'the same rivers, the same mountains and some of the same problems'. O'Neill copperfastened the developing relationship when he accepted an invitation to visit Dublin four weeks later.

While such encounters undoubtedly indicated an improving situation there were still limits to what was happening. On neither of the occasions when the two leaders met was there any discussion of political issues. Instead both meetings focused on areas of economic co-operation. At the same time parallel discussions took place between northern and southern ministers on issues with cross-border significance such as tourism.

O'Neill followed up his contacts with Dublin by extending the hand of friendship to Northern Ireland's nationalist community. His policy took a number of forms but mainly centred on making connections with religious rather than political leaders. It included visiting Cardinal William Conway, Archbishop of Armagh and spiritual leader of Ireland's Catholics, offering official condolences to the Catholic Church on the death of Pope John XXIII (1958–63) in June 1963, visiting Catholic schools and increasing the financial support provided by the state for Catholic hospitals and educational institutions.

Reactions to O'Neill's policies

O'Neill's economic and political policies were unheard of in the history of Northern Ireland up to that point. Not surprisingly, the brave new world that he seemed to be heralding raised a mixture of fear and expectation within Northern Ireland's two communities.

While it might have been expected that there would be wholesale opposition to O'Neill's policies from within the unionist population this was not strictly true. There was no immediate public outcry against the Lemass visit while evidence suggests that many moderate unionists were fully in favour of reform, seeing it as essential if Northern Ireland was to survive and prosper. This interpretation seemed to be confirmed by the results of the 1965 General Election where the Unionist Party enjoyed its usual high level of success.

However, it is fair to say that bubbling beneath the surface there was a degree of fear and apprehension at what the outcome of O'Neill's overtures to nationalists would be. Nor was such apprehension limited to those outside the UUP. The fact that O'Neill did not see fit to inform his own Cabinet colleagues of Lemass' visit in advance indicates that he was concerned about their possible reaction. Of course it also leads one to speculate that the idea for the visit was his alone. If that were the case it did not bode well for the prospects of change. Could one man convince the majority of the population of the need for change if he did not even seem willing – or able – to convince his own Party?

Evidence suggests that O'Neill was right (and wrong) to circumvent his senior colleagues. Confirmation of the divisions within the Party was forthcoming when Brian Faulkner publicly condemned his leader's failure to consult his cabinet.

The emergence of Revd Ian Paisley

However, O'Neill had much bigger problems to worry about. There was strong objection to the policies that O'Neill was implementing from Revd Ian Paisley, the Co. Armagh-born founder and Moderator of the Free Presbyterian Church. Apart from his reflection of long-standing Protestant concerns about the influence of the Catholic Church in the Republic, Paisley objected to any links with the south, especially as its Constitution laid claim – in Articles II and III – to the whole island of Ireland.

Violence and division

Of course, as with all dawns, this new dawn did not last. Before long the situation in Northern Ireland had deteriorated to a significant degree. Tensions increased in 1966 in the aftermath of the commemorations for the fiftieth anniversaries of the Easter Rising and the Battle of the Somme. One outcome was the outbreak of rioting in various parts of the north. Yet worse was to come. Two Catholics lost their lives in May and June 1966, the consequence of a series of gun attacks by the UVF (a paramiliary group that adopted the name of the 1912 organization). These deaths are seen by some as marking the first shots in what would become known as 'the Troubles'.

O'Neill acted swiftly and decisively by banning the UVF. However, as the situation worsened, he found that support within his own Party – never strong at the best of times – was weakening. In September 1966 he publicly exposed a plot by UUP backbenchers to remove him as leader. There was also increasing speculation about how much support O'Neill now had within his own Cabinet. In particular there were doubts about the loyalty of colleagues such as his Deputy Prime Minister, Brian Faulkner and the Minister of Agriculture, Harry West.

It might seem strange to report that O'Neill's policies received similarly mixed reactions from the nationalist community. At first Catholic leaders – both political and religious – reacted warmly to the Prime Minister's attempts to hold out the hand of friendship. Lemass' visit to Stormont, itself a political milestone, was soon followed by another. For the first time in its history the Nationalist Party decided to take up the role of official opposition in Stormont.

However, these actions also raised expectations, some of which were unlikely to be met, given the growing fissures within O'Neill's own Party and community. There was outrage within nationalist circles at the decision of the Minister of Development, William Craig, to name the new city linking Portadown and Lurgan Craigavon, in honour of Northern Ireland's first Prime Minister. Such exasperation was most effectively articulated by a new generation of Catholics, those who had benefited from the educational reforms first introduced in the late 1940s.

There were also increasing accusations from within the nationalist community that O'Neill's much-heralded economic policies favoured the Protestant east of the province at the expense of the Catholic west. To support this accusation it was pointed out that with the exception of Derry, all the places earmarked for economic development were in Protestant areas. The resulting high levels of unemployment and the decision not to build the university in Derry seemed to provide concrete evidence to support such a contention.

On top of this no significant efforts were made to increase Catholic membership of Northern Ireland's various health and education bodies. This detail alone led the pro-O'Neill *Belfast Telegraph* to comment exasperatedly that a 'nonsense' was being made of attempts at bridge building. The implication was that O'Neill's writ did not extend much beyond his own immediate sphere of influence. The truth of this assessment seemed to be borne out with the foundation of the civil rights movement in 1967.

The emergence of NICRA

The Northern Ireland Civil Rights Association (NICRA) was established at the start of 1967. There can be little doubt that NICRA took much of its inspiration from the civil rights movement led by Dr Martin Luther King in the United States. One of NICRA's founder members, Paddy Devlin, later wrote in his autobiography *Straight Left* that the group was 'inspired by the Civil Rights campaign to get justice and equality for blacks in the USA'. At the same time, NICRA soon tapped into other sources of inspiration, most notably the student demonstrations that took place in France in 1968 and the example of events in Czechoslovakia in the same year.

It was not difficult to see why the American movement would have appeared attractive to reformers in Northern Ireland. From their initial success in the Montgomery bus boycotts, Martin Luther King's campaign had employed non-violent methods of civil disobedience in an effort to achieve equal opportunities for blacks. By 1967 a series of marches and protests, particularly those held in Washington, had led an initially unwilling US Congress to pass laws outlawing public discrimination and guaranteeing voting rights. Such developments were widely reported in Europe.

NICRA's aims

From the very start NICRA was careful in its efforts to ensure it attracted the widest levels of support possible. Established as a non-sectarian movement, NICRA did not seek to end partition – a position that was calculated to provide some degree of reassurance to unionists. Rather it hoped to end what it perceived to be a number of serious abuses that created inequality in the existing political, social and economic system.

Through its aims NICRA identified seven specific injustices that it sought to remedy. The first four of these centred on the abuses that existed in the system of local government.

1 The introduction of 'one man – one vote'. This would allow a vote to all people over the age of 18. It would also remove the right of business owners to cast multiple votes, a situation that helped perpetuate unionist domination of local government.

2 Ensuring the fair allocation of council houses. At this time the possession of a vote in council elections depended upon being a ratepayer – basically a houseowner. The fewer the number of Catholics who possessed a property, the fewer the number of Catholics who could vote.

3 Bringing an end to the practice of gerrymandering, where electoral boundaries were drawn in such a way that served to benefit one community over the other. Perhaps the most infamous example of the practice was in the city of Derry where the unionist dominated council ruled over a Catholic population of 20,102 compared with a Protestant population

of 10,274. (These are the 1966 figures from the Report of the Cameron Commission set up by O'Neill's government to investigate the disturbances of 1968 – see below.)

4 The establishment of a formal complaints procedure against local authorities to report breaches in the above areas.

The remaining aims focused on reversing particular aspects of government policy that had bedevilled the Catholic population since the state's foundation in 1921.

5 The prevention of discrimination in the allocation of government jobs. The Cameron Commission found widespread evidence of favouritism towards Protestants in the allocation of jobs. There was similar evidence of under-representation of Catholics in other areas of government employment, including the senior civil service and the judiciary.

6 The removal of the 1922 Special Powers Act which still allowed the government to arrest and detain people without holding a trial to see if they were guilty or not.

7 The disbandment of the B Specials, the sole remnant of the three-pronged Ulster Special Constabulary established 47 years previously to help fight the IRA during the War of Independence.

The achievement of the last two aims in particular would hold particular resonance within the nationalist community.

Support and reaction

While it is true to say that support for NICRA came from across the community, it was certainly more obvious from one side. In particular it came from the new generation of Catholics that had benefited from the introduction of free education in the late 1940s. This group had witnessed the growing self-confidence of Catholics elsewhere, not least in the US where John F. Kennedy had been elected President in 1960. Significantly they were also far from impressed by the rather anodyne performance of their own Nationalist Party whose only policy still appeared to be the ending of partition.

Support for NICRA also came from other groups within Northern Ireland including a number of liberal Protestants who sympathized with some of NICRA's demands, communists, academics and trade unionists.

Yet, despite its efforts to distance itself from what might be seen as specifically nationalist demands, there was much suspicion about the emerging movement from within the unionist population. Although its desired reforms would have benefited many on both sides of the political divide, a significant percentage of the unionist population suspected that NICRA was only interested in Catholic rights. Still more were of the opinion that NICRA was nothing more than a front for the (still moribund) IRA.

In many ways at least some of these suspicions were understandable. To the uninformed observer it did indeed seem that civil rights meant Catholic rights, as most of them would particularly benefit members of the minority community. What such an interpretation failed to understand, however, was the fact that by and large it was the Catholic community alone which had had its rights wilfully undermined by the Northern Ireland government.

NICRA's tactics and O'Neill's response

It was not until August 1968 that the first NICRA protest march took place in Northern Ireland. Mirroring the tactics that had been employed with such success by the American movement, NICRA organized a march between the Co. Tyrone towns of Coalisland and Dungannon. The occasion for the protest was the decision of Dungannon Rural District Council to allocate a council house in the village of Caledon to a 19-year old single Protestant woman.

It was the Nationalist Party MP for East Tyrone, Austin Curry, who first suggested the possibility of a march. His initial reaction to the allocation had been to squat in the house, but once he had been evicted he sought a more public demonstration against one of the main abuses that NICRA had been set up to eliminate. The march duly took place and passed off without incident even though it had been rerouted by the RUC. Unfortunately subsequent marches would not pass off quite as peacefully.

Violence in Derry

The second NICRA march took place in Derry in October 1968. Again the thorny issue of housing was the precursor of the protest; NICRA felt that the Londonderry Corporation's record of inequality in the allocation of council houses was deserving of public recognition.

The route chosen for the march meant that it would travel from Derry's Waterside across the Craigavon Bridge to the centre of the city. That prospect was too much for members of the unionist community and the city's Apprentice Boys (a group founded in 1814 to commemorate the shutting of Derry's gates against the forces of King James II in 1688) threatened to hold a rival march. The chance of violent confrontation was high and so the government responded by banning the holding of any march east of the river Foyle or within the historic city walls.

The organizers of the march decided to ignore this decision and the demonstration went ahead as planned. It didn't get very far; just yards from its starting point it was confronted and attacked by a cohort of RUC officers. The crowd was small and the incident might have passed off relatively unnoticed outside the province but for two facts. Four Westminster MPs had accompanied the marchers and, more importantly, a camera crew from RTE, the Irish national broadcaster, was filming the event.

Later that night television news programmes across the world broadcast the images recorded in Derry. These showed more clearly than any reporter's words the heavy-handed tactics that had been used by the police to break up the gathering. On that night it became obvious to many people that Northern Ireland was on the verge of a potentially insoluble crisis.

The *Five Point Reform Programme*

Clearly members of the London government watched the news. It wasn't long before the British Prime Minister, Harold Wilson, summoned O'Neill and two of his senior ministers to London to find out exactly what was going on. The meeting clearly exerted the type of pressure on the beleaguered Northern Ireland Prime Minister that NICRA could only dream about. On 22 November, a reform programme was announced. It included five main proposals, all of which were to be in place by the end of 1971.

The proposals went some way towards satisfying NICRA's demands. A points system for the allocation of council houses was introduced while there were also to be reforms within local government including the ending of extra votes for business owners. Londonderry Corporation was to be replaced by a

Development Commission while some provisions within the Special Powers Act were similarly pensioned off. To make sure that there were improvements in the provision of public services, an ombudsman was appointed to investigate complaints.

Clearly some progress had been made but the package had signally failed to deliver some of NICRA's key demands. 'One man – one vote' had not been granted while much of the detested Special Powers Act remained on the statute books. Moreover, there had been no mention of any change to the position of the B Specials. O'Neill himself later dismissed the package as too timid, an admission perhaps of the way in which he found himself constrained by the difficult political position he was in.

The Prime Minister's opinion of the reforms was also shared by NICRA's leadership and in the short term their protests and unionist counter-protests continued. O'Neill, however, could clearly see the chasm into which the north was staring and so on 9 December he appeared on television to hammer home to people the starkness of the position in which Northern Ireland now found itself. In particular, he appealed to NICRA's leaders to help to restore calm to the province.

Initially the broadcast seemed to have had the desired effect: all further street protests were called off. However the breathing space O'Neill had won proved to be very short-lived. While he might have managed to calm the civil rights movement, the reforms, limited as they were, had caused dismay among the unionist community. Many of them felt that their once secure position was now under threat.

To make matters worse O'Neill now faced increasing resistance to his policies from within his own Party. Home Affairs Minister William Craig publicly condemned his leader's television broadcast and argued that the Prime Minister was acting under pressure from the British. Craig was sacked for his public insubordination, however even more opposition was appearing on the horizon.

The People's Democracy march

NICRA might have called for a halt to its campaign; however its decision was ignored by another civil rights pressure group, the newly formed People's Democracy. Populated mainly by university students, People's Democracy had developed demands broadly similar to those of NICRA. However unlike NICRA they were not prepared to accept that O'Neill's reform programme was his last word on the subject and announced that they were planning to hold a march between Belfast and Derry, from 1–4 January 1969. Fearing its impact on an already tense situation the decision was condemned by both NICRA and nationalist leaders. However the condemnations were ignored and the demonstration began on schedule.

Since much of the planned route would have taken the marchers through staunchly Protestant areas, the police were obliged to re-route it so as to avoid confrontation. However, on the third day confrontation took place; the marchers were the target of a violent ambush at Burntollet Bridge on the outskirts of Derry. Not only were some of those involved in the assault off-duty members of the security forces, but the situation was aggravated by the RUC seeming to do little or nothing to protect the marchers.

Worse was to come. On the same night and for no clearly discernable reason connected with the preservation of law and order, police rampaged through nationalist areas of Derry, raising tensions further still. Not surprisingly such actions did little to endear the RUC to members of the minority community.

Aftermath

NICRA's reaction to the events in the north-west was to start marching again. The first march was held in the border town of Newry. Again violence resulted. O'Neill responded by establishing the Cameron Commission to investigate the increasing levels of unrest. This was too much for two members of his cabinet and they resigned from the government. One of the departing ministers, Brian Faulkner, argued that O'Neill did not possess the strength to control the deteriorating political situation.

It seemed that Faulkner was not alone in questioning O'Neill's leadership abilities. Early in the New Year 12 backbench MPs publicly called for his resignation. O'Neill ignored their calls and instead announced that he would hold a General Election – which he termed the 'crossroads election' – in an effort to prove that, even if elements of his Party were not behind his efforts to modernize Northern Ireland at least the public were. Given that the unionist majority was clearly uneasy at the recent turn of events, this was a highly risky strategy. However, O'Neill was probably hoping for some support from nationalist voters.

A game of snakes and ladders? The *Daily Telegraph's* comment on O'Neill's
unenviable position, February 1969. The danger comes from Revd Ian Paisley.

The 'crossroads election'

The poll took place on 24 February 1969. Unfortunately – if not
wholly unexpectedly – the result was not what O'Neill was
hoping for. Neither section of the Northern Ireland voting
public had rallied to his side. There was a reduction in unionist
support and there was also little or no evidence of the hoped for
support from Catholic voters. Even those MPs who had been
elected under the Party banner were lukewarm in their support
for their leader. Perhaps most embarrassing of all, O'Neill, who
had never before had to face a challenger in his own Bannside
constituency, only polled 1,414 votes more than his high profile
opponent, Revd Ian Paisley.

Although O'Neill was now fatally compromised he still refused
to resign and struggled on as leader for another two months.
However it was now clearly just a matter of time. With the UUP
hopelessly divided and with the political situation further
damaged by renewed violence and confrontation, O'Neill
bowed to the inevitable and resigned on 28 April 1969.

The final nail in O'Neill's political coffin was a series of bombings. At the time these attacks appeared to be the work of the IRA; in reality they had been carried out by loyalist (extreme unionist) paramilitaries in the style of the IRA in an attempt to force O'Neill to go. Writing later in his *Autobiography*, O'Neill reflected that the bombs 'quite literally blew me out of office'.

While that might have been true in a literal sense, it is fair to say that his hold on power had been tenuous for some considerable period of time. O'Neill's ambition had been to create an atmosphere where 'those sterile forces of hatred and violence which have flourished for so long [would] at last be crushed by the weight of public opinion'. Public opinion had indeed played its part, but not in a manner foreseen or wanted by Northern Ireland's beleaguered and hapless fourth Prime Minister.

Another new leader

The resulting leadership election – the first in the Unionist Party's history – saw O'Neill being succeeded by his cousin, Major James Chichester Clark. Born in 1923, Chichester Clark had seen action during the Second World War and had been wounded at Anzio. In the election Chichester Clark triumphed over Faulkner by a single vote (ironically O'Neill's casting vote). The new Prime Minister mustn't have been able to believe his luck. Less than a week earlier he had resigned from the government in protest at O'Neill's decision to introduce 'one man – one vote' in time for the next council elections. Then Chichester Clark had argued that the timing of the measure was completely wrong; now he declared he would continue with O'Neill's reform programme. A week was clearly a very long time in politics.

13 countdown to chaos: 'the Troubles' begin

This chapter will cover:

- the summer of 1969
- the deployment of the British Army
- the re-emergence of the IRA
- Protestant paramilitaries
- a change of leadership
- the formation of new parties
- the introduction of internment
- Bloody Sunday
- Direct Rule
- power-sharing and Sunningdale
- the UWC strike.

The summer of 1969

The leadership of the UUP might have changed but the problems facing the government most certainly had not. Tensions continued to increase as the civil rights protests – themselves becoming increasingly confrontational – were followed by serious civil unrest in Belfast. To make matters worse there was clear evidence of a growth in paramilitary activity of both republican and loyalist hues.

If all of this wasn't bad enough, the forthcoming annual Orange Order commemorations threatened to tip Northern Ireland over the edge and into a bottomless chasm of violence. Not surprisingly, the governments in London and Dublin were becoming increasingly apprehensive to the extent that they began to take some sort of action. The British government established a Cabinet Committee on Northern Ireland while their Dublin counterparts, anxious about the safety of the minority community, sent an intelligence officer to the north to monitor developments.

A long hot summer

Violence broke out in Belfast first, but it didn't take long for the unrest to spread to Derry. In Belfast it took the form of widespread house burning, mostly carried out by loyalists. In Derry the conflict began after the annual Apprentice Boys parade on 12 August. It soon spread to the city's nationalist Bogside area.

In total, the rioting of what became known as the Battle of the Bogside lasted for 50 hours. An uneasy calm was finally restored to Derry when the decision was taken to withdraw the now exhausted RUC and replace them with a small number of British troops; however violence soon flared up in a number of provincial towns and more particularly in Belfast where sectarian conflict was particularly intense.

In the middle of this period of intense and frightening violence the Taoiseach, Jack Lynch, issued a statement outlining his grave concerns at the deteriorating situation. This statement, and the accompanying movement of Irish troops and field hospitals to the border, did little to ease tension or apprehension on the unionist side.

The need for political solutions

History is full of what are known as turning points and the history of Northern Ireland is no exception. The events of August 1969 are now seen as having provided just such a turning point in the development of what became known as 'the Troubles'. In particular they are seen as being directly responsible for the deployment of the British Army on the streets of Northern Ireland as well as the eventual re-emergence of the IRA.

Using the Army might help to curb the spiralling levels of violence, but it could never provide a solution for Northern Ireland's problems. It was new political thinking that was needed. The question now was where such ideas would come from. Recent experience had suggested that new thinking from within the Northern Irish body politic was doomed to failure, usually condemned as giving away too much for one side and too little for the other.

That seemed to leave Westminster as the most likely source of new initiatives. London had left the government of the province to the local parliament for decades without interference; could that now be allowed to continue? More importantly, could Westminster succeed where O'Neill had failed and introduce policies that would reconcile nationalists while reassuring unionists?

The *Downing Street Declaration*

While the flames of violence were still smouldering in Belfast and Derry, James Chichester Clark travelled to London to meet Harold Wilson. It seemed as if this external influence was always necessary for constructive action to be taken. Their deliberations resulted in the publication of the *Downing Street Declaration*. This aimed to achieve the almost impossible task of providing reassurance for both communities.

Nationalists were informed that 'every citizen of Northern Ireland is entitled to the same equality of treatment and freedom from discrimination as obtains in the rest of the UK irrespective of political views or religion'. Meanwhile, to appease unionists the *Declaration* stated – in a manner similar to the 1949 Ireland Act – that 'Northern Ireland should not cease to be part of the UK without the consent of the people of Northern Ireland'.

Words were fine but for nationalists it was action that was needed. In the following weeks a range of sweeping reforms was announced or introduced. In an effort to address the remaining NICRA demands a committee on policing was established under Lord Hunt, a single housing authority was established, taking over housing functions from local councils, and measures to prevent discrimination in public employment were announced. At the same time, the Scarman Tribunal was set up to investigate recent disturbances.

The political reforms were accompanied by the announcement of capital investment aimed at improving the economy.

Reactions

It should come as no surprise to report that the unionist population did not greet these initiatives with unbounded glee. Notwithstanding the clear reassurances provided for them by the *Downing Street Declaration*, many unionists were alarmed at what they saw as continuing concessions to nationalists.

The final straw came when the Hunt Report into policing was published. It recommended the disarming of the RUC and the disbandment of the B Specials. In place of the latter it suggested the creation of a new part-time force under British Army control. This would later come into being under the title of the Ulster Defence Regiment (UDR).

Loyalist anger at the proposed loss of such a cherished force knew no bounds and once again violence erupted. This time the location was the Shankill Road, one of the heartlands of Belfast loyalism.

The re-emergence of the IRA

The unrelenting pressure being experienced by some nationalist communities resulted in the re-emergence of the IRA. Since the collapse of its border campaign in 1962, the IRA seemed to have become more interested in theoretical Marxism. When the summer of 1969 was at its hottest, in a literal and metaphorical sense, the IRA had been nowhere to be seen. 'I Ran Away' was the accusation most frequently levelled at the organization because of its failure to defend Catholics during this period. It was an accusation that stung some of the movement's younger, more militant members. They resolved to do something about it.

In the last days of 1969 therefore, the IRA split into two parts. One group became known as the Official IRA. It continued to focus on establishing a socialist Ireland. At the same time it remained prepared to use violence if required. The other section was christened the Provisional IRA (PIRA). This group claimed for itself the movement's traditional role of defender of the nationalist community.

Within a few months the new Provisional IRA had declared its objectives. Apart from the expected focus on the defence of the nationalist population and the achievement of civil rights, the group stated that its aim was to ensure the destruction of the Stormont government and the removal of 'British imperialism' from the island of Ireland.

The PIRA and the British Army

The last aim in particular made it inevitable that the PIRA would come into conflict with the British Army sooner rather than later. There was a real irony in this situation. Initially the Army had proved more acceptable to nationalists – as a source of protection against loyalist violence – than it had been to the unionist population. However, although initially welcomed by the Catholic community, the Army soon found itself in an impossible situation, trying to maintain order while a political solution was imposed. With some truth the epitaph 'piggy in the middle' was applied to the position in which the Army found itself.

It was the middle of 1970 before the PIRA's campaign began to take off in earnest. The Army responded by imposing a 34-hour curfew on the nationalist Lower Falls area of Belfast while a house-to-house search for weapons was carried out. Although a number of weapons – as well as ammunition and explosives – were discovered politically the search was a complete and utter disaster. It has been credited with helping to increase the membership of the PIRA and with weakening the good relationship that had been built up between the Army and parts of the nationalist community.

What else could the Army have done? If it had stood back and allowed the PIRA to build up strength it would have been putting itself in the firing line; the PIRA's aims made that very clear. Yet by attempting to limit the PIRA's growth, the likelihood of a broader conflict – albeit perhaps a more limited one – became an absolute certainty.

Protestant paramilitaries

It wasn't just the PIRA that wanted to destroy the existing government. Protestant paramilitaries also wanted to see the end of the current regime, albeit for very different reasons. They sought a return to the 'good' old days and the certainty that came with unquestioned unionist domination. The UVF had re-emerged, grown and prospered against the background of the civil rights campaign and O'Neill's perceived appeasement of Catholics. It had developed a military-style organization and had, as historian Sabine Wichert argues in her book *Northern Ireland since 1945*, 'increasingly found reasons to pre-empt and counter PIRA violence'.

If the UVF felt any degree of loneliness in its defence of the unionist population, it was not to last. In September 1971 the Ulster Defence Association (UDA) was set up with the aim of filling a perceived gap in the defences of the loyalist community. The UDA regarded itself as a defensive grouping that would resist republican aggression. Within a year it could boast a membership in excess of 30,000. As such, it was – rather interestingly – viewed by the authorities as too large to ban.

Faulkner replaces Chichester Clark

Within the vacuum created by political uncertainty the levels of violence and destruction mushroomed. Stormont's reaction was to demand a more robust response from the Conservative government that had recently taken office in Britain. However, little happened: the Tories were unwilling to do anything that might further alienate the nationalist community. Faced with London's reticence, Chichester Clark felt that he had no option left but to resign. He did so on 20 March (soon becoming Baron Moyola of Castledawson) and was replaced by Brian Faulkner.

There is no doubt that the 49-year-old, Dublin-educated, Faulkner had a better grasp of the situation than his predecessor; however, he too was unable to effect a reduction in the spiralling levels of violence. By the time the marching season arrived in July–August 1971, violence was at an all-time high, particularly in Derry. Almost in despair and seeing few other options, the Stormont government decided to go for an old chestnut and order the re-introduction of internment, despite the opposition of the Westminster government.

Political realignments

Political uncertainty and civil unrest were mirrored by, and more than likely an influence on, the significant changes that took place in the party system in the early 1970s. There had been some efforts at political realignment throughout the history of Northern Ireland, mostly with regard to the Unionist Party. By and large such challenges had been successfully met and the *status quo* maintained. This time would be different; the new parties that emerged would provide a stiff and, in one instance, fatal challenge to the existing nationalist and unionist groups.

As should now be clear, the UUP had been divided in some shape or form for most of the 1960s. These divisions came to a head in March 1970 when a number of MPs were expelled because of their failure to support the government's security policy.

The divisions within the Party were mirrored by a more widespread dissatisfaction with the government's policies and performance. Just how deep the voting public's displeasure was became clear when, in the by-election for the Bannside seat formerly held by O'Neill, Revd Ian Paisley was elected as a Protestant Unionist. O'Neill meanwhile had turned his back on local politics and, having been ennobled as Baron O'Neill of the Maine, took up residence in London.

This by-election victory was a spectacular success and Paisley followed it up in June 1970 with his election to Westminster as MP for North Antrim. Fifteen months later the Protestant Unionist Party was renamed the Democratic Unionist Party (DUP). Its stated aim was to defend the Constitution of Northern Ireland while pursuing an assortment of more progressive social policies.

The year 1970 also witnessed an attempt to break free from the traditional unionist/nationalist cleavage with the launch of the Alliance Party. Although the new Party opened its doors to supporters irrespective of their religious affiliation, the emergence of a 'third way' was not quite as radical as it might initially have appeared. The new Party was broadly unionist in its ideas and was hoping to achieve the implementation of the parts of O'Neill's reform programme that had not yet been introduced.

The changes that took place within nationalism were even more noteworthy as they resulted in a major realignment within nationalist politics. By the start of the 1970s the old Nationalist Party had more or less faded away and in August 1970 the Social Democratic and Labour Party (SDLP) was established to fill the gap.

Led by West Belfast MP Gerry Fitt, the SDLP was moderately left wing on social and economic issues. At the same time the Party sought the eventual re-unification of Ireland. The SDLP immediately became the main Opposition Party in Stormont, although it withdrew in July 1971 after the Stormont administration refused to launch an enquiry into two suspicious deaths in Derry that had involved the British Army.

Internment

The introduction of internment – through Operation Demetrius – on 9 August 1971 was a huge gamble on Faulkner's part. It was a gamble that failed spectacularly. It is no exaggeration to suggest that the political situation in Northern Ireland was markedly worse after its introduction than it was before.

So what went wrong? There were two main weaknesses, one in the planning of the operation and one in its execution. Of the 452 men arrested, not one was a leading member of PIRA; the intelligence used was entirely out of date and related to the pre-Provisional IRA. Moreover, despite the high levels of loyalist violence, all those targeted for internment were either nationalists or civil rights supporters. The first loyalists were not interned until February 1973, over 18 months later.

Reactions to internment

An orgy of violence and destruction followed the introduction of internment. The outcome was many fatalities and thousands from both communities left homeless. In the remaining months of 1971 nearly 150 people lost their lives, the victims of either bombings or shootings. To put this figure into some kind of perspective, it was nearly five times as many as had died in the first eight months of the same year.

Nor – despite what the focus of internment might have been seen to imply – did the violence all come from the one side. The recently formed UDA (see above) was responsible for the

December bombing of McGurk's Bar in Belfast. In this attack, 15 people lost their lives, the worst single atrocity of a very bloody year.

Increasing violence was one reaction to the introduction of internment, but it was not the only one. Along with other Nationalist and Republican Labour representatives, the SDLP responded by calling for people to withhold payment of rents and rates and for a withdrawal from local government. The civil rights movement also got in on the act; a new series of marches were organized in protest at the introduction of internment.

Bloody Sunday

Concomitantly the Army's attitude also seemed to be hardening. A civil rights protest held at Magilligan Internment Camp in January 1972 was met with baton charges, rubber bullets and CS gas from members of the Green Jackets and the Parachute Regiment. The confrontation with the latter regiment in particular was an unfortunate portent of things to come.

Just over a week later another civil rights march was organized, this time for Derry. As the march was breaking up a riot developed and the Parachute Regiment was ordered in to restore order. Over the course of the next 30 minutes or so 13 unarmed civilians were shot dead. An additional 13 were injured, one of whom subsequently died of his wounds.

The subsequent official inquiry headed by Lord Widgery failed to provide a satisfactory conclusion to the events of what became known as Bloody Sunday. Published in April 1972, Widgery's report was immediately condemned as a whitewash by nationalist politicians. While the judge accepted that the actions of some of the soldiers had 'bordered on the reckless', he also concluded that – although it could not be proven – there were strong suspicions that some of the deceased had handled bombs or firearms.

The announcement by Tony Blair of a second inquiry in 1998 was a clear admission that the conclusions arrived at by Lord Widgery were fundamentally flawed. At the time of writing the Saville Inquiry still has to report its conclusions, however it is expected to do so in mid 2005.

Apart from the immediate outpourings of disbelief, grief and anger, the events of 30 January 1972 had more disquieting if predictable results. Catholic hostility to and alienation from the

201
countdown to chaos:
'the Troubles' begin

13

state was markedly increased, and that from an already worryingly low base. A sadly predictable consequence of this was a further swelling of the ranks of the IRA (both hues) and an escalation of republican violence. In response, the number of British Army personnel grew to the extent that by the middle of 1972 they numbered in excess of 20,000.

Such violence and the government's continuing failure to deal with it found a new reaction within the unionist community. In February 1972 the Ulster Vanguard movement was established. Headed by former Stormont minister William Craig, Vanguard was portrayed as a co-ordinating body for traditional loyalist groups. It was a powerful group; one of its largest meetings, held in Belfast's Ormeau Park, attracted a crowd of 70,000. It was a powerful indication of the levels of unionist dissatisfaction.

Direct Rule

The situation was now so grave that Faulkner again attempted to return to the discredited security strategies of the past. He demanded the power to rearm the RUC and re-establish the B Specials. However, the Conservative Prime Minister Edward Heath was clearly no longer convinced that Stormont was capable of ensuring the maintenance of law and order. He demanded that his government be given control of law and order and justice. Not surprisingly Faulkner refused.

On 22 March 1972 senior members of the Northern Ireland government travelled to London. They were under the impression that they were attending top-level talks with the British government about the situation in Northern Ireland. This was not the case; instead they were being relieved of their control of security and potentially their control of Northern Ireland. Heath informed them that his government was planning radical changes which would impact on the security and political development of the province.

Apart from confirming that authority for security was being removed and that internment would be phased out, Heath told them that he was planning to hold a referendum on the future of the border. He also made clear that the years of single party domination were over and stated he would be holding talks with other parties in Northern Ireland in an attempt to establish a 'community government'. This was the first hint of the type of settlement that would be attempted over the next three decades.

Finally, and in an indication that Westminster was intending to keep a much closer eye on the province than had been the case, Heath announced that he was planning to appoint a Secretary of State for Northern Ireland.

Such changes would have rendered the Northern Ireland government impotent. This was too much for the Stormont Cabinet to accept and after lengthy negotiations the entire government resigned. Heath's response was immediate and decisive. He suspended the Stormont parliament, initially for a year (later extended), and introduced what became known as Direct Rule. From now on Northern Ireland was to be governed directly by the British government in London with a team of ministers, led by a Secretary of State, taking over the functions of the Stormont Cabinet. The genial and avuncular William Whitelaw was appointed as the North's first Secretary of State.

Reactions to the end of Stormont

After 50 years of self-government the Northern Ireland parliament was gone. Reactions were predictable; the prevailing sentiment amongst the vast majority of unionists was one of horror. Their parliament – which they had relied upon as a barrier against a united Ireland – was no more. Just as a family gathers round the bedside of a dying relative, so Stormont's final hours of existence were played out before a grieving crowd estimated at 100,000.

This gigantic wake was accompanied by a series of massive strikes and shutdowns, organized by Vanguard in protest at the suspension. The strikes were undoubtedly successful at shutting down much of life in Northern Ireland over a two-day period; however they were unable to achieve their stated objective – opening up Stormont again.

On the nationalist side the reaction was markedly different. Few tears were shed for Stormont with the SDLP and the Dublin government both welcoming the chances for a new beginning. Somewhat ironically, while the PIRA had achieved one of its aims, the introduction of increased control by London reinforced the continuation of their second bugbear, the British presence in Ireland. The organization therefore declared its opposition to Direct Rule and announced its determination to continue its struggle to achieve a united Ireland.

1972: the blackest year

The death of Stormont paled in significance against the backdrop of real carnage that marked the remaining months of 1972. Despite supposed improvements in security – resulting from the introduction of internment and Direct Rule – and even the existence of a two-week PIRA ceasefire, 1972 turned out to be the worst year of 'the Troubles' in terms of the numbers of deaths. By the end of the year 496 people had lost their lives in a never-ending cycle of appalling carnage.

Two events in particular stood out as being particularly heinous, even though every single death is equally deserving of recollection and condemnation. On 21 July the PIRA detonated 20 bombs around Belfast in just over one hour. Nine civilians died on a day that became known as Bloody Friday. Ten days later and without a warning a PIRA bomb exploded in the picturesque village of Claudy in Co. Derry. In total, nine civilians lost their lives.

The government's response was 'Operation Motorman'. This military manoeuvre aimed at restoring some semblance of law and order to the paramilitary-controlled no-go areas which had sprung up in Belfast and elsewhere. The success of this operation encouraged the British government to make moves towards a political settlement. By the end of 1972 it was holding discussions aimed at establishing a government which could enjoy cross-community support.

Power-sharing

The new year began in the same manner in which the old one had ended – with ever-increasing levels of violence. The constant cycle of loyalist-induced bloodshed finally convinced the government to introduce internment for those other than republicans. Yet this was akin to shutting the stable door after the horse had bolted. Clearly some form of political progress was crucial and on 20 March 1973 the British published their proposals for the future of Northern Ireland.

The proposals envisaged the creation of a new law-making assembly (rather than the more pejorative – in Northern Ireland terms – parliament). This would be elected by PR, a fairer system of election long since abandoned by the old regime. However, in an admission of local politicians' recent failures, the new assembly was not to be given control over security or justice. There would also be an Executive, which would act as the government of Northern Ireland.

There was more. For the plan to work successfully the British insisted that two other conditions would have to be fulfilled. In the context of Northern Ireland both these were revolutionary. There was to be the forced sharing of power between Catholics and Protestants. In itself this was an admission by the British of their belief that unionists could not be trusted to rule Northern Ireland in a manner acceptable to the nationalist minority.

If that wasn't bad enough for members of the majority community, there was still worse to come. The British insisted that there would have to be the formal recognition by the north's political parties of what was termed an 'Irish Dimension'. Translated this meant that there would have to be a role for the Republic of Ireland in the running of Northern Ireland. It was envisaged that this would take place through the creation of a Council of Ireland. This body – which shared its name with an ill-fated element of the 1920 Government of Ireland Act – would allow for the discussion of interests common to Belfast, Dublin and London.

Reactions

If Secretary of State William Whitelaw had ever hoped – perhaps in some moment of hallucinatory madness – that his experiment would be universally welcomed he was to be sorely disappointed. However, it wasn't entirely a case of wholesale unionist rejection either, as might have been expected. That grouping proved to be divided in its reaction to the plans and the extent of these splits became clear when the results of the Assembly elections were announced at the end of June.

The results revealed that, with 26 seats, the number of anti-power-sharing unionists elected (including the UUP, the DUP and the Vanguard Unionist Progressive Party (VUPP), set up by William Craig to oppose power-sharing) was greater than the number of unionists elected who supported power-sharing (with 24 seats). Alongside the pro-power-sharing unionists were 28 other members supporting the project; 19 from the SDLP, eight from Alliance and a single representative from the Northern Ireland Labour Party.

Right from the start, therefore, it was clear that there were going to be serious problems in working the new system. While there was a clear overall majority of Assembly members in favour of power-sharing, the fact that over half of the unionist representatives elected were vehemently opposed to the concept meant that the prospects for the success of the new venture were far from certain.

206
countdown to chaos:
'the Troubles' begin

13

An Executive is formed

It took five months of excruciating horse-trading before Whitelaw was able to announce, in November 1973, that the size and membership of a power-sharing Executive had been agreed. There would be 11 ministries in total, all of which would go to supporters of power-sharing. Six were to be held by unionists, four by the SDLP and one by Alliance. There would also be four non-voting members of the Executive: two of these positions would be allocated to the SDLP, one to the unionists and one to Alliance. Brian Faulkner, the last Northern Ireland Prime Minister, was also going to be the first power-sharing Chief Executive. The SDLP leader, Gerry Fitt was to serve as his Deputy.

Sunningdale

Two of the three elements of the new system were now in place. All that remained was to reach agreement on the form and powers of the most contentious component, the Council of Ireland. That was going to be much easier said than done.

The discussions about the proposed Council of Ireland opened on 6 December at the Civil Service College at Sunningdale in Berkshire, well away from the hothouse atmosphere of Northern Ireland politics. The meeting brought together a powerful assortment of politicians from across the British Isles. Heath led the British delegation, supported by Francis Pym, who had just – somewhat inexplicably – replaced the highly effective William Whitelaw as Secretary of State. The Irish delegation was headed by Taoiseach Liam Cosgrave (son of the former Cumann na nGaedheal leader) and the Foreign Minister, Garret FitzGerald. Last but not least was the Northern Ireland team. It included Faulkner and Fitt as well as Alliance Leader Oliver Napier.

In what might be regarded – with hindsight – as an understandable if shortsighted decision, there were no anti-power-sharing politicians present. The Irish government and other local parties had suggested that their presence would serve only to disrupt what were extremely delicate negotiations. At one stage Paisley and Craig were asked to attend but only to give their views. Naturally this offer was rejected out of hand.

Terms of the Agreement

After three days of complicated negotiations what became known as the Sunningdale Agreement was signed. It started off by setting out the general positions of the London and Dublin governments vis-à-vis the reunification of Ireland. This provided an update of the guarantees contained in the 1949 Ireland Act, which had been based on the will of the now-abolished Stormont parliament. Now London agreed that it would not oppose Irish unification if a majority of the Northern Ireland population desired it. At the same time Dublin moved further than it ever had before regarding its position on the border. It accepted that Irish unity could only ever be achieved peacefully and with the consent of the majority of the people of the north.

The Agreement also contained more practical details on the make-up of the Council of Ireland. It was to have 14 members, seven from the north and seven from the south. Its powers were left deliberately (and – as it transpired – dangerously) vague but it was agreed it would help with the development of co-operation between north and south and would eventually be given decision-making powers. Finally, the Agreement stated that the Dáil and the Assembly would elect a 60-member Consultative Assembly at some future date.

A lot of this was deliberately ambiguous; yet even so, certain other elements of the Agreement were put on the long finger. It was agreed that at some future (unspecified) date control over internal security issues would be returned to the Assembly at Stormont. Furthermore it was established that approval of the decisions made at Sunningdale would take place at some future conference.

Problems for the future

The fact that agreement had been reached at all on such contentious issues was remarkable; however, this seeming triumph lost a great deal of its initial shine when it became clear just how such diverse positions had miraculously been reconciled. It soon transpired that the unionist and nationalist representatives involved believed that they had agreed to something entirely different.

On the one hand the SDLP viewed the Agreement as paving the way towards the creation of closer ties between north and south. At the same time, however, Faulkner saw Sunningdale as a mere token, which he had only agreed to as a way of getting Dublin to accept the position of Northern Ireland as part of the UK.

Of course once these diverse interpretations became clear they would have a significant impact on the chances of success for power-sharing. In the meantime, however, Faulkner had more serious problems to worry about. On 10 December loyalist paramilitaries announced that they had established an Ulster Army Council (UAC) to resist the introduction of any significant 'Irish Dimension'. Nor did the PIRA seem any more satisfied. It welcomed the signing of the Agreement by detonating a series of bombs in London in the week before Christmas.

A house of cards?

The power-sharing Executive finally took up the reins of power on 1 January 1974. After nearly two years of Direct Rule, Northern Ireland could boast its own parliament again, albeit one with significantly fewer powers than its predecessor. Almost immediately, however, its chances for success were undermined by events within the UUP.

At a meeting on 4 January of the Party's ruling body, the Ulster Unionist Council (UUC), it was decided to reject the Sunningdale Agreement. Faulkner immediately resigned as Party leader to be replaced by Harry West. However as Faulkner retained the support of 19 of the 21 unionist Assembly members he was able to remain as Chief Executive.

If the members of the power-sharing Executive thought that things couldn't get any worse they were sadly mistaken. Political developments across the Irish Sea provided further unneeded problems. Prime Minister Edward Heath dissolved the Westminster parliament and a General Election was called for 28 February. This would provide the first test of public attitudes towards the signing of the Sunningdale Agreement.

Immediately a struggle for the hearts and minds of unionist voters developed between the pro-Faulkner unionist candidates and the anti-Sunningdale United Ulster Unionist Council (UUUC). The latter grouping had been established in January 1974 to campaign against Sunningdale. Its leading light was that constant thorn in the side of UUP leaders, Revd Ian Paisley.

A house of cards? Clearly the *Observer* wasn't holding out much hope for the power-sharing executive's prospects of success.

The 1974 Westminster election

The election result was almost a whitewash for the UUUC and it was a complete and utter disaster for the pro-Faulkner unionist candidates. Of the 12 Northern Ireland Westminster constituencies, 11 were won by anti-Sunningdale candidates. The only exception was the West Belfast constituency, which was retained by SDLP Leader Gerry Fitt.

Closer examination of the results revealed just how big a defeat the election was for Faulkner and his supporters. Anti-Agreement unionists received nearly four times as many votes as were cast for their pro-Agreement opponents.

The UUUC had cleverly portrayed the election as a referendum on the Sunningdale Agreement. The results clearly indicated that a significant majority of the Northern Ireland electorate was opposed to what had been agreed. It could justifiably be argued, therefore, that the Assembly was no longer a true reflection of public opinion in the north.

This was certainly the viewpoint expressed by the UUUC. Given the huge levels of support it now enjoyed, it demanded that there should be new elections for the power-sharing Assembly. Not surprisingly the British government chose to ignore their request.

The election also resulted in a change in government in London with Labour returning to power under Harold Wilson. In local terms Merlyn Rees replaced Francis Pym as Secretary of State; however a small Labour majority in the House of Commons meant that Rees was forced to spend much of his time in London going through the voting lobbies. This absentee landlord style of administration was exactly what the already ailing system did not need.

Of course these political developments took place against a background of continuing violence. In turn this was coupled with regular public protests against the signing of the Sunningdale Agreement. Although the British government continued to insist that there was no alternative to the Agreement, it was clear that within unionism there was a determination that the system would fail. Since the UUUC's electoral mandate was being conveniently ignored by the British and because nothing else attempted seemed to have worked, the weapon chosen to destroy Sunningdale was a massive strike.

The shutdown begins

On Tuesday 14 May 1974, the Assembly voted to continue its support for the Sunningdale Agreement. The politicians had been warned what would happen if they took this line. Later the same evening a general strike began. The strike was organized by the Ulster Workers' Council (UWC). Set up in 1973, this umbrella grouping of Protestant trade unionists had gained substantial amounts of political and paramilitary support. Its purpose was to demonstrate the depth and strength of unionist opposition to the Sunningdale Agreement.

Interestingly, to begin with public support for the strike was limited; but that soon changed. A combination of UDA intimidation and improved co-ordination by the UWC ensured that by the end of the first week much of Northern Ireland had come to a standstill. Industries had closed down, there were regular electricity blackouts, fuel supplies were strictly controlled and there were hundreds of roadblocks. Recently released Cabinet papers reveal that the British government contemplated bringing in nuclear submarines to provide power, but nothing came of this idea.

The future of the government of Northern Ireland was now on a knife-edge. The palpable tension in the province was further heightened by the news on 17 May that car bombs, believed to have been planted by loyalists in Dublin and Monaghan, had claimed 27 lives (with five more of the injured dying later of their wounds). This became and remained the worst single day's death toll during the entire period of 'the Troubles'.

This tragedy provided an ideal opportunity to show public opposition to the tactics being employed by the UWC. Along with a number of local trade unionists, the Trades Union Congres (TUC) therefore helped organize a back-to-work demonstration on 21 May. However the initiative met with little support – only 200 marchers turned up. At the same time a UDA press official commented in relation to the attacks on the south, 'I am very happy about the bombings in Dublin. There is a war with the Free State and now we are laughing at them.'

Wilson's fatal intervention

So what options were there for the government to take? Basically they boiled down to force or negotiation. However, it seemed as if London was not prepared to entertain either. Although there was no shortage of soldiers in the province, the Army was hesitant about taking on the strikers. In their view the strike was political and not a terrorist action. The other option was negotiation however Harold Wilson was losing patience with the situation. He famously appeared on television on 25 May to denounce the strike and its organizers. Wilson condemned the strike as 'undemocratic and unparliamentary' and accused the strikers of 'spending their lives sponging off Westminster.'

If this intervention was intended to weaken support for the UWC (which the government believed to be limited) it achieved completely the opposite effect. Indeed so beneficial was the speech in terms of hardening loyalist resolve that there was talk (albeit tongue-in-cheek) of making the Prime Minister an honorary UWC member. Over succeeding days certain unionist politicians were seen sporting pieces of sponge on their jacket lapels!

The government finally acted on 27 May when the Army was ordered to take control of fuel supplies. The UWC responded by ordering a total shutdown. With no obvious solution on the horizon and with the British and SDLP refusing to negotiate with the UWC, Faulkner himself acted. On 28 May he announced his resignation as Chief Executive of the power-sharing Executive. The other unionist members of the Executive resigned with him.

Thus ended the power-sharing experiment. Having achieved its goal, the UWC ended its strike on 29 May. A day later the power-sharing Assembly was suspended and Direct Rule was re-introduced. It was to remain in place for the next quarter of a century.

14

the search for a solution: 1974–85

This chapter will cover:
- seeking a solution
- the Peace People
- the hunger strikes
- the ballot box in one hand and the armalite in the other
- the New Ireland Forum
- the Anglo-Irish Agreement.

Continuing the search

For the remainder of the 1970s and the early years of the 1980s successive British governments experimented with a variety of initiatives – some more ingenious than others – in an effort to solve the Northern Ireland problem. They also responded to the continuing violence by introducing a series of enhanced security provisions. While these were successful in lessening levels of violence within Northern Ireland the PIRA simply moved the focus of its 'war' elsewhere. It launched a campaign of violence in Britain, exploding bombs in cities such as Guildford and Birmingham. In the case of the latter, 21 civilians lost their lives.

Following the failure of power-sharing, Britain's next attempt at a political solution was the 1975 Constitutional Convention. This might have been seen by cynics as little more than an attempt to pass the buck by providing a Forum for local politicians to suggest their own solution. However such an accusation would have underestimated the thinking that lay behind this change of tactic. Returning ownership of the solution to local politicians was a clear recognition by London that imposed solutions were never going to work. A long-term resolution would only be possible if local politicians agreed a solution among themselves.

Membership of the Convention was chosen by election. The result was yet another resounding defeat for Faulkner. His recently-founded Unionist Party of Northern Ireland (UPNI) won only five seats compared to the UUUC's 46. A year later Faulkner retired from politics. He died in early 1977 following a hunting accident, shortly after being appointed to the House of Lords. In the same year the UUUC itself disintegrated, its collapse the result of internal policy differences. The various groups that had made up its membership now went their own ways.

By that time the Constitutional Convention was itself dead and buried. It had collapsed in November 1975 without ever reaching agreement. Indeed, its only concrete proposals had pointed to a solution that would have marked a return to pre-power-sharing thinking. The unionist parties had proposed the reintroduction of majority rule with the addition of some minority rights.

Not surprisingly, both the British government and the SDLP rejected this suggestion. However, the majority population were not so easily deterred. Another loyalist strike was held in May

1977 in an effort to persuade the government of the merits of the proposals. This time the outcome was markedly different from 1974; the strike failed to persuade the British to change their minds. Of course the context was also somewhat different given that there was no local parliament to bring down.

New security policies

Whilst making efforts to deal with the continuing political fragmentation, the British government also turned its attention to dealing with the ongoing paramilitary violence. Secretary of State Merlyn Rees and his successor Roy Mason pursued policies that were christened Ulsterization and criminalization. The former, similar in its thinking to Richard Nixon's policy of Vietnamization, involved reducing the strength of the Army in Northern Ireland while increasing the size of the RUC and UDR. The latter saw the end of special category status for those that had been convicted of terrorist offences.

Special category status had been introduced in 1972. It had allowed those who claimed that they had broken the law for political reasons to live as prisoners of war (POWs) rather than being treated in the same way as those incarcerated for non-political crimes. Its removal meant that those convicted of terrorist offences after March 1976 would be treated in the same way as other criminals. They would be housed in a newly constructed prison that had been built at the Maze outside Belfast. The most notable feature of this new prison was the shape of its individual units; they had been constructed in the shape of the eighth letter of the alphabet. These H-Blocks would become famous, or infamous, throughout the world.

Ulsterization had some effect on the levels of violence. However, although the numbers of deaths began to decrease in the latter years of the 1970s, there were still some appalling individual incidents of brutality. Chief among these was the PIRA's 1978 firebombing of the La Mon House hotel outside Belfast, resulting in the deaths of 12 people.

The Peace People

As the government did not seem to be having much success in restoring normality to Northern Ireland, a group of ordinary people thought that they would have a go. Thus was born the movement that became known as the Peace People. Led by Mairéad Corrigan and Betty Williams, this pressure group sought to use mass demonstrations to force an end to 'the Troubles'. The Herculean efforts of the two leaders secured them the 1976 Nobel Peace Prize, however they were unable to change the thinking of those involved in the violence and in a bitterly divided society the movement eventually faded.

As a second decade of violence dawned, violence was again on the increase and a solution seemed as far away as ever, despite the election, in April 1979, of a new Conservative government led by Margaret Thatcher. Indeed not long after Thatcher's victory, two separate PIRA operations resulted in the deaths of 22 people. In one of the operations Earl Mountbatten, the last Viceroy of India and a senior member of the British Royal Family, lost his life. In the other, 18 soldiers were killed. Even the heartfelt pleas for an end to violence made by Pope John Paul II (1978–) at Drogheda on 30 September 1979 seemed to fall on deaf ears.

The hunger strikes

PIRA prisoners detested the policy of criminalization. They viewed themselves as soldiers fighting for Ireland's freedom, not as ordinary criminals, which is what they were now being treated as. From the time of the ending of special category status in 1976 the scene was set for a confrontation between prisoners and the British government.

The initial reaction of republican inmates was to refuse to wear prison-issue clothes; instead they covered themselves with blankets. This 'blanket protest' was followed in 1978 by the 'dirty protest', whereby prisoners smeared their cell walls with excrement rather than having to slop out. By late 1980 over 340 of the 837 republican prisoners were involved in the campaign. It must have been an unpleasant experience. Indeed the Archbishop of Armagh, Cardinal Tomas Ó Fiaich, stated after visiting the prison:

> The nearest to it that I have seen was the spectacle of hundreds of homeless people living in sewer pipes in the slums of Calcutta. The stench and filth in some of the cells with the remains of rotten food and human excreta scattered around the walls was almost unbearable.
>
> (Catholic Press Office release)

A variety of forms of pressure was also exerted outside the walls of the Maze Prison. However, numerous public demonstrations in support of the protests met with little success. Nor indeed was the use of violent intimidation any more successful. A series of attacks on prison warders proved ineffective as the new Conservative Secretary of State, Humphrey Atkins, refused to compromise with the prisoners.

In late 1980, therefore, the PIRA turned to a tactic beloved throughout the course of the twentieth century. The organization began a group hunger strike as a last method of achieving their demands. This was called off in December, as the prisoners believed that they had achieved a deal on the wearing of their own clothes. They were wrong however; despite claims to the contrary the British still refused to make concessions on the issue of special category status.

On 1 March 1981 a second hunger strike began. This time the tactics employed by the prisoners had changed. Unlike the group structure of the previous strike, this time it was decided that prisoners would join the protest at intervals so as to maximize its impact. The first prisoner to refuse food was Bobby Sands, the PIRA inmates' Officer Commanding.

The hunger strike gained huge publicity for the PIRA yet it still did not change government policy. The republican movement searched around for something else that would enhance their campaign just that little bit more. Their opportunity came when Frank Maguire, the sitting MP for Fermanagh–South Tyrone died. Republicans saw the chance to increase pressure on the British and so put Sands up as a candidate. On the fortieth day of his hunger strike Sands – standing as an Anti-H Block candidate – was elected to Westminster.

By now the hunger strike was headline news around the world. Yet despite huge amounts of international pressure on both sides, neither side would compromise and on 5 May Sands died. The hunger strike continued until 3 October 1981 by which time nine other republican prisoners had died. In the same period 61 people had died as a result of violence outside the walls of the Maze Prison.

Concessions granted?

The British government had not made a single concession during the duration of the hunger strike although towards its end concessions were being hinted at. Within a week of the strike's end, however, James Prior, the new Secretary of State, announced that a number of the concessions that the prisoners had sought would be granted. It was agreed that prisoners would be allowed to wear their own clothes at all times; the 50 per cent reduction in length of sentence lost by those involved in protests would be restored; an increased number of prison visits would be permitted, as would a greater degree of association among prisoners.

These concessions were enough to bring closure to what had been a particularly inflexible and bloody period in the history of 'the Troubles'. By the end of October 1981 the protests in favour of special category status had all but ended.

The ballot box in one hand and the Armalite in the other

In a political sense Bobby Sands' victory in the Fermanagh–South Tyrone by-election was hugely significant. His victory suggested to the republican movement that there was much to be gained from involvement in the political process. Nor could his win be explained solely as a sympathy vote, although there was undoubtedly an element of that in it. That it was not a total fluke was proved when his election agent, Owen Carron, won the seat at the by-election following Sands' death. The two victories could also be argued to have indicated the increasing depth of nationalist alienation from the state.

The republicans' official adoption of the policy of exploring the political avenue came at the 1981 Provisional Sinn Féin *Ard Fheis*. At this conference the republican party's delegates approved the movement's plan of contesting elections while also continuing to support extra-constitutional methods to achieve its aims. Before the motion was passed, Danny Morrison, Sinn Féin's Director of Publicity, had rhetorically enquired of the delegates if anyone among them would object if 'with a ballot paper in this hand and an Armalite in this hand, we take power in Ireland?'

'Rolling devolution'

While all of this was happening there was more clearly than ever a need to put in place some form of political solution. Prior's answer was the introduction of what became known as 'rolling devolution'. This quite ingenious plan proposed the election of yet another Assembly to which decision-making powers would be rolled out only if there was cross-community support for power-sharing.

Elections for the new Assembly were held in October 1982. However there was no real enthusiasm for the initiative amongst the north's parties (with the exception of Alliance). Indeed no nationalists ever sat in the Assembly during its three-and-a-half year existence, making the devolution of any powers impossible. The Assembly was finally dissolved in June 1986 in the aftermath of the signing of the Anglo-Irish Agreement (see below).

Yet even if the Assembly itself changed nothing, the results of the elections for its membership revealed a considerable amount about the changes that were taking place within nationalist politics. They showed that, with 10 per cent of the popular vote, there was clear growth in support for Sinn Féin among nationalist voters. Clearly the dual strategy adopted at the 1981 *Ard Fheis* was already paying dividends. Of course, some of the support could be attributed to the residual sympathy felt towards the dead hunger strikers.

This achievement was followed by an even bigger triumph in June 1983. In that year's Westminster General Election, the Party's President, Gerry Adams, defeated former SDLP leader, Gerry Fitt, for the West Belfast seat (Fitt was then elevated to the House of Lords). Both the Irish and British governments were now growing increasingly concerned that Sinn Féin might replace the SDLP as the main nationalist party in the province. For that reason they increased their levels of co-operation in search of the elusive solution.

Concern for the SDLP

Naturally, the prospect of being overtaken by Sinn Féin also worried the SDLP. Now led by John Hume, the Party started looking more and more to Dublin for means of shoring up its support. This was not a forlorn hope. With London and Dublin co-operating ever more closely in the face of Sinn Féin's growth, there was the possibility that the SDLP might again have a significant input into the future direction of the province, something the Party had not really enjoyed since the failure of power-sharing in 1974.

At the same time the levels of violence – while now noticeably lower than they had been in the early 1970s – were still giving considerable cause for concern. As with previous years there was still no shortage of spectacular republican attacks. In December 1982 17 people, 11 of whom were soldiers, died when a republican splinter group, the Irish National Liberation Army (INLA), exploded a massive bomb in Ballykelly, Co. Derry. The INLA had emerged in 1975 from a split in the Official IRA.

The New Ireland Forum

As a result of the pressure being applied by the SDLP leader, John Hume, the Irish government, now led by Garret FitzGerald, decided to set up a think tank to provide possible solutions to the Northern Ireland conflict. The New Ireland Forum, as it was called, first met in May 1983.

Hume hoped that the Forum would enable Ireland's nationalist parties to recognize that unionists had genuine fears about a united Ireland and that these fears would have to be addressed urgently. He believed that if this happened progress could be made and support for Sinn Féin would dwindle.

While FitzGerald was also keen to see a decline in support for Sinn Féin, he hoped that by implementing Hume's idea he would be able to effect further improvements in the Republic's relations with the British government which had reached an all-time low in the aftermath of the 1981 hunger strikes.

Despite invitations being issued to all interested parties – with the exception of Sinn Féin – attendance at the Forum was limited to Ireland's constitutional nationalist parties. Sinn Féin had been deliberately excluded, as FitzGerald had demanded that all participants reject the use of violence for political ends. Given the source of the invitation the north's unionist parties declined to attend. In this way the prospects of success for the Forum were fatally undermined. Whatever recommendations it came up with would be devalued because of the lack of unionist input.

Nevertheless the work went on and the Forum published its *Report* in May 1984. This document made a number of key points with regard to 'the Troubles'. In particular it criticized the sort of policies that had been pursued by the British government since the late 1960s. It concluded by offering three possible solutions to the Northern Ireland conflict. These were a united Ireland achieved by agreement and consent, a federal arrangement with a parliament for the north within a united Ireland, and joint authority where London and Dublin would have equal responsibility for running Northern Ireland.

Not unexpectedly, the unionist parties rejected all of the options contained within the *Forum Report* outright. What was more telling, however, was the reaction of the British government, which was delivered against a background of supposedly improving Anglo-Irish relations.

Thatcher's first public response to the *Report* came on 19 October, shortly after a PIRA attempt to kill her and senior members of her cabinet at the Conservative Party's annual conference in Brighton. The Prime Minister firmly rejected all of the Forum's proposed solutions in an infamous 'Out! Out! Out!' diatribe. For a time Anglo-Irish relations deteriorated again, yet the dangers of leaving a political vacuum to develop were too great and within a short time both governments were working closely together to effect change within the north.

The Anglo-Irish Agreement

On 15 November 1985 Margaret Thatcher and Garret FitzGerald arrived at Hillsborough Castle, the official residence of the Northern Ireland Secretary of State. There both premiers signed the Anglo-Irish Agreement, an accord that would transform the political situation in the north.

Commentators have suggested a number of different reasons as to why this Agreement was signed, not all of which are mutually exclusive. One interpretation – already hinted at – is that both constitutional nationalists and the British government were afraid that Sinn Féin might overtake the SDLP and become the principal nationalist party in the north. This would make the chances of agreement between the different traditions in the north more difficult. Moreover it might worsen the security situation and threaten the stability of Ireland.

Another interpretation is that Thatcher's main reason for signing the Agreement was based on security considerations. She realized that unless she dealt with nationalist alienation in Northern Ireland, she would not be able to improve the province's security situation. At the same time some believe that FitzGerald hoped that the Agreement would help reduce nationalist alienation with the state. He believed that this, coupled with reform of the security forces in Northern Ireland, would undermine the minority's toleration of the PIRA.

What was agreed?

Although the Anglo-Irish Agreement did not come anywhere near establishing any of the solutions so recently proposed by the New Ireland Forum, it did give the Republic a voice in the running of the north. This resurrection of an 'Irish dimension' flew in the face of every attempted solution since Sunningdale, all of which had deliberately excluded this element in the knowledge of how unionists would react to it.

There were other differences too, but perhaps the biggest change from all previous solutions was that the Agreement did not establish an assembly or an executive. It was purely an agreement between the two governments. In this way, it was reasoned, institutions that did not exist could not be pulled down. Thus a repeat of the Sunningdale debacle could be avoided.

Similarly to the Sunningdale Agreement Dublin accepted that a united Ireland was a long-term goal that would only materialize with the agreement of a majority of the province's population. In terms of structural changes, there were two key elements to the Agreement. One was the establishment of an Intergovernmental Conference, headed by the Secretary of State and the Irish Foreign Minister. This would deal with issues such as security, legal matters, political questions and improving cross-border co-operation. The second was the creation of a permanent secretariat, made up of northern and southern civil servants, which would provide administrative support to the Conference. It was also accepted that devolution would only occur in the future if there were agreement on the sharing of power.

Reactions

Whilst the Agreement was clearly acceptable to the Fine Gael and Labour Parties that made up the Republic's coalition government, the Fianna Fáil Opposition Party led by Charles Haughey condemned it. Fianna Fáil was dismayed by the recognition being given by Dublin to Britain's right to be in Northern Ireland. A number of individual Irish politicians were also strongly opposed. A prominent Irish Labour Party Senator, Mary Robinson (later President of Ireland), resigned from her Party because the Agreement was unacceptable to the unionist community.

Unlike the Dáil, the Agreement enjoyed overwhelming cross-party support at Westminster. However individual members of the British parliament were not so happy. Ian Gow, a Treasury

Minister and formerly the Prime Minister's Parliamentary Private Secretary, used the principle of collective responsibility to resign from his position in the government. He argued that the Agreement had been won by violence and would make the situation in the province worse rather than better.

Like Ian Gow, the unionist MPs at Westminster were also opposed. One of their number, Harold McCusker, memorably stated in the House of Commons 'I never knew what desolation felt like until I read this Agreement last Friday afternoon.' His views expressed the feelings of both main unionist parties. Back at home there was complete agreement between the UUP and DUP with regard to the Agreement. Unionists of all shades and opinions were appalled with what had been agreed at Hillsborough. They felt that they had been abandoned by their own government and believed that they were now in a process that would eventually result in a united Ireland.

What annoyed them the most, however, was the way in which they had been kept in the dark during the negotiations leading up to the Agreement while it looked as if the SDLP had been at least consulted during the negotiating process. Among unionist parties, only the Alliance Party did not condemn the Agreement outright.

The reaction within the nationalist community was rather more divided. As a result of its close relations with the Dublin government the SDLP had been given more of a role in the creation of the Agreement than any other party in the north. It was therefore able to view the accord as an opportunity to create a better way of life for all those living in the province.

Sinn Féin condemned the Agreement outright, albeit for rather different reasons from the unionists. They argued that rather than bringing a united Ireland closer, it had actually made the division of Ireland more permanent. Their argument here was similar to the one put forward by Fianna Fáil; by signing the Agreement the Irish government was recognizing the existence of Northern Ireland.

The unionist campaign of opposition

To where could unionists look for ways of making sense of their feelings of despair and betrayal? To where could they turn for the political support that would be necessary to sustain a successful campaign of opposition? The short answer was nowhere. The only other groups opposing the Agreement – Fianna Fáil and Sinn Féin – were not what might have been described as traditional political soul mates for unionism.

Unionist leaders therefore decided that the most effective method of opposing the Anglo-Irish Agreement would be a campaign of non-cooperation with the British government. However, they were also keen to demonstrate, by strength of number, the depth and breadth of unionist opposition to what they termed the 'Dublin Diktat'. This 'depth and breadth' became very clear when a huge protest rally was held at Belfast's City Hall on 23 November 1985. This demonstration of opposition was attended by at least 100,000 people although some commentators put the figure significantly higher.

The British and Irish governments were made aware of this same 'depth and breadth' through a variety of other forms of protest. These included marching to the headquarters of the new Anglo-Irish Secretariat, set up to support the working of the Agreement, which was located just outside Belfast. On a number of occasions these marches degenerated into violence. The old chestnut of a strike was also utilized when a 'Day of Action' was arranged for early March 1986. Although much of the province was brought to a standstill peacefully, in a number of places the protests also resulted in violence. Finally unionist politicians launched a campaign of civil disobedience with measures including the shunning of British ministers, the refusal to set rates in unionist council areas and a boycott of the British parliament.

However, potentially the biggest gun in the unionists' arsenal of opposition was the decision of all 15 unionist MPs to resign their seats at Westminster in December 1985 and then stand for them again in the resulting by-elections. Their intention was to show the strength of unionist opposition through the total number of votes the candidates received.

Yet the outcome of this strategy was something of a mixed bag. The strength of unionist support was clear for all to see. The unionists gained a total of over 420,000 votes, but the sweet taste of victory was somewhat spoilt by the results of the poll in Newry and Armagh. Here the UUP candidate lost his seat to Seamus Mallon of the SDLP. There were other interesting conclusions to be drawn from the election statistics. Sinn Féin's share of the nationalist vote fell from nearly 42 per cent to just over 35 per cent. This suggested that one of the key aims of the

Agreement's architects – the destruction of Sinn Féin – might just be achievable.

Alongside these mostly peaceful forms of opposition a more sinister response also made an appearance. Loyalist paramilitaries began a campaign of violence and intimidation against members of the largely Protestant RUC. The explanation as to why they were attacking a force mostly peopled by their own community was that the support of the police was seen as essential to the success of the Agreement. In addition, in November 1986 Ulster Resistance was formed. Its stated aim was to 'take direct action as and when required' to end the Anglo-Irish Agreement

Results of the campaign

The unionists' methods of opposition were many and varied. By and large, however, their tactics failed to have any impact on the British government, which was determined to stick by the Agreement. The absence of (now) 14 MPs out of a total in excess of 650 was not particularly noticed at Westminster. As the Conservative government had a healthy majority their votes were not needed – something that would not be the case a decade later. Moreover, since Northern Ireland's local councils had few powers as it was, their refusal to use these powers made little or no difference and the government simply struck new rates on their behalf.

In September 1987, unionist leaders agreed to talk to British ministers again. By making this decision it was clear that they had accepted that their campaign to destroy the Anglo-Irish Agreement had failed miserably.

15 the beginning of the end: 1985–97

This chapter will cover:
- Sinn Féin and constitutional politics
- the Hume–Adams talks
- suggestions of a breakthrough
- the 1994 cessations
- violence renewed
- all party talks
- the Good Friday Agreement.

Sinn Féin and constitutional politics

The Armalite and ballot box strategy that had been adopted by Sinn Féin in 1981 had initially proved successful in mobilizing support for the republican movement. However, in the aftermath of the signing of the Anglo-Irish Agreement, the republican movement seemed to have come up against a number of difficulties with its twin strategy approach. While support for the Party had grown rapidly at first, it had then bottomed out and Sinn Féin still lacked a decisive mandate. At the same time the PIRA was coming under considerable pressure from the security forces, even though it was still able to mount effective operations such as a mortar attack on Newry RUC Station in February 1985 that left nine officers dead. In many ways, it could be argued, the republican campaign had reached an impasse.

It was against this background that a strategic rethink began within Sinn Féin. As a result of this the movement made a number of significant adjustments to its traditional position. These included the acceptance in 1986 of the reality of the existing Irish Republic, and the abandonment of its possession of what senior member Martin McGuinness had termed the 'high altar of abstentionism'. This decision allowed its representatives to take up any seats won in the Dáil. At the same time the Party had begun to indicate its willingness to compromise over its short-term political demands and to engage in dialogue with other constitutional nationalist parties.

Initially the modification of policy did not result in any great change in fortunes. In the 1987 Dáil elections the Party managed to attract significantly less than 2 per cent of the vote, albeit by only standing in a minority of constituencies. That same election saw the return to power of Fianna Fáil in coalition with the recently formed Progressive Democrats, itself a splinter from the former Party. Once back in office Fianna Fáil announced that, previous opposition notwithstanding, it would now support the working of the Anglo-Irish Agreement.

Nor was Sinn Féin's performance in the same year's British General Election much better. It secured close to 20,000 votes less than had been achieved in the 1983 General Election. At the same time the SDLP achieved its highest ever share of the vote and managed to top off a successful campaign by ousting the sitting South Down MP, Enoch Powell. This gave the Party three seats at Westminster and seemingly the right to refer to itself as the main voice of the minority community.

The Hume–Adams talks

Despite Sinn Féin's diffident performance, the SDLP leader John Hume still believed that much could be gained from talking to the Party's leadership. In a 1987 interview Gerry Adams had suggested his willingness to consider an 'unarmed struggle' to further the search for independence. It was on this basis that late in the same year dialogue commenced between Adams and Hume, initially brokered by Belfast-based Redemptorist priest Fr Alec Reid. At significant cost to his own reputation (obvious subsequently from the stream of invective directed towards him when the talks became public knowledge in 1993), Hume's willingness to engage with Sinn Féin was arguably the first step in an embryonic peace process that ultimately brought the republican party in from the political cold.

Of course it wasn't the first time that Adams had been involved in cloak and dagger talks. During internment he had been involved in secret discussions that were held between the British government and the republican movement.

Perhaps more than the negotiations themselves it was their timing that brought such odium down on Hume. The talks had begun just months after the 1987 'Poppy Day' bomb in Enniskillen when a PIRA device killed 11 Protestants attending a service of commemoration. Another of the injured died much later from injuries received on that day. Not surprisingly there was revulsion at home and abroad. Not least in its impact was the denunciation uttered by U2's lead singer during a concert in the US that same evening. Bono asked the audience 'Where's the glory in bombing a Remembrance Day parade of old-age pensioners...that leave[s] them dying or crippled or dead under the rubble of the revolution that the majority of the people in my country don't want?'

The carnage was to continue. Around the time the meetings began, two plain clothed British soldiers who had happened upon the funeral of a PIRA volunteer were apprehended, beaten and executed. Almost all of this took place in the full view of television cameras. These operations did such damage to perceptions of the republican campaign that a dialogue between Adams and Hume must have seemed a more attractive option to Adams than it did to Hume. Yet the SDLP leader went ahead with the meetings, which leads one to conclude that he saw a prize both attainable and worth striving for.

If one views the talks in terms of an immediate outcome then they were a failure. However, they were more to do with finding out about positions at first. The two leaders had very different views of the role that Britain was playing within the north. Adams viewed it as essentially selfish, concerned with strategic and economic requirements. Hume, however, viewed the British stance as increasingly one of neutrality. In the context of Irish politics, however, the Hume–Adams talks convinced the SDLP leader that Sinn Féin sought a different route for achieving their goals. Overall the negotiations marked the beginning of a longer-term process that would help transform the political landscape.

The talks lasted six months and all the while the violence continued. Indeed the end of the negotiations followed shortly after the killing of eight soldiers near Ballygawley, Co. Tyrone. Overall, the late 1980s and early 1990s bore witness to a never-ending series of individual and collective killings. Apart from its usual targets the PIRA broadened out its campaign to take in those that had any sort of dealings with the security forces. This 'declaration of murderous violence against the community itself' – as Seamus Mallon termed it – included within its remit contractors, civil servants and caterers, among others. Chief among the casualties of this element were eight Protestant construction workers blown up in January 1991 at Teebane Cross in Co. Tyrone. All told, 1991 could point to having the highest numbers of deaths since 1976. Not a particularly proud boast.

No end to the violence

The PIRA also broadened out its range of tactics, employing the 'proxy' bomb and targeting mainland Europe. The former entailed forcing someone, invariably an innocent civilian, to drive a bomb into a security target where the driver – and others – went up with the detonation. In Europe a number of British military personnel – and a significant number of civilians – were targeted in countries such as West Germany and Holland.

Clearly the PIRA weren't running out of ideas; nor were they running short of munitions. In late 1987 the French Navy intercepted the *Eksund*, a freighter laden with guns and explosives and heading for Ireland en route from Libya. While there was initial euphoria at this significant breakthrough, it later transpired that the Libyans had dispatched four previous loads of a similar nature, including Semtex which found employment as a primer in the increasingly large bombs that the PIRA were producing by the early 1990s. It could be argued that the 'long war' had potentially a lot longer to run.

While the republican and loyalist paramilitaries dealt their deadly hand of death – the latter groups targeting an increasing number of Catholic civilians – the security forces fought fire with fire in an attempt to gain the upper hand. Chief among the latter's actions were the 1987 SAS killings of eight PIRA volunteers on a bombing mission in Loughgall, Co. Armagh (the PIRA's biggest single loss of life since 1921), the killings of three PIRA operatives in Gibraltar ten months later and the SAS-caused deaths of three men suspected of planning the aforementioned Ballygawley atrocity. Such operations revived, at least in some minds, memories of the so-called 'shoot-to-kill' deaths of the early 1980s when six unarmed Catholics had been gunned down by the security forces.

The investigations into this last series of incidents gave rise to another enduring element of the Northern Ireland problem, that of collusion. The inquiry by Greater Manchester's Deputy Chief Constable, John Stalker, into these deaths lost credibility when Stalker was removed in highly questionable circumstances. The investigation was continued by Colin Sampson but remains unpublished. Likewise, the 1989 killing of Belfast solicitor Patrick Finucane has remained an issue of controversy, with allegations of security force complicity given some degree of weight by the British government's agreement in 2004 to hold inquiries into this and an number of other contentious killings (see below).

Political progress?

There was still much progress to be made and the publication in 1992 of *Towards a Lasting Peace* indicated just how far Sinn Féin's policy was beginning to shift. This paper revealed a considerable reduction in the republican movement's emphasis on armed struggle. Instead considerable weight was placed on developing the concept of self-determination while the republican leadership suggested that it was particularly Britain's responsibility to persuade unionists that their interests would best be served within the context of a united Ireland.

Towards a Lasting Peace argued that all Irish nationalist parties needed to join together to form a front, whose purpose was the achievement of constitutional change in Ireland. This all-Ireland coalition would, in turn, reduce the unionist majority within Northern Ireland to a minority within the whole island and, it was reasoned, when Britain realized that they would be unable to continue to shore up unionism as a minority grouping, it would be prepared to deal with the republican movement.

That this wasn't just wishful thinking on Sinn Féin's part had been proven by noises being made by the Secretary of State, Peter Brooke, over the previous number of years. In 1989 Brooke had suggested – in an effort to correct the republican movement's understanding of Britain's position – that if the PIRA called a ceasefire the British government would react in an imaginative manner. Perhaps even more significantly Brooke had stated in November 1990 that his government had no 'selfish strategic or economic interest' in remaining in Northern Ireland. It was precisely this neutrality that Hume had been attempting to convince a sceptical Adams of in their talks.

Of course not all the exchanges were happening in the public eye. Whilst speaking out in public, Brooke had also approved the establishment of the 'Back Channel'. This was a private line of communication with the republican leadership. While difficulties remain in understanding exactly who started, or what came out of, these covert contacts, the very fact that both sides were prepared to talk at some level was an indication that there was new thinking on both sides. That such talks should continue for a number of years was also something of a miracle, given the PIRA's ongoing campaign in England which included the 1991 attempt to mortar 10 Downing Street; the April 1992 bomb in the City of London, which caused three quarters of a billion pounds worth of damage; and the March 1993 Warrington bombs which killed two children.

Brooke also attempted to launch a new round of discussions between the main constitutional parties regarding a political settlement. However, the main stumbling block with regard to unionist engagement remained the odious Anglo-Irish Agreement. To assist the process the Intergovernmental Conference element of the 1985 Agreement was temporarily suspended to allow talks to begin.

Some progress was made although it remained difficult to tell that this was the case. Agreement was reached that any settlement of the Northern Ireland question would have to involve three elements or strands. These were intercommunity relations, north–south co-operation and intergovernmental negotiations. Agreement would only be recognized when accord was reached in each of these areas. That was about as far as the negotiations got; by the middle of 1991 the whole initiative was dead and buried. The discussions collapsed over the agreement of a timetable for each strand and over the issue of who would chair the Strand Two element.

Resurrecting hope

By the middle of 1992 the British General Election had taken place and Sir Patrick Mayhew had replaced Brooke as Secretary of State. Significantly that election saw not only a reduction in Sinn Féin's share of the vote but the loss – to the SDLP's Joe Hendron – of Adams' trophy seat in West Belfast. Despite fears that his appointment would result in a more uncompromising British policy, Mayhew also initiated a talks process utilizing the same broad three-stranded framework introduced by his predecessor. However, as with the previous incumbent's efforts, these discussions also collapsed within a matter of months.

While all of this was taking place – or not as the case may be – discussions between Hume and Adams recommenced. In April 1993 the two leaders issued a joint statement in which they reaffirmed their intention of achieving self-determination for the people of Ireland. The discussions gave birth to a draft document in which Sinn Féin stated that it was prepared to acknowledge the necessity of unionist consent with regard to the future constitutional development of Northern Ireland.

Even if politics seemed to be inching things forward, violence seemed determined to drag Northern Ireland back to its bloodiest past. October 1993 in particular saw the highest number killed in a single month for 17 years. A PIRA attack on a fishmonger's shop on the loyalist Shankill Road left ten dead (including the bomber) and a further 57 injured. The PIRA later claimed that the intended target of the bomb was a meeting of the paramilitary Ulster Freedom Fighters (UFF – a cover name for the UDA) that was believed to be taking place in a former UDA office above the shop. The loyalists' response was swift and equally brutal. Gunmen entered a pub in the mainly Catholic village of Greysteel, 13 km (8 miles) to the east of Derry on Halloween night. Yelling 'trick or treat' they sprayed the bar with automatic gunfire. Eight civilians lost their lives.

The *Downing Street Declaration*

The British and Irish governments had not been idle while these developments were taking place. Despite the developments in republican thinking evident in the Hume–Adams statement they found themselves unable to accept it as a basis for peace given the intimate connection that Adams had with it. London and Dublin began to draw up their own document and in December 1993 they jointly produced the *Downing Street Declaration* (the second time such a title had been used), which outlined their approach to the removal of conflict. In this paper both sides publicly reaffirmed many of the positions that they had been taking of late while recognizing the legitimacy and right of expression of the different traditions within the island.

The British undertook to 'uphold the democratic wish of a greater number of the people of Northern Ireland on the issue of whether they wish to support the Union or establish a sovereign united Ireland'. At the same time they reaffirmed Brooke's 1990 declaration that they had no 'selfish strategic or economic interest in Northern Ireland'. They concluded that 'it is for the people of the island of Ireland alone, by agreement between the two parts respectively, to exercise their right of self-determination on the basis of consent, freely and concurrently given, North and South, to bring about a united Ireland'.

Meanwhile Dublin accepted that a united Ireland had to be the result of majority consent within Northern Ireland rather than arbitrary imposition. Significantly they accepted that significant elements of the 1937 Constitution were repugnant to unionists and in light of this undertook – in the context of an overall settlement – to put forward and support changes to the Irish Constitution.

Just in case people got carried away with what was being suggested, the British government put a number of important qualifications on its position, mainly as a way of countering the unionist sense of alienation that had originated with the signing of the Anglo-Irish Agreement. London stated that its position on the future of Northern Ireland was essentially a neutral one. It would not persuade unionists to join such a new union nor would it commit itself to how long such a development might take. In case anyone thought that they had gone soft on the issue, the British also reaffirmed that they still held sovereignty over Northern Ireland and did not contemplate sharing this with Dublin.

Political reactions

Qualifications aside, the *Declaration* was a significant development. Not least in terms of importance was the British acceptance that the desire to see a united Ireland was a legitimate aspiration to hold. Yet the qualifications were still too much for republicans and they found themselves initially unable to accept the Declaration. Sinn Féin argued that even if they were glad to see that Britain was at least accepting the concept of self-determination, the document's language allowed unionists a veto over its exercise.

The response from the different unionist parties was equally circumspect. While the UUP were comforted by the British government's qualifications, they were less than happy with what they termed the *Declaration's* 'green tinge'. It was a similar reaction from the DUP although they argued that, more than having a green tinge, the *Declaration* was yet another step towards the reunification of the island.

On the whole the unionist parties remained unpersuaded by key elements of the *Declaration*. In particular they were concerned at the vague nature of the Republic's pledges to change its Constitution. They argued that the language used would permit Dublin to decline to change the Constitution if it was dissatisfied with the 'overall settlement'. Moreover, they argued that if the Republic was satisfied it would be an indication that its long-standing constitutional claim over Northern Ireland had been achieved. That would not exactly be a cause for celebration either.

The PIRA cessation

At first glance the *Declaration* might not have been the political panacea for which the PIRA was looking. In the end, however, careful explanation of the thinking behind the *Declaration* – carried out by Irish government representatives – enabled the republican movement to use the document as a basis for its 'complete cessation of military operations' as of 31 August 1994. The months between the *Declaration* and the cessation had been taken up with discussions and negotiations between the main players at home and providing reassurances for republicans at home and abroad. Chief among the latter were those Irish Americans who feared that too much was being given away. The task of reassuring them fell to Adams who, despite vehement British objections, was granted a visa for entry into the US by President Bill Clinton for this very purpose in January 1994.

The PIRA statement of August 1994 recognized the 'potential of the current situation' but warned that 'a solution will only be found as a result of inclusive negotiations'. In other words Sinn Féin would have to be fully included in any talks process.

If Sinn Féin had hoped that the cessation would provide their passport for entry into substantive talks they were to be sorely disappointed. Almost immediately the debates about semantics began with regard to the language employed by the PIRA in its August statement. The British government announced that it wanted to hear the PIRA use the word 'permanent' in connection with its cessation and they added that they would require a period of quarantine to test the republican movement's actions rather than its words. Sinn Féin argued that the silence of the PIRA weapons and their own pre-existing mandate provided more than enough justification for their immediate inclusion in talks.

Yet some sense of a thaw in the relationship between the two sides was evident. Talks were held between Sinn Féin and British government officials (as opposed to MPs) and the British rescinded the ban that they had imposed in 1988 on Sinn Féin members' voices being broadcast.

In contrast to British prevarications, both Dublin and Washington initially proved less circumspect in their reactions. Just a week after the PIRA cessation took effect Taoiseach Albert Reynolds shook hands with Gerry Adams when the two of them appeared publicly on the steps of Government Buildings along with John Hume. Just over a month later Dublin announced the establishment of a Forum for Peace and Reconciliation, to be attended by representatives of all Irish parties, while in early December nine PIRA inmates were released on licence. Meanwhile, President Clinton allowed Adams back into the United States and organized a myriad of conferences aimed at supporting the peace process with economic investment.

Within four months however the Dublin part of this support network had crumbled. In December 1994, Reynolds's Fianna Fáil administration was replaced by a Fine Gael–Labour– Democratic Left coalition. Neither the Taoiseach, John Bruton, nor Proinsias de Rossa, the leader of Democratic Left, were known for their love of republicanism. Within a week Bruton had proved this by echoing London's demands for PIRA decommissioning. It was for making such pronouncements that Albert Reynolds once memorably described his Fine Gael opponent as 'John unionist'!

The loyalist response

Meanwhile the loyalist paramilitaries waited a further six weeks after the PIRA declaration before they announced their own ceasefire on 13 October 1994. Recent revelations from then

Taoiseach Albert Reynolds reveal that he travelled to Belfast's Shankill Road and personally discussed the terms of the loyalist ceasefire with the umbrella Combined Loyalist Military Command (CLMC). Yet they weren't just waiting. At 10.05 p.m. on 1 September – over 22 hours into the PIRA cessation – loyalist paramilitaries murdered a Catholic civilian. How this was in response to an PIRA attack – a frequent loyalist mantra of justification – is extremely hard to see.

The loyalist statement was read by a certain Gusty Spence who had been imprisoned for his involvement in one of the earliest UVF killings that actually predated the beginning of 'the Troubles'. It warned that the continuation of the ceasefire would be 'completely dependent upon the continued cessation of all nationalist/republican violence'.

The loyalists' ceasefire also began to pay political dividends for their political representatives, the Progressive Unionist Party (PUP) and the Ulster Democratic Party (UDP). By the close of the year both groups were engaged in exploratory discussions with representatives of the London government.

The *Framework Documents*

In February 1995 the London and Dublin governments put two further progress papers forward. The aim of the *Framework Documents* was, not surprisingly, to provide a framework for taking the nascent peace process forward.

The first paper, *A Framework for Accountable Government in Northern Ireland*, outlined Britain's proposals for new political institutions for the north. These included a 90-strong assembly that would exercise powers similar to its 1974 power-sharing antecedent. A range of mechanisms was also suggested to provide protection for the nationalist minority.

The second Framework Document, *A New Framework for Agreement*, was produced jointly by London and Dublin. It was based around the principles of self-determination, consent, non-violence and parity of esteem. To help develop relationships within Ireland it proposed the establishment of some form of north–south body while east–west relations (those between Britain and Ireland) would be underpinned by structures similar to those established by the Anglo-Irish Agreement.

Reactions

As usual reactions from the local parties were mixed. Unionists saw too many similarities with Sunningdale and abhorred the possibility of the development of north–south links into some form of institutions with executive powers. Not long afterwards, the UUP leader, James Molyneaux, resigned to be replaced by Upper Bann MP David Trimble. Molyneaux (who was appointed to the House of Lords) had always claimed to have the ear of the British; the Anglo-Irish Agreement and the *Framework Documents* seemed to have proved this assertion to be somewhat misplaced. He left behind a divided and demoralized party.

Initially Trimble looked like a hardline replacement. His somewhat unexpected candidacy had not been harmed by his recent highly visible role in the 1995 standoff at Drumcree, on the outskirts of Portadown. Here a traditional Orange Order march had initially been banned from travelling through the nationalist Garvaghy Road area. Then as the threat of widespread loyalist opposition grew, the march was pushed down the road – literally – by the RUC. Moreover this was not Trimble's first foray into hardline opposition. In a previous existence he had been a vocal opponent of the 1973–4 Sunningdale Agreement.

Sinn Féin also had issues with the *Framework Documents* but these went in the opposite direction from those of the unionists. They argued that the *Documents* provided mechanisms by which unionists would be able to veto progress. Only the SDLP and Alliance reacted positively to what had been proposed.

While there was no doubt that plenty was being written, there was little or no evidence that anything was being said. The continuing absence of face-to-face talks between the British government and republicans began to impact severely on the stability of the peace process.

Decommissioning

The main problem for the British was the absence of PIRA decommissioning of its weapons. The British and unionists were demanding this as a prerequisite for entry into negotiations. For the PIRA such a demand was tantamount to an admission of defeat and surrender; two things which they were unlikely to ever sign up to. Its frustration boiled over and instead of continuing to follow the lead of the Sinn Féin leadership, the PIRA began to plan for a return to military operations.

Unaware of what was being planned, London attempted to find a way around the impasse by establishing a commission, chaired by former US Senate Majority Leader George Mitchell, to look into the issue of decommissioning. The Mitchell Commission reported its findings in early 1996. Its solution to the deadlock was christened the twin track approach or parallel decommissioning. In layman's terms it suggested the handover of weapons in parallel with talks taking place, but not before. The Commission also put forward proposals or principles of non-violence, to which all parties would have to sign up in order to demonstrate their commitment to peace.

Mitchell's work should have provided a way out of the impasse, but before long there were yet more obstacles to overcome. One was the decision to hold elections to a Peace Forum – an idea first raised by the Mitchell Commission – as a way of providing a mandate for the participants. The other was the not wholly unexpected collapse of the PIRA cessation in February 1996 when they exploded a bomb at London's Canary Wharf. This was proof enough for all of the doubters that the republican movement had never seen its cessation as anything more than a tactic.

The PIRA placed the blame for their decision to return to violence on the British government's continued reluctance to move the peace process forward at a sufficient speed. It has been suggested that one of the main reasons for this was the precarious position that the Conservative government found itself in by that time. There might have been some truth in this suggestion. John Major – who had succeeded Thatcher as British Prime Minister in 1990 – had been returned to power in 1992 with a small majority. Within a few years the loss of several by-elections and the withdrawal of the whip from a number of Conservative MPs over their opposition to the government's policy on Europe had left the Prime Minister reliant on UUP support to stay in office. He could only push the process forward at a pace with which the unionists were comfortable. At that time, that was very slowly indeed.

Violence also began to emanate from other republican sources, most notably the Continuity IRA which split from the main movement in the aftermath of the 1994 cessation. However, by and large the official loyalist ceasefires continued to hold, albeit if one excludes the activities of the Loyalist Volunteer Force (LVF). Based in the mid-Ulster area, the LVF was, under the leadership of Billy Wright, taking a particularly hard line against what it perceived as nationalist-demanded encroachments into traditional Protestant rights. In particular the issue of Orange Order marches through nationalist areas of Portadown was continuing to cause severe problems.

Forum elections

Unionists supported the Forum plan but nationalists were furious. They simply did not see the need for participants in the peace process to have to prove their mandate further. In their view the plan was yet another stalling exercise, an example of the malign influence that the unionist parties in general and the UUP in particular were exercising over John Major's Conservative administration.

Yet in spite of their hostility to the plan both the SDLP and Sinn Féin put forward candidates for the Forum elections. However, as far as Sinn Féin was concerned, that was as far as their involvement would go. They announced that they would boycott the resulting assembly. The SDLP were only slightly more accommodating. They announced that they would make up their minds to attend the Forum on a day-by-day basis depending on what the agenda was.

The election results revealed that support for the DUP and Sinn Féin had increased. The UDP and PUP were also successful in winning seats, which meant that they would be able to attend any future peace talks. This was probably one of the most positive outcomes of the decision to hold elections. It provided for broadly based negotiations that at least had the potential to bring all the key players in the process along.

The peace talks

The peace talks finally began in June 1996. However, the Canary Wharf bomb and the continuing absence of a PIRA ceasefire ensured that Sinn Féin was not present. Moreover, they did not have the same voices to plead their case as earlier in the process because the end of the cessation and the change of government in Dublin (see above) had weakened the pan-nationalist front that had been built up by Hume, Adams and Reynolds.

If truth be told, the entire peace process was in some form of limbo throughout 1996 and on into the first half of 1997. It appeared that no real progress would be possible until a stronger government had been installed in London. As there had to be an election in 1997 and as it seemed more than likely that the Conservatives would be defeated, attention turned to the likely impact that a Labour government would have on the stuttering peace process.

New Labour

The 1997 General Election transformed the political map in Britain and provided the stimulus for developments in Ireland. The New Labour administration wasted no time in getting things moving again by announcing that if the PIRA renewed its ceasefire Sinn Féin would be allowed to enter the talks. For its part the election had proven extremely successful for Sinn Féin too; Martin McGuinness had won a seat in Mid Ulster thus doubling the Party's potential representation at Westminster and indicating that electoral support for the republican movement's strategy was once again increasing.

At the same time an election in the south had seen the electorate's rejection of the current administration and a return to power of Fianna Fáil, partnered by the Progressive Democrats. Bertie Ahern became Taoiseach.

Tony Blair, the British Prime Minister, had warned the republican movement that the peace process train would leave the station with or without them. In the event they were on board. Having been assured that they would be included in talks six weeks after calling a new cessation, the PIRA ceasefire was renewed on 20 July 1997, shortly after a number of horrendous murders including those of two RUC men in the Co. Armagh town of Lurgan. Then, having signed up to the Mitchell Principles of Non-Violence, Sinn Féin entered the talks in September.

Sinn Féin's entry was the signal for some of the unionist parties to absent themselves from the process. Revd Ian Paisley's DUP and the minority United Kingdom Unionist Party (UKUP), led by Robert McCartney, refused to even consider proximity negotiations, a position not shared by the UUP nor indeed by the parties representing the loyalist paramilitaries. Paisley's absence and thus disconnection with the final outcome would ultimately allow him to take up a position of opposition to the Agreement (in electoral terms).

The Sinn Féin entry also caused some problems within that organization. It was important that the Sinn Féin leadership would be able to negotiate without the PIRA going back to war as had happened at Canary Wharf in 1996. At a General Army Convention called to agree a change to the PIRA's constitution that would allow the organization's Army Council (which the Sinn Féin leadership controlled) to decide on possible concessions, cracks appeared. The leadership's victory resulted in a section of the republican movement shearing off to form the Real IRA. Apart from their defeat at the Convention this group were less than happy at the Party's agreement to sign up to the Mitchell Principles.

It had been decided that the negotiations would be based around three strands. Strand One would concentrate on establishing a suitable internal governmental structure for Northern Ireland; Strand Two would be concerned with relationships between the two parts of Ireland while Strand Three would deal with British–Irish relations. At the same time an Independent International Commission on Decommissioning was launched under the chairmanship of Canadian General John de Chastelain.

The final countdown

The talks were initially held at Castle Buildings, Stormont. In January 1998 they moved; first to London and then on to Dublin. They returned to Belfast in early February. During these early months there was something of a political merry-go-round as first the UDP and then Sinn Féin left and then re-entered the process. The UDP absented themselves before they were asked to do so. The reason was an admission by the UFF, the paramilitary group to which the UDP was close, that it had engaged in terrorist activities. Their absence, however, lasted only a number of weeks.

Sinn Féin also went although not voluntarily. They were excluded by the two governments in the aftermath of two murders, which were blamed on the PIRA. After just over two weeks the Party was allowed to return. From then until Holy Week the negotiations continued. At that stage the two Prime Ministers, Tony Blair and Bertie Ahern, joined the talks.

The governments had introduced a deadline of Holy Thursday, 9 April, as the final deadline for the talks. In the event that deadline was overrun. Then, just when it seemed that UUP objections might lead to the collapse of the process, Tony Blair called on the persuasive powers of US President, Bill Clinton, to keep the negotiations going. Clinton's intervention seemed to do the trick and at 5.30 p.m. on the evening of Friday 10 April 1997, Good Friday, the deal was done.

6

the Good Friday Agreement and its aftermath

This chapter will cover:
- terms of the Agreement
- referenda
- disagreements remain
- stop–start devolution
- the emergence of 'the Extremes'
- logjam.

The terms of the Agreement

As with many of the documents produced over previous decades aimed at solving the Northern Ireland problem, the Good Friday Agreement was capable of significantly different interpretations depending on which political perspective one took. Given that it was a document to which both republicans and unionists were preparing to sign up, such potential flexibility in interpretation should not come as any great surprise.

The Agreement was divided into three strands reflecting the distinctions that had developed at the time of the Brooke and Mayhew talks. Strand One dealt with the internal political settlement. It established a 108-member Assembly that was to be elected by PR. This body would enjoy full legislative and executive authority over areas previously administered by the Northern Ireland Office (the government department that ran Northern Ireland).

Strand Two focused on relations within the island of Ireland. It established a North–South Ministerial Council that would be responsible for cross-border co-operation in a range of areas including language, agriculture, health, tourism and trade. Meetings of the Council would include the relevant ministers from both jurisdictions depending on the issues under discussion.

Strand Three centred on east–west relations namely those between Ireland and Britain. As part of this aspect there would be a Council of the Isles or British–Irish Council comprising members from all parliaments and devolved assemblies within the British Isles. Its purpose was to facilitate consultation and co-operation in a range of areas including drugs, agriculture, energy and regional issues. There would also be a British–Irish Intergovernmental Conference with a remit similar to the institutions established between London and Dublin by the 1985 Anglo-Irish Agreement.

There were other significant areas of agreement. The Irish government undertook to renounce its constitutional claims to Northern Ireland as contained within Articles II and III of the 1937 Irish Constitution. Meanwhile London agreed to replace the 1920 Government of Ireland Act. There were also to be prisoner releases coupled with the decommissioning of paramilitary weapons. It was the latter issue that would become the real bugbear of the Agreement.

Crucifying the guns – The Times' take on the decommissioning aspects of the Good Friday Agreement.

Policing

One of the key elements in the creation of a new political beginning in Northern Ireland was reform of policing. Both communities regarded the RUC significantly differently. To the unionist population they had been and remained the defenders of law and order against decades of republican violence. Nationalists, however, saw the existing police force as a partial organization that had helped and continued to help maintain decades of discrimination. A police force that could attract the support of both communities was, therefore, essential.

The Agreement provided a roadmap for reform of policing. Under its terms an Independent Commission on Policing in Northern Ireland was established under the chairmanship of Chris Patten, former Conservative Party Chairman and last Governor of Hong Kong. The Patten Commission (as it became known) spent close to a year taking detailed evidence from all interested parties. The upshot was a series of recommendations including a name change – from RUC to Police Service of Northern Ireland (PSNI) – changes in emblems, a reduction in numbers, new accountability boards and a 50–50 recruitment policy with regard to both communities.

The key changes were in place by early 2002. They were accepted with great reluctance by the unionist community given the way in which members of the force and their families had suffered during the course of 'the Troubles'. The award of the George Cross to the RUC as a whole brought some comfort, but overall it was a bitter pill to swallow. Nor was the reaction from Sinn Féin much more positive. It regarded the PSNI as little more than the RUC under new management and refused to endorse the changes introduced.

Reactions to the Agreement

Even before the Agreement was signed it was clear that there were going to be difficulties in selling it, particularly within the unionist community. The absence of the DUP and the UKUP from the negotiations has already been noted; however more ominously public divisions were beginning to emerge within the ranks of the majority UUP. The first sense of this came when Jeffrey Donaldson – one of the members of the UUP negotiating team – walked out of Castle Buildings just as the deal was nearing completion.

That this Pilate-like act was not an isolated reaction was soon clear. It soon emerged that six of the UUP's ten MPs had set their faces against the deal, creating a very difficult situation for David Trimble. In May all the unionists opposed to the Agreement – including UUP dissidents – set up the United Unionist Campaign to co-ordinate their campaign of opposition. Their slogan became 'It's Right to say No'.

Initially somewhat contradictory reactions from within republican ranks provided further cause for concern. On the last day of April the PIRA issued a statement suggesting that the Agreement fell somewhat 'short of presenting a solid basis for a lasting settlement'. The organization further added that it would not be decommissioning any of its weapons.

However, a few days later, the Sinn Féin leadership advised its supporters to back the Agreement. At the Party's *Ard Fheis* members voted to change their constitution so as to allow members to take seats in the Northern Ireland Assembly. This was an historic moment in the history of the Party. For the first time it was prepared to take up seats in what it itself might have previously termed a 'partitionist parliament'. That in itself suggested tacit recognition of the existence of the Northern Ireland state.

Referenda

The first substantive test of the Good Friday Agreement would be how the voting public would react to it. Referenda were held on both sides of the border on 22 May 1998 to ascertain the electorate's reactions. These were preceded by a pro-Agreement campaign that enjoyed almost overwhelming cross-party support in all political jurisdictions within the British Isles. Of course there were notable exceptions: the DUP, UKUP, a number of senior UUP members and a number of individuals including Margaret (now Baroness) Thatcher.

Within Northern Ireland 71.12 per cent of those that voted indicated their support for the Agreement. The overall turnout was 80.98 per cent, a figure significantly higher than that produced at most election times. This result was an overwhelming endorsement or a clear rejection of the Agreement, depending on which party one was asking.

As the vote was carried out on the basis of Northern Ireland as a single constituency, it was impossible to give an accurate breakdown of support levels within the two communities. Insofar as estimates can be relied upon, it seemed that close to 97 per cent of nationalists were giving the Agreement their support while the comparable figure within unionism stood at about 52 per cent. This limited majority, while better than the figures achieved at the time of the 1973 power-sharing elections, still gave significant cause for concern.

The figures for the referendum in the Republic were predictably clear. There 94.4 per cent agreed with the Dublin government's plans to amend Articles II and III of the Irish Constitution as agreed at the peace talks.

Assembly elections

The elections for the new Assembly were held in late June. On the surface it seemed that there was a clear majority of members elected in favour of power-sharing (75 per cent of the votes resulting in 80 out of 108 Assembly seats) however this failed to take account of two important caveats. First, not all of the 28

UUP members elected were in favour of the Agreement even though the UUP was meant to be a pro-Agreement Party. Second, and more important, the Agreement dictated that certain decisions (called key decisions) called for majority support from both nationalist and unionist communities. Given the fine balance between pro- and anti-Agreement unionist support that was going to be easier said than done.

The results also revealed interesting developments regarding the relative positions of the main political parties. For the first time in its history the SDLP topped the poll in terms of its share of first preference votes although in terms of seats won the UUP came first (28 seats to the SDLP's 24). The DUP won 20 seats and just over 3 per cent less of first preference votes than the UUP. Sinn Féin was also not that far behind the SDLP. It gained 18 seats and just over 4 per cent less first preferences than the main nationalist party.

A brighter future?

The new Assembly gathered for the first time on 15 July 1998 with the Alliance Party's Lord John Alderdice having been appointed Presiding Officer by the Secretary of State. David Trimble, UUP leader, and Seamus Mallon, SDLP deputy-leader, were elected as First and Deputy First Ministers (Designate). At the same time a number of business committees were established, as was a 'Shadow Assembly Commission' to assist with the transition from Direct Rule to devolved power.

To those of a sanguine disposition it might have seemed as if things were looking up, however this was Northern Ireland and political life was certainly never quite that simple. The PIRA's marked reluctance to decommission its weapons led unionists to suspect that their campaign was not over. Certainly the fact that the war was not over for some within the republican family became abundantly clear on Saturday 15 August 1998.

On that day the Real IRA detonated a massive bomb on the main street of the Co. Tyrone market town of Omagh. As mentioned before, this group had emerged out of a split in the republican movement resulting from the Sinn Féin decision to take up seats in the Stormont Assembly.

Although this heinous act ultimately failed in its efforts to destroy the peace process, it succeeded massively in destroying the lives of a great number of innocent civilians. Thirty-one lives were lost on that day, including those of two unborn children. The victims were old and young, male and female, native and foreign, Catholic and Protestant. It was, and remains, an act beyond comprehension.

In the aftermath of the atrocity, and the associated outpourings of public revulsion, the Real IRA announced a suspension of operations whilst its future direction was decided. A ceasefire was subsequently declared although it was later abandoned.

Stalled progress

A further year of stop–start negotiations got the process nowhere and by September 1999 the new system was still in the starting box. The continuing failure to advance the decommissioning issue had meant that unionists were not prepared to go into government. The British government responded to the impasse by inviting the Houdini of the peace process, Senator George Mitchell, back to chair a review of the Agreement. By the time this ended in November 1999 Gerry Adams and David Trimble had held their first face-to-face meeting – progress of a sort. There had also been a change of Secretary of State, Mo Mowlam (who had held the position since 1997) having been replaced in October by New Labour guru Peter Mandelson.

The review seemed to provide the necessary impetus and the Assembly was convened on 29 November to elect the full quota of ministers. The go-ahead for UUP involvement was provided by its ruling body, the Ulster Unionist Council (UUC). This in itself followed on from a PIRA agreement to appoint an 'interlocutor' to treat with the Decommissioning Commission. However there was still work to be done. The UUC endorsement was for a limited period (until February 2000) and would be withdrawn if PIRA decommissioning was not forthcoming.

When the Assembly met on 29 November 1999 ten ministers were nominated (including two from the DUP who would continually refuse to attend Executive meetings with Sinn Féin present). Three days later power was devolved. At the same time the Anglo-Irish Agreement was replaced by the British–Irish Agreement and later on the same day Articles II and II of the Irish Constitution were replaced. Within three weeks, meetings of the bodies established in Strands Two and Three had taken place. For the first time in 25 years Northern Ireland had a power-sharing Executive. It seemed as if a bright new future was finally dawning.

Failure

Unfortunately and like so many previously, the dawn did not last. Again the decommissioning issue reared its ugly head. At the end of January 2000 the Head of the Decommissioning Commission announced that no acts of decommissioning had taken place. It looked as if the blame for suspension was going to be placed squarely at the feet of the republican movement. Then, minutes before suspension was to be announced, the PIRA made it known that it was now willing to consider how decommissioning could occur.

Whether this was a genuine offer or simply a way of removing the heat of blame from republicans is hard to tell. In any case it was too late: at midnight on 11 February 2000 the Secretary of State suspended the Assembly and Direct Rule was reintroduced. The devolved institutions had held power for ten weeks and two days. Soon after the PIRA withdrew its last minute offer.

The suspension lasted for four months during most of which intensive negotiations took place. Then in late May the UUC bit the bullet – literally – and agreed to resume power-sharing with Sinn Féin. The reason for their change of heart was a PIRA offer to 'put its arms beyond use'. However the UUP was clearly fracturing under the pressure of the Agreement. Evidence of the difficulties Trimble found himself in had already come in the Spring of 2000 when he escaped defeat by a relatively small margin in a leadership challenge by UUP MP, Revd Martin Smyth.

In the meantime as a confidence-building measure, the PIRA agreed to allow independent inspectors to inspect its arms dumps. Martti Ahtisaari, the former President of Finland, and Cyril Rhamaphosa, the former Secretary General of the African National Congress, were given the task of inspecting the weapons and ensuring that they remained secure. Inspections took place in June and October 2000.

Devolution restored

Despite the attempts to resolve the decommissioning issue it continued to haunt the process. With no real progress made beyond the PIRA's words of intent, Trimble began to seek out other ways of putting pressure on the republican movement short of another suspension. In December 2000 he announced that in future he would refuse to permit Sinn Féin ministers to attend meetings of the North–South Ministerial Council.

Although Sinn Féin got round the ban by meeting their southern counterparts informally, they referred the matter to the courts and were vindicated when Trimble's actions were declared *ultra vires*. Despite losing again on appeal Trimble decided to continue with his ban until the autumn of 2001. Shortly after it was lifted the courts (delivering a reserved judgement) again declared the ban illegal.

Continuing impasse

These tactics still failed to achieve the Holy Grail of decommissioning. In frustration Trimble threatened to resign as First Minister at the start of July 2001 if progress still had not been made. This was not just a way of putting more pressure on republicans; his harder line was a way of gaining support at the forthcoming General Election; of course it also helped paper over some of the divisions that were emerging within his own Party.

In the event, the June General Election was not a good one for the UUP or, for that matter, for the SDLP. The main victors were Sinn Féin and the DUP. The UUP went from holding nine seats to just six while the DUP increased their representation from three to five. The SDLP retained the three seats that they held while Sinn Féin – taking two seats off the UUP – went up from two to four MPs.

Further talks between the parties took place at Weston Park in England in July. By that stage Trimble had carried out his threat to resign. In his place he nominated fellow UUP minister Reg Empey thus leaving (under the terms of the Agreement) a six-week gap until a new First Minister and Deputy First Minister (who automatically lost his position when Trimble resigned) had to be elected. Initially, it appeared that there had been no breakthrough, and when the two governments eventually published their own proposals for progress they received what could at best be described as a lukewarm reaction.

Then in early August the Decommissioning Commission announced that it had reached agreement with the PIRA on the methods of weapons disposal. However this breakthrough was still not enough for the UUP. The PIRA agreement with the Decommissioning Commission had still not included a timetable for the process. Trimble announced that he was withdrawing his Party's ministers from the Executive.

The Secretary of State, Peter Mandelson, had decided there was no option but to suspend the Agreement and initiate another review, when a chink of light appeared. It became clear that the SDLP – following on from a similar endorsement by the Catholic Church – was finally going to take up its seats on the new Policing Boards, an accountability mechanism established by the Agreement. This would make them the north's first nationalist party to endorse the region's policing arrangements. This concession was enough for Trimble to postpone his resignation threat, at least temporarily. The Assembly limped on.

However the small matter of Trimble's resignation remained to be dealt with. If it came into effect (for example, if he or some other UUP member were not (re)elected within a six week window) the Good Friday institutions would fall. The new Secretary of State, Dr John Reid (Mandelson had been forced to resign when implicated in a passport scandal back in Britain), then made use of an obscure clause in the Agreement to suspend the institutions for a single day. This temporary suspension then resulted in the creation of a new six-week gap until the re-election of the First Minister, which allowed further negotiations to take place. The PIRA was not impressed, however, and withdrew its decommissioning offer and its contacts with the Decommissioning Commission.

Colombia and Bin Laden

At that point events far beyond Ireland conspired to effect a change on the development of the political process. The genuineness of the PIRA's 1998 ceasefire was called into question when three republicans – claiming to be tourists – were arrested in Colombia and charged with training Colombian FARC guerrillas in terrorist techniques. (They were eventually acquitted in mid-2004 although convicted of carrying false passports. However, this verdit was overturned on appeal.)

Then, on 11 September 2001, New York and Washington came under attack from Islamic Fundamentalists. While there was never any question of republican involvement in the Al Quaeda sponsored attacks, the mood in the American administration turned severely against homegrown support for movements with terrorist connections, particularly in terms of stopping financial support. Coupled with US annoyance at recent events in Colombia, Sinn Féin began to worry that a significant source of funding might be cut off. Meanwhile, the PIRA re-engaged with the Decommissioning Commission yet again.

In the meantime the shenanigans continued at Stormont. The Assembly was suspended and then restored again, allowing for yet another six-week gap. During this period, which was due to end on 3 November, the UUP again announced that its quota of ministers would vacate their positions by 25 October. The DUP ministers would have little choice but to follow suit.

It looked as if the prospects for an acceptable resolution were poor, however, just two days before the UUP resignations were to take effect, the Decommissioning Commission announced that an act of PIRA decommissioning had taken place. This followed on from a public announcement by Adams that he had advised the PIRA to initiate such a process.

This was enough to halt the UUP's resignation plans; but there were more complicated matters to deal with. Since Trimble had resigned as First Minister (thus triggering also the resignation of the Deputy First Minister since both were elected as a team), he had to stand for re-election to the position. Such a significant vote required majority support from the representatives of both communities. The problem was, however, that some of Trimble's own Party no longer supported his policies and might be prepared to vote with the DUP against his reappointment. This would mean that he would not achieve a majority of unionist support and thus could not return to the job.

Re-electing Trimble

To get around the difficulty of re-electing Trimble both members of the Northern Ireland Women's Coalition (NIWC) decided to change their party designation to secure the re-election of the First and Deputy First Ministers. The reason that they were forced to take this step was that the votes of those members of the Assembly who had chosen on the first day not to designate themselves as 'nationalist' or 'unionist' but instead as 'others' did not count in these cross-community votes.

For the NIWC to do this required a change to the rules of the Assembly, which duly took place. However the support from the NIWC still wasn't enough. At this point the Alliance Party announced that to save the Agreement three of its MLAs (the title given to Assembly members) would follow the NIWC's example and redesignate as unionists. In return they were to be offered a review of the current voting system in which their votes had not counted when it had mattered most. The Secretary of State also extended the deadline for suspending the Assembly by a further two days.

The second re-election attempt took place on Tuesday 6 November. This time the vote was more pleasing to the pro-Agreement side. Trimble was re-elected as First Minister and the SDLP's Mark Durkan was elected as Deputy First Minister, Seamus Mallon having decided that the time was right to stand down. Not everyone was pleased, members of the DUP were so angry at the generous manner in which the rules had been interpreted that they had already sought a judicial review of the Secretary of State's actions. Their attempts were unsuccessful. Then, in the aftermath of the successful vote, a very public scuffle broke out live on TV between the two sides. Wags christened it the 'brawl in the hall'.

Devolution dead

In early April 2002 the PIRA announced that it had put more of its weapons 'beyond use'. However these piecemeal concessions were still not enough for the UUP. The following September Trimble announced that the UUP would withdraw from the Executive by the middle of January 2003 if it was still not clear that the PIRA had finally renounced violence. He also announced that his ministerial colleagues would no longer attend North–South meetings.

The stimuli for this particular ultimatum were the continuing events in Colombia and evidence that the PIRA was linked to a break-in at an intelligence centre in Castlereagh, the headquarters of the PSNI. Trimble's immediate concern was a need to prevent the seemingly inevitable split of his Party, given the growing opposition of Jeffrey Donaldson.

In the end, other developments conspired to ensure that the Assembly and Executive were long gone before Trimble's deadline had passed. In early October Sinn Féin's Stormont offices were raided by the PSNI and a range of items were removed. The raid was part of an investigation into alleged republican intelligence gathering. Trimble responded by demanding that the British government take action against Sinn Féin. He, in turn, was responding to a DUP announcement that its ministers would resign from the Executive if no action was taken against Sinn Féin.

The unionists' ultimatum was effective, and from midnight on 15 October the Secretary of State suspended the Assembly and Executive once again and reinstated Direct Rule. Speaking in the aftermath of suspension the Prime Minister, Tony Blair, challenged the republican movement to follow the correct 'fork in the road' and engage in 'acts of completion' as a way of getting the process up and running again.

The PIRA responded by once again breaking off contacts with the Decommissioning Commission. Meanwhile Sinn Féin reacted by arguing that the necessity for 'acts of completion' was not just limited to one side. They stated that the other signatories to the Agreement also had obligations to fulfil. Over the next few months both sides got down to more behind-the-scenes, piecemeal negotiations.

Elections – or not?

At the time of the re-election of the First and Deputy First Ministers the Secretary of State (John Reid, soon to be replaced by Paul Murphy) had announced that the elections for the Assembly would take place in May 2003. As that date drew nearer it became obvious that the British government was unwilling to let the poll take place for fear of what results it would yield. It was becoming increasingly clear that the likely victors in such a poll would be the DUP and Sinn Féin. If the Agreement was experiencing difficulties in its current form, what chances would it have with the 'extremes' of nationalism and unionism holding the reigns of power?

In the end, this prospect was too much for the government to face and at the start of May Blair announced that he was suspending the elections, initially for four weeks, and then until the autumn. In announcing the longer postponement Blair attempted to focus the blame for his decision on the PIRA's continuing refusal – during their behind-the-scenes negotiations – to call a complete halt to its activities by responding in a clear and unequivocal manner to the position that had been laid down by the two governments in their *Joint Declaration*.

The *Joint Declaration*, also released at the start of May, had been London and Dublin's proposals for removing the final areas of disagreement within the Agreement. In return for 'acts of completion' by the republican movement – namely the ending of all PIRA activities – the British envisaged measures such as further demilitarization and the devolution of policing and justice powers to the Assembly. To oversee the decommissioning element the two governments proposed to establish a four member Independent Monitoring Commission.

Unfortunately the *Joint Declaration* caused further problems for Trimble within the UUP. By this stage there was little or nothing of surprise in this opposition. In June, Donaldson challenged Trimble for the Party's leadership. Again the latter triumphed. Then, no sooner had Trimble obtained the Party's backing – albeit narrow – for the governments' proposals, than three of his MPs announced that they were resigning the Party whip at Westminster to enable them to oppose government attempts to pass legislation linked to the *Joint Declaration*. Martin Smyth, David Burnside and Jeffrey Donaldson claimed that their actions were in protest at the policies their leader was pursuing.

Trimble moved fast to have the three rebels expelled from the Party, however he was halted in his tracks when a judicial review of his actions overturned the initial decision to suspend the three MPs in preparation for their ultimate expulsion from the UUP. The peace process was in trouble but so too was the leadership of the major unionist party. Its internal divisions could only benefit the DUP, which gleefully called on the three rebels to join its ranks.

In September one element of the government's plans took shape when the planned Independent Monitoring Commission was established. Its remit was to pass judgement on the quality and permanence of the various paramilitary ceasefires.

Polling day

In late October the date for the much-postponed election was finally announced as being 26 November. On the same day the head of the Decommissioning Commission, General John de Chastelain revealed that the PIRA had put a further amount of weapons beyond use. This was but one element in what was meant to be a carefully choreographed series of speeches by the Sinn Féin and UUP leaderships leading to a renewal of power-sharing after the election. It finally seemed as if the pieces for a rescue deal were slowly falling into place.

However at the last minute the whole process collapsed. David Trimble dismissed the Decommissioning Commission's report on the PIRA's actions as lacking in transparency. He had wanted much more detail about the actual decommissioning process. De Chastelain, however, was bound by a confidentiality agreement made with the PIRA and would not tell Trimble what he wanted to know. In exasperation the UUP leader pulled the plug on the attempt to put a pre-election deal in place. It had been, some wits proclaimed, a day (paraphrasing Seamus Heaney's poem *Doubletake*) when 'hype and history rhymed'.

Even though the prospects for a post-election settlement were growing weaker by the second, Blair confirmed that the elections would take place as planned. With all potential deals off, the campaign was little more than a political free-for-all, with the contest being particularly bitter within unionism and nationalism.

The results were as predicted: most of the smaller parties were blown away and the DUP and Sinn Féin emerged as the big winners (30 and 24 seats respectively in comparison with 27 for the UUP and the SDLP with 18). Their numbers would entitle them to nominate party members for the positions of First Minister and Deputy First Minister respectively when – and if – the Assembly first met. Such a meeting would now depend on whether these two parties, never exactly natural political bedfellows, could reach some form of accommodation.

Of course the main difficulty was going to be the reconciliation of their very different aspirations. The DUP was looking for a 'fair deal', a new agreement that would be acceptable to unionists as well as nationalists. For their part Sinn Féin was looking for their 'entitlement', the full implementation of the Agreement as it already stood. Both parties could point to strong respective mandates for pushing their respective positions.

As it stood the Assembly could not meet. Its rules, which demanded cross-community support for the election of the First and Deputy First Ministers, simply would not work with Sinn Féin standing for the latter post and with a majority of the unionist members now anti-Agreement. With no progress possible on that front, attention turned to a review of the workings of the Agreement.

The DUP's and Sinn Féin's victories were not the only political realignments that were taking place. Shortly before Christmas 2003, UUP rebel Jeffrey Donaldson announced that he and two of his fellow MLAs were quitting the Party. After a decent interval of consultation and rumination, the three confounded no expectations and joined the DUP, increasing its representation to 33 seats and strengthening its numerical superiority over the UUP still further.

Another spanner in the works!

The all-party review of the workings of the Agreement started in early February 2004. Just over a fortnight later its future was thrown into doubt when the PSNI intercepted a van in which a dissident republican was seemingly being held against his will. The Chief Constable placed the blame for the kidnap attempt at the door of the PIRA.

The British government responded by asking the recently established Independent Monitoring Commission to investigate the circumstances of the abduction. That organization later agreed that the PIRA – which it categorized as being still 'in a high state of readiness' – had been involved and recommended that the government impose financial sanctions against Sinn Féin. At the same time it recognized the continuation of loyalist paramilitary activities and likewise suggested that financial penalties be imposed on the PUP.

At around the same time, the British and Irish governments published the reports of a series of investigations into collusion, which had been undertaken by a retired Canadian judge, Peter Cory. Cory had recommended the holding of inquiries into all cases and while the British government agreed to set up inquiries into three, it was their continued reluctance to order an inquiry into the murder of the fourth victim, Belfast solicitor Pat Finucane, that attracted most headlines. The Irish government agreed to establish inquiries into the two cases involving alleged collusion in their jurisdiction.

In any case, before the Independent Monitoring Commission report had been released the review process had broken down. The UUP argued that the government's response to the attempted kidnapping fell far short of what was required. Trimble argued that Sinn Féin should have been excluded from the review and led his Party out of the process. The review broke down due to their absence and was put on ice until the forthcoming elections to the European parliament had taken place.

The European elections were European only in the sense that it was seats in the Strasbourg parliament that were up for grabs. The issues debated owed more to local constitutional affairs than they did to politics in Brussels. Nevertheless, the results confirmed the electoral trend which became clear with the previous year's Assembly elections. Even though the talismanic Revd Ian Paisley had decided not to stand again, the DUP candidate topped the poll. Indeed, the Party took nearly two thirds of the unionist votes cast.

The loss of the equally talismanic John Hume (honoured, along with David Trimble, with the 1998 Nobel Peace Prize) as the SDLP's candidate was not as happy an experience for that Party. Hume had nearly topped the poll at the previous European election, this time the Party finished a distant fourth, leaving the last seat for the UUP candidate. The second seat went to Sinn Féin, a winner in this particular poll for the first time. Their ascendancy over the SDLP was clear if one considered that they took over 62 per cent of the total nationalist vote.

Leeds Castle

With the election out of the way, attention returned to the task of forging some sort of agreement between the north's parties. It was decided that yet another set of make or break talks would be held in the luxurious surroundings of Leeds Castle, Kent, in September 2004. In the lead-up to these discussions Blair tried to increase the pressure for a deal by making clear that these talks would be the last attempts to put the Humpty Dumpty that was the Agreement back together again. Of course that left the tantalizing question of what would happen if agreement were not possible. Little enlightenment on this issue was forthcoming from the London government. All the Prime Minister would speak of was 'a different way forward'.

The talks duly took place although the UUP did not attend and the DUP would not negotiate directly with Sinn Féin. The discussions were based upon four key areas of an end to all types of paramilitary activity; decommissioning; refinements to the existing institutions; and policing and criminal justice powers. Although there were reports in the media of substantial progress on areas such as decommissioning (apparently to be completed before the end of 2004) and the future of the PIRA (reportedly being prepared to 'stand down'), the talks failed to reach agreement within the allotted time frame.

The sticking point was the failure of other parties – particularly Sinn Féin – to accept DUP proposals for changes to the levels of accountability experienced by devolved ministers. The DUP wanted changes that would make it possible for unpopular ministerial decisions to be blocked by the votes of 30 Assembly members. The nationalist parties regarded this as interfering with the painstakingly negotiated terms of the Good Friday Agreement and as putting in place a new version of majority rule given that the DUP had just this number of MLAs.

After Leeds Castle

Just before the talks at Leeds Castle broke up, the two governments put forward their own proposals, trying to find some middle ground between the different parties' positions. However, when the politicians met up again back at Stormont no agreement was reached; indeed it looked as if things were getting worse rather than better. It seemed that – as had happened so often in the past – hopes had again been raised for nothing.

Yet such pessimistic thoughts were premature (although in the end not totally misplaced). Discussions between the various sides continued on throughout October and into November. During these negotiations the first ever face-to-face political talks took place between the DUP and the Irish Government in Dublin – an unprecedented and historic event. As these negotiations continued it became more and more obvious that progress was being made in a significant number of the remaining areas of contention, not least demilitarization, a particular bugbear of republicans. That progress was being made in this element in particular became clear from another unprecedented and historic event – the meeting that took place in Downing Street between Gerry Adams (accompanied by other senior Sinn Féin leaders) and the Chief Constable of the PSNI, Hugh Orde.

The key issue remaining was that of decommissioning and as the end of November approached it seemed more and more likely that a breakthrough was on the cards. An exhaustive series of bilateral meetings resulted in the London and Dublin governments preparing a set of proposals, which, they believed, outlined the agreed steps by which a final resolution of the peace process' outstanding issues could take place. President George W Bush even got in on the act at this stage, telephoning both Revd Ian Paisley and Gerry Adams in an effort to push both men the extra mile to an agreed final solution.

Say cheese!

However at this point Groundhog Day reared its head again. Just as had happened so often in the past the whole thing began to unravel at the last minute. Again – just as had happened so often in the past – the outstanding issue was decommissioning. This time, however, there was a new slant on the position of the main players. As the details of the potential deal became public it transpired that the crunch issue was not the actual process of decommissioning, which had now been agreed, but whether or not photographs of decommissioning could be taken and then published.

The photographs were a DUP demand (although the idea was being supported by the two governments), what that Party termed a 'visual aspect'. Given the lack of transparency in previous acts of decommissioning, the DUP argued that only photographic evidence, as opposed to the words of any witnesses, would convince the Northern Ireland public that what had been claimed to have taken place had actually happened. This new requirement was in spite of the PIRA already having agreed to allow two clergymen – one Protestant and one Catholic – to witness the acts of decommissioning.

Witnesses were bad enough, however the taking of photographs (even though they would not be released until the Assembly and Executive were fully up and running again) was a bridge too far for the republican movement. Nor did they seem to be overly enamoured with the DUP leader stating that the PIRA should don 'sackcloth and ashes' and atone publicly for the crimes that they had committed over the course of 'the Troubles'. The PIRA therefore refused to subject itself to what it termed 'an act of humiliation'. In response the DUP revealed that it would not sign up to the rest of the deal.

The 'deal'

At the start of December the British and Irish leaders travelled to Belfast not to announce publicly that a deal had been reached (as had been intended), but to publish their proposals to restore devolution. Their intention in going ahead was to demonstrate just what had been achieved and to allow the public to reflect on that same progress. Indeed, although both prime ministers were clearly bitterly disappointed at not being able to announce a final resolution, Tony Blair still spoke of 'remarkable' progress having been made while acknowledging that more remained to be done.

It was clear from the terms that what Blair had said wasn't just spin and that a significant amount of progress had indeed been made. The proposals indicated that had all of the elements of a deal been put in place the PIRA would have engaged in decommissioning of its weapons to the extent that total decommissioning would have been completed by Christmas 2004 'if possible'. That organization would then have entered into what it termed a 'new mode'. The proposals were not over exaggerating when it termed these developments as 'momentous'.

Shortly after the completion of decommissioning the Assembly and Executive would have been re-established in shadow mode (to enable adequate preparations to be made) and would then have moved speedily towards full devolution. At the same time there would have been major developments in the area of security with significant numbers of British Army personnel leaving Northern Ireland and with republicans finally providing their imprimatur (after convening a special *Ard Fheis*) for policing arrangements within the north. There would also have been substantive steps taken towards the devolution to the Assembly of power over justice, an issue withheld up to this point.

Of course it wasn't just concession on the part of the republican movement that these proposals were demanding. All of this would also have meant the DUP agreeing to work power-sharing fully – something it had failed to do fully when the Agreement had been up and running before – while also being fully involved with the North–South bodies established by the Good Friday Agreement – again something that it had refused to do at all in the Agreement's previous existence.

Changes to other elements of the Good Friday Agreement were also contained within the governments' proposals. Some of these were of concern to the SDLP which called particular attention to the proposal to elect all ministers together as opposed to the First and Deputy First Minister being elected separately from all other Executive members, which had been the practice up to this point. SDLP leader Mark Durkan suggested that this was to provide a way out for the DUP MLAs from having to vote directly for a Sinn Féin Deputy First Minister (the DUP's original negotiating position was to have both First and Deputy First Ministers elected separately). He argued that such a change was a move away from the spirit of partnership government as contained in the Good Friday Agreement.

Other adjustments included a proposal to introduce a new ministerial code, which would have ensured that all members of the Executive accepted fully the principles of cross-community power-sharing. This commitment would have been further reinforced by a revised pledge of office. At the same time the Assembly would have received enhanced powers of scrutiny and the British government would have removed its ability to suspend the institutions in the future.

Whose fault?

Not surprisingly there were some efforts by the main players to lay the blame at the door of the other side. The DUP made it clear that as far as they were concerned the republican movement had reneged on the deal. Sinn Féin argued that it had been clear from the first mention of photographs (shortly before the Leeds Castle negotiations) that the PIRA was never going to agree to photographs being taken while the PIRA stated that it believed the issue of photographs had been used by the DUP as a way of rejecting the whole deal. At the same time Gerry Adams argued that the PIRA's announcement of its intention to move into a 'new mode' was a 'declaration of peace'.

What next?

Although success was tantalisingly close no final agreement was possible before the end of 2004 and both political commentators and politicians began to speak of further progress being unlikely before the next Westminster General Election. This is believed to be likely to take place in May 2005.

In the final analysis, this phase of the never-ending peace process had ended without the Holy Grail being achieved. However, although no ultimate deal was forthcoming it would be churlish to suggest that no progress had been made. At the very least the whole process had revealed that the two Parties once deemed unlikely to ever be a party to the same deal were now on the verge of doing just that, something that would be very hard to go back on. Moreover the process had broken down not over whether or not there should be decommissioning, but as to how it should be recorded. That was a major advance on what had been achieved in the past.

Speaking in the aftermath of the failed deal Bertie Ahern spoke of the DUP and Sinn Féin positions being similar to two trains on the same track, going alongside each other but never meeting. Tony Blair, meanwhile, commented on what he saw as the 'inevitability' of the process. The hope must be that the two trains will sooner or later – as they must – arrive at the same, shared destination, thus allowing Heaney's utopian day of hope and history to rhyme.

17 the Republic of Ireland since the 1960s

This chapter will cover:
- Ireland under Lemass
- the impact of 'the Troubles'
- the Fine Gael–Labour Coalition
- the Haughey years
- FitzGerald's new agenda
- Fianna Fáil implodes
- a decade of scandals
- Ireland in the new millennium.

The Lemass years

By the late 1950s the generation of state-founders that had governed Ireland since the foundation of state were beginning to relinquish the reigns of power. In 1959 deValera made the move from Leinster House to Áras an Uachtaráin (the President's official residence) when he was elected President. His long-time deputy, Seán Lemass, succeeded him. Born in 1899, Lemass had played a part in the 1916 Easter Rising and in the subsequent fighting between 1919 and 1923. A founder member of Fianna Fáil he had once famously described the organization as 'a slightly constitutional party'.

Around the same time, Fine Gael leader Richard Mulcahy stood aside and was replaced by James Dillon, son of the last leader of the Home Rule Party.

Even though Lemass was as involved as anyone else in as many of the struggles surrounding the foundation of the state, he was still under 60 and came from a completely different generation ideologically. His main preoccupation became the stimulation of economic growth, a process that had begun with the introduction of the 1958 *Programme for Economic Expansion*. As previously indicated this had focused on developing manufacturing and its export.

A second plan followed five years later, but because of balance of trade problems had to be abandoned before it was due for completion in 1970. A third *Programme for Economic Expansion* did follow in 1969, but while considerably more modest than its predecessors, it too had to be abandoned in the early 1970s at a time of a worldwide economic downturn.

It wasn't all doom and gloom, and while problems did remain, the Irish economy began to emerge out of the darkness it had occupied for several decades. New industries established themselves and the country benefited considerably from its membership of the European Economic Community (EEC) after 1973 (see below). One particularly positive result emanating from this period was an increase in the Irish population, much of it, naturally, young.

Educational changes

Hand-in-hand with this focus on economic development came a renewed emphasis on educational reform. The Fianna Fáil governments of the late 1950s and 1960s instituted a campaign of modernization that aimed to drag Irish education out of the nineteenth century. Under the guidance of a series of innovative ministers including the future Taoiseach, Jack Lynch, a series of far-reaching reforms were introduced including curricular reform, improved financial provision (resulting in free education) and infrastructural development.

Yet it wasn't all roses for the new dispensation. When Lemass called a snap election in 1961 he was rewarded by a loss of eight seats leaving the Party three short of an overall majority and having to rely on independents' support. As a result the government found its survival threatened at various stages. This electoral setback came at the end of a difficult year for the administration. Industrial unrest was – and remained – rife at home while nine Irish peacekeepers serving with the United Nations (UN) were killed in the Congo. Moreover, the Irish attempt to join the European Economic Community (EEC) was rebuffed by the veto of Charles de Gaulle. This 'non' was a matter of significant regret to the Taoiseach.

During his tenure Lemass was also to the forefront in developing a new relationship with Northern Ireland (see Chapter 12). His seminal meetings with Terence O'Neill in 1965 set the tone for a period (albeit short) of significantly improved co-operation between both jurisdictions. This new dawn was a far cry from the mutual suspicion and antagonism that had characterized previous decades and, while it lasted, useful economic co-operation took place. Yet in 1966 the relationship was soured somewhat by the jingoistic celebrations of the fiftieth anniversary of the 1916 Rising.

Fine Gael

Initially Fine Gael, even with a new leader, was unable to compete with the greater dynamism within Fianna Fáil. It was given a chance to forge a new identity through the publication of 'Towards a Just Society' in 1965. The work of a group of 'Young Turks' including Declan Costello (son of the former Taoiseach), the document urged the Party to adopt a more Keynesian approach with respect to economic policy.

The policy platform was adopted by Fine Gael – with varying degrees of enthusiasm – in time for the 1965 General Election. It is fair to say, however, that the Party's conservative leadership found it too difficult to embrace such radical new thinking in a fully genuine manner. As a result, defeat followed and in its aftermath Dillon resigned as leader to be replaced by Liam Cosgrave, the son of the first President of the Executive Council. Although Cosgrave had supported the 'Just Society' paper, he remained relatively conservative in his politics.

A year later Lemass also resigned as Fianna Fáil leader and Taoiseach, seemingly at the height of his powers. His replacement in both positions – after the Party's first ever leadership election – was the Minister for Finance, Jack Lynch, a former hurling star with his native county, Cork. For the first time the Taoiseach didn't carry as much personal historical baggage either. Lynch was born in 1917, a year after Pearse had stepped out under the portico of Dublin's GPO and read his *Proclamation of Independence*.

The 1960s was a period of social, cultural and economic change that also had a profound impact on Ireland, for good and for bad. Of particular note were the developments in the areas of art and literature which pursued new themes – and old – in a different way. That said, the hand of the censor sometimes stymied progress in the latter medium.

There were also significant changes within the Catholic Church, owing their origin to the modernizing Second Vatican Council summoned by Pope John XXIII in 1962. The emergence of a more modern type of Catholicism found its mirror in the desire of the state to create a more pluralist aspect religiously. To that end, the special recognition afforded to the Catholic Church in the 1937 Constitution was removed in 1972. However, the constitutional ban on divorce remained, and there were other areas where the Church's teachings remained unchanging; the 1967 encyclical Humanae Vitae reaffirmed its ban on contraception.

Lynch's sure touch ensured the governing party an overall majority in the 1969 General Election. This electoral security should have ensured the Fianna Fáil administration a serene period of office over the coming years. Within a year, however, unfolding events north of the border were to have a shattering impact on the Republic.

The impact of the north

As violence began to erupt across the border Lynch came under increasing pressure to deploy the Irish Army in the north or to supply the nationalist minority with weapons. The Taoiseach withstood such pressures although he did speak out forcefully and somewhat ambiguously when confronted with developments in Derry in August 1969.

The Taoiseach's intentions always seemed to have been peaceful but others within his Cabinet were advocating more active forms of reform when it came to Northern Ireland. Chief among these was the Donegal minister, Neil Blaney, however Lynch was not prepared to tolerate dissent from within the Cabinet and at the Party's 1970 *Ard Fheis* he told his opponents to 'put up or shut up'.

That was not to be the end of the matter. In May 1970 Lynch was forced to demand Blaney's resignation along with that of Charles Haughey, Minister for Finance (at the same time Kevin Boland, the Minister for Local Government resigned in protest at the dismissals). The occasion was evidence of a high level plot to divert government money to import arms for use within the north.

While the government managed to survive the crisis in the short term, the two sacked ministers were arrested and, along with a former intelligence officer, Captain James Kelly, were accused of conspiracy to import arms. In the event charges against Blaney were dismissed while Haughey and Kelly were acquitted.

The whole affair caused deep divisions within Fianna Fáil. Lynch faced a period of protracted opposition to both his Northern Ireland policy and his leadership from a faction within the Party. However by 1971 his policy had won the day and those opposed to it had either parted company with the Party (not all voluntarily) or, in the case of Haughey, had repaired to the backbenches to lick their wounds.

Nor was the Republic immune to the violence that was sweeping across the north. The bombs exploded in Dublin in December 1972 and again in May 1974 (in the latter case along with Monaghan). The loss of life in the latter attacks made the combined death toll on that day the worse of the entire period of 'the Troubles'.

By 1973 Fianna Fáil had been in power for 16 years. There were clearly parallels to be made with the 16 years of Fianna Fáil rule in the years between 1932 and 1948. Not least in this regard was the sense of ennui that was clearly being experienced by the body politic by the time a General Election was called for in February 1973. The government could point to a not unimpressive record, not least its success in achieving what Lemass had failed to do a decade earlier, namely gaining admittance to the EEC.

However it was not enough and the government was ousted in favour of a Fine Gael–Labour coalition even though it secured a bigger proportion of first preference votes than in 1969. Liam Cosgrave became Taoiseach, the first and thus far only son to hold the same position as his father in the Irish system.

The coalition government's record was mixed. Its lowest point was in all probability the resignation of President Cearbhall Ó Dálaigh in 1976. This perhaps extreme action was occasioned by the uttering of insulting remarks about the President by a government minister. The injudicious remarks were themselves occasioned by a previous decision by the President to refer a Bill to the Supreme Court (as was his prerogative) to test its constitutionality. When the minister showed no signs of resigning the President took that course himself, arguing that it was the only way to preserve his own integrity and the dignity and independence of the institution he represented.

There were other lows. Most notable was the impact of the worsening international economic situation in the mid-1970s. Yet when Cosgrave called the election earlier than was necessary in 1977 the government was convinced it could not lose. However, the effects of the economic downturn played large in the minds of the people and compared very unfavourably with the brave new economic world that was being promised by the Fianna Fáil manifesto. In the event, that was probably enough and Lynch returned to power with 84 seats and an overall majority – the largest ever achieved in the history of the state.

In from the cold: Haughey as Taoiseach

Within two years, however, the Fianna Fáil administration was about as unpopular as its predecessor had been at the time of the General Election. Much of the reason for this lay with continuing economic problems. This unpopularity was expressed through the lack of votes cast for Fianna Fáil in both European (for the first time) and local elections. Dissatisfaction with Lynch's leadership began to grow and in December 1979 he resigned as Taoiseach and leader of Fianna Fáil.

The available evidence tends to suggest that Lynch resigned when he did in the belief that his preferred successor, George Colley, could defeat the most likely other challenger, Charles Haughey, whom Lynch had brought back onto the front bench in 1975 and into the Cabinet two years later. In reality, the two men's calculations were seriously wide of the mark. Haughey won the contest and became Fianna Fáil leader and Taoiseach-elect just over nine years after his political career seemed dead and buried.

Haughey's Ireland

Despite significant opposition to his appointment amongst the other parties, Haughey was elected Taoiseach by a comfortable majority. However his zone of comfort did not last as the condition of the Irish economy continued to give cause for concern at a time of worldwide economic recession. So serious was the situation that Haughey went on television in early 1980 to warn the people that they could not continue to live beyond their means. Advice, it would become clear much later, that the Taoiseach had no intention of following himself.

The period up until the General Election of May 1981 was a difficult one for both Haughey and his administration. The weakness within the economy was not the only deterioration at this time. Relations between Dublin and London began to deteriorate as the political situation within Northern Ireland took a marked turn for the worse.

Initially the relationship between Haughey and the equally recently elected British Prime Minister, Margaret Thatcher, was businesslike, even cordial and great claims were made by Haughey of a new beginning in Anglo-Irish relations. What set the cat among the pigeons were the 1980 and particularly the 1981 hunger strikes. Dublin's failure to get the British to treat the republican movement with respect resulted in the emergence of a form of cold war between the governments of the two islands. By the time the hunger strike had ended ten men were dead inside the Maze Prison, many more had lost their lives outside its walls and Haughey had lost power.

Too many elections!

With the loss of six seats from their 1977 figure, Fianna Fáil found itself displaced by a Fine Gael-Labour coalition (with independent support) in 1981. Garrett FitzGerald, Fine Gael leader since 1977, became Taoiseach. His task was immense; the economy was in a mess and the coalition was forced to introduce a supplementary budget in an attempt to balance the books. However, it was the government's first full budget that signalled its demise after only eight months. An attempt to impose VAT (Value Added Tax) on children's clothes and shoes led one of the government's independent supporters to switch sides and bring the coalition down.

Fianna Fáil figures tried to prevent an election by attempting to persuade President Hillery to allow them to form a government. The President quite rightly resisted this highly unusual and improper pressure and a poll was held in February 1982. The outcome was the election of another minority government. This time it was a Fianna Fáil one.

The government's conrol of the Dáil was tight – it had been partly achieved by agreeing to fund investment in the constituency of one of the independent TDs, Tony Gregory. Moreover, that wasn't the only weakness. Haughey's own position was not as secure as he might have wanted with a number of senior Party figures expressing extreme dissatisfaction with his leadership.

This dissatisfaction had returned by October 1982 when two Cabinet members, Martin O'Donoghue and Desmond O'Malley resigned from the government. The cause of their displeasure was a number of scandals involving Cabinet members, in particular the Minister for Justice, Sean Doherty. Haughey survived this immediate threat, but lost a subsequent vote of confidence in the Dáil. Another General Election was, therefore, scheduled for November 1982.

This time it was FitzGerald who was triumphant, albeit with support from the Labour Party which was led by the 32-year-old former Irish rugby international player Dick Spring. Again Haughey faced a heave against his leadership. Again he survived. The occasion for this move – apart from the loss of yet another election – was recently-revealed evidence that the Minister for Justice in the last administration – Sean Doherty – had authorized the tapping of the phones of two journalists, ostensibly in an effort to stop leaks from the Cabinet. Haughey denied any knowledge of or involvement in these activities.

Meanwhile FitzGerald got down to the business of improving relations between Dublin and London. His first effort, the New Ireland Forum, met with little support from Thatcher, yet just over a year later the two governments signed the Anglo-Irish Agreement in an effort to pull the carpet from under Sinn Féin.

Constitutional crusade

FitzGerald's other big focus was his so-called 'constitutional crusade'. Chief among his aims was a reduction in the Catholicity of the Irish state – particularly evident in elements of the Constitution and legislative framework. He argued that 'If I was a Northern Protestant today, I can't see how I could aspire to getting involved in a state which is itself sectarian.' He stated that he sought the creation of a 'genuine republic', one that would have been recognizable to and acceptable to Tone and others, in other words, a secular state. To this end referenda were held with a view to changing the Constitution position vis-à-vis divorce and abortion. Although the former was lost and interpretations of the latter disputed, it was increasingly clear that traces of secularism were entering Irish society. (A referendum permitting divorce was narrowly passed in 1995.)

The Fine Gael–Labour coalition lasted until 1987 when Labour pulled the plug in opposition to planned spending cuts in that year's budget. In the ensuing election Fianna Fáil again returned to office, once more as a minority administration. One of the big winners in this election was the Progressive Democrat (PD) Party with 14 seats. That Party had been formed in late 1985 by Desmond O'Malley and Mary Harney, both formerly of Fianna Fáil. The immediate cause of the split was their rejection of Fianna Fáil's opposition to the Anglo-Irish Agreement; at a deeper level, however, it was the result of years of opposition to Haughey's style of leadership.

The Ides of March?

For no compellingly apparent reason, Haughey called another General Election in 1989, fully three years before he was obliged to do so. The Party's poor performance saw it remaining in government only with the support of the PDs. This was Fianna Fáil's first experience of coalition government and given the Party in question it could hardly be described as a marriage made in heaven!

Ironically, the coalition worked well – for a while. However by the turn of the decade it was coming under stress and strain. The first clear evidence that all was not well came during the 1990 campaign for the presidency, where Fianna Fáil's Brian Lenihan was facing Mary Robinson, formerly of the Labour Party and still supported by them in this campaign.

In the event Robinson won, Lenihan's campaign having been fatally undermined by rumours of his involvement in efforts to persuade President Hillery not to call a new election in 1982 (see above). It was the first time that Fianna Fáil had contested a presidential election and lost. Even worse, because of PD pressure, Haughey had been forced to sack Lenihan from the Cabinet late in the campaign.

Worse was to come. As Fianna Fáil support continued to haemorrhage, Haughey was forced – following further internal dissent – to dismiss two more ministers, Albert Reynolds and Padraig Flynn. Then, just as it must have appeared that he had got the upper hand over his enemies – at least the internal ones – the 1982 phone-tapping scandal again reared its ugly head. The then Minister for Justice, Sean Doherty, first implied – none too subtly – and then claimed outright, that Haughey had been aware of the decision to tap the phones of the two journalists.

Haughey was forced out in early February 1992 to be replaced by the recently dismissed Albert Reynolds. Under his leadership the coalition with the PDs continued, although there was no doubt that Reynolds had no great taste for anything other than single-party government. However in the end, deteriorating relations between the two coalition partners led to its collapse and to the 1992 General Election. The election result was bad for Fianna Fáil and Fine Gael but a triumph for Labour, which won an extra 17 seats. Dick Spring led his Party back into government with Fianna Fáil.

Crisis renewed

Relations between the new coalition partners were not always what they might have been. Despite significant progress being made in terms of the economy and particularly with the Northern Ireland Peace Process, a topic with which Reynolds closely identified (see Chapter 15), a number of different controversies served to create mistrust and tensions between the two parties and particularly their leaders. This mistrust eventually led Dick Spring to withdraw from the coalition in December 1994, shortly after Reynolds had resigned as Fianna Fáil leader and Taoiseach.

The immediate cause of Reynolds's departure was a crisis over his appointment of the Attorney General, Harry Whelehan, as President of the High Court. While Labour were unhappy at the appointment, what caused them to voice their opposition to the development publicly was the appearance of evidence that Whelehan had allowed a request from the RUC for the extradition of a priest accused of paedophilia to languish in his Department for a number of months.

Despite Labour's opposition Reynolds went ahead with the appointment whilst also intending to pour balm on the choppy waters of his relations with Spring. However worse was to come; evidence appeared of another case which had also languished in the Attorney General's Department. This news caused even greater division within the coalition and when it became clear that Reynolds had had knowledge of its existence, knowledge not communicated to Spring, the Labour leader removed his support for the coalition and Reynolds resigned as Party leader and Taoiseach. He was replaced by Bertie Ahern.

Normally such events would have resulted in an election, however in this case – and for the first time in the state's history – another solution was found. Spring was initially considering returning to power with Fianna Fáil now that they were under new management, however when it became clear that Ahern and others had been in possession of the same information that had resulted in Reynolds' resignation, this was not possible. Instead, Spring negotiated a new coalition with Fine Gael, now led by John Bruton, and with Democratic Left. The new administration was christened the 'Rainbow Coalition'.

A decade of scandals

The new government greatly benefited from being in office at a time when the Irish economy seemed to be taking off, a phenomenon that became known as the 'Celtic Tiger'. It is not as well remembered for the progress that the Peace Process made during its watch. However, while there was prosperity in the Irish Republic, there was also the opportunity for malpractice by those holding positions of trust and the remainder of the decade seemed to reverberate, almost on a daily basis, to revelations about one new financial, political or religious scandal or another.

Many senior Irish politicians were implicated in these scandals. None was more senior than the former Taoiseach, Charles Haughey. He, like many others, was found to have benefited from dubious financial practices, which involved offshore accounts and a severe lack of payment of taxes. This had enabled him to live a life of luxury at a time when he was cautioning others to tighten their belts (see above). Faced with these revelations, the government established a number of different tribunals in order to enable whatever degree of truth possible to be discovered.

Politicians from both Fianna Fáil and Fine Gael had been caught up in the unfolding scandals. Even though there were many more from Fianna Fáil, they were victorious in the 1997 General Election, returning to government once more, albeit with the support of the PDs, now led by Mary Harney. Labour lost a significant number of seats while Fine Gael remained relatively steady on 54.

Even then there were more rocky days ahead for the new coalition. Another minister was forced to resign as a result of revelations about his political and business dealings. At the same time, one of the tribunals reported in a highly critical manner in the matter of Charles Haughey's profligate lifestyle and its financial origins. Ahern was forced to set up even more tribunals to investigate these new revelations. It began to look as if the past was catching up with Fianna Fáil and that the electorate might abandon it.

Skeletons in the cupboard – comment on the raft of scandals facing Fianna Fáil leader Bertie Ahern.

Yet this turned out not to be the case. In 1997 the Fianna Fáil candidate, the Belfast-born lawyer and academic Mary McAleese, was victorious in the Irish presidential election. The results of the same election saw the end of Dick Spring as Labour leader. His Party's candidate performed so poorly in the poll that he concluded he had no option but to resign. His successor was Ruairi Quinn, but his reign was remarkably short, ending just two years later in the aftermath of the 2002 General Election.

It wasn't just politicians who were exposed in the scandals of the 1990s and beyond. The Catholic Church also came under the spotlight for a number of reasons. Apart from questions over the way in which some members of the hierarchy dealt with allegations of abuse against priests in their care, the Church was rocked by revelations that the Bishop of Galway had fathered a child. More numerous still were the allegations of sexual or physical abuse levelled against members of religious orders who had run various types of institution within the state.

Into a new millennium

Labour's uninspiring performance in 2002 resulted in Quinn's replacement by Pat Rabbitte, formerly a member of the now subsumed Democratic Left. A similarly dismal Fine Gael performance (it lost 23 seats) saw its leader, Michael Noonan, resign to be replaced by Enda Kenney. Noonan had himself only been in the job for a few months. He had succeeded John Bruton when the latter had been forced out in early 2001, the victim of the Party's increasing lack of identity and direction. As might be surmised, Fianna Fáil was again victorious and was returned to power, again with the support of the PDs.

In the succeeding two years much of the coalition government's attention was taken up with the shoring up of the Peace Process north of the border. At the same time frantic preparations were made for the introduction of the Single European Currency (the Euro) on 1 January 2002. Yet despite the continued (if more muted) roar of the 'Celtic Tiger', many in Ireland still failed to benefit from its bounty and an ever-widening gap between the 'haves' and the 'have-nots' seemed to emerge. Furthermore, the need to provide reforms within the education and health sectors remained clear. Indeed it might be fair to argue that some of the ensuing discontent may have resulted in Fianna Fáil's exceedingly modest performance in the European and local elections of the summer of 2004.

Yet with no General Election on the horizon the government was able to continue relatively serenely on its way – at least until the last few weeks of 2004. In an effort to revitalize the administration Bertie Ahern engineered a major reshuffle of his cabinet, which saw all but three members being either removed or replaced. The government was also able to bask (to a certain extent) in the reflected glory of Mary McAleese upon her unopposed re-election as President at the start of October.

That said, the government did not have quite as close a link to the sole candidate this time. Under the provisions of *Bunreacht na HÉireann* a sitting President is able to nominate themselves for the position, a clause that McAleese took advantage of presumably as a way of distancing herself from too close association with any party. As a result of her decision to do this, none of the other parties put up a candidate against McAleese, but if truth be told, her immense popularity with the Irish electorate would have meant that any other candidate would have been whitewashed, thus reflecting badly on the nominating party.

Once more it was the peace process that was again to provide the Dublin government with potentially its biggest achievement and also its biggest headache as 2004 drew to a close. The excruciating negotiations did yield some positive elements not least the first face-to-face political talks between the Irish government and the leadership of the DUP. On top of that the outline of the likely future development of the peace process became clear through the proposals published by the two governments in early December.

However these positive elements were leavened by two more sobering aspects. First was the failure of the deal to take shape (as outlined in Chapter 16) because of the issue of photographic evidence of decommissioning. Second, was the public outcry that followed the Taoiseach's admission that if the deal had panned out as intended the Dublin government would have recommended the release from prison of the four PIRA volunteers who had been jailed for the manslaughter of Detective Garda Gerry McCabe in June 1996.

The reason that this admission caused such consternation was that up to this point the government had consistently rejected Sinn Féin demands for the men to be released – as all other paramilitary prisoners had been – under the terms of the Good Friday Agreement. This seeming about face left a very bad taste in the collective mouths of the Irish body politic.

Equally concerning for some was the acknowledgement by the Minister for Foreign Affairs, Dermot Ahern, that it was only a matter of time before Sinn Féin was involved in a future coalition government in the Republic. While there was some attempt at drawing back from this admission from other members of the Fianna Fáil Party, there is no escape from the fact that the nature of the Irish political system combined with Sinn Féin's recent solid electoral performances in the Republic means that that Party's involvement in governments on both sides of the border will happen sooner rather than later.

abbreviations

ACA	Army Comrades' Association
ARP	Air Raid Precautions
CLMC	Combined Loyalist Military Command
DUP	Democratic Unionist Party
EEC	European Economic Community
ESB	Electricity Supply Board
GAA	Gaelic Athletic Association
IDA	Industrial Development Authority
INLA	Irish National Liberation Army
IRA	Irish Republican Army
IRB	Irish Republican Brotherhood
ITGWU	Irish Transport and General Workers' Union
LVF	Loyalist Volunteer Force
MLA	Member of the Legislative Assembly
MP	Member of Parliament
NICRA	Northern Ireland Civil Rights Association
NIWC	Northern Ireland Women's Coalition
PD	Progressive Democrats
PIRA	Provisional Irish Republican Army
POW	Prisoner(s) of War
PR	Proportional Representation
PSNI	Police Service of Northern Ireland
PUP	Progressive Unionist Party
RAF	Royal Air Force
RUC	Royal Ulster Constabulary
SAS	Special Air Service
SDLP	Social Democratic and Labour Party
TDs	*Teachta Dála* – Dáil Deputies
TUC	Trades Union Congress
UAC	Ulster Army Council
UDA	Ulster Defence Association

UDP	Ulster Democratic Party
UDR	Ulster Defence Regiment
UFF	Ulster Freedom Fighters
UKUP	United Kingdom Unionist Party
UPNI	Unionist Party of Northern Ireland
UUC	Ulster Unionist Council
UUP	Ulster Unionist Party
UUUC	United Ulster Unionist Council
UVF	Ulster Volunteer Force
UWC	Ulster Workers' Council
VAT	Value Added Tax
VC	Victoria Cross
VUPP	Vanguard Unionist Progressive Party

glossary

abdication crisis The 1936 British constitutional crisis which arose when Britain's new King, Edward VIII, abdicated so that he could marry an American divorcée, Wallis Simpson.

Air Raid Precaution (ARP) Established by the Westminster Parliament in 1938, ARP wardens were charged with preparing British people from attacks by air during the expected war with Germany.

Apprentice Boys A loyalist (see below) club set up in 1814 to remember the group of apprentices who closed the gates of Derry against the armies of King James II in 1688. The main annual event organised by the Apprentice Boys is a march in Derry on a date close to 12 August.

Ard Fheis Annual Party Conference (Irish).

Ascendancy The ruling class in eighteenth century Ireland.

Blueshirts The popular name given to the National Guard (itself formed from the Army Comrades' Association). This movement (whose members wore blue shirts) developed a programme based on vocationalism, a theory of government closely related to corporatism.

Continuity IRA The name given to a splinter group which split off from the Provisional IRA (see below) in the aftermath of that organization's 1994 cessation. The Continuity IRA has not declared a ceasefire as of yet.

cultural nationalism A movement that emerged in the latter years of the nineteenth century with the aim of ensuring that Ireland's rich Gaelic heritage was not totally eroded.

Dáil Éireann The Lower House in the Irish Parliament (Irish).

Direct Rule A term used to describe the state of affairs when Northern Ireland is ruled directly from Westminster rather than by its own devolved parliament.

disestablish The removal (by a law of 1869 which took effect in 1871) of the State's recognition of the Church of Ireland as Ireland's official religion.

Emancipation (Catholic) The Act of Parliament (1829) that permitted Catholics to sit freely as Members of Parliament (MPs).

Fenian The popular name of the Irish Republican Brotherhood (IRB – see below). The movement was founded in 1858 – in both the United States and Ireland – with the aim of achieving an independent Ireland through the use of force.

Fourteen Points A series of suggestions (1918), put forward by US President Woodrow Wilson, as a way of preventing another World War. They included concepts such as national self-determination.

Gaelic Athletic Association (GAA) Founded in 1884 by a group of individuals who feared the increasing influence of 'English' games such as rugby and soccer, the GAA was established to provide a countrywide structure for the playing of indigenous sports such as football and hurling.

Garda Síochána The Irish police (literally guardians of the peace – Irish).

gerrymandering The practice of drawing electoral boundaries in a way that benefits one particular group (usually a minority) at the expense of another (usually the majority).

Home Rule The nineteenth and early twentieth century campaign for Ireland to be granted a devolved parliament by Westminster.

internecine Mutually destructive conflict.

Irish Dimension The idea that the Irish government should have some input into how Northern Ireland is governed.

Irish National Liberation Army (INLA) A paramilitary republican group that emerged in 1975 from a split in the Official IRA (see below). The organization called a ceasefire in August 1998 but has refused as of yet to decommission any of its weapons.

Irish Republican Army (IRA) The IRA's origins lie in the Irish Volunteers (founded in 1913). This movement split in 1914 over the issue of whether or not to fight for the British in the First World War. The part that refused to fight retained the name Irish Volunteers and part of it was involved in the 1916 Rising. In the struggle for independence that began in 1919 the Irish Volunteers was renamed the IRA. This movement too split in 1922 over whether or not to accept the Treaty. One part did eventually become the Irish Army, and one part that refused (known as the Irregulars – see below) fought and lost a Civil War and then became an underground organization, re-emerging occasionally to strike again for its goal of a united Irish Republic, particularly during the period 1956–62. In late 1969 the IRA split into the Official IRA and the Provisional IRA (see below) after a dispute over whether to pursue a political or military strategy.

Irish Republican Brotherhood (IRB) The official name of the Fenian movement (see above).

Irish Volunteers A private army established in 1913 with the express purpose of ensuring Ireland was granted Home Rule. The movement split in two at the start of the First World War with the vast majority going off to fight for the British (being renamed the National Volunteers) and a minority refusing to support Britain (retaining the name Irish Volunteers). An element of this group organized and executed the 1916 Rising. Later on the group became known as the Irish Republican Army (IRA – see above).

Irregulars The section of the IRA (see above) that opposed the Anglo-Irish Treaty and fought a civil war against the government forces.

Keynesian (economics) The ideas of economist John Maynard Keynes as expressed particularly in his 1936 book *A General Theory of Employment, Interest and Money*. This volume argued that the lack of demand for goods and rising unemployment could be countered by increased government expenditure to stimulate the economy.

Laissez faire Laissez faire is short for '*laissez faire, laissez passer*,' a French phrase meaning to 'let things alone, let them pass'. When applied in an economic sense it refers to avoiding state regulation of the economy.

League of Nations An international body established by the Paris Peace Settlement (1919) in an attempt to provide a place where leaders could talk together and so avoid wars. It was superseded by the United Nations after the Second World War.

Loyalist A hardline supporter of Northern Ireland's continued link with the United Kingdom.

Loyalist Volunteer Force (LVF) Believed to have been set up in 1996 by members of the Ulster Volunteer Force (UVF – see below) who opposed the loyalist Paramilitaries' ceasefire of 1994. Although opposed to the Good Friday Agreement the LVF declared a ceasefire of sorts in May 1998. In December 1998 it became the first paramilitary organization to decommission a number of weapons.

Luftwaffe The German air force (literally air weapon – German) first established during the First World War, banned by the Treaty of Versailles and re-established by Adolf Hitler in 1935.

Marshall Plan Linked in with the 1947 Truman Doctrine by which the US undertook to protect 'free peoples who are resisting attempted subjugation by armed minorities or by outside pressures'. The Marshall Plan (named after the then US Secretary of State General George C Marshall) or the European Recovery Program (ERP) offered American financial aid to European nations to assist with a programme of European economic recovery.

New Ireland Forum A think tank established by the Irish government in 1983 to provide possible solutions to the Northern Ireland conflict. Its 1984 Report suggested a number of possible solutions all of which were rejected by the British Prime Minister, Margaret Thatcher.

Northern Ireland Civil Rights Association (NICRA) A cross community organization established in 1967 with the purpose of achieving equal rights for all of Northern Ireland's citizens. It took its inspiration from the US civil rights campaign and employed similar tactics of peaceful demonstrations.

Official IRA One of the groups formed after the 1969 IRA (see above) split. The Official IRA continued to focus on establishing a socialist Ireland although it was not above using violence. It declared a ceasefire in 1972 and remained largely inactive thereafter.

Oireachtas The Irish parliament consisting of Dáil Éireann and the Seanad (Irish).

Orange Society/Order Established in 1795 with the aim of defending 'the king and his heirs as long as they shall maintain the Protestant ascendancy'. The organisation's most public action is its annual commemoration of the 1689 Battle of the Boyne.

Pale The region surrounding Dublin during the late middle ages symbolizing the reduction in Norman control of Ireland (from the Latin *pallus* denoting the stakes used to mark the borders of the area).

Paris Peace Settlement The collective term given to a number of treaties drawn up at the end of the First World War.

plantation In Irish history the policy of colonising an area with those of a different nationality and or religion so as to ensure political control.

pocket borough Parliamentary constituencies within large estates that returned the members that the owners of those estates wanted.

Police Service of Northern Ireland (PSNI) A new police force established in November 2001 on the recommendations of the Patten Report to replace the RUC (see below).

proportional representation A system of voting designed to create a result more in line with the way in which people voted. Seats are allocated roughly in proportion to the percentages of votes cast for each party.

Provisional IRA (PIRA) One of the groups formed after the 1969 IRA (see above) split. The Provisional IRA aimed to use violence to remove British influence within Northern Ireland and to achieve a united Ireland.

Real IRA A faction of the Provisional IRA (see above) that emerged in 1997 following that movement's decision to agree to a change to the IRA's constitution that would allow the organization's Army Council (which the Sinn Féin leadership allegedly controlled) to decide on possible concessions.

repeal To reverse the Act of Union (1800).

Royal Irish Constabulary (RIC) The police force of Ireland between 1822 (established by the Irish Constabulary Act of that year) and 1922 when it was replaced by the Royal Ulster Constabulary (RUC) (see below) in Northern Ireland and the Garda Síochána (see above) in the Irish Free State. The RIC was the first police force in the British Empire to be permitted the use of the prefix 'Royal'.

Royal Ulster Constabulary (RUC) The Northern Ireland police force between 1922 and 2001.

rotten borough Parliamentary constituencies that returned MPs for areas where there were no inhabitants.

Seanad The Senate, the upper house in the Irish parliament (Irish).

sectarian To think or act in a way that discriminates against those of another religious group.

socialism Economic and political theory that places the means of production and distribution in the hands of the community.

special category status The recognition in the early to mid 1970s that those convicted of crimes connected with 'the Troubles' had acted for political and not criminal reasons.

Stormont The name given to the Northern Ireland Parliament building opened on the outskirts of Belfast in 1932.

Surrender and regrant A Tudor policy introduced as a method of controlling Ireland that was cheaper than all-out warfare. By this policy many of the main Gaelic Irish chiefs submitted to the English monarchy and in return received titles of nobility from it. The policy also demanded that they should abandon the Gaelic language and traditions and their loyalty to Rome.

Taoiseach The prime minister of the Republic of Ireland (Irish).

Teachta Dála (TD) Dáil Deputies – members of the Dáil (Irish).

U-Boat German name for a submarine (literally undersea boat).

Ulster Army Council Set up in December 1973 by loyalist paramilitaries to resist the introduction of any significant 'Irish Dimension' (see above).

Ulster Defence Association (UDA) Formed in September 1971 up with the aim of filling a perceived gap in the defences of the loyalist community. The UDA regarded itself as a defensive grouping that would resist republican aggression. It regularly used the cover name of Ulster Freedom Fighters (UFF – see below) to claim responsibility for acts of terrorism. The UDA was not declared illegal until 1992.

Ulster Defence Regiment (UDR) A part time and locally recruited section of the British Army established on the recommendations of the Hunt Report (1969) to replace the B Specials. The UDR was merged with the Royal Irish Rangers in 1992.

Ulster Freedom Fighters (UFF) A cover-name used since 1973 by the UDA (see above).

Ulster Resistance Established in November 1986 to 'take direct action as and when required' to end the 1985 Anglo–Irish Agreement.

Ulster Special Constabulary (USC) Established in 1920 to deal with the growing unrest in what was to become Northern Ireland. Most of its members were drawn from the UVF (see below). It was divided into three sections, A, B and C classes.

Ulster Unionist Council (UUC) The ruling body of the Ulster Unionist Party (UUP).

Ulster Vanguard Established in February 1972 by former Stormont minister William Craig as a co-ordinating body for traditional loyalist groups.

Ulster Volunteer Force (UVF) A paramilitary group originally initially set up in 1912 to oppose the introduction of Home Rule to Ireland. It went off to fight for the British in the First World War. Some of its members joined the Ulster Special Constabulary (USC – see above) on its establishment in 1920. In 1966 the same name was adopted by a loyalist paramilitary grouping set up to oppose the liberal reforms of Terence O'Neill.

United Ulster Unionist Council (UUUC) Established in January 1974 to campaign against the Sunningdale Agreement.

Ulster Workers' Council (UWC) Set up in 1973 (with the purpose of demonstrating the depth and strength of unionist opposition to the Sunningdale Agreement) this umbrella grouping of Protestant trade unionists gained substantial amounts of political and paramilitary support. It co-ordinated the May 1974 UWC strike which brought down the 1974 Power sharing Assembly and Executive.

Wall Street Crash As a result of a collapse of confidence in the Wall Street Stock Exchange (in New York) in October 1929, the value of stocks and shares collapsed. This impacted negatively on the entire US economy and, due to the influence of the same throughout the world, on the world in general.

Books

There are literally thousands of books available, covering all aspects of Irish history. The following selection is designed to provide those readers wishing to develop their understanding further with useful starting points.

Bardon, Jonathan. *A History of Ulster*

Bartlett, Thomas & Jeffrey, Keith. (Eds) *A Military History of Ireland*

Beckett, J. C. *The Making of Modern Ireland 1603–1923*

Brown, Terence. *Ireland: a Social and Cultural History 1922–85*

Connolly, S. J. (Ed) *The Oxford Companion to Irish History*

Cullen, L. M. *An Economic History of Ireland since 1660*

Dudley-Edwards, Ruth. *The Faithful Tribe*

Duffy, Sean et al. *Atlas of Irish History*

Elliot, Marianne. *The Catholics of Ulster: A History*

English, Richard. *Armed Struggle: the History of the IRA*

Ferriter, Diarmaid. *The Transformation of Ireland 1900–2000*

Flanagan, Laurence. *Ancient Ireland: Life Before the Celts*

Foster, R. F. *Modern Ireland 1600–1972*

Harbinson, Peter. *Pre-Christian Ireland: From the First Settlers to the Early Celts*

Hoppen, K. T. *Ireland since 1800: Conflict and Conformity*

Jackson, Alvin. *Home Rule: An Irish History 1800–2000*

Kee, Robert. *The Green Flag*

Lee, J. J. *Ireland 1912–85: Politics and Society*

Lyons, F. S. L. *Ireland Since the Famine*

Martin, F. X. & Moody, T. W. (Eds) *The Course of Irish History*

McDonald, Henry. *Trimble*

McKittrick, David et al. (Eds) *Lost Lives*

Ó Gráda, Cormac. *The Great Irish Famine*
Stewart, A. T. Q. *The Narrow Ground: Aspects of Ulster 1609–1969*
Taylor, Peter. *The Loyalists*
Taylor, Peter. *The Provos: The IRA and Sinn Fein*

Films

Ireland and its history – particularly since the nineteenth century – have been portrayed in many ways on film. The following list (which is by no means definitive) will give readers the opportunity to see how some of the events and people mentioned in this book have been portrayed on the silver screen.

The Informer (1935)
The Plough and the Stars (1936)
Captain Boycott (1947)
Odd Man Out (1947)
The Fighting Prince of Donegal (1966)
The Violent Enemy (1969)
The Molly Maguires (1970)
A Sense of Loss (1978)
Angel (1982)
Harry's Game (1982)
Acceptable Levels (1983)
Cal (1984)
A Prayer for the Dying (1988)
The Field (1990)
Hidden Agenda (1990)
Mountains of the Moon (1990)
The Crying Game (1992)
In the Name of the Father (1993)
Nothing Personal (1995)
A Further Gesture (The Break) (1996)
The Ghost in the Darkness (1996)
Michael Collins (1996)
Some Mother's Son (1996)
Bogwoman (1997)
The Boxer (1997)
Resurrection Man (1997)
One Man's Hero (1998)
Titanic Town (2000)
Bloody Sunday (2001)
H3 (2001)
Sunday (2001)
Omagh (2004)

Websites

There is a plethora of material available on the Web relating to the history of Ireland. Not all of what is available is equally good and the reader should exercise a degree of discernment.

http://www.bbc.co.uk/history/war/troubles/
Through a series of articles, media clips and photographs 'the Troubles' website takes the reader through Northern Ireland's turbulent history.

http://www.bbc.co.uk/northernireland/education/stateapart/
A State Apart is an interactive chronicle from the BBC covering the 30 years of conflict in Northern Ireland.

http://www.chirl.com/
An excellent resource which presents chronological information on people and events connected to Ireland.

http://historical-debates.oireachtas.ie/
This Historical Debates website contains the full text of the Official Report of the Parliamentary Debates of the Irish Parliament.

http://www.historylearningsite.co.uk/ireland_1848_to_1922.htm
This website has material on a full range of Irish historical events from the nineteenth and early twentieth centuries.

http://www.islandireland.com/Pages/history.html
The links on this useful website will take the reader to numerous resources on Irish history.

http://www.oireachtas.ie/
Website of the Oireachtas (Irish Parliament).

http://www.schoolhistory.co.uk/gcselinks/britishworld/britainireland.html
Website on British and Irish History – some useful links.

http://www.ucc.ie/chronicon/
Chronicon is an electronic journal of history. It publishes articles relating to history with a particular focus on Irish history.

http://cain.ulst.ac.uk/
This superb site contains information and source material on all aspects of 'the Troubles' and the subsequent peace process.

index

Why not try another book from
the **teach yourself** series?
Read on to sample a
chapter from **The Middle East**
since 1945.

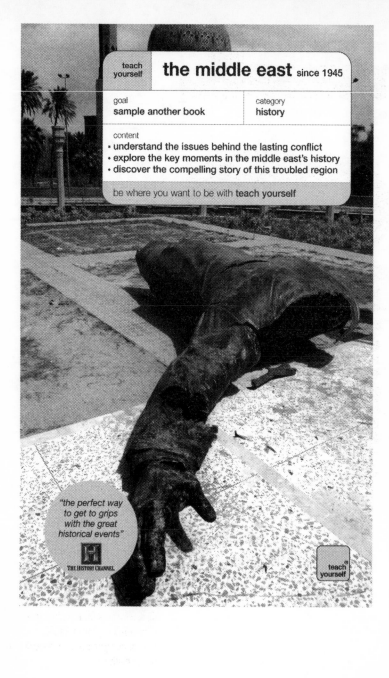

10 Intifada

This chapter will cover:
- unsuccessful attempts to solve the Israel-Palestine problem in the 1980s
- the emergence of Palestinian nationalism

Fruitless negotiation

Time of strife

During the early 1980s the Middle East was as strife-torn as it had ever been. In the east, to satisfy the ambitions of their dictator-rulers, the people of Iran and Iraq were dying in their tens of thousands. Iranian fundamentalist fervour was beginning to seep across the region, bringing with it a new wave of unstoppable terrorism in the form of the suicide bomber. Egypt's discontent had manifested itself in the assassination of its well-intentioned president.

The Israeli invasion of Lebanon had gone horribly wrong. It brought none of the political or strategic gains intended, and ended in a shameful withdrawal. The massacres at Sabra and Shatilla left the Israeli government in deep disgrace and the nation bitterly divided. The PLO had been defeated and its leadership now languished in distant Tunisia. The people it purported to help remained stateless, impoverished and largely hopeless. The only beam of light, appearing in the middle of the decade, was the emergence of Nicholas Gorbachev as leader of the Soviet Union. His leadership would end the Cold War that had so often fuelled the Middle East's bitter quarrels.

Lebanese endgame

At about the time that Saddam Hussein was wondering whether war with Iran was such a good idea after all, several thousand miles away Yasser Arafat was also contemplating the future with some alarm. Now based in Tunis, for the first time in its existence the PLO had no common frontier with Israel. The armed struggle to replace Israel with a single democratic Palestinian-Jewish secular state had clearly failed.

Arafat, as PLO chairman and instigator of its policies, was inevitably blamed. Senior figures within the Palestinian National Council were tired of his inefficiency, favouritism and corruption. They wanted him removed. Back in Lebanon, open fighting broke out in the Baqa Valley between remnants of Fatah loyal to Arafat and Syrian-backed PLO dissidents. Keen to be at the front, Arafat shaved off his beard, donned a smart suit and dark glasses and sneaked into the battle zone via Cyprus.

After Shia bombs killed 241 US marines and 59 French paratroopers, mediators were eager to restore some semblance of order to the battered country. They eventually managed to separate the warring Palestinians and once again Arafat sailed off into the sunset with a US guarantee that the Israelis would not interfere with his flight.

Talks about talks

The bewildering details of the criss-cross network of proposals and talks going on at this time, some secret, some open, are too obscure to be relevant here. Many were simply talks about talks – efforts to decide an agenda and who would be allowed to participate before the negotiations proper began. The Israelis and the USA, for example, would not talk with the PLO because they regarded it as a terrorist organization. For this Arafat had only himself to blame. Because he claimed, arrogantly and inaccurately, to speak for all Palestinians and control their paramilitary activities, he was also held responsible for their actions. This sometimes rebounded unpleasantly on him.

In 1985, for instance, a PLO hit squad – acting with or without Arafat's knowledge – killed three Israelis on a yacht in Cyprus. The Israeli government reacted by bombing the PLO HQ in Tunis, killing 56 Palestinians and 15 Tunisians. Small wonder several Arab states had said they were unwilling to harbour the PLO when it was expelled from Beirut. Arafat miraculously survived the raid on his compound. He was, he said, out 'jogging' at the time. Those who knew him smiled. Arafat was never a jogger – he had been simply taking a walk.

A few weeks later Arafat was again put in a difficult position. This time it was by his friend Abu Abbas, the pro-Iraqi bandit and leader of the Popular Front for the Liberation of Palestine. Abbas arranged for four young, frightened and poorly trained would-be freedom fighters to hi-jack the cruise liner *Achille Lauro* as it sailed from Alexandria. On board were 556 passengers and crew, including some Americans. Arafat immediately took responsibility. He would, he told the world, sort the matter out peacefully and discipline the hi-jackers. In fact, he did neither.

The hi-jackers shot dead a disabled American passenger and dumped his body overboard. When the ship returned to Egypt, an Egyptian aircraft was ready to fly the hi-jackers and Abu Abbas to Tunis. US fighter aircraft intercepted it *en route* and forced it to land in Italy. The Italian authorities, not wishing to get involved, eventually released all the hi-jackers.

Not only were the Israelis and the Americans unwilling to talk to the PLO, but the PLO itself refused to accept the crucial UN Resolution 242 (backed by the 1973 cease-fire Resolution 338) which the US made a central pre-condition for negotiation. Arafat's understandable objection was that 242 talked of peace between the 'states' of the Middle East and not of self-determination for the Palestinians. Even when Arafat said he would accept Resolutions 242 and 338 in return for Palestinian self-determination, US president Ronald Reagan rejected the offer out of hand.

Around the time that Israel went into Lebanon there were three peace suggestions in the air. The Reagan Plan wanted to take matters on from where they had been left at Camp David. Another plan, drawn up at an Arab summit at Fez, suggested a return to the two-state solution envisaged by the UN in 1947. The third idea was that somehow Jordan should merge with Palestinian-inhabited territory to form a state or confederation. Something on these lines was agreed between Arafat and King Hussein in 1985. Two years later Hussein made another agreement, this time with Israeli Prime Minister Shimon Peres. Along with all the other proposals, neither produced any lasting or tangible result.

Israel's National Unity

Depressed by the death of his wife and haunted by what was happening in Lebanon, Prime Minister Begin resigned in 1983. He was briefly replaced by Yitzhak Shamir, the one-time Stern Gang member. After the following year's elections neither the Labour nor the Likud coalitions were able to form a stable government. With the country under pressure from its friends over Lebanon and inflation running at 400 per cent a year, a political crisis was the last thing Israel needed. A way out of the difficulty was found by establishing a Labour-Likud Government of National Unity. Labour leader Shimon Peres became prime minister, while Likud leader Shamir acted as his deputy and foreign minister. Then, 25 months later, their roles were reversed.

Peres initiated the phased withdrawal from Lebanon (see page 107), leaving a security zone in the south of the country under the nominal control of the South Lebanese Army. Under both Peres and Shamir the policy of planting Israeli settlements in the occupied territories, especially the West Bank, continued apace. Indeed, Shamir refused even to talk of the 'West Bank' – to him it was 'Judea and Samaria', two provinces of the Old Testament Kingdom of David. The Jewish population in the area tripled between 1982 and 1986, bringing perhaps half of the land there and over 80 per cent of the water into Israeli hands.

The motives for this were two-fold. First, settlements appealed to the ultraconservatives to whom the Likud was increasingly beholden for political support. Second, with each settlement built it became more difficult for Israel to abandon its conquests of 1967. By the end of the 1980s, the government could claim with some justification that things had changed so much since the Six Day War that proposals made then were no longer relevant. The answer, they suggested somewhat cynically, was not for the Israelis to leave the territories, but for the Palestinians to do so.

At this point, for the first time in the long and unhappy saga, the ordinary Palestinians took matters into their own hands. They had had enough of being a political football kicked about by Israelis, the PLO, the Americans, the Soviets, the Egyptians, the Syrians, the Jordanians, the Iraqis, and just about everyone else who took a passing interest in the Middle East. Despairing of ever being listened to amid the hullabaloo of international politics, they let out a long, instinctive, heart-rending scream of pain.

The Palestinians

The West Bank and Gaza Strip

The Palestinians of the West Bank and Gaza Strip called their uprising the *Intifada*, meaning 'trembling' or 'shaking off'. With the benefit of hindsight, it is perhaps surprising that they endured so much for so long before losing patience. It may help, therefore, if at this stage we remind ourselves just who these people were.

When the state of Israel had been created out of the mandated territory of Palestine, the area contained some 1.3 million Arabs. Few of these people regarded themselves as Palestinians. Rather, their loyalties were to clan, tribe, faith, and the wider Arabic-speaking community. The enormous upheaval caused by the First Arab-Israeli War left around 150,000 Arabs within the new state of Israel. Although technically Israelis, they were very much second-class citizens. For almost 20 years they lived under military controls. To discourage the development of a distinct

Arab identity, the administration referred to them not as Arabs but as 'Druze', 'Bedouin' and so forth.

The remaining 1.15 million Arabs from the Palestinian mandate were scattered three ways. Over 20 per cent went to live in neighbouring Arab lands, settling either in refugee camps just over the border or in the towns. The largest group, around 100,000, went to Lebanon.

A second group fled to the West Bank, joining the Arabs already living there to swell its population to about 700,000. In this rugged region, with the city of Jerusalem on its south-western edge, they lived as shepherds, farmers, craftspeople, labourers and managers of small businesses. The hills of the north-west received sufficient annual rainfall for grazing and the harvesting of cereal crops. Elsewhere, water from the River Jordan or pumped from beneath the ground irrigated fields of fruits and vegetables.

The third group of Palestinian Arabs pressed into the Gaza Strip. Its boundaries determined by a 1949 cease-fire line, this was an area of 363 sq km (140 sq miles) that had surrounded Egypt's 1948 military headquarters. Only 8 km (5 miles) wide at its broadest, it was an arid band of poor and desperately overcrowded territory with little to recommend it. The bulk of the refugees lived in camps managed by the United Nations. Here, as on the West Bank, it was more than ten years before all the tents had been replaced by concrete huts. Water and sewage provision were poor. Education and medical facilities were generally rudimentary, and employment opportunities extremely limited.

For most of the time until the Six Day War the West Bank was administered, though not formally annexed, by Jordan. Egypt ruled the Gaza Strip with considerable harshness. Its inhabitants, for example, were not given Egyptian citizenship. Jordanian rule in the West Bank was reasonably sympathetic.

The emergence of a nation

Both the Gaza Strip and the West Bank were overrun by the Israeli army in 1967 and thereafter administered by Israel. Some Arabs fled the Israeli advance, others were forced to leave. Those who remained behind rapidly developed a national consciousness, becoming the first generation of true Palestinians.

Two factors helped the emergence of Palestinian nationalism. One was the PLO, with its network of semi-independent affiliates. The organization gradually became more than just a resistance movement. Recognized as the voice of the Palestinian Arabs of the West Bank and Gaza Strip, it came to regard itself as a government in waiting. Its pronouncements and propaganda filtered through to the crowded dispossessed, instilling in them a sense of what they believed ought to be and hoped one day would be.

The second influence on the growth of Palestinian nationalism was the behaviour of the Israeli conquerors. For ten years, guided by Moshe Dayan, the occupied territories were governed with a comparatively light hand. Those dwelling in the West Bank benefited from new roads (built for military purposes but useful for getting goods to market), better housing, and improved medical services. This changed dramatically with the formation of Begin's Likud government in 1977.

Israeli oppression

The most obvious sign of the Israeli government's new approach to the occupied territories was the settlement policy. In ten years the number of Jewish settlements rose from 36 to over 100. Most were small and the soil they farmed was generally poor, but to their Arab neighbours they were an obvious affront. The Israelis said the land they built on was either barren or not owned by anyone. The Arabs complained that, barren or not, the land was not just there for the taking. Furthermore, much of the land for whom no owner could be found had belonged to Arabs who had fled during the various wars. New settlers dug bore holes that drew upon the West Bank's precious underground reserves of water. Some sources say the average Israeli was allocated 12 times as much water as the average Palestinian.

Israeli settlers were given grants and tax advantages, and provided with good roads, schools and medical services. Their Arab neighbours looked on with increasing resentment. The settlements attracted some of the most intolerant and racist elements of Israeli society, too. Vigilante groups, like Gush Emunim, attacked Arab shops and houses. When apprehended, the perpetrators of this anti-Arab terrorism were generally let off lightly. Arab resentment grew still more bitter.

Life was made difficult for the Arabs in all kinds of little ways, too. They were subjected to road blocks and strict searches of their vehicles and property. Large-scale meetings were prohibited and taxes were increased. Failure to pay led to imprisonment. If Palestinians tried to get redress, the legal system was weighted against them. Verbal and minor physical abuse were commonplace, adding to the general feeling among the Palestinian Arabs that they were an unwanted and despised people.

In 1985, the Israeli cabinet voted to tighten the screw still further. Its 'Iron Fist' policy, devised by Foreign Minister Rabin, had a double aim: to destroy all opposition to Israeli rule, and persuade Palestinians that life would be better for them outside Israeli-governed territory. This tied in with the 'Greater Israel' policy of gradually absorbing the occupied territories into the state created in 1948.

Iron Fist led to an increase in so-called 'administrative punishments', which included deportation and preventative detention. The latter meant holding people without trial or appeal on suspicion that they might commit a crime. The use of physical intimidation increased, too. Palestinian youths were regularly rounded up, beaten, tortured and made to confess to crimes they had never committed. The courts turned a deaf ear to accusations of malpractice.

One comparatively mild example is illustrative of thousands of similar cases. The Palestinian lawyer Raja Shehadeh recalls the case of a 14-year-old shepherd boy who lived near Ramallah. One day, as he was grazing his sheep on the hills near Jenin, an anti-Israeli demonstration took place which involved throwing stones at Israeli soldiers. When he returned to Jenin, the young shepherd was arrested and taken to a special prison for youths that occupied a former British army barracks in the Faraa Valley.

He had done nothing, the boy told his interrogators. He had been out on the hills with his sheep all day. 'Confess!' screamed his persecutors. The lad did not even know to what he was supposed to confess. He was beaten until one of his arms fractured, then released. The Israelis believed such behaviour would break the back of Palestinian resistance. In fact, it had the opposite effect.